**Tiffany Reisz** lives in Lexington, Kentucky. She graduated with a BA in English from Centre College and is making her parents and her professors proud by writing erotica under her real name. She has five piercings, one tattoo and has been arrested twice. When not under arrest, Tiffany enjoys Latin dance, Latin men and Latin verbs. She dropped out of a conservative seminary in order to pursue her dream of becoming a smut peddler. If she couldn't write, she would die.

Also by Tiffany Reisz:

The Original Sinners

THE PRINCE
THE ANGEL
THE SIREN

E-Book Novellas

THE MISTRESS FILES

THE GIFT
(previously published as SEVEN DAY LOAN)

IMMERSED IN PLEASURE

SUBMIT TO DESIRE

The story's not over quite yet!
Watch for THE PRIEST
coming soon from Mills & Boon SPICE

# THE
# MISTRESS

## TIFFANY REISZ

Dedicated to Mistress Jeanette, Mistress Amiko, Mistress Astria, Mistress Sade Ami, Mistress Michelle Lacy and all the Dominatrixes who make the world their footstool.

I kneel at your feet and kiss your boots.

Your Servant Always,

Tiffany

# The story so far...

At the end of *The Prince,*
the following statements were true:

**1.** Erotica writer Nora Sutherlin and her former
intern Wes Railey are engaged.

**2.** Marie-Laure (the long-thought-dead sister of
King of the Underground Kingsley Edge) is alive.

**3.** Nora Sutherlin, Søren's lover for fourteen years,
has been kidnapped but is unharmed.

**4.** Søren, who Kingsley wants to steal from
Nora, is a Catholic priest.

At the end of *The Mistress,*
only *one* of these statements will be true.

And we know that all things work
together for good to them that
love God.
to them who are the called
according to His purpose.

—Romans 8:28

**The lady or the tiger?**

—Frank Stockton

**Part One**

# CAPTURE

# 1
# THE QUEEN

When Nora came to she was fifteen years old again. She had to be. What else could explain the cold, industrial chair she sat in, the unforgiving metal of the handcuffs on her wrists and the terror in her heart?

Inside her aching and addled mind, Eleanor Schreiber opened her eyes and raised her head. Across from her in the interrogation room at the police station sat the new priest at Sacred Heart—3:00 a.m. on a Saturday morning and here he was before her, a mere twenty-nine years old in the face but with eyes ancient enough they'd probably seen Christ in the flesh. She kind of hoped he had. She'd always wondered how tall Jesus was.

The priest—Father Stearns to the church but Søren to her—said nothing. He merely stared at her with a little smile lurking on his lips. At least someone was enjoying her misery. Where was her father? Her dad should be here now. She needed her father, not her Father. Her dad was the reason she'd ended up arrested in Manhattan in the hours before dawn. But no, she only had her priest and the desire to wipe the smile off that perfect face of his.

"So I've been meaning to ask you…" She decided to take control of the moment and be the first to break the silence. "Are you one of those priests who fucks the kids in the congregation?"

Whatever reaction she'd hoped for from her priest, she didn't get it.

"No."

Eleanor took a deep breath and exhaled heavily through her nose.

"Too bad."

"Eleanor, perhaps we should discuss the predicament you're in at the moment."

"I'm in a real pickle." She nodded, hoping to annoy him. A useless plan. They'd met twice before tonight and she'd done her damnedest to get under his skin both times. No dice. He'd treated her with kindness and respect both times. She wasn't used to that.

"You were arrested on suspicion of grand theft auto. Supposedly five luxury vehicles with a combined value of over a quarter of a million dollars have disappeared from Manhattan tonight. You wouldn't know anything about that, would you?"

"I take the fifth. That's what I'm supposed to say, right?"

"To the court, yes. To me, you will tell the truth always."

"I don't think you want to know the truth about me, Søren," she said, her voice not much more than a whisper. She wasn't stupid. She only had to look at him to know that he and she had nothing in common. He looked liked money, talked like money. He had the whitest fingernails she'd ever seen and hands that belonged on a statue or something. All of him looked like a work of art—his hands, his face and lips, his height and beauty…. And here she was, chipped black nail polish, wet from the rain she'd been arrested in, hair falling in lank waves into her face, her school uniform a sodden mess, no money, no hope, and her whole life a fucking train wreck.

"There is nothing I don't want to know about you," Søren said, and seemed to mean it. "And I assure you, nothing you tell me will shock or disgust me. Nothing will make me change my mind about you."

"Change your mind? You've already made up your mind about me? What's the verdict?"

"The verdict is simply this—I am willing and capable of helping you out of this mess you've gotten yourself into."

"Can we call it a 'pickle'? Pickle sounds less scary than mess."

"It's a disaster, young lady. You could easily spend years in juvenile detention for what you did tonight. One of the cars you stole belonged to someone important and influential, and he's apparently determined that you don't see sunlight until age twenty-one. Keeping you out of juvenile detention will take a great deal of doing on my part. Blessedly, I have some connections. Or, more accurately, I have someone who has connections. The time and expense will be considerable," he said in a tone that seemed to imply he relished the time and expense, which made no sense. But nothing about the man or his interest in her made any sense at all.

"And you'll go to all this trouble for me…why?" Eleanor lifted her head a little higher and stared straight into his eyes.

"Because there is nothing I wouldn't do to protect you, Eleanor. Nothing I wouldn't do to help you. And nothing I wouldn't do to save you. Nothing."

A chill passed through Eleanor's whole body. Someone walked over her grave, as her grandmother would say. She never understood that phrase, that feeling before. Now she did.

"But my assistance doesn't come without a price."

"Right." Eleanor smirked at him. "So this is when we get back to my first question and the fucking of the kids at church. Oh, well, if you insist."

"Do you value your worth as a child of God so little that you think the only thing I could possibly want from you is sex?"

The question hit Eleanor so hard she almost flinched. But she wouldn't let him see he'd gotten to her. Her mom would disown her for this. Her dad was probably eight states away by now. Her grandparents were seven minutes from death. Her entire future was about six feet under. Still she wasn't about to let anyone take away her pride. She at least had that. For now, anyway.

"So that's a no?"

Søren raised his eyebrow at her and she almost giggled. She was beginning to like this guy. She'd fallen in love with him already—utterly, completely and until the end of the world or even after. Never guessed she'd end up liking him, too.

"That would be a no. I will require something of you, however, in exchange for my assistance."

"Do you always talk like this?"

"You mean articulately?"

"Yes."

"Yes."

"Weird. So what price am I paying? Hope it's not my first-born child. Don't want kids."

"My price is simply this—in exchange for my assistance, I only ask that you do what I tell you to do from now on."

"Do what you tell me to do?"

"Yes. I want you to obey me."

"From now on? Like…how long?"

And he smiled then and she knew she should have been

afraid but something in that smile… It was the first time that night she felt safe.

"Forever."

*"Wake up, Sleeping Beauty."*

She heard a voice tinged with a French accent and tried to ignore it as she always tried to ignore French-accented voices. The last thing Nora wanted to do was wake up. In her dream she was with Søren and he was twenty-nine and she fifteen and their story had only begun. And she knew if she opened her eyes, she could very well be facing the end of their story. She wanted to stay in her dream and would have stayed in it forever but for the cold, delicate fingers dancing across her face like spider legs.

Nora opened her eyes.

# 2
## THE KING

Kingsley Edge stood in front of the mirror in his large walk-in closet studying his wounds as he changed from his torn shirt into another. The layers of marble-colored bruises Søren had left on him after their one night together had already turned from red to black. He could have hated the priest for the reminders upon his body of a night he feared would never be repeated. Still, he cherished the bruises now as much as he did when they were boys at school. Far more than the scars on his chest, gifts from enemies with guns, he wore them as badges of honor.

He raised his hand to the worst of his old wounds—a scar on the left side of his chest a few inches below his heart. A strange injury that looked more like he'd been stabbed than shot. Who knows? Maybe he had been.

The mission that had left him with that scar, with two of his four bullet wounds, he remembered almost nothing of. His mind had buried the memory, and he had no desire to dig it back up. Waking up in the hospital in Paris… That moment he would never forget. He would probably think of it on his deathbed. That hospital bed…it should have been his death-bed, could have been…

But for the visitor.

He had come to consciousness slowly, arduously, crawling through the deep dark on his way back into the light. He had dragged himself up through the trench of drugs and pain, bit-ter pain and the failure of the mission. Sensing white light in the room, he'd kept his eyes closed, unable yet to confront the sun.

From over his shoulder he'd heard low voices—one female, crisp and careful, and one male, authoritative and unyielding.

"He will live," the man's voice said in French. It wasn't a question he asked the woman, but an order given.

"We'll do what we can for him, of course." Of course, she said. *Bien sûr.* But Kingsley had heard the lie in her voice.

"You will do everything for him. Everything. From this moment on he is your only patient. He is your only concern."

"*Oui, mon père. Mais…*" *Mais*…but… Her voice betrayed her fear. *Mon père?* Kingsley's muddled mind had tried to wrap itself around the words. His father had been dead for years. Who was the father she spoke to?

"Consider his life as precious as your own. Do you under-stand that?"

There it was. Kingsley would have smiled in his half sleep were it not for the tubes down his throat. He knew a death threat when he heard it. *Consider his life as precious as your own….* That was French anyone could translate. *He lives and you live. He dies and…*

But who cared enough about him anymore to make even an idle threat? When joining *le Légion* he'd put one name down on his next-of-kin line. One name. The only family he had left. And yet, he wasn't family, not at all. Why would he of all people come to him now?

"He will live," the woman had promised, and this time she spoke no *"mais."*

"Good. Spare no expense for his comfort and health. All will be accounted for."

The nurse, or perhaps she was a doctor, had sworn again she would do everything. She'd pledged that the patient would walk out whole and healthy. She'd promised she would do all she could and then some. Smart woman.

Kingsley heard her high heels retreating on the tile, the sound of her shoes as crisp and efficient as her voice. The sound died and Kingsley knew he and the visitor were now alone in the room. He struggled to open his eyes but couldn't find the strength.

"Rest, Kingsley," came the voice again. And he felt a hand on his forehead, gentle as a lover's, tender as a father's.

"My Kingsley…" The voice sighed and Kingsley heard frustration mixed with amusement. Amusement or something like it. "Forgive me for saying this, but I think it's time you find a new hobby."

And even with the tubes in his throat, Kingsley had managed a smile.

The hand left his face and he felt something against his fingers. The dark came upon him again, but it wasn't the deep dark this time, merely sleep, and when he awoke again the tube was gone and he could see and speak and breathe again. And the thing that had touched his fingers was an envelope containing paperwork for a Swiss bank account someone had opened in his name—a Swiss bank account that contained roughly thirty-three million American dollars.

He took the money and he took the advice of his one and

only hospital visitor. He returned to America, to the country where he'd once experienced true happiness.

And in America he did as he'd been ordered.

He found a new hobby.

Kingsley finished dressing. He tucked his shirt in and pulled on and buttoned his embroidered black-and-silver vest. Once more he looked dashing and roguish all at the same time. The household knew something had happened and for their sake he would act the part of their fearless leader as always if only to comfort their minds. In truth, he'd never been so scared in his life, not even that day in the hospital.

He yanked on his jacket as he stepped away from the mirror. Never before had he dealt with a crisis of this magnitude in his world. As soon as he'd built his Underground, his Empire of S&M clubs that catered to the wealthy and the powerful as well as the scared and the shamed, he'd begun stockpiling blackmail fodder on all the police chiefs and politicians, on the media and the Mafia, anyone who could potentially threaten his borders. Now the thing he'd feared most, harm—real harm to a citizen of his kingdom—had befallen them. And he had only himself to blame.

As soon as he left his bedroom, his night secretary, Sophie, met him in the hallway. She rattled off half a dozen messages and meetings.

"Cancel all the meetings," he ordered as they reached the stairs. "Ignore the messages."

"*Oui, monsieur.* Master Fiske is in your office."

Good. Griffin was on time today.

He dismissed Sophie and headed to his private office on the third floor. When he reached it, he found Griffin standing by the window talking in hushed tones to the young man with him. Kingsley watched them a moment, waiting for them to notice him. But they had been afflicted with the tunnel vision of new love. Griffin raised his hand and cupped the face of Michael, his new lover. One kiss turned into a second one followed by a whisper. Michael nodded and leaned into Griffin, and when Michael's silver eyes finally looked at something other than Griffin, Kingsley saw the terror in them.

He could sympathize.

"You should have left your pet at home," Kingsley said, unable to resist goading Griffin.

Griffin raised his chin as he wrapped an arm possessively around Michael's shoulders, pulling him tight against his chest.

"Somebody has Nora, King. I'm not going to let Mick out of my sight until we get her back."

"Your pet is not in danger. I don't think *la Maîtresse* is, either. Not yet." He spoke the words with confidence and hoped they believed the half-truth.

"I don't care. We protect our property. You and Søren taught me that."

*"C'est la guerre."* He sighed. Kingsley had no counterargument. Wasn't that why he'd sent Juliette away? To protect his property?

"Hey, where is Søren, anyway?" Griffin asked.

"He's tied up at the moment." Kingsley chose not to elaborate on the literal truth of that statement.

"What do we know? Anything?"

Kingsley shrugged.

"It's a long story. Too long to tell. A waste of time. The priest and I, we have an old enemy we'd thought long dead. She's not. I don't know what her game is, but rest assured, it is a game."

"Nora's been kidnapped. What the fuck kind of game is this?"

"A very dangerous one. Luckily I'm something of an expert at dangerous games."

"I'll break any legs you tell me to," Griffin offered, and Kingsley gave the slightest laugh.

"I appreciate the offer, *mon ami*. I think a more subtle approach might be necessary with this adversary. What I need from you is this..." Kingsley reached into his pocket and pulled out a silver key ring adorned with a *fleur de lis*. On it were eight keys—one to each of his clubs and the town house. "I will be occupied for some time dealing with this nasty business. Someone needs to keep an eye on the Empire for me."

Griffin's dark eyes widened. He held out his hand and Kingsley placed the keys in Griffin's palm.

"The keys to the Kingdom," Griffin said. "I'd say thank you for the honor but I know you're only giving them to me because you don't have any other choice."

"I have dozens of staff on my payroll, many choices. I trust you. You can keep everyone in line until I come back."

"Do you know where Nora is? Do we know anything? Do you think we should call—"

"The police? I know who we're dealing with and I'm fairly sure what she wants. I wouldn't call the police unless you want *la Maîtresse* dead."

Michael inhaled at the word *dead* and Kingsley had to stop himself from rolling his eyes. The poor boy, so young and innocent. He wouldn't stay innocent long under this roof.

"If anyone hurts Nora..." Griffin let the words hang in the air, the unspoken threat more potent than any words.

"If anyone hurts Nora, you will have to stand in line for your retribution. I know a few who have the greater claim to her."

"Point taken."

"Now go see Sophie. She knows everything you'll need to

know. Remember, in this world it is better to be feared than loved. Keep everyone in line. Use a firm hand. You can stay in the house if you wish. Your pet, too. Although whatever you do, don't go into my room."

"Do I want to know why not?"

"*Non.*"

Griffin nodded and shoved the keys into his pocket.

"I'll take care of the Empire. You find Nora, okay?"

"That is the plan."

Griffin, with Michael trailing behind, headed toward the door. In the doorway, Michael paused and turned around.

"Mr. Edge?"

"What is it, Michael?"

The young man went silent for a moment and Kingsley waited. Usually he would have scolded someone for calling him Mr. Edge. It was *monsieur,* Kingsley, Mr. K., or nothing at all. But today he couldn't care less.

"It's only…" Michael began again, and Griffin put a comforting hand on Michael's back. "Nora's one of my friends."

"I know she is."

"I don't have a lot of friends."

"I'll find her," Kingsley promised. "We'll bring her home."

"Thank you. I mean…*merci.*"

Kingsley gave Michael a smile as he and Griffin left him alone in the office. One of his dogs, Max, ambled in and nudged Kingsley's hand. As Kingsley petted the dog, he thought of Sadie, the lone female of his rottweiler pack. She'd died, stabbed in the heart. Had his own sister done that? Put a knife into the chest of an animal? Surely she had help with her games. Say what one would about Nora Sutherlin, but the woman was a survivor, strong and resilient and could have easily fought off another woman. She'd been born strong and iron had sharpened iron. Submitting to a sadist had made her unbreakable. Becoming a Dominatrix had made her vicious. She'd even broken him a time or two. But that was all play. Men paid for the privilege of letting her break them. Now she was in real danger. This wasn't sadism or some role-play between consenting adults. This was violence, real violence and danger, the most pressing danger. He'd seen her lash bloody tiger stripes onto the body of a masochistic client with her whip skills, but he'd also seen her freeze in terror when a mentally unbalanced fan had attacked her at a book signing with a knife.

With a sigh, Kingsley ran his hands through his hair and rubbed hard at his face. If only the phone would ring, if only the letter would come with the demands and the threats. This dangerous game had only started. Marie-Laure had the board set up. What would be her opening move?

"Marie-Laure…" he whispered to himself. "What are you waiting for?"

*"Monsieur?"*

Kingsley turned around and glared at his secretary.

"Sophie, anything you need now must go through Griffin."

"But, *monsieur,* there's someone here to see you."

"He can see Griffin."

"He says he's only here to see you."

"He better be important." Kingsley strode toward the door. Perhaps Marie-Laure had moved her first pawn.

"I think he is," Sophie said with wide, scared eyes. "He says he's Nora Sutherlin's fiancé."

# 3

# THE KNIGHT

This couldn't be happening. This wasn't happening. How could it be happening? The questions stomped through Wesley's mind like a spooked stallion, trampling all other thoughts, all other questions. From the moment he'd gotten off the phone with Søren he'd been moving through the hours like a robot. He'd lost feeling in his hands. His ears wouldn't stop ringing. The world buzzed with white noise and the only thought he could hold in his head was, *Why?*

He'd woken up yesterday on the floor in one of the stables. Blood on his head, static in his brain, and no Nora anywhere. He'd called Søren, who'd hung up on him the moment Wesley had told him Nora was gone and the words *I will kill the bitch* were written on the stable wall. With a pounding skull, Wesley had thrown a few things into his car, left a vague message for his parents about visiting friends with Nora and headed north. He didn't dare fly. He couldn't risk being unreachable for four hours. What if Nora had been kidnapped for ransom? He'd pay every penny he had and steal whatever else he needed to buy her back again. He stopped only for gas on the way from Kentucky to New York and to down painkillers for his splitting headache. Surely he had a concussion from whatever had hit him. But that was the least of his worries now.

All that mattered was getting Nora back. Whatever the price.

And this was part of the price, coming to this house that he'd never entered before but already hated. Nora had said on at least a dozen occasions that, love him or hate him, Kingsley was her go-to man for any crisis she couldn't solve on her own. *I trust Kingsley and I have good reason to. Even Søren goes to Kingsley when there's a shitstorm,* she'd said. *And if I'm involved there's usually a shitstorm.* Wesley had decided then and there he never wanted to meet this Kingsley person, whom he considered to be nothing more than Nora's pimp. Kingsley called her all the time on that damn red phone of hers and sent her into all sorts of dangerous situations that left Wesley in borderline panic attack mode until she got home again.

But he couldn't deny this was the shitstorm to end all shitstorms. Only for Nora would he come to Kingsley begging for help.

Wesley paced as he waited and knew if someone didn't get him in five seconds, he'd go hunt Kingsley down himself. Kingsley Edge—who the hell was this guy, anyway? Wesley looked around the room for any clues and found nothing but a well-appointed music room complete with grand piano, antique furniture in various patterns of black-and-white and no hint whatsoever about what kind of person owned this house except that he had good taste and a lot of money. Nora didn't talk too much about Kingsley except to complain about him overbooking her back in her days as a Dominatrix. Although once she'd had a little too much to drink and spilled a few secrets about him, secrets she probably hadn't remembered telling him the next day. But other than that, Wesley knew nothing about him except that he was French. He imagined Kingsley was older, much older than Nora, and probably not very attractive. If he was attractive Nora probably would have had much nicer things to say about him other than muttering her usual vitriol at him. If she wasn't calling him "Kingsley" she was calling him "the Frog" or the "fucking Frog" more likely. She called him that so often that whenever Nora said "Kingsley" Wesley always pictured an actual frog wearing a beret. He hoped his imagination was somewhat close to the mark.

"So the future Mr. Nora Sutherlin has come to visit," came a voice from behind him, a voice with an unmistakable French accent.

Wesley turned and discovered a prince where a frog should be—shoulder-length dark hair, olive skin, riding boots and a frock coat, handsome beyond reason. Did Nora not have *any* ugly men in her life?

"I think Nora Railey sounds better." Wesley stood up as straight as he could and met Kingsley's eyes from across the room.

"I'll have my secretary start engraving the invitations." Kingsley came into the room slowly. "Let's hope we can find the bride before the big day arrives."

"You know about Nora?" Wesley's heart leaped, hoping against hope.

"I know she's been taken. I know who has her. Where she's been taken, I do not know that."

"Does Søren know anything?"

"Søren knows more than you and I combined. Unfortunately, he doesn't know where she is, either."

"But you know who has her?"

"*Oui.*"

Kingsley turned around and started to leave the room. Wesley raced after him and grabbed the back of his long coat. Before he knew what had happened, Wesley found himself with his back planted hard into the wall and Kingsley's face inches from his own.

"Young man, I wouldn't do that if I were you." Kingsley held Wesley immobile. "I used to kill people for a living. I never officially retired."

"You don't scare me." Wesley hoped the pounding of his heart against his rib cage didn't betray him. Kingsley dressed like someone off a romance novel cover but Wesley discerned genuine danger in the Frenchman's eyes. Nora worked for this man? Called him the Frog to his face? She was braver than Wesley had ever given her credit for.

"You're more attractive in person than you are in your photographs," Kingsley said, giving Wesley's face a close inspection. "I'm still not quite sure what she sees in you, however. Unless she lied to me about wanting a child of her own."

"I'm not a child."

"Not quite a man yet, either. Don't worry. You will grow up quickly in this house. *Peut-être…*" Kingsley moved an inch closer to Wesley's face and stared deep into his eyes. "She sees in you what I see in you."

"What's that?"

Wesley attempted to wrest himself out of Kingsley's grasp. Kingsley didn't let go.

"Everything she doesn't see when she looks in the mirror." With that, Kingsley released him and Wesley wrenched himself away. He felt a wave of nausea as if his brain bashed against his skull. But he didn't give in to it. He breathed through his nose and stood his ground.

"I want to see Søren. Now," Wesley said.

Kingsley straightened his jacket and smoothed his vest.

"Answer two questions first. Then I'll let you see him."

"Whatever. Fine. What?"

"Question one—is it true that you are affianced to her?"

Wesley narrowed his eyes at Kingsley, who stood waiting, tapping the toe of one of his stupid boots against the floor.

"Yes. Right before she got kidnapped, we went horseback riding. I asked her to marry me. When we got back to the stables, she said yes."

Kingsley nodded as he rubbed his bottom lip with his fingertip before raising two fingers.

"Second question. Did you ask her to marry you before or after your head injury?"

"Has anyone ever told you that you're an asshole?" Wesley asked, coming up to him again. Cautiously this time, however. If Kingsley pushed him into the wall again, Wesley knew he'd lose whatever nothing was in his stomach for sure.

"*Oui*. But only once. I made sure they never said it again. Come along. You want to see the priest? I'll show you the priest."

Kingsley started up the stairs and Wesley had no choice but to follow. He noticed Kingsley wincing slightly as they turned a corner and headed to the third floor. Was he injured? Had someone attacked Kingsley, too?

"Are you all right?" Wesley asked, his loathing temporarily giving way to his better instincts. Kingsley might be the asshole of the universe, but Wesley hated to see anyone in pain.

"It is safe to say I've been better."

"Did someone attack you, too?"

"I wouldn't call it an attack."

"Then what would you call it?"

"I'd call it one of the better nights of my life."

Kingsley said nothing more as he led them down a hall to a room on the right.

"I'm afraid *le prêtre* won't be much good to you."

"I don't care. I need to talk to him."

"If you insist." Kingsley opened the door to a room at the end of the hall. Wesley's eyes widened when he took in the scene. On the floor, at the end of the biggest red bed he'd ever seen in his life, sat Søren, his blond head bowed, his eyes closed. "Talk away. He may not talk back, however."

"What the hell…?"

"He threatened to call the police," Kingsley said matter-of-factly. "The police, the church and all city, state and federal authorities. I couldn't allow that. For his sake."

"So you…"

"Sedated him. And handcuffed him. He'll be out another hour at least with the shot I gave him."

"You drugged Søren?"

"I have a very well-stocked medicine cabinet in case of emergencies."

"You're crazy."

Kingsley gave a shrug so nonchalant it could only be described as French.

"Turnabout is fair play, *non?* His turn to wear the handcuffs."

Wesley could only stare at Søren on the floor. Even unconscious he had a certain broken nobility to him in his black clerics and his white collar. The one time Wesley had spoken face-to-face with the man, he'd been wearing secular clothes.

"He's a priest," Wesley said as the reality of Søren's profession finally sank in. He knew, of course. He'd known from the beginning. Nora never hid that from him. But seeing the collar…

"He is. And possibly the finest priest in America if not the world. And if he wants to remain a priest and get his lover back, then it's for the best we leave the authorities out of this. I can only protect his secrets so much. He'll thank me later."

Kingsley closed the door and started back down the hall.

"Kingsley, we have to call the police. I don't care what happens to Søren or you or even me. We're wasting time. We don't even know where she is."

"You call the police if your car gets stolen. You don't call them for anything that matters. I know who has your fiancée, and believe me, if you value your beloved's life at all, you will trust me—calling the authorities would equal a death sentence for her."

The truth of the words shone in Kingsley's eyes. As much as Wesley didn't want to believe him, something told him that whatever happened to Nora, it wasn't some kidnap for ransom, wasn't some prank or game.

"The woman who has your fiancée is willing to kill. She's done it before. She's also willing to die. Something else she's done before. A dangerous combination. We raise the alarm, the siren sounds, Nora dies."

"How do you know this person's willing to die?"

"Because, *mon petit prince,* she pissed me off. That is a good indictor she had a death wish."

Kingsley's brash words failed to give any comfort.

"They're going to kill Nora, aren't they? The words on the walls…" Wesley whispered, his heart clenching as he remembered the fear upon seeing the French words, even not knowing what they meant. "Søren said they mean 'I will kill the bitch.'"

"If it comforts you at all, 'the bitch' is not your Nora. I'll leave the story for the priest to tell."

"No way. You knocked him out so now you're going to tell me." Wesley stared Kingsley down. Kingsley might be strong and dangerous, but he was also in pain and pain made him vulnerable. Wesley wouldn't back down this time. "And you're going to tell me now."

Kingsley exhaled heavily through his nose before shrugging again.

"Those words—*I will kill the bitch*—were uttered thirty years ago by the woman the priest married at age eighteen. His wife, Marie-Laure…my sister."

"Thirty years ago…Søren was married to your sister?"

"Yes. A marriage of convenience. That was what it was supposed to be. That is what he told her it would be. She wanted more, more than he could give."

"She was in love with him?"

"*Oui,* or whatever she had in her heart that passed for love. *Obsession* would be a more accurate word. When she found out he loved another she said those words as a threat. For whatever reason she waited thirty years to carry out her threat."

"Nora would have been four years old then. She didn't even meet Søren until she was fifteen, which is bad enough. No way could Nora have been the other woman at four years old."

"*Exactement.* That's why I say you can take some comfort in that threat. That's why I know she's alive and safe…for the time being. *Le prêtre* was in love with someone else at the time. But your fiancée was not the bitch my sister meant."

"Who was she, then? Maybe we should talk to her."

Kingsley turned on his booted heel and gave Wesley a gallant mock bow.

"You already are, *mon ami*. The bitch…at your service."

# 4
# THE ROOK

As soon as she got to the hotel, Grace Easton decided she'd stay only one night. What was the point of such a beautiful room with a view of the ocean if she didn't even have Zachary with her to share it? She stared out the window onto the beach and saw two birds dancing at the edge of the water, dancing and biting each other. A mating ritual, perhaps? Or fighting? Or both? Nora would say both, wouldn't she? Grace smiled as she dug her phone out of her purse and called Nora's number. When voice mail picked up, Grace left a quick message.

"*Nora, it's Grace. Zachary had to fill in for someone at a conference in Australia. I'm all alone in Rhode Island on holiday. Thinking of coming to the city. I'd love to get into some trouble with you.*"

Grace knew such a message would surely get Nora's attention. That woman had been threatening Grace with all sorts of scandalous fun if Grace ever dared cross into Nora's territory again. Nora had said she would introduce Grace to Søren if she was feeling up to the challenge. Hopefully Nora would call back tonight so Grace could make some new plans. Nothing more depressing than staying alone in a honeymoon suite at a New England B and B. Why had she come, anyway, other than habit? She and Zachary had vacationed here almost every year of their marriage. It was the one time Zachary could see his best mate Jason from university who'd moved here ten years ago. But now Zachary was trapped at a conference and Jason and his wife had canceled on them because of a family emergency. Grace was trapped alone on holiday in America. What would be better than getting into a little trouble with the one and only Nora Sutherlin? Maybe…maybe Nora was the reason she'd come without Zachary. Nora had practically dared her to take a walk on the wild side with her. Grace did love a challenge.

With a jet-lagged sigh, Grace pulled away from the window and dug through her carry-on bag. From it she pulled out her eReader and stretched out on the bed, deciding to read until she heard back from Nora. She'd gotten to the good part of the book right as her plane had landed.

*"Harry?"*

*"You can do better than that," came a voice from behind him. Blake turned around and saw Harrison sitting cross-legged on the floor. He'd laid down a plaid blanket and had a lantern sitting by his knee. The light from the flickering wick cast a golden shadow across his face. During the day at school all anyone saw of Harrison were his black retro glasses and the books that never left his hands. But Blake saw past the glasses, past the books.*

*"Better than what?"*

*"You're really going to call me 'Harry' down here? While we're alone together?"*

*"What am I supposed to call you? Mr. Braun? Sir?"*

*"I wouldn't stop you if you did."*

*"I'm not calling you 'sir.'"*

Harrison shrugged as he turned a page in the textbook in front of him.

*"Suit yourself. You're the one who started this."*

Blake considered turning around and leaving. This was the stupidest idea ever, anyway. He'd never forgive Mr. Pettit for forcing him and Harrison to write that paper together. One late night on Harrison's bed arguing about the morality of Machiavelli's political philosophy had brought him here to this moment.

*"Me? You kissed me, remember?"*

*"You were begging for it."* Harrison glanced up at Blake over the top of his glasses. *"Three chairs in my room and you sit on the bed next to me?"*

*"Why do you have so many fucking chairs in your room, anyway?"* Blake sat down on the blanket across from Harrison.

*"To see if you'd sit in them or choose the bed."*

*"You were testing me?"*

*"Yes."*

*"Great. I failed the first test."* Blake ran a hand through his hair and shook his head.

*"You sat on the bed next to me. I kissed you. You kissed back. Hate to tell you this, but you passed."*

Blake stared at Harrison and willed himself to hate him. It should have been easy to hate Harrison. Captain of the academic team, every teacher's pet, only a junior but already he had scholarship offers from two Ivys. On top of that he was the one guy at their Catholic school who'd come out as gay. He'd done it on purpose, practically daring the school to expel him, expel the straight-A student, captain of the debate team, smartest fucking kid in school who'd won as many academic awards as Blake's team had brought home soccer trophies. He wanted the fight, the publicity, the day in court. The more the other *guys at school taunted and tortured him, calling him a "fag" and shoving him into lockers, the quieter, calmer and more determined he seemed to endure it with dignity. He always introduced himself as "Harrison" but everyone who hated him called him "Harry" just to be petty. Harrison didn't blink, didn't cry, didn't act like he noticed the hate hurled his way.*

*It was Harrison's noble stoicism in the face of torture that first caught Blake's eye. That and that perfect fucking face of his that he hid behind those hipster glasses.*

*Harrison slammed the book shut and Blake jumped.*

*"Look, it's 8:13 already." Harrison took off his glasses and for the first time Blake saw his naked face. God fucking dammit, why did he have to feel this way for another guy? "They lock us up at nine. You came to me. You said you couldn't stop thinking about me. You said you've never done anything with a guy before but you had to know for sure and maybe could we hang out and talk and…remember all that?"*

*"I remember."*

*"Was that a lie? Or are we playing a game?"*

*"This isn't a game to me," Blake pledged.*

*"What is it, then?"*

*Because he couldn't hold back anymore, Blake leaned forward and kissed Harrison. Unlike the first kiss on the bed two weeks ago, a kiss that had been slow and sensual and had left Blake questioning everything he ever wanted, thought or believed, this kiss fell flat on Harrison's unmoving lips.*

*"What's wrong?" Blake asked, terrified of the answer.*

*"You're doing it wrong." Harrison gazed at him with narrowed, hooded eyes. Their lips were only an inch apart.*

*"How do I do it right? Tell me…you've done this before."*

*"Lesson one—don't stop breathing."*

*"What do you—"*

*Before Blake could finish asking his question, Harrison had him by the throat.*

*"I let the whole world fuck me over by day. But you and me, when we're alone, it's you who gets fucked. You get to run the school by day. At night, with me, you're mine. I own you. You want to do this, you never forget that. So...do you want to do this?"*

*Blake swallowed and felt his Adam's apple hitting Harrison's hand.*

*"Yes, Harrison."*

*"At least you finally got my name right."*

*Harrison released Blake's throat and without apology or further preliminaries rose up onto his knees and pulled his shirt off. Blake knew nothing of what Harrison did after school. Homework, right? But he must have been doing something other than studying to get those muscles in his biceps and on his stomach. Blake didn't get much more time to stare because Harrison unzipped his jeans, grabbed Blake by the back of the neck and pulled his head down.*

*"Take it," Harrison ordered, and Blake wrapped his mouth around him and sucked deep. He knew he should have been grossed out by this, by sucking off another guy. But he wanted it, wanted him, and couldn't get enough.*

*On his hands and knees with Harrison's cock down his throat, Blake felt, for the first time in his life, like he was doing exactly what he was supposed to be doing.*

*"Lesson two..." Harrison reached down and grabbed Blake by the chin, stopping him. "You get me this turned on and there will be consequences."*

*"What kind?"*

*Harrison grabbed Blake's shirt and pulled. The shirt came off first and then the jeans, the boxers right along with them.*

*"This kind."*

Grace finished reading the scene and let the eReader slide out of her hand as she closed her eyes. Her swollen clitoris pulsed against her fingers and every muscle in her back tightened like a coiled spring. The images flashed through her mind—the two teenage boys hiding their hunger for each other from the world, the bitterness that they had to hide making them all the more desperate for each other, the young mouths meeting, their bodies joining…. She came hard, rocking against her hand as her vaginal walls contracted against nothing.

She pulled her hand from between her thighs and lay gasping on the bed. Between gasps she heard something vibrating. Not a vibrator, though—she hadn't packed hers.

Finding her phone, Grace raised it to her ear without checking the number.

"Hello," she said, taking another breath.

"How's my Gracie?"

"Amazing…" She gave a throaty laugh and heard Zachary chuckling on the other side of the world.

"Are you going to tell me why you're amazing or are you leaving it to my imagination?"

"I've been reading."

"Horrible idea. I hate books. Reading's for bellends."

"It's one of your writers."

"Writing's for bellends."

"What about editing? Do you recall editing one called *All Hallows High?*"

"Oh, God."

Grace laughed again as she sat up in bed and rested against the headboard.

"What is that for? That 'oh, God'? It's fantastic."

"I think Nora wrote it to test me."

"It's a romance novel. Not a very hard test."

"It's an erotica novel between two teenage boys at a Catholic school."

"And?"

"And she's trying to get a rise out of me with it."

"She got one out of me. With my husband on the other side of the earth she'll probably get another one out of me before the night's over."

"I'm glad you find a book that includes illegal sexual acts so erotic. The underage boys fuck each other."

"You remember I'm a teacher. Teenagers, even the boys, do that sort of thing."

"Oh, yes, and the teacher fucks the boys, too."

"Dear Lord. Do the boys also—" she dropped her voice to a stage whisper "—smoke marijuana?"

"You're mocking me."

"You do remember that you lost your virginity at thirteen, and that I lost mine at eighteen to my own teacher, who happened to be you?"

"Please don't call me out on my hypocrisy when I'm trying to be hypocritical."

"Zachary."

"What?"

"Stop being so vanilla."

Zachary fell silent on the other end of the line and Grace could only cover her mouth to stifle her laughter.

"Grace."

"Yes?"

"I love you."

"I know you do." She grinned to herself, having much too much fun teasing her husband.

"So you're enjoying the latest work of Ms. Sutherlin? Sounded like it from how breathlessly you answered the phone."

"Love it. I slept with her editor to get an advance copy."

Grace stood up and found an empty glass. She tucked the phone under her ear while she filled it with water. Her little reading session had been a workout. Nora's books left her as breathless as her characters.

"Should I be worried that my wife is reading Nora Sutherlin's books?"

"Why? Because she's Nora Sutherlin the writer or because she's Nora Sutherlin the woman you slept with last year?"

"Can you tell me the right answer before I give my answer?"

"'Neither' is the right answer. You have nothing to worry about."

"My wife is masturbating to my ex-lover's books. Nothing good can come of this."

"Orgasms came of it."

"Other than that."

"Your wife knows her husband is in love with her and is devoted to their marriage. Your wife knows that Nora Sutherlin isn't a threat to her marriage. And your wife knows all of this even knowing her husband still carries a torch for Ms. Nora Sutherlin."

"Now that's not true at all. I adore her, yes, even if she will be the death of me someday. But the feelings are entirely of the friendship variety. Nothing more."

"It must be so much easier to lie to me on the phone instead of face-to-face." Grace pulled the covers down on the bed and slipped in.

"It is, come to mention it."

Grace sighed as she pulled her leg to her chest and rested her chin on her knee.

"I borrowed your coat the other day. Your gray trench.

Couldn't find mine and it was raining. Stuck my hand in the pocket and guess what I found?"

She almost laughed aloud at the sound of Zachary's heavy guilty sigh coming from the other side of the world.

"A black tie?"

"A black tie…that for some reason smelled of hothouse flowers. I only ever remember meeting one person in my entire life with that scent on her. Beautiful woman with green eyes and black hair and spectacular cleavage. Sound familiar at all?"

"Vaguely familiar."

Grace remembered how her hand had trembled when she saw the black silk tie, smelled it. That day she met Nora, she remembered that scent, the scent of flowers that thrived in captivity even if they didn't belong there.

"She put it in my pocket, and I didn't know she'd done it. It was a joke, not some precious souvenir."

"And you kept it in your pocket for over a year because…?"

"You never know when you'll need a spare tie."

Grace stopped talking and took a drink of her water.

"Are you angry?" Zachary asked, and she heard real concern in his voice. They teased each other often about that year they spent apart, he in America, she still in London. That year had been so hard and so hellish for the both of them that the only way they could face the memory of it was by mocking it, defying it to have any power over their marriage.

"No, I'm not angry. I think I'd worry about you if you weren't still attracted to her. My only worry is…"

"What?"

"I'm sure this won't make any sense but…do you miss her? Or do you miss it? Nora's quite specific. There's no one like her so I understand if you miss her. But if you miss it, miss the sort of sex you had with her that you and I don't have, then I'd be worried."

"I miss her," he said, and Grace believed him. "I won't lie. She and I had an amazing passionate night together. I saw another world with her, a world I never even dreamed existed. It was eye-opening to say the least, and I'm certainly glad I got to see it. But it's not my world. You're my world."

"You're my world, too," she confessed, smiling through tears. They'd only been apart two days and she was already getting emotional and maudlin. Damn Zachary for being so lovable, so missable.

"So we're all right? You forgive your husband for occasionally having fond reminisces about a wild American girl he once—"

"Once?"

"Or twice. Or...more than twice."

"It's unfair. I know I'm supposed to be jealous that you had a night of sex with a beautiful woman who writes torrid books and lives a scandalous life," she said in her most dramatic *Masterpiece Theater* voice. "But really I'm jealous that you got to see that world. What does she call it?"

"The Underground."

"Yes, you got to see the Underground. S&M clubs and Dominatrixes and wealthy and powerful deviants. Meanwhile, I was falling asleep in my tea while Ian droned on about bloody exchange rates."

"So you're telling me that you're not jealous that I slept with Nora Sutherlin and still miss her from time to time. You're jealous that I had more fun committing adultery than you did."

"Entirely correct."

"You're not far from the city. Call Nora. Tell her to show you the Underground. Have some fun adultery for once."

Grace felt her conscience bite her. Not much of a bite. More a nibble.

"I did call Nora already," Grace confessed. "Got her voice mail. Thought we could meet for a drink."

"Nora doesn't have one drink. She has drinks—plural. And kinks—plural. Be prepared for a long night if you end up in the passenger seat of her car."

"I'll say my prayers. Are you sure you'll be fine with me spending some time with her?"

She heard him sigh and her heart clenched to hear it. She could picture his face right now, so striking with his ice-blue eyes and thoughtfully furrowed brow.

"Gracie, I know you've been under so much stress lately. I know how hard this has been on you."

He didn't have to say what "this" was. This was their failed quest to get pregnant that had left them both emotionally exhausted.

"A little," she admitted in a choked whisper.

"Go have fun, darling. You deserve a night off."

"So…how much fun are you willing to let me have?"

"As much as you want. I had mine. You go have yours. Be careful and don't give me any details about it the next day. Ignorance is bliss."

"What if you find a black tie in my coat pocket that smells like some handsome bloke?"

"I'll think positively. I'll pretend you murdered a stranger and kept the tie as a memento."

"Fair enough."

"Call Nora again. Give her my lust. And tell her to please write a book that isn't specifically designed to get us all arrested next time. Oh, and remind her that her edits are due on Monday."

"I'll pass the message along. If you need me, I'll be in the Underground. So try not to need me."

"Have a good time. Be safe. Stay away from men in collars."

"Are the male submissives dangerous?" she asked, feeling rather proud she knew the terminology.

"I was talking about priests."

They bid their good-nights and Grace hung up the phone. Priests…as if she could stay away from Nora's priest. Ever since Zachary first told her about Søren, Grace knew she had to meet this man someday. During her first phone call with Nora, she'd grilled her relentlessly, fascinated to speak to a woman who had a Catholic priest for a lover.

*A priest…really?*

*My priest. He's been my priest since I was fifteen years old. I hope you're scandalized. It's no fun if you're not scandalized.*

*Thoroughly scandalized. Is he handsome?*

*Is the pope Catholic?*

*I'll take that as a yes. Zachary's not very fond of him.*

*Zach has terrible taste in men.*

*He said Søren wasn't nice.*

*Søren isn't nice. But he's good.*

*Good? How good?*

*He's the best man on earth.*

*That's quite a claim. I'll have to meet this man if he's the best man on earth.*

*I'll introduce you someday. One word of advice—show no fear.*

*Show no fear?*

*Seriously. He's like a big cat with a catnip toy if you give him your fear to play with.*

*How big of a cat are we talking about?*

*Lion. Big damn lion.*

*You make him sound dangerous.*

*Oh, he is dangerous. Just part of his charm. But he's not half as dangerous as Kingsley is. Søren calls the shots. Kingsley's the trig-german.*

*And what do you do?*

*You already know the answer to that, Grace. Anything I want to.*

Grace found herself smiling again at the memory of the conversation. Zachary did say he trusted her, and she had to admit she'd rather regret not taking him up on his offer. She and Zachary almost always vacationed in Rhode Island in August, the week before her school year started again. Only his conference in Australia had been moved and now they were on opposite ends of the earth. Would be nice having a little adventure. And she did want to meet this priest of Nora's. Any man who scared her husband, the infamous London Fog of publishing, that was a man she had to meet.

Grace picked up the phone again and dialed Nora.

This time someone answered.

But it wasn't Nora.

# 5
## THE PAWN

Laila slipped off her shoes and socks and stepped onto the lush green grass eager for the reunion she knew was at hand. She crossed the lawn toward the dense copse of trees. The sidewalk could have taken her there but she'd much rather dig her bare feet into the earth. All her life she'd dreamed of America, dreamed of this country so much larger than her own. Maybe it was even big enough to hold all her hopes and dreams. Denmark felt like an old relative she'd long worn out with courtesy visits. America seemed new and fresh to her, not covered in the dust of dead kingdoms.

Her steps slowed. She found the house hidden deep in the trees and smiled at the sight of it. No wonder her uncle Søren loved it here so much. No wonder he never let them send him anywhere else. Such a pretty house, this little two-story Gothic cottage that looked like something off the cover of a mystery novel.

Laila knocked once and received no answer. Another knock.

Still nothing. Strange…she would have thought at least one of them would be waiting for her at the rectory. Last week she'd received an email from her tante Elle offering to fly her to the States for a week. "*Shh…*" read the note. "*Let's give your uncle a big surprise.*"

So where was her aunt? And where was her uncle? With a nervous hand, Laila turned the doorknob and found the door unlocked. The flight had been delayed an hour in London. Maybe her aunt and uncle were home. Perhaps they were… occupied. She wouldn't put it past them to steal a spare hour. Laila found herself smiling as she stepped into the kitchen.

She'd worn that smile before when she'd caught them in an embrace during a visit last year. An embrace and a whisper, a whisper and a kiss… Laila had seen the glint in a pair of green eyes, a glint that hinted the embrace was merely a prelude to a nighttime symphony.

"Wipe that smile off your face, young lady," her uncle had ordered her as he'd pulled back and crossed his arms across his broad chest.

"Why?" she'd asked. "Am I not supposed to know about—" and she dropped her voice to a whisper "—sex?"

"No, you are not." He'd given her a look so stern it nearly scared her. Or would have scared her had someone else not reached up and flicked him on the ear.

"She's seventeen. She's allowed to know about the birds and the bees and that you and I very often engage in the birds and the bees. More bees than birds. Like last night, for example. And this morning. And—"

And whatever came after the "and" got muffled under her uncle's hand.

"Laila," he said with deliberate, menacing calm to Laila and the woman he gently, playfully suffocated under his hand, "is

not to know about sex or talk about sex or have sex. Ever. I'll
never have children. She is therefore my honorary daughter.
With her love of animals, Laila was no doubt destined for the
Franciscans. I have the perfect convent picked out for her.
Her room is already reserved. Now I have spoken. Nod if
you understand."

And Laila and the woman in his arms nodded even as she
giggled all the way back to her bedroom.

Of course she knew about sex. She knew he had it all the
time with her "aunt," as she and Gitte, her sister, thought of
her. Not that it bothered her. She wasn't Catholic, after all.
Why should she care if he had a lover?

And such a lover he had... No one seeing her could blame
him for what he'd done. Then again, no one seeing him could
ever blame her, either. As a younger girl, she'd envied her aunt
in a way. Her feelings about her uncle made her ashamed of
herself sometimes until she got a little older and realized she
didn't want him so much as she wanted what they had, her
onkel Søren and tante Elle. What they had...it seemed like
magic to her. She even thought of it as not a thing so much or a
feeling, but as a place. The Enchanted Kingdom of Adulthood,
she'd dubbed it. Adults alone lived in that world and as a girl
she'd longed to gain entrance into it and learn all its secrets.

Whenever around her aunt and uncle she felt like she stood
outside the gate and could see through the bars. She only
needed the key. Love. That was the key. Adult love. Private
love. Passionate love between two people who told secrets
with their bodies. She'd learned about love watching her aunt
and uncle doing nothing but talking to each other. There had
only been those few visits, once a year, sometimes twice, but
they were enough to teach her that love wasn't something one
found only in books. The kind of love that knights fought

for and kings died for and ships were launched for and poets recorded for posterity—it was real. She'd seen it. She wanted what they had, wanted that secret that they told each other without even saying a word. She'd seen it pass between them with every glance. Maybe she would have that someday, she wished every time she'd seen it. Maybe she'd find it here in America.

Silence filled the rectory. She heard nothing, no one. What if he was with her now in his bedroom? Maybe that's why the quiet all about her resonated with restless energy. In a house so small surely she could hear the sounds of passion even upstairs and behind closed doors. Or was it possible to make love entirely in silence? She doubted her aunt could. As a girl of ten, Laila had discovered that if she sat on the floor with her ear to the wall, she could hear them at night. That young she never quite understood what she heard—breathy gasps, warm, illicit murmurs, a moan followed by silence. Sounds of pleasure caused by…what? Then she hadn't known. She'd heard other sounds, too—whimpers, cries, quiet noises that sounded far more like pain than pleasure. It gave her the strangest feeling in her stomach to sit by the wall at night and force herself to stay awake and listen to them in their bedroom. Sometimes she felt something like jealousy. Sometimes her whole body shuddered with a need for something she couldn't name.

Shuddering…that's what it was. The house seemed to shudder as soon as Laila stepped foot into the kitchen. Laila's happiness here started to falter. Something didn't feel right. Never before had she breached her uncle's home, but she knew the house, like him, would be meticulous, nearly immaculate. And it was. Nothing out of place. Nothing disturbed. Nothing wrong. But still…everything seemed wrong. She passed through the kitchen and into the living room. Beautiful, of course. A thousand books. One perfect grand piano. A fireplace naked without a fire. She found a staircase and took it to the second floor. She found the bathroom, the office.... When she stepped into the bedroom, she almost blushed.

Laila couldn't look at the made bed without imagining the sheets askew. Four years ago, her aunt and uncle had come to her grandmother's funeral, and as usual after everyone had gone to bed, Laila pressed her ear to the wall and listened. She'd expected to hear the usual sounds of passion, of pain. Or maybe only talking. But that night she heard them doing something she'd never heard them do before in the Enchanted Kingdom of Adulthood—fighting.

"I don't want to discuss this with you, Eleanor."

"The funeral's tomorrow. We need to talk about it."

"You brought it with you?"

"Of course I did. I thought you might want...she might have wanted..."

"No, she wouldn't. She gave it to you. She wanted you to have it. Unless it means nothing to you anymore." Laila heard the bitterness in her uncle's voice.

"It means as much to me as it always did. I only thought that since I left you, you might want to bury it with her."

"You might have left me, but I never left you. Keep it if you want it at all."

"At all?" Her aunt sounded aghast. "It's my most precious possession."

Laila's stomach had clenched so hard at her tante Eleanor's words and the fervency in her voice. As was her habit, she reached up to her neck and wrapped her hand around the locket that rested in the hollow of her throat for comfort.

"As you are mine."

Then Laila had almost stopped listening. The sorrow in her uncle's voice cut into her, his words sharp as a knife.

"Don't...don't make this harder than it is."

"It couldn't be any harder than it is, Little One."

Silence came after that but only for a moment before she heard her uncle's voice again, tender and careful.

"Forgive me. I'm so grateful you're here. For me...for them."

"They don't know, do they? You haven't told them I left you."

"I only told Freyja. Laila and Gitte worship you. I didn't want to hurt the girls."

Laila heard laughter then, but it did nothing to untie the knots.

"What are you laughing at?" The mirth in her uncle's voice calmed her momentarily.

"You saying you didn't want to hurt the girls. Not your usual style, is it?"

"You keep smiling like that, and I'll turn you over my knee."

"Now that's more like it."

An intimate silence filled the room again—a silence that hinted at kisses and other more private acts.

"I'll stay as long as you want or need me to. And I'll keep this until the day I die. But if one of the girls asks me about us...I won't lie to them."

War had broken out in the Enchanted Kingdom of Adulthood. She wanted to hear no more. But she couldn't stop listening.

Laila backed out of her uncle's empty bedroom, a bedroom she knew she didn't belong in, and returned to the kitchen. She'd hoped to find sanctuary here but now she felt only troubled. The very air in the entryway seemed worried, as if someone had left in a great hurry and offered the house no explanation.

She wandered around the kitchen, afraid for some reason to venture out but also afraid to stay put. Maybe she should call the church. She had that phone number. He might be gone but his secretary could be working there. Maybe she had an emergency number.

Laila went to the kitchen phone not wanting to use her cell. When she reached it she discovered at last a cause for her concern.

The rectory had a landline still. Had he been there, she would have teased her uncle for being part of a church so old-fashioned they still used big black rotary phones with dangling cords. But her small smile died when she lifted the receiver and found a crack in the cradle. More than a crack, the phone was marred by a huge ugly gash. The handset, too, was damaged. She stared at the phone in her hand before resting it gently onto the cradle again. Someone had been on the phone and hung it up so violently and with such force the phone had cracked open. As a small child she'd hung off her uncle's arms like a monkey on a tree—sometimes she clung to his biceps with her hands, sometimes she hung upside down from her knees. It seemed he could keep her suspended in the air forever. As long as she hung and she'd swung, she'd never once feared he would drop her. And he never had. She'd never met a man stronger than her uncle. Only a man of incredible strength could have done this kind of damage with one fierce slam.

Even as her body started to shake, Laila's mind began to race. She needed to get out and seek safety. She picked up her suitcase and raced to the door, but the sound of footfalls on the hardwood stalled her steps.

She spun around ready to thank God her uncle had come back and would make everything okay again like he always did.

But it wasn't him.

And nothing was okay.

# 6
# THE QUEEN

A smiling woman stood before Nora. She wore an elegant black-and-purple dress, understated lipstick and a maleficent gleam in her dark eyes. Nora's chair faced a large window. The sun had already set; the diaphanous curtains moved in the evening breeze like green smoke surrounding her. The woman, whoever she was, looked about forty-five years old and had long dark hair classically coiffed. And for some reason something about the set of her lips, the line of her jaw, reminded her of Kingsley.

"Who are you?" Nora said, her voice groggy with pain. She didn't follow up with "Where am I?" because she didn't want to know.

"You don't know?"

"If I knew, why would I ask?"

Nora pulled on the handcuffs behind her back. She had small hands and could sometimes squeeze out of handcuffs if she had enough wiggle room. But they were clapped on tight, too tight, and no lock pick set or hairpins were to be found.. Her heart thundered in newfound panic.

"I'll give you a hint," the woman said with a smile that held no friendliness at all. "You've slept with my husband."

"That doesn't winnow the field down as much as you think it would."

The woman narrowed her eyes at Nora and something in that look seemed so familiar, she suddenly knew exactly who it was who faced her. Terror, real terror, gripped Nora's heart with hooked talons.

"You're supposed to be dead," Nora whispered.

"You're Catholic. Haven't you ever heard of resurrection?"

"Marie-Laure." Of course she was. She looked so much like Kingsley it was as if she was a house he haunted.

"Marie-Laure Constance Stearns. *Comment ça va?*"

Nora swallowed.

"I've been better," she said in answer to Marie-Laure's question. "Usually when I'm handcuffed it's consensual."

"Only usually?"

"I get arrested a lot."

Marie-Laure came toward her and bent over. She stood so close and studied her with such scrutiny that Nora could smell her perfume—cypress—and see the crow's feet mostly hidden by an impressive makeup job under her eyes.

"See something you like?" Nora asked as she leaned back in the chair trying to move her head as far from Marie-Laure's as possible.

"Simply trying to see what he sees in you. My husband, I mean. I'm not finding it yet."

"I give great head."

The retort was answered with a slap, hard and fast, to her left cheek.

Nora winced and blinked her now-tear-filled eyes.

"You are seriously good at that," she said. "Wow." Søren had slapped her harder than that but only once ever, on the night she'd gone back to him.

"I thought my husband was a man of refined tastes."

"In wine and books and music, he is. Terrible taste in women, though. Obviously."

Nora braced herself for another slap. It didn't come.

Marie-Laure took a few steps back until she stood at the window again. Something about that window, this room... Nora had a feeling she'd been in this house before, but when? She remembered it like she remembered a dream—all haze and feeling, no substance.

"I was only twenty-one years old when I got married. And he'd turned eighteen on our wedding night. We weren't much more than children then, so I forgave him for not loving me."

"How Christian of you."

"You see...shortly after we married, I discovered the truth about him and my brother. They tried to keep it from me. But I knew. I saw them whispering together at times, saw the way my husband looked at my brother when he should have been looking at me. Kingsley boasted of his female conquests. As a girl I thought he was exaggerating. Then when I knew about him and my husband, I thought he'd been lying the whole time. Embarrassed, a cover-up."

"Kingsley's not gay. Neither is Søren. Not that there's anything...well, you know."

"I realize that now. Then I thought they were, that they were deeply in love with each other. I knew my marriage was ostensibly for money—that's what he said, anyway—but I agreed to it because I knew he'd love me eventually. Why wouldn't he?"

"I can think of a few reasons," Nora said, determined to piss Marie-Laure off as much as possible. What a fucking lunatic. If she survived this, Nora would kill Søren for marrying Marie-Laure all those years ago. On paper it had seemed like the perfect solution. Marie-Laure and Kingsley had had no money. Søren had his trust fund just waiting for him to get married or turn twenty-one. If Søren and Marie-Laure married, no one could say a word about all the time Kingsley and Søren spent alone together. They could have lived in the same house. And Marie-Laure would have been rich and free to do whatever she wanted with whomever she wanted. But it was Søren she wanted, the one man whose love she would never have. And the plan that looked so perfect on paper, the marriage that meant everyone would win...for Kingsley, Søren and Marie-Laure, it had been the beginning of the end of everything. Maybe even Nora's life.

"Everyone loved me at that school. I had every boy there falling all over himself for me. When I knew my husband had no interest in me, I even took one of them up on his offer. One of the students, a boy named Christian. Perfect, *non?* Oh, and one of the priests."

"That's shocking."

"They'd never seen a girl as beautiful as I was. How is that shocking?"

"Other than Søren I've never met a priest who was interested in women."

Marie-Laure gave her a smile so sweet Nora almost wished the woman would slap her again. Anything other than that smile.

"He must love beating you."

"He's a sadist. Of course he does."

"Does that bother you? That he's a sadist? That he needs to inflict pain to become aroused?"

"You're going to interrogate me about my relationship with Søren?"

"You have other plans?"

Nora had her hands cuffed behind her back and it felt like the cuffs themselves were attached to the chair.

"Guess not. What do you know about Søren, anyway? You haven't seen him in thirty years. How do you even know what he's into? How did you even find me? What do you want?"

The questions finally poured out of Nora as she gave in to her fear.

"What do I want?" Marie-Laure repeated the final question. "That I will tell you. I want to have a long talk with my husband."

"You could have called him. Phone at the rectory. He's got a cell phone, too, although the church pays for it so he tries not to use it for personal calls. He's anal like that."

"No...I tried to talk to him before when we were together. I asked him over and over again what was wrong with him that he didn't want to be with me."

"Maybe he just wasn't that into you," Nora offered, but Marie-Laure ignored her.

"So if I had someone he loved here, someone he wanted to protect, then perhaps he might finally answer the questions I have. I can't quite believe he does love you, though. Especially now that I've met you."

Nora looked down at herself, her stained jeans, her bloody white tank top, her hair in lank, dirty waves. No doubt she looked as bad as she felt.

"This isn't me at my best, I promise."

"I've seen you at your best. I still wasn't impressed."

"Jesus, tell me how you really feel."

"I cannot quite fathom that he cares as deeply for you as I would need him to, so I brought in a little...what's that phrase? Backup?"

She called out a name then; it sounded like "Damon."

A man entered the room. She knew it was a man from the sound of his footsteps even though Nora couldn't see him.

He and Marie-Laure spoke to each other in French, which Nora caught most of. She heard "handcuffs" and "Bring in the girl."

The girl? This couldn't be good.

Whoever he was stood behind Nora and uncuffed her from the chair.

Nora brought her arms around and massaged her wrists. She almost felt more secure cuffed to the chair. If they uncuffed her it was probably because they weren't afraid of her. She didn't like being the woman in the room no one was afraid of.

Nora stayed in her chair and didn't turn around when she heard the door open behind her again. But when the door opened a third time, she heard the pained cry of a young woman. She stood up and spun around.

"Laila?" Nora recognized the girl at once—Søren's niece. The man let Laila go, and she rushed into Nora's arms.

"Tante Elle," Laila cried as they sunk to the floor together. Nora pulled her close and held tight to the girl's trembling body.

"You psycho bitch, what the fuck are you doing?" she demanded, turning back to Marie-Laure.

Laila clung to Nora, who could only pull the girl closer and rock her in her arms. She seemed mostly unharmed. A cracked lip, a bloody bruise on her cheek. She must have fallen in some sort of struggle.

"Are you all right?" she whispered to Laila in the little Danish she remembered.

"Okay," Laila whispered back. "I was at Onkel Søren's house. They grabbed me and—"

"You two look very sweet," Marie-Laure said. "And aren't we a lovely trio? We have the wife, the mistress and the niece all here together. I thought about taking one of his sisters, but the little girl's better. Men always do prefer the younger ones. Look at you…" Marie-Laure studied Laila's face. "Such a beautiful thing. You look like him. Different eyes, though. Sweet blue eyes, not gray. All the boys must be in love with you."

Laila shuddered in Nora's arms.

"No one is in love with me," she said, and Nora kissed the top of her head and whispered, *"Jeg elsker dig"* into Laila's ear—*I love you*.

"Don't worry. Love is overrated. But tell me something about love, Laila," Marie-Laure said, coming close to where Nora and Laila sat huddled on the ground. She sensed the man hovering behind them so she made no move to escape. It was too dangerous, especially now with Laila there shivering in her arms almost paralyzed from fear.

"What?" Laila asked, her voice quaking. Nora ran her hand up and down Laila's back, trying to instill some comfort into the girl.

"Does your uncle love this woman?" She inclined her head toward Nora. "This whore of his? Does he love her?"

Laila looked up at Nora, who only nodded her head, indicating Laila should tell the truth as best she could.

"Yes," Laila said. "Of course he does. She's…" Laila's voice broke and tears started to stream down her face. Nora started crying then, too, in simple fear for Laila. "She's everything to him. She's like his wife."

Marie-Laure's eyes flinched but she only turned back to Nora.

"What about her?" Marie-Laure said to Nora. "Does he love his niece?"

"Of course he does, you lunatic. She's like a daughter to him."

"The pretend wife or the pretend daughter? So hard to

choose… I need to keep one of you here. But one of you needs to go to him and deliver a message. But who does he love more? Whom should I keep? Whom should I send? Whoever stays, we'll have a wonderful time together, me and my houseguest."

The man, Damon, stepped forward and into Nora's field of vision. Had she seen him on the street she would have thought him homeless as gaunt and bitter as he looked. Thin and short, but those traits only made him look more menacing. He had a deadly tilt to his mouth and a roughness about his edges despite his expensive gray suit. He had the same look in his eyes that Kingsley had—the look of a man who'd killed without caring and could still sleep at night.

"I know…" Marie-Laure continued. "I'll let you two decide. Choose. Who stays? Who goes? Quick, quick. Tell me."

A smile of pure malice swept across Marie-Laure's face. Laila gasped and started to speak.

Nora clapped her hand over Laila's mouth.

"I'll stay," Nora said immediately and without hesitation. "Send Laila with whatever stupid fucking message you have. I'll be your houseguest as long as you want."

Marie-Laure shrugged seemingly unimpressed and unsurprised by Nora's answer.

"*C'est la vie.* I think you'll be more fun to play with, anyway. Damon?"

The man stepped forward, grabbed Laila by the arm and hauled her to her feet. Marie-Laure met her eye to eye.

Nora started to stand up but Damon shot her a warning look. Nora sank back down the floor. Instead, she reached up and clasped Laila's hand.

"Tell your uncle, my husband…" Marie-Laure dropped her voice to a whisper. "That I gave him my death as a gift. And now I'm taking my gift back."

# 7
# THE KING

Even knowing how futile it would be, Kingsley made phone calls to a few of his better sources—one in the upper echelons of the NYPD, another in the FBI. They both pledged to quietly investigate but they made him no other promises. He would have made more calls but couldn't afford the risk. Only being a priest brought Søren the same measure of peace that owning Nora did. If it got out that not only was Søren still married somehow but also had a lover, the justice of the church would come down swift and merciless. Only last year Kingsley had read a story in the news about a Catholic priest who'd fallen in love with a woman and married her. The consequence? Excommunication. Strange justice. Priests who molested children were put into counseling. The priests who fell in love with adults were damned. And Søren wondered why Kingsley had never converted.

Not a week ago Kingsley had wished to see a world without Nora Sutherlin in it. Had that stray, bitter whim brought this upon them? He was no fool. A world without Nora Sutherlin was a world without Søren. If the priest lost his Little One, especially if her death happened because of something Søren had done, no matter how inadvertently, it would mean his destruction. Søren couldn't live in a world without Nora. Kingsley couldn't live in a world without Søren. Her death would be like the sinking of a great ship. She would take them all down with her.

Marie-Laure… Kingsley sat on the edge of his desk, his forehead in his hand. *Ma soeur,* what have you done? And what had they done, he and Søren, as boys? How much guilt did he bear for this crime? He knew Søren had told Marie-Laure their marriage would be one in name only. It would be for the money and nothing else. But Marie-Laure, vain and mad with love, refused to accept that.

*Did he say he loved you?*

*Non…but he should. He must. He's my husband.*

*He told you why he married you. He did it for us, Marie-Laure, to help us.*

*I don't want his money. I want him.*

*You can't have him.*

*Why not?*

And to that question—*pourquoi pas?*—Kingsley had no answer. No, he did have an answer but one he couldn't tell her, wouldn't tell her. *Because he's mine, not yours,* he could have said. *Because he loves me, not you,* he wanted to say. *Because I'd rather see you dead than let him touch you the way he touches me.*

That final treacherous thought was the one that haunted Kingsley for the past thirty years. He never uttered it, only in his mind, his heart, and yet he still carried the guilt of how much he'd meant the words at the time. Sitting on the edge of his desk, staring out onto the midnight city, he conjured that horrible memory of his sister's body in the snow on the ground. His targets were all demons back in his days as a Jack-of-all-deadly-trades for the French government. The world slept better when Kingsley put a bullet in those chests. He aimed for the heart and left easily identifiable corpses. They might be demons but they came from somewhere and he knew someone would want a body to bury in an open casket. He could at least give them that. After all, the body he'd seen at his feet the day he thought Marie-Laure had died...nothing before or since, not even seeing his parents in urns, had turned his stomach like that. The rock had shattered her face. Nothing but gray matter oozed from the broken skull. The body, too, was broken, nothing but a bag of bones. Only her left hand had survived the fall. The wedding band on the ring finger had shone clean and bright and golden in the sunlight. Not dented, not scraped, not bloodied. That's how he should have known the ring had been planted on the dead girl's hand.

And the dead girl...who was she? Kingsley had barely glanced at the newspaper article Søren had uncovered. A young runaway from Quebec coming to America for a better life. What did she run from? An abusive father? A broken heart? Poverty? Or was she running to something, or someone? Whatever reason, she deserved better than to die like that, her body so torn up by the rock that had killed her they'd had to carry her away in two bags. It seemed too convenient to imagine the girl had been the victim of a simple accident, falling from the cliff to her death. He and Søren had had to abandon the hermitage where they'd had their assignations. Perhaps the girl had taken refuge there in the winter and Marie-Laure had met her on one of her long walks. Had his sister befriended the girl? Had they shared confidences? Did Marie-Laure tell the girl all about her marital troubles? The husband who wouldn't touch her? Did Marie-Laure lure her to the edge of the cliff and push her to her death? Her shock at seeing him and Søren kissing seemed genuine at the time. Kingsley had wanted her to see them together, had timed his confrontation with Søren in the hopes Marie-Laure would discover them in some state of passion or undress. Then she would know the truth without either of them having to tell her. Then she could see how much Søren loved Kingsley, not her. Then she would understand the truth and move on.

Foolish boys they were. Children playing dangerous games after dark, as Søren had said. So foolishly wrapped up in lust for each other they never even noticed that Marie-Laure was playing her own dangerous game with them.

Now Nora could end up like that runaway on the snowy ground. And that left Kingsley with no choice but to do now what he merely fantasized about thirty years ago.

He would see his sister dead.

The phone rang and Kingsley answered it in an instant.

"Report."

"I miss you, *monsieur,*" came a rich, honeyed voice on the other end of the line. "How is that for a report?"

Kingsley sighed as he felt tension releasing from his body like air from a popped balloon.

"Jules, you're breaking the rules," he teased. Hearing her voice, her laugh, was everything he needed and the last thing he wanted.

"You can punish me for it when I come home. I know you told me not to call until you said I could, but I had to hear your voice. It's been a week."

"A very long week, my Jewel. And it's only getting longer."

Kingsley ran a hand through his hair and wished it was Juliette's hand on him. Søren had destroyed him during their night together. He needed Juliette's touch to restore him again. But that would have to wait.

"Let me come home. Let me take care of you. It's my place."

"You have to take care of yourself now. It's not safe here."
He wanted to say more, to tell her the truth of what had happened. The risk was too great, however. No woman in the
world submitted more beautifully in the bedroom and acted
so independently outside of it. If she knew how bad it had gotten, she'd be on the next flight back to the city, his orders be
damned. "You can come home when it is safe. No sooner."

"Is it going to be like this from now on?"

*"Oui,"* he said without apology.

"Have you told *le prêtre?*"

*"Non.* He has too much on his mind now."

"You try to protect us all," Juliette said, and he heard the
love in her voice—the love and the exasperation. "You must
let someone take care of you. Let me take care of you."

"I'm fine. I am. We all are."

"Is he? Did Nora come back?"

Kingsley swallowed. He hated lying to his Juliette. She was
as much his confessor as Søren was Nora's.

"He's been better. And *non,* she is not back yet. Juliette…"
He paused to gather his words. With so many lies he had to
give her some truth. "Søren and I, we were together."

He heard that musical laugh of hers all the way from Haiti.

"No wonder you sound so tired."

"It's part of it, *oui.*" He laughed, too, but the laugh quickly
died. "My Jewel, you know—"

"I know," she said quickly and simply and without the
slightest hint of judgment or fear in her voice. "I know you
love him. I know he loves you, too."

"He loves me? From your lips to God's ears. He loves only
her."

"You forget we love more than one person. You do, she
does, he does…I do."

"You've fallen in love already?"

"*Bien sûr.* You'll have to share me now."

"As long as I have you at night."

He pictured her now, his Juliette, standing on the balcony staring at the ocean, her statuesque beauty, her dark skin glowing in the fading evening sunlight. They'd met on a beach at the edge of the ocean, and he couldn't see rising water without thinking of her. He'd never forget the first time he saw her. Some children on vacation had been pelting a native bird's nest with stones. Juliette decided to give them a taste of their own medicine. A grown woman throwing rocks at the spoiled scions of white American tourists. He'd been doomed from the start.

"Every night, my love. All my nights are yours."

Kingsley heard the front bell at the door and voices in the hall—Griffin and a woman's voice. A woman's voice he'd never heard before.

"I must go. No rest for the wicked," he said.

"*Mon roi,*" she whispered, and Kingsley's heart clenched at the name she called him only in their most private moments. "Please, be safe. I need you."

A thousand times she'd whispered that to him…breathed it across silk sheets as she crawled to him, moaned it into his ear as he entered her. But those words had a new meaning now that had nothing to do with passion anymore.

"I need you, too," he said. "I need you to do as I tell you. Stay there. Stay safe. You'll be home soon."

"Promise?"

He paused before answering. He could promise her nothing now, should promise her nothing.

"I promise." Sometimes a needful lie was less a sin than the truth.

He hung up the phone and forced thoughts of Juliette from his mind. No time for emotion or sentimentality. No time for love, not when he had a job to do. And while no one on earth admired or adored women more than Kingsley, a battlefield was no place for them and he could not deny that his world had turned into a war zone. He and Søren would find a way to get Nora back. And her fiancé, Wesley, who was young but certainly no coward. Any man who braved the bed of Nora Sutherlin and the wrath of *le prêtre* could be called many things, but not a coward.

Kingsley stood up straight and took a deep breath. He felt better now. Juliette was safe and far away from all this madness. The three of them—Wesley, Søren and he—would find a way to deal with this crisis on their own. They'd put no more women at risk. He should ban them all from the house for the time being. He would exile them, send them all away. They were too fragile, too at risk in such a dangerous time.

He started toward the door to his office but it opened before he got to it.

A beautiful redheaded woman, her pale skin painted with freckles, swept into the office ahead of Griffin.

"Ma'am, you can't barge in—" Griffin said, and Kingsley raised his hand.

"Hello," the woman said, facing Kingsley.

"May I help you?"

"Yes, you can tell me what the hell is going on. Where's Nora?"

"I would tell you if I knew, *madame*. Perhaps you could tell me who the hell you are?"

"My name is Grace Easton, and I know that means nothing to you, but I'm friends with Nora. I tried to call her and got Wesley. He told me someone had taken her and…"

She continued speaking in her light and musical accent. While she spoke Kingsley walked over to one of his filing cabinets, opened it and thumbed through files. He pulled one out, walked back over to her and let her finish her speech.

"…and I'm not leaving until someone tells me what's going on or at least lets me speak to Wesley. I know I seem like a madwoman showing up out of nowhere and you have no idea who I am but I promise—"

"Grace Easton, neé Rowan, age thirty," Kingsley said, opening the file. "Irish mother. Welsh father. Fluent in Welsh, I see. I think that's the one language *le prêtre* doesn't speak. You're much more beautiful now than you were back in school, and you were *très jolie* back in your school days. No wonder Professor Easton deflowered you on his desk. Although had it been me, it would have been the desk, the floor, the wall, back on the desk but from behind…"

He pulled a photograph of a twenty-two-year-old Grace Easton on her graduation day standing with her husband, Zachary Easton, and held it up to her.

She stared at it with wide turquoise eyes.

"My God…Nora wasn't exaggerating."

Kingsley put the photograph back into the file.

"Welcome to hell, Mrs. Easton. Now if you wouldn't mind, get out."

# 8

## THE KNIGHT

Wesley stood in the bathroom of the guest room Kingsley had escorted him to and pressed a wet washcloth to the back of his head. He'd seen enough head injuries working at the hospital that he knew his was minor enough he didn't have to worry about it. He needed a Band-Aid, though. Otherwise, he was going to be bleeding into his hair for a week.

What did it matter? Wesley dropped the bloody washcloth into the sink and went back into the bedroom. On any other day he might have admitted to finding the room beautiful, even opulent. Nora had told him about Kingsley's house—the four-poster beds in every room. Better for bondage, she'd said, and Wes could see the marks on the footboard, remnants of metal handcuffs probably. Silver and pale blue, the room looked like something out of a Founding Father's house, one he'd visited as a kid on vacation with his parents. Wes's foot slammed against something under the bed. He knelt down and found a metal briefcase. Curious, he opened the latches and saw a dozen different types of sex toys, plus condoms and lubricant. Behind so much beauty lay so much sin. He slammed the case shut and shoved it under the bed with such force his head started to ring. Forget it. His pain didn't matter. Nothing mattered except getting Nora back. He couldn't believe he had to trust her life to Kingsley, the biggest asshole he'd ever met in his life, and to Søren, who was apparently still unconscious. These were the men Nora trusted more than anyone else on the planet? Her judgment was getting worse all the time. Agreeing to marry him might have been good evidence of that.

He sat on the bed and rubbed his aching temples. His hands shook a little. Was it from low blood sugar? Or from the fear, the bitter aching gaping fear the likes of which he'd never felt before? Both probably. He should be planning his wedding right now curled up in bed with Nora. Not here. Anywhere but here.

This was stupid. He didn't need to be thinking about the future, anyway. Nothing mattered, nothing at all, except for getting Nora back as fast as they could. Every minute that passed put her deeper into danger. He wished he knew where she was. He'd take her place in a heartbeat.

Wesley jumped as Nora's cell phone started to ring again. He grabbed at it, praying it was the kidnappers with information.

"Yes?"

"Wesley, this is Grace again. I'm in Kingsley's house."

"So am I."

"Good. Could you help me? He's trying to kick me out."

Wesley hung up and raced from the bedroom. He didn't find Kingsley in his office or anywhere on the second floor.

Finally in the front room of the house he found a redheaded woman with freckles arguing vociferously with Kingsley.

"Hey, what's going on?" Wesley inserted himself between the two of them.

"I'm attempting to rid myself of an intruder in my home," Kingsley said. "I've shown her the door. She simply needs to walk through it."

"I'm not leaving until someone tells me what's going on with Nora. No, that's not true. I'm not leaving until I *see* Nora."

"I think she means it," Wesley said, standing at Grace's side.

"*Mon Dieu,* the entire vanilla world has taken over my house. Fine. Both of you stay. Have tea. Turn everyone in my house boring. If you need me I'll be trying to find Nora if only to get rid of you two."

Kingsley turned and stormed out of the front room.

"Charming, isn't he?" Grace turned to Wesley. "Thank you."

"So you're Zach's wife?"

"That would be me."

"I'm Nora's fiancé."

The look of shock on Grace's face prompted Wesley's first laugh in over twenty-four hours.

"I know. Long story," he said.

"Nora never ceases to shock me. I'm not even going to ask."

"Good idea."

"I will ask this—do you know anything about what's going on?"

"Really, *really* long story."

"I'd like to know it. This may come as a shock to you, but Nora's about my only female friend in this world."

Wesley walked over to the sofa and sat down, sinking deep into the black-and-white-striped cushions. He felt light-headed, tired, lost. He knew he needed to eat something, check his blood sugar, take care of himself. But he didn't have the energy for it, didn't have the will.

"Nora doesn't have many female friends, either. She says she scares women."

"I'm not scared of her. Maybe I should be but I'm not." Grace sat next to him on the sofa and spun her wedding band on her finger. "When Zachary and I reunited after our separation, my closest friends were furious at me for taking him back. He'd run off to America, had an affair with another woman. I forgave him but they wouldn't. The only person who seemed to be genuinely happy for us was—"

"Nora."

Grace nodded. "She's been a good friend to both of us. I'm sick to my stomach with worry. Zachary's in Australia at a conference and now the one friend I had in the States I wanted to see is... God, Wesley, what on earth is happening here?"

"I probably shouldn't tell you." He leaned forward and rested his elbows on his knees and his forehead in his hands. He couldn't remember ever feeling this sick or this tired or anywhere near this scared. "But I guess it doesn't matter now. When Kingsley and Søren were teenagers, they had a relationship."

"They were lovers?"

"Yeah. That. They were in school together. It was a—"

"Catholic school, wasn't it?"

"Yeah, it was."

"This is starting to sound familiar."

Wesley told her what he knew of the story. Kingsley and Søren falling in love, the sister, Marie-Laure, coming to visit, Søren marrying her so that she and Kingsley wouldn't have to live an ocean apart anymore. But the sister had fallen in love with Søren and when she discovered that *he* loved her brother...

"She faked her own death?" Grace asked, aghast.

"By killing a runaway who had the same color hair as her. The body had on her wedding ring. Nobody even guessed it was someone else. Kingsley thinks his sister crossed the border into Canada and lived in Quebec for a while. According to him she was the most beautiful girl in the world. Easy to find a rich man to take care of her."

"But why all this? Why take Nora now after all these years?"

"No idea. He doesn't know what set her off, either. Something must have."

"Where's Søren now? Can I speak to him?"

"He's in Kingsley bedroom. Third floor. Door at the very end of the hall."

Grace stood up.

"I don't think you'll get much out of him, though."

"Why not?" Grace asked from the doorway.

"He's unconscious."

"What?"

"Kingsley gave him a shot of something. Apparently Søren was going to call the cops and the rest of the world. Kingsley said it would be the worst idea ever."

"Unconscious or not, someone should check on him."

"He's all yours."

Grace started to leave but hesitated in the doorway. She turned back around, came to him and dropped a quick kiss on his forehead.

"She'll be all right. I have faith in her," Grace said, squeezing his shoulder. It was the first kind thing anyone had done or said to him all day. He could have wept from simple gratitude alone.

"Thank you," he said, and could barely hear himself speak.

Grace said nothing, either, merely smiled at him before leaving the room.

Alone in the front room, Wesley prayed. He prayed helplessly, not even knowing what to pray for other than a miracle. That's what they needed now. A miracle. A sign from God. Something to tell them everything would be all right, Nora would be safe, the world hadn't spun out of God's control even if it felt like it had.

Somewhere nearby Wesley heard the sound of a car door slamming. He ignored it.

If Nora were here she'd tell him to relax, to take deep breaths, to take care of himself. *Stop worrying about me so much,* Nora would say to him, had said to him a thousand times. *I'm a big girl. I can take care of myself.*

But he was supposed to take care of her. Søren had entrusted Nora to him and he'd let her get taken by some lunatic with a thirty-year-old grudge. And now he felt forsaken. Losing Nora was his punishment for not taking better care of her while they were together. He'd thought she'd be so much safer with him than with Søren, and now she was gone. Stolen from him. He'd failed her, failed them all.

*Please,* he prayed once more. *Give me a sign you're still listening.*

Wesley heard a sound then, a knock on the front door. He waited, not knowing if he should be answering the door in someone else's house or not. But then it came again, louder this time. The door had a bell. Why was the person knocking instead?

He went to the door and opened it. A girl lay curled up on the landing, bleeding from a cut on her face.

She opened her eyes—bright blue eyes, intelligent and scared.

"Hello?" He knelt down and met her face-to-face.

"I have to deliver a message," she said, her voice strangely accented.

"From who?" Maybe it had happened. Finally. A message from the kidnappers.

"From God."

# 9
# THE ROOK

Grace walked down the third-floor hallway, leaving the men of the house to their own devices. They were all terrified—Wesley, Griffin, who'd let her in the house, even Kingsley, although she could see he had much more practice at hiding his fears than the rest of them.

*Nora…* Grace prayed her name as she neared the bedroom she'd been warned away from. She could put together no other words for a prayer. All the possibilities she could pray against were too terrible to imagine. Wesley said Kingsley's sister had Nora. His sister…a woman. Better a woman than being taken by a man. A woman kidnapped…surely his sister had help, had men around her. Impossible to think any lone woman could get the better of Nora Sutherlin. Dear God, Nora. It turned Grace's stomach to even consider what might be happening to Nora right now.

Outside the door to Kingsley's bedroom, Grace paused and wondered for a moment what she was doing. She merely wanted to see him...this man, this priest, the one person her usually fearless husband ever admitted to being afraid of. Nora seemed the ultimate free spirit to Grace—she trod across the world in leather boots with black sails flying. And yet when she spoke of Søren she called him the man who owned her. Owning Nora sounded as dangerous as owning a nuclear bomb. Valuable and powerful it may be, but who would want that sort of thing under one's own roof?

Grace turned the knob on the door and peered inside. A small lamp had been left on and pale gold light filled the room. On the floor at the end of the grand red bed sat a man with his blond head bowed as if in prayer. The door made the slightest squeak as it opened but the man on the floor didn't move. Whatever Kingsley had drugged him with clearly hadn't worn off yet.

Shutting the door behind her, Grace moved closer to get a better look at the man. Her heart contracted with sympathy. He'd be in agony when he came to. Sitting on the floor had to be uncomfortable, and far worse, when he woke up it would be to a world where Nora was still gone. Kneeling on the floor at his side Grace studied his face.

Good God, Nora hadn't been exaggerating at all. Is he handsome? Calling this man handsome would be like saying Einstein was fairly decent at his sums. He was so handsome she wanted to demand an apology from him. He had blond hair long enough to run one's fingers through but still short enough to give him a civilized air. Nora had called him dangerous but Grace couldn't see the threat at all. He was tall, definitely. Even sitting on the floor with his hands cuffed behind his back, Grace could tell he must have stood well over six feet. But no, certainly not dangerous. In fact, he looked rather kind, especially around his eyes. Nora often extolled his virtues as a priest to her—how he treated everyone at the church with equal respect, how he listened without judging, how he treated the children like adults and forgave the adults like they were children, how he gave and gave and gave of himself to them and asked nothing in return, only that they remember all blessings come from God, even the ones in disguise.

No, he certainly wasn't dangerous. Perhaps only to someone who tried to harm Nora. But it was madness to have him locked up in this bedroom like some sort of wild animal. Surely she could find the key somewhere. She'd unlock the handcuffs, let his arms relax into a more natural position.

Grace stood up and looked around. There it was, the key to the cuffs hanging on a blue ribbon off the back of the door. When he'd woken up he would have seen the key staring right at him. Cruel of Kingsley to do that if he, in fact, had done it on purpose. And something told her he'd most certainly done it on purpose.

Once more she knelt at his side and reached behind him. It would be awkward getting the key in the lock from this position. She'd practically have to wrap her arms around the man. But he slept on, oblivious to her presence. So Grace turned toward the bed and pressed close to his body. She couldn't resist breathing in the scent of him. He smelled cool, clean, like a new fallen snow on a deep winter's night. Nonsense. What was she thinking? The fear and panic were clearly getting to her. Who on earth smelled like winter?

She took a deep breath, shook off her poet's musings and started to bring the key around his hip. She found the cuffs on his wrist and felt the slight depression of the keyhole.

"Almost there," she whispered to herself. "We'll get these off."

At that he raised his head and Grace found herself staring

at the hardest eyes in the most dangerous face she'd ever seen in her life.

"I wouldn't do that if I were you."

Gasping, she dropped the keys and scrambled back a few feet on the floor.

"Father Stearns," she said, almost panting from the sudden scare. "I'm so sorry. I only wanted—"

"Welsh accent...you're Mrs. Easton, yes?" Father Stearns raised his chin an inch higher and waited for her answer. She felt like an utter fool sitting on the floor trying to keep her skirt from riding up her legs while a Catholic priest studied every line of her face.

"Yes. I'm Zachary's wife. I was on holiday and called Nora. Wesley answered..." The words poured out her in a wave of nervous energy. "He told me what happened, where he was going. I came straightaway."

"Have we heard anything about Eleanor?"

Grace's stomach sank. She would have given anything to be able to tell him any news.

"Nothing anyone's told me."

Father Stearns nodded and leaned his head back against the bed with his eyes closed.

"I'm so sorry," Grace whispered. "Nora, we care about her, Zachary and I."

"That's very kind of you to say, Mrs. Easton."

She smiled. "Please call me Grace. Nora's told me a great deal about you."

"No wonder you're so nervous."

Grace laughed nervously, proving his point.

"She's only told me good things, I promise."

He opened his eyes again and stared at her for a long silent moment, searching her face for something. For what, she couldn't imagine. But she didn't quite mind his gaze on her. It felt intimate without being inappropriate.

"I refuse to believe that," he finally said. "I know Eleanor too well."

"Well, perhaps it all wasn't good per se. But nothing bad. Fascinating definitely. She did seem to imply you were the one usually putting the handcuffs on, not ending up in them. I could take those off if you'd like."

"I would like. But as I said, I don't recommend it."

"Why not?" She moved a little closer to him, feeling a bit more comfortable now that they'd started talking.

"I'm a pacifist. I don't believe nonconsensual violence is ever justified. I am trying to remember that I'm a pacifist so I don't murder Kingsley where he stands."

Grace laughed again, less nervously this time.

"I don't think murder will help the situation."

"It might not hurt it."

The words should have been a joke but Grace heard no mirth in his tone.

"I'll go now if you like." Grace started to stand. "I didn't mean to be so nosy, but I saw you on the floor and—"

"No. Don't go. Please."

He sounded so humble that Grace couldn't help but sink to her knees again.

"Of course."

"Stay and talk to me. Distract me from all the thoughts in my head."

She heard a note of desperation in his voice.

"I'll stay. I'll stay as long as you want me to." Grace moved a little closer to him on the floor. "Do you want to talk about the thoughts in your head?" she asked, as if she were talking to one of the children in her class. "If they're half as awful as mine, it might help to get them out."

He said nothing at first, only opened his eyes and stared at something only he could see.

"We're all terrified," Grace whispered. "I've never been so scared in my life. This doesn't happen to people you know. This happens in movies, or in foreign countries and the stories get turned into movies, and it's all madness. I almost died when I was nineteen having a miscarriage, and I'm telling you now, I've never been this frightened."

"I was eleven years old when I looked death in the face the first time. In my early twenties I spent a few months in a leper colony. I have dug my fingers into a teenage boy's sliced-open wrists to try to stop him from bleeding to death on the floor of my church. I thought I knew terror before today. I was wrong."

"I keep telling myself to stay strong, that Nora would be strong for me so I have to be strong for her. Falling apart won't help her. We can't despair." Brave words but all Grace wanted to do was dissolve into tears.

"Don't despair? That's usually my line."

"I imagine even a priest needs words of comfort sometimes."

"All the time, Grace."

He fell silent after that and she feared the thoughts in his head as much as she imagined he did.

"I don't want to know what's going on in your mind, do I?"

"Terrible thoughts. Vengeance. Brutality. What I want to do to anyone who hurts my Little One."

"You call her Little One?"

"I always have. She was a teenager when we met. A very ill-mannered teenager. She demanded to know why I was so tall. She insinuated I had grown this tall simply for attention."

"Only Nora could be rude and flirtatious at the same time."

"I explained to her that I was tall so I could hear God's

voice better. And since I was taller and could hear Him better, she should always listen to me. That didn't sit very well with her. She retorted the next day with a verse from Psalm 114. 'The Lord keeps the little ones.' Her biblical proof that God prefers short people. I started calling her Little One after that. It helped us both remember she belonged to God first."

"And you second?"

"A close second," he said, giving her a quick but devilish grin.

"These are good thoughts. Keep telling me good thoughts. Maybe we can get you over your murderous inclinations and out of the handcuffs."

"I have no good thoughts right now."

He fell silent and closed his eyes. Grace knew that whatever was going on in his mind right now was nothing she wanted to know.

"You shouldn't be here," he said, his eyes still closed. "It's not safe here. You should be with your husband."

"Zachary's at a conference in Australia. And I'm not going anywhere, not until Nora's back. I don't care if my husband divorces me, Kingsley has me arrested and I get fired for missing school, I'm staying."

"Missing school?"

"I'm a teacher. School starts next week. But it will start with or without me."

"What do you teach?"

"Year 11 English Lit. Teaching Shakespeare to seventeen-year-olds is not unlike herding cats."

He smiled then and opened his eyes.

"I used to be a teacher," he said. "I taught Spanish and French to ten- and eleven-year-old boys."

"Sounds like hell."

"It was. I rather liked it, though."

"It is rewarding in its own way. If you get through to one student a year, see that spark of understanding, see that little hint of the adult they'll become and you know you've somehow helped him or her along that path…it's worth all the work, all the sacrifice."

"It was like that with Eleanor when she was a girl. The moment I saw her at age fifteen, I saw exactly who she would become."

"No wonder it was love at first sight."

"Love, lust, fear, wonder and joy—such joy. I considered it my mission in life to make sure she survived her teenage years to become the woman I saw in her."

"Survived? I recall being a teenager as rather difficult, but certainly not life-threatening."

"Eleanor's were not the typical teenage years."

"I don't believe Nora has had a typical anything her entire life."

"That would be an accurate statement."

"If it helps any, I think you did a good job with her. She's a rather impressive person."

"I tried not to fail her. Everyone else in her life had—her father was a criminal, her mother considered Eleanor a mistake. It gave me great pleasure to take her from them. More pleasure than I should admit to."

"You smiled. Would you like me to take the handcuffs off now?"

"I would like that, but I'm still picturing Kingsley in the morgue. And of course, I'm only focusing my anger at him because he's here. I know I'm not actually angry at him. I keep trying to tell myself that."

"He was trying to save you from yourself. You are a priest, after all. Can't be telling the police and the FBI and the whole wide world that someone has your lover."

"I couldn't begin to care less what the whole world thinks of my relationship with Eleanor. All that matters is getting her back."

"Of course," she said, smoothing her skirt over her knee. "But will the police help? I'm asking a genuine question. If you think they could help, I'll call them myself and Kingsley be damned."

Father Stearns turned his eyes from her and exhaled.

"No, they won't help. They can't. It's been thirty years, but I haven't forgotten what Marie-Laure was like. Obsessive nature. Clearly she wants revenge. On me. On Kingsley. Eleanor will be that instrument of revenge. She's not trying to steal a jewel and abscond in the night. She wants to hurt us. She's died before. I don't think she's afraid to die again. My fear is that she plans to take Eleanor with her. Police involvement will only put Eleanor's life at greater risk."

"Marie-Laure…Kingsley's sister was your wife?"

"Was…*is* my wife apparently. Kingsley missed her terribly back when we were in school. After their parents died, he and Marie-Laure had little but each other and even then they were separated by an ocean—she in Paris, he in America. I thought it would make him happy to see her again."

"She came to your school?"

"I arranged to bring her over. It had been over a year since they'd seen each other—brother and sister. And yet less than a week after being reunited, Marie-Laure simply announced that she was in love with me."

"That must have been something of a shock. For you and Kingsley."

"It was an unpleasant shock. My heart was very much elsewhere, but I didn't want to hurt the girl. Kingsley seemed so happy to have her back with him. I remember that day like yesterday. I'd gone for a walk alone. Marie-Laure followed me, asked if she could join me. We'd barely gone a mile when she stopped and confessed she'd fallen in love with me. I tried to stay calm, rational. I said to her that I was sorry, but I didn't feel the same. But she shouldn't take it personally. I told her I wasn't capable of loving her like someone else could. She said she didn't care."

"She cared. I promise, she cared."

"I told her that if she wanted, we could be married, but it would be a marriage in name only. I told her about the trust fund I'd receive if I married. She and Kingsley could have every penny of it. God knows I didn't want a cent from my father. I would ask nothing in return from her. She could be as free as she wanted to be with anyone she wanted. All I asked was that she let me finish out the school year at Saint Ignatius. For legal reasons I thought it would be best if we at least lived together for a few months."

"She agreed to that?"

"Readily. She said she understood, and that it was kind of me to offer. Kind, she said. More like stupid and foolish. I'm not stupid very often, Grace. That was stupid."

"You were in love, not stupid. They're two very different diseases with identical symptoms."

"I was in love. I'd never felt anything like that before. I wanted to tell her but Kingsley wanted to wait. I thought she'd understand eventually."

"But she didn't understand." It wasn't a question. If Marie-Laure had kidnapped Nora, clearly the woman didn't understand.

"I didn't even allow us to kiss at our wedding. That was one of the conditions. I knew it would hurt Kingsley too much to see. And yet, on our wedding night, as soon as we were alone, she threw herself at me. Everything I told her, everything she'd agreed to, she pretended like it hadn't happened.

She acted as if the only words I'd said to her that day in the woods were 'We can be married.'"

"Love can give you tunnel vision. I know I had it with Zachary. I only saw the possibilities, never the danger."

"Love made Marie-Laure very dangerous. She touched me constantly. I hated it. Especially being touched in my sleep." Something flashed across his eyes—an old memory, perhaps, and a very bad one at that.

"Was it difficult to rebuff her advances? After all, if she looked anything like Kingsley, she must have been beautiful."

"Many thought her so. Some who saw her declared her the most beautiful girl they'd ever seen. But she held no interest for me. None whatsoever. All her beauty was on the outside. I cared for her because Kingsley did. That was all."

"I'm sure she thought you'd change your mind eventually. Women do that, convince themselves men will change when they won't. If Marie-Laure believed in the power of her own beauty, I'm sure she thought she could change your mind. Must have been a great blow to her ego when she couldn't."

"She was less than pleased, obviously."

"I've known my fair share of women like that. Beautiful, dangerous girls. Any man who didn't fall at their feet…they considered it an insult and a challenge."

"You speak of beautiful women as if you weren't one. I assure you, you are. The freckles are an especially nice touch."

Grace hoped the low light in the room masked the blossoming blush on her face.

"I'm not sure I agree with you. My husband would, but Zachary's a freckle fetishist, if there is such a thing."

"Your husband and I have excellent taste in women."

The blush deepened at the insinuation. Grace took a deep breath. *Show no fear,* Nora had cautioned. Now she knew why.

"Nora was right about you."

"About what?" Father Stearns asked. "Or do I not want to know?"

"She told me you'd play with me, play with my mind. You intimated that you know my husband has slept with Nora. Trying to gauge my reaction?"

"Perhaps. It's not typical wifely behavior to show such concern over a woman who her husband has been with."

"You can play all the mind games you want with me. I do care about Nora. My marriage is better than it's ever been because of her. It's the two of us in our marriage for the first time ever. Me and Zachary. Not me and Zachary and his guilt."

"Doth the lady protest too much?" Father Stearns narrowed his eyes at her and Grace found herself squirming under the intensity of the gaze.

"No, I'm simply speaking the truth. I love Nora. She's a dear friend, and considering I slept with someone even before Zachary had his night with your Nora, I think all is forgiven between us and then some. And Nora was absolutely right about you."

"Was she?"

"She told me to show no fear around you. Said you'd play with it like a cat with a catnip toy."

At that, a laugh filled the room, warm, rich and masculine. It made every nerve in Grace's body want to stand at attention and salute someone.

Then the laugh died and Father Stearns closed his eyes again. Once more he leaned his head back against the bed. He seemed to be in prayer.

"Forgive me, Grace," he exhaled his apology. "I try not to—" he paused as he seemed to search for the right word "—*inflict* this side of myself on the unwilling or unsuspecting. I'm afraid it simply comes out at times."

Grace scooted a little closer to him again so that their legs were mere inches apart. She reached out and laid a hand on his thigh right above his knee. She wasn't sure what possessed her to do that other than she'd touched Zachary a million times that way when offering support or comfort.

"The woman who you've loved for almost twenty years has been taken. You were drugged and handcuffed to a bed. You're a Catholic priest and if any of this gets out, your reputation and career will be ruined. Please..." Grace squeezed his leg and felt muscle hard as steel under her hand. "Please do not apologize to me. God knows I can't do anything to help this horrible situation at all. If at the very least I can be a sympathetic ear, then please, inflict whatever you need to on me."

Father Stearns raised his eyebrow at her, and Grace sensed even the shadows in the room scuttling into the corners and pressing their backs to the wall.

"I didn't mean it like that," she said, removing her shaking hand from his leg.

"Are you sure about that?"

"You are terrible. Seriously," she said, trying to laugh off her nervousness. "I'm going to take the handcuffs off you now, but I can tell I'm going to regret it."

"You will."

"How on earth can anyone concentrate with you being... you?" she teased as he reached behind the bed and found the keys again. "You must delight in scaring women."

"Men, too. Ask your husband."

"Oh, he's told me."

"I should apologize to him. When we met I was feeling unnecessarily territorial. Eleanor never brought outsiders into our world. I knew he had to be very special to her to show him that side of her. I took my irritation out on Zachary."

"Don't apologize. He's shredded the egos of so many writers I've lost count. It's only poetic justice you shredded his a bit."

"You have no sympathy for the male ego, do you?"

"Of course not. I'm a wife. I'm rather glad you terrified him a little."

"You don't seem terrified."

"I am, I assure you. But Nora warned me how terrifying you are. I'd prepared myself."

He smiled then, a genuine smile entirely devoid of guile or artifice.

"Eleanor is not even remotely afraid of me."

"I find that hard to believe." Grace came up to her knees and reached behind Father Stearns. Here she was a grown woman married for twelve years and she felt as awkward as a schoolgirl around her secret crush.

"I assure you it's true. I learned long ago that it was for the best that I erect a very high wall between myself and the rest of the world. She and Kingsley are the only two people I've ever met who simply ignored that wall as if it didn't exist."

Grace's hands fumbled to find the keyhole. She found it with a fingertip and pushed in the key.

"Kingsley and Nora ignored your wall. I have to ask… what is the reward for getting past that wall of yours? Or is it a punishment?"

"Both reward and punishment."

"How so?"

Father Stearns turned his head to her and the handcuffs popped open. At that moment their faces were so close together if she leaned in an inch they'd be kissing.

"I fucked them."

Grace sat back on her knees, the keys falling from her hand.

Father Stearns brought his arms around and removed the cuffs. He massaged his wrists and Grace could see purple bruises peeking out from underneath the black cuffs of his clerics. Even drugged he'd clearly put up a fight.

"Thank you, Grace." Father Stearns came to his feet. "I no longer wish to kill Kingsley. No more than usual, anyway."

"You're welcome, Father." Grace's voice quivered but Father Stearns was polite enough not to point it out. Perhaps he'd had enough playing with her mind tonight. Pity. She already rather missed it. At least it had distracted her from the gnawing terror for a few minutes.

He reached a hand down to her, a hand she took with more pleasure than she felt comfortable admitting to herself.

"You're welcome to call me Søren. I'd prefer it if you did."

"Of course…Søren. That's what Nora always calls you. She says she can't call you 'Father Stearns' without wanting to giggle," she said, coming to her feet. She straightened her clothes, which had gotten rumpled while sitting on the floor. "Søren's a Danish name, yes? What does it mean?"

"It means 'stern.' A good name for me, I've been told."

"I beg to differ. I don't think you're quite as stern as you're letting on."

"Careful, Grace…it's dangerous behind the wall."

His tone was teasing but she heard a real warning in his words, a warning she decided to heed.

"So, what now?" she asked, deciding a change of subject might be for the best. "What should we do?"

"The only thing we can do is wait. For a week now she's been playing a game with us. Sending photographs, breaking into homes—my sister's, Eleanor's… She stole a file from Kingsley's office. This is a woman who wants to play a mind game with us. Eleanor will stay alive as long as Marie-Laure enjoys playing the game."

"She will be fine. Nora will," Grace said again, more for her sake than his. "I mean if any woman can get through this, it's Nora. Isn't it?"

"She's strong, intelligent and cunning. She's well-trained.

If forced to defend herself, she can. She knows how to hurt people and hurt them badly. As a teenager she got into a few fights, but as an adult, she's never hurt anyone without their consent. She may have to now." He paused and Grace watched as his large hands curled tight into fists before he relaxed his fingers once again. "I would pay any price to save her from this."

She took his hand in hers and held it a moment.

"I know you would. I'd give anything to know something…anything. What is Marie-Laure waiting for?"

"I don't know. But surely she knows the silence and the waiting are the worst of tortures."

"It has to end. It's been a day already. Something has to—"

The sound of heavy footsteps in the hallways cut off the end of Søren's sentence. She heard doors opening and slamming shut. She and Søren stepped into the hall. The man who'd escorted her to Kingsley's office, Griffin, exhaled with relief at the sight of him.

"Søren," the man said, almost panting in his panic. "There's a girl here asking for you."

"A girl?"

"She's down in the front room."

He looked at Grace and she knew it had happened. Finally. Marie-Laure had started the game.

"Did she tell you her name?" Søren asked as they strode down the hall, Grace following close behind.

"Nope. But she's looks about eighteen, she's blonde, she sounds foreign and she's fucking gorgeous. You got a daughter you never told anyone about?"

"No," Søren said, his pace quickening. "But I have a niece."

# 10
# THE PAWN

Laila pulled her knees to her chest on the sofa and shivered. Why was it so cold in here? Was it cold? Somewhere over her head one man spoke to another man. Although she spoke English almost as well as her native Danish, their words did not register with her. She heard static, white noise, and could only stare with fixed eyes at the doorway.

"What's your name?" a gentle male voice asked in English. "Can you tell me your name?"

Finally the words cut through the static.

"Laila," she whispered.

"Laila. That's a pretty name. I'm Wes."

"Hi, Wes." She blinked and looked at him. Her eyes finally started to focus and she at last saw the person who'd carried her into the house. Before he'd just been a presence, male and tall. Now she saw him. He had shaggy blond hair and warm brown eyes and easily the most handsome face she'd ever seen on a man in her life. Man? Maybe not. He didn't look that much older than her. Nineteen? Twenty, maybe.

"Are you hurt anywhere?"

She shook her head.

"I don't think so."

"Your face is bleeding a little. It looks like you scraped it on the concrete. We'll clean it up and you'll be okay."

"Okay."

He spoke with such quiet confidence that Laila believed him immediately even if he meant only the cut on her face would be okay.

He took her hand in hers and she clung to it, desperate for comfort from this stranger. He didn't feel like a stranger to her, though. He didn't ask her questions about what had happened to her, how she'd gotten here. He knew somehow. He was part of this. They were part of this together.

"Laila?" A familiar voice cut through the haze and she sat up immediately, throwing herself in her uncle's arms. The one moment of peace she'd felt looking in Wes's eyes disappeared as the floodgate broke. She sobbed against his shoulder as he gathered her to him on the sofa. In between her choking sobs, she told him the story. She'd come to surprise him. She'd gone into the rectory. She thought no one was home. She heard footsteps…something covered her head. She fought, she struggled, but no amount of thrashing would get her free. They'd taken her somewhere in the trunk of a car. It felt like days in the car but probably only a few hours. When the car stopped, someone pulled her out and when they yanked the blindfold off, she saw…

"I saw Tante Elle. They have her," she said, switching to English. Other people had come into the room while she was speaking—a beautiful woman with red hair and freckles and a man with dark hair, olive skin and dangerous eyes. They looked as scared as her uncle, as scared as her.

"Who?" Wes asked, over Laila's shoulder.

"Eleanor," Søren explained, kissing Laila on top of her head. "Laila and her sister consider Eleanor their aunt. Go on, Laila."

"She was there on the floor."

"Was she hurt?" Wes asked.

Laila shook her head. "She has some bruises on her arms, on her face. There was another woman there and a man with a gun."

"What did the woman look like?" asked the man with shoulder-length dark hair. He spoke in a French accent. Kingsley, that was his name. Her aunt had told her about the handsome Frenchman who she called the bane of her existence. From her tante Elle it had sounded like a compliment.

She stared at him.

"She looked a little like you." The man shook his head and he swore under his breath. He turned his back to the room. "But older," Laila continued. "And angry. She was smiling but she looked very angry."

"What did she say?" Her uncle brushed the hair off her face.

"She said awful things…" Laila returned to her Danish, not wanting anyone else to hear. She told her uncle everything the woman had said, everything her aunt said in defiance. And she told him about the choice they had to make. Laila buried her head against his chest when she confessed what her aunt had done and how powerless she'd been to stop her.

"Søren?" The redheaded woman with the freckles came closer. "What did she say?"

Laila only listened as her uncle recited her tale in English. He left out the part about the woman calling her tante Elle a "whore."

"Marie-Laure made them choose," he said, his voice low

but steady. "She told Eleanor and Laila that one of them could leave and deliver a message to me. The other one had to stay behind as…entertainment. Eleanor…"

He paused to clear his throat and Laila began to cry again, sobbing silently against his chest.

"What?" Wes asked. "What happened?"

"Eleanor covered Laila's mouth so she couldn't volunteer. So Laila was allowed to leave with her message."

He fell silent and no one in the room spoke. The confession of her aunt's sacrifice had made mutes of them all.

"Dammit, Nora…" Wes was the first to speak. She winced at his words, felt her own failure to speak in time, felt more than anything shame over how relieved she was that she'd been allowed to go free.

"She gave me a note to give you." Laila dug in her jeans pocket and pulled out the paper. "She said to tell you that she gave you her death as a gift and now she was taking her gift back. She said God had a message for you, too."

Kingsley exhaled noisily and with great and very French disgust.

"And what does God have to tell us?" he demanded.

"She said that God says no more sinning. Time for atonement."

No one said anything as Laila held out the note to her uncle. Without any show of emotion he read the words before handing it to Kingsley. Kingsley took it from his hand and opened the note.

"What does it say?" Wes demanded. Laila was grateful he'd asked. She hadn't gotten to read it. "Is it a ransom note? I'll pay whatever they ask."

"Not a ransom." Kingsley balled up the note. "And it doesn't matter what it says because we're not going to let her play us."

"It does matter what it says." Wes stood up and walked over

to Kingsley. "I'll play any game I have to if it means getting Nora back."

"You're not the one she wants to play with, Wesley," Søren said, and Laila looked up at him. "Kingsley and I are the ones she's angry with, the ones she's trying to hurt."

"So what are you going to do about it?" Wes faced her uncle with fury in his eyes. She'd never seen anyone look at her uncle like that.

"Whatever I have to." Her uncle said the words simply and without a trace of fear. For some reason his lack of fear and the quiet determination in his voice scared her more than her own kidnapping had.

"And then what?" Wes asked.

"I get her out," Kingsley said.

"*You* get her out?" Wes turned to Kingsley. "You and what army?"

"I don't need an army."

"What? Are you the French James Bond or something?"

"Of course not. James Bond is vanilla."

"I feel so much better now," Wes said as he scraped his fingers through his hair. "Kinky James Bond is going to rescue Nora. Thanks but maybe it's time we get the cops involved."

"Call the police if you want her dead. By all means, call them. They love to blare their sirens so the whole world knows they're coming. Do you know how easy it is to kill someone like…" Kingsley raised his hand and snapped his fingers loudly in Wesley's ear, so loudly Wesley flinched. "Like that. The speed of sound is 342 meters per second. The speed of a bullet is four times that. She'll be dead before they can even knock on the door. I promise you, she's guarded. Every minute of every hour someone with a gun is within shooting distance of her. One wrong step equals one bullet."

"We have to do something. We don't even know where she is," Wes said.

"I do." Laila sat up and wiped her face. "I know where she is."

"Where?" Wes looked down at her and she saw hope in his eyes.

Laila reached up and unclasped her necklace. She flipped open the locket and passed it to her uncle.

"That room."

"What room?" The redheaded woman leaned over her uncle's shoulder and stared at the picture. Laila didn't have to look. She'd worn the silver heirloom locket for most of her life, knew the photographs in it better than she knew her own face. On one side of the locket was a picture of her grandmother holding her mother as a newborn baby. On the other side of the locket was a photograph of her grandmother holding her uncle Søren as a newborn. Her grandmother had kept a box of photographs that she looked at from time to time. They all seemed to be taken in the same room—a library with a fireplace. Gold walls, green curtains. She'd asked her grandmother about it once and her grandmother had said she would rather not talk about her time living in America. All that mattered, her grandmother said with a sad smile, was that she gave birth to her son while in that country. He made up for everything.

"Are you sure?" her uncle asked.

She nodded. "I saw the pictures in Mormor's box. There was one where she sat by a fireplace holding you. She wasn't smiling. But it was that room in my locket, the one Tante Elle is in. I know it was."

"Søren?" Wes's voice prompted her uncle to look up from the locket.

"Eleanor's at my half sister's house. She's at Elizabeth's."

"Your sister's house?" Wes asked. "Is she involved in this, too?"

Søren shook his head. "No, I told Elizabeth to leave the country and travel, to stay on the move. I'd been afraid something like this would happen. She and her sons left last week. She's not home. She's not part of this."

"We're sure she's at your sister's?" Kingsley asked.

"Yes." Søren looked at Kingsley, who nodded as if Søren had given him some kind of telepathic message.

"We'll go, then," Kingsley said. "I'll call him right now."

"Call who?" Wes asked. "Go where?"

"We have a friend who lives near his sister's," Kingsley explained as he pulled a phone out of his trouser pocket. "Only ten miles away. I'll be able to plan better if I'm closer. I may have to come and go several times. I need a base. His house is perfect."

"A friend of yours? Can we trust this guy?" Wes stared aggressively at both Kingsley and her uncle. For the first time she wondered who he was, what he was to her aunt that made him so deeply a part of this nightmare.

"We can trust him. He owes me. He owes him, too." Kingsley nodded at Søren as he scrolled through the numbers on his phone. "And he owes our missing *Maîtresse* most of all."

Laila sensed excitement in the air. Not excitement, no. More like anticipation and even a measure of relief. They knew something now, something more than they did before. And even more, they knew something the woman who had her aunt didn't know they knew. They knew where to find her.

"He doesn't owe you anything," her uncle said with obvious exasperation.

"He kicked me out of my own bedroom. He owes me."

"Who is he? Nora's life is on the line here. If you won't even let me call the police—"

"He's on our side, I promise," Kingsley said. "Trust me, you'll like him. He's nice and dull. Married, a family man. He's even...honorable." Kingsley said the last word like it left a bad taste in his mouth.

"A nice and honorable family man?" Wes repeated, sounding utterly shocked Kingsley would associate with such a person. "Then why are you friends with him?"

"Because he's kinky as hell, and I used to fuck his first wife."

"Kingsley, please," Søren said, scowling.

"This is why no children are allowed in my house." Kingsley winked at Laila. "You turn everyone vanilla."

"I'm eighteen now," Laila protested.

"I was talking about him." Kingsley pointed at Wes with his phone. Laila smiled at Wes, who rolled his eyes.

Kingsley raised the phone to his ear. Someone on the other end answered as Kingsley grinned like the devil himself.

"Wake up, Daniel. I'm calling in that favor you owe us."

Part Two

# EN PASSANT

# 11
## THE QUEEN

For what felt like an hour, Nora paced the room with the green curtains. They hadn't handcuffed her, hadn't gagged or bound her; they'd simply left her to walk unencumbered. She tried the window first and found it locked and barred. She'd need a blowtorch to get out that way. The door seemed too dangerous. Anyone could be standing behind it with a gun waiting to shoot on sight. Still, if no one came back for her in another hour or two, she'd give it a try. Better to die on her feet than huddled in a corner crying.

She kept moving about the room, trying not to give in to panic. Where was she? She felt like she should know. The furniture was elegant but old and dated. She'd guess someone had decorated the house in the 1960s and no one had bothered updating the decor since then. It gave the room an eerie feel, like she'd fallen into another time. Or that time stopped in this room. When she paced she pushed against old stale air that had probably wasted away in this room as long as the furniture had.

What the fuck was happening? She thought she knew everything about Søren's marriage to Marie-Laure. Thirty years ago, Søren had brought Marie-Laure from Paris to visit Kingsley in lieu of the *Je t'aime* that she knew Kingsley had longed to hear. Søren told her that he'd never considered the possibility of marrying Marie-Laure until he'd seen how happy Kingsley became in her presence, and once he'd thought of marriage, he realized it could be the perfect solution. But Marie-Laure had ignored Søren's cautions that he would never love her back and she'd fallen head over heels for him. Head over heels…how it began. How Nora thought it had ended. Marie-Laure catching Søren and Kingsley in an intimate moment… Marie-Laure running through the winter woods in shock and grief. She slipped on ice, perhaps—or maybe it hadn't been a simple slip—and plunged a hundred feet to her death, her body shattering on a rock below. Now she knew it had been a lie. Marie-Laure had learned long before that moment she walked in on Kingsley and Søren that they were lovers. Did she think she'd done them a favor? She would die and leave Søren a widower, and he and Kingsley would fall into each other's arms and be happy together forever?

*I gave them my death as a gift…and now I'm taking my gift back.*

Nora stopped her caged pacing long enough to glance out the window again and peer between the bars. The stars danced high in the night sky. What time was it? How long had she been here? She wore the same clothes she'd had on in the stables with Wesley back in Kentucky. She still had on her black snakeskin cowboy boots she'd worn riding. Still had on…

Nora glanced down at her left hand. On the ring finger sat a diamond that outshone the stars in the sky outside the window.

"Wes…" she whispered, staring at the ring. God, poor Wesley. He must be out of his mind with panic now. What had he done? She prayed he hadn't called the police. Getting the police involved would only make things worse. This woman might be crazy but she was dangerously crazy. She had to be intelligent to fake her death and make a life for herself for thirty years. If Marie-Laure wanted revenge on Søren it would be easy enough—kill Nora. She knew Søren would rather see his own heart cut out than allow anything to happen to her. If the sirens started screaming, it would be quick work to slit her throat and disappear back into whatever secret hellhole Marie-Laure had been hiding for the past thirty years.

Footsteps in the hallway alerted her she had perhaps only a few more seconds alone. At one end of the library stood a fireplace, and by the fireplace hung a row of antique bronze fireplace tools, including a poker. She felt a strange something when she picked it up. The heft of it surprised her. There was a weightiness to it greater even than its actual mass. She sensed history in it and didn't understand why. Didn't matter. It was the same length as a riding crop and she gripped it just the same. Kingsley Edge had been the first man to put a riding crop in her hand. A riding crop used properly merely stung like fire when applied to the body but it sure as fuck could do a lot of damage if used improperly. Kingsley's number-one word of warning to her when he gave her the first of her little red riding crops—never go near the face, never go near the eyes. *I met a boy in India who'd been blinded when a rich man hit him across the eyes with a riding crop. Don't get me sued, chérie.*

The door started to open. Nora strode toward it.

A man stepped in the rom.

Nora aimed for the eyes.

From the look on his face, he'd been expecting an attack, but not of this variety. He caught the brass bar an inch from his skull and with his other hand grasped Nora by the wrist and slammed her into the floor. She hit hard and the air rushed from her lungs.

"You should have seen that coming, Andrei," came Marie-Laure's mocking tone from above her. Nora put up a struggle but gave up when the man, Andrei, put his full weight into the knee holding her down.

"I saw it coming. Thought she'd go for the groin," the man said.

"I only do CBT when paid," Nora grunted through gritted teeth. She could hardly breathe with this Andrei bastard on her back. The other guy, Damon, probably weighed one-fifty wet. This guy weighed two tons dry.

"CBT?" Marie-Laure repeated.

"Cock and ball torture."

A trilling laugh filled the room and Nora saw Marie-Laure floating down to the floor in a sea of diaphanous black satin.

"You're delightful." Marie-Laure pushed a stray strand of black hair off Nora's face. "This is good. I'm having so much fun right now. I have my husband dancing for me. I danced for him thirty years ago. Now it's his turn."

"What do you want with Søren?"

"Only to play awhile." Marie-Laure took another lock of Nora's hair in her hand and twirled it girlishly around her finger. "I'm being so silly with him. I burned his bed. And Damon, he killed one of my brother's dogs. He even wrote a message in blood." Marie-Laure giggled like a schoolgirl. "It's ridiculous. I even gave him until noon on Friday to make up his mind about us. High noon. I've seen too many movies, haven't I?"

"And not enough therapists."

The dig didn't seem to make any impact. Marie-Laure kept grinning.

"Pull her up," she said, nodding at Andrei. The man grabbed Nora by the upper arms and dragged her to her feet.

"You're disgusting." Marie-Laure looked Nora up and down. "And you smell."

"I'm doing the French thing. I'm down to one shower a week."

"Is pissing yourself a French thing?" Marie-Laure batted her eyelashes at Nora and wrinkled her nose like a little girl.

"Your fault for knocking me out. I'll take a shower if you'll let me. I have a nice shower back at my house. I can find my own way there. I'll see myself out."

Wanting to test the waters, Nora took a step forward and Andrei swiftly and efficiently pushed her into the wall. He did a good job with it—pushed hard enough to make a point, not so hard she hurt herself. Nice technique.

"You promised to be my houseguest, remember?" Marie-Laure reminded her. "The little girl is on her way to my brother's with her message for my husband. And you're staying with me. I'm looking forward to it. I don't spend much time with women. I much prefer the company of men."

"I don't have many women friends, either. Less drama, more cock. I get it."

"You never stop talking, do you?" Marie-Laure tilted her head to the side and studied Nora like she'd encountered some sort of alien species.

Nora replied by saying absolutely nothing.

Marie-Laure nodded. "You're funny," she said in an approving tone. "It's *très chère*. Is that why my husband loves you? Because you make him laugh?"

"I'm pretty entertaining, but I don't know if that's the main reason he loves me."

"Any theories?" Marie-Laure gave a dismissive shrug that was so very French Nora wanted to slap her.

"None that make sense."

"That's what I want to understand." Marie-Laure looked

Nora up and down again. "I want to know…why you? Long ago I thought, *peut-être,* he could love only another like himself, a man, a boy. I forgave him for not loving me because he couldn't help it. I even left so he and my brother could be together. But he *can* love a woman and of all the women in the world—elegant women, intelligent women, women of poise and breeding and loyalty." At that Marie-Laure glanced down at Nora's left hand. Nora felt the ring on her finger heavy as deadweight. "So many better women in the world, and he picks you."

"I know. Nuts, right? If you figure it out, be sure to let me know."

"We will figure this out, you and I. Come along. You'll stay with me. But first we have to clean you up. I can hardly look at you. Andrei, bring her, *s'il vous plaît.*"

Marie-Laure spun around to the door, graceful as the dancer she once was. The man took Nora's elbow in his stern grip and escorted her to the door.

"Do you mind if I ask where we are?" Nora glanced around the hallway. It all seemed so familiar and yet…

"You don't know?"

Nora tried not to roll her eyes.

"I know I've been here before."

"Have you? I'm surprised he brought you here. I imagine he comes here as little as possible."

"Søren brought me here?" As she said the words, Nora noticed a painting hanging in the hallway. A young girl of about eight in a white dress sat in a rocking chair, a small stuffed horse clenched in her hand. The artist had painted a smile on the girl's face but left her violet eyes empty of hope and happiness.

Nora had seen those eyes before.

"Elizabeth…" she whispered, meeting the painted child's broken gaze. "We're in Elizabeth's house?" Once Nora made the connection, the memories of her one trip here came flooding back. Søren's father's funeral. Nora had been only seventeen years old. Ostensibly he'd brought her to the funeral for the sake of Claire, his half sister, who was about her age. But Nora knew better even then. Something had happened in this house, something bad, something Søren wanted to tell her but had been waiting for the right time. When his father was dead and buried six feet under, that had been the right time.

The fireplace poker…now she understood why it had felt like a memory in her hand. An eleven-year-year-old Søren had wielded it against his own father in that room to stop him from raping Elizabeth. And Elizabeth had wielded it herself to stop her father from killing Søren.

"Where's Elizabeth?" Nora demanded. "And Andrew?"

"Gone." Marie-Laure waved her hand dismissively. "My husband apparently told her to leave the house and take her sons with her. Too bad. I would have liked to have met my sister-in-law at last."

"Sons?" Nora caught a glimpse of a family photograph at the end of the hallway. Elizabeth, who was about Marie-Laure's age, stood under a tree with her son Andrew at her side and a much younger boy in her arms.

"Oh, *oui*. She adopted another son three years ago. His name is Nathan. You didn't know?"

Nora shook her head. Three years ago… Back then she did everything she could to stay out of Søren's life. She knew if she stayed one second too long in his world, she'd never leave it again. Or she thought she'd never leave again if she went back. She thought Søren would never have let her. But he had and now she'd ended up here with his maniac dead wife.

Never before had she more longed to be chained up to his bed with nowhere to go. Not for sex this time but for safety.

"I didn't know. He doesn't talk about Elizabeth much."

"Never thought such a brave man would be so scared of his sister," Marie-Laure said in a tone so taunting that Nora briefly considered trying her luck on a double murder/escape attempt.

"Not *scared of* his sister. *Scarred by* his sister. There's a difference."

"Scarred? Perhaps. Kingsley told me about Søren and Elizabeth...what they did together as children. He thought it would convince me that I'd married a man too scarred to love. I believed it for a day or two, wanted to believe it. But..."

"But what?" Nora asked, not sure she wanted the answer. Still it seemed expected of her to ask so she decided to play along for the time being.

"Damaged, my brother called my husband. Broken. Lies, obviously. He wasn't broken. He was stronger than anyone I'd ever met. So I thought perhaps he was too strong to love me. Love makes one weak, makes one vulnerable. Perhaps he didn't love me because he would not allow himself to be so weak. But he was weak."

"Søren is not weak. Not now. Not ever."

"Is that so? Let me show you something."

Marie-Laure continued down the hall and Nora followed, the bodyguard Andrei right next to her not speaking but never once taking his eyes off her.

She entered a bedroom, large and opulent. One of the nicer guest rooms, Nora guessed, as it held no photographs or personal items that seemed to belong to the house or its inhabitants. Although Marie-Laure had clearly made herself quite at home. She sat on the cream-colored silk covers and gathered her robe around her like some princess in repose. From the nightstand she picked up a Bible with a white leather cover.

"One of the priests at the school gave me this as a wedding gift," Marie-Laure said, caressing the engraved words on the front. "Father Henry. He even wrote the date of our marriage inside with our names."

Marie-Laure smiled wanly at the book. She brought it to her lips and pressed them to the cover before looking at Nora again.

"I had such dreams for us. This Bible was my most precious possession. I loved to open it and see our names inside and our wedding date. I thought he wasn't touching me because we still barely knew each other. I thought in a week or two, he'll be more comfortable with me. If I give him enough time, then he'll make love to me."

"I'm sorry he couldn't be what you wanted," Nora said, mustering a modicum of real sympathy. But not sympathy for Marie-Laure, the kidnapping psycho on the bed. Only sympathy for the girl she'd once been, the girl who'd loved someone who would never love her back.

"No, you aren't sorry. If he could have loved me back, we still would have been married. And where would you be if he hadn't been your priest?"

"Dead." Nora said the word quickly and simply and without hesitation. She said it because it was true. Had Søren never come into her life, she would have followed in her father's footsteps. She would have followed them right into the grave.

"Dead. So love saved your life. It ended mine."

If only, Nora thought, but decided to keep that remark to herself. Her cheek might not survive another slapping.

"I wanted to show you proof. You say my husband is not weak. I disagree. This is my Bible. My husband had his own Bible, too. He always kept it with him, and read from it all the time."

Nora suppressed a mad, tired laugh. *All zee time.* Wherever

Marie-Laure had been living, she hadn't completely lost the French accent there.

"He is kind of gay for the Bible," Nora agreed. "So what?"

"So, I watched him one night opening his Bible. He turned to a page and smiled. I'd never seen him smile like that. I know he didn't see me watching him. I know he wouldn't have smiled like that for me to see."

"Smiling at the Bible? Must have been reading Song of Solomon."

"Not quite."

Marie-Laure opened her Bible and took out a scrap of paper, yellowed slightly with age.

"He'd stepped out for a moment. Father Henry came for him. Alone with his Bible, I told myself I simply wanted to see if he'd written our names and the date of our marriage in it. He hadn't, of course. My heart broke but still I turned the pages. Perhaps I'd find some comfort in this book he read so much. I found no comfort, but I did find this."

She handed the note to Nora. The bodyguard made no move as Nora reached out and took it from her. Carefully she unfolded it and read the words.

*You Blond Monster, I'd give my right arm for another night like last night. Knowing you, you'd take it.*

At the bottom of the note were two more words.

*Je t'aime.*

French for *I love you.*

Kingsley had left Søren a love note in his Bible, and Søren had kept it.

"There were dozens of them," Marie-Laure continued, the

mad smile now gone from her face. "Dozens of notes from my brother to my husband. Most were like that—a mix of hate and love. Some were only love. Some only hate. One note…" Marie-Laure paused to laugh. "One note simply said, 'Bad news—I'm pregnant. It's yours.' My brother and his sense of humor." She shook her head like an older sister would at the stupid joke of her younger brother.

Nora wanted to laugh, too, at young Kingsley's thirty-year-old dirty joke, but at the sweetness of it, the silliness, the absolute intimacy implied by the stupid crack that Kingsley felt the need to write down and tuck into Søren's Bible for him to find and laugh over later. No one finding those notes could have missed the meaning of them. Kingsley and Søren—it wasn't sex or lust that brought them together again and again. They'd been in love. Nora knew it. She'd known it for years. But Marie-Laure hadn't known it until that moment.

"I kept this one note as evidence if I needed it," Marie-Laure said, her voice now cold and emotionless again. "I left the rest where I found them. My husband…I'd never met anyone so intelligent. And yet, love made him so weak and so foolish that he left two dozen pieces of evidence of his affair with my brother inside his Bible. Oh, yes, my husband was weak. Love made him weak. And I realized then love had made me weak, too. I didn't want to be weak anymore."

"I know they would have told you in time about them. Kingsley doesn't like talking about that part of himself. But he would have. Eventually I know he would have."

"Doesn't matter. They lied by omission. They used me."

"Used you? Søren told you that he wasn't in love with you. You knew that before you married him. He thought you wanted the money, thought you needed it."

"I wanted him, loved him. And he didn't love me. My own brother didn't even love me. Kingsley loved my husband more than his own flesh and blood. My husband loved my brother more than his own wife. I didn't know what to do. The notes I'd read…the words were burned into my mind. I prayed all the time. Days and days of walking alone in the woods trying to clear my head, trying to find an answer. Instead, I found the hermitage…their hermitage. And I got the miracle I'd prayed for."

"What miracle?"

"A girl, a runaway, hiding out in the hermitage. Long dark hair, almost my height. It was meant to be. Destiny. She was perfect."

"Perfect for what?"

"I'd given all the options so much thought. I could tell Christian what was happening. He loved me, worshipped me, thought my husband insane for never touching me. If I'd asked him he would kill my husband for me…kill my brother. But then I thought of those notes and how much they must love each other. And I did love Kingsley even though he'd stolen my husband's affections from me. So I knew what I would do. I would kill myself."

"But you didn't. You killed that poor girl."

"She had nothing. Nothing at all. She thought she'd find a new life in America. I merely saved her the heartache of disappointment."

"By murdering her? Yeah, you're all heart."

"She was a gift. She made it so easy to disappear. No one even looked for me. I found the road, hitchhiked into Canada, found someone to take care of me…so easy to die."

"You didn't die. You murdered someone."

Marie-Laure only shrugged as she sat her white Bible back on the bedside table.

"Someone had to die for their sins, their lies. But I'm starting to think…"

Her voice trailed off and she tapped her chin.
Fear shivered over Nora's skin.
"Think what?" she whispered.
"That one death was not enough."

# 12
## THE PAWN

Laila watched as her uncle and Kingsley spoke to each other in hushed French. She ached to know what the note said that she'd delivered. As the carrier, she felt she deserved to be told what it said. The anguish on her uncle's face, his naked fear, however, kept her from demanding more answers. He'd tell her in time if she needed to know. No matter how scared she was, she trusted him.

"Hey," came Wes's soft voice at her shoulder. "Let's go get your face cleaned up. Okay?"

She let him take her by the hand as she stood up on shaking legs. He led her to a bathroom at the end of the hall. While Wes dug through drawers she sat on the countertop by the sink.

"Wow."

"Wow what?" she asked, keeping her back to the mirror behind her. She didn't even want to see how bad she looked.

"There is, like, an entire hospital full of first-aid supplies in this bathroom. I'm not even going to think about why."

Laila smiled. "I can probably guess."

Wes washed his hands in the sink for a solid two minutes. He scrubbed his nails, used tons of soap and scalding water and dried them on a new clean towel.

"You wash your hands like a surgeon," she said.

He smiled ear to ear, a smile so bright it was like a sunbeam breaking through the clouds. But the cloud came back in an instant and both sun and smile were gone again.

"I work in a hospital. Part-time orderly stuff. I want to be a doctor someday, though." Wes tossed the towel aside.

"I work in an animal clinic. I'd be too scared to work with people. They talk back."

"That's my problem with working with animals. They can't tell me where it hurts." He stood directly in front of her so that her knees almost touched his hips. "Can you tell me where it hurts?"

"I think I'm okay. I'm sore all over."

"You must have put up a fight. I'm going to touch your face now."

He took her gently by the chin and turned her face toward the light.

"I tried. He was too strong."

"Don't feel bad. They got me, too." He pointed to the bandage on his temple. "Whoever it was did a good job knocking me out without actually hurting me. I think these people are professionals. That scares me more than anything."

"Did they take you, too?"

He shook his head and she sensed his regret.

"I wish they had. We were at my house in Kentucky. I got hit or something and when I came to a few seconds later, she was gone."

"She was with you?"

He nodded as he raised a wet cotton ball and started to stroke her cheek with it. From the corner of her eye she saw the cotton ball turning pink with blood.

"Yeah. We're…friends. She was visiting me. We went horseback riding and came back to the stables. We talked about something and then…it all went black. When I came to, she was gone."

"That's awful. Are you okay?"

"As okay as anyone would be, I guess."

"You don't look okay." He didn't. He might be the most gorgeous guy she'd ever seen in her life, but he also happened to be the most gorgeous guy she'd ever seen in her life who looked like he would pass out any minute. "You look bad."

"Your English is really good. Too good."

She laughed as he tossed the cotton ball and picked up a clean one.

"I'm sorry. Everyone in Denmark learns English. My uncle's been making me speak it to him all my life so I would get better at it. I didn't mean you look ugly. You look sick."

"Don't apologize," he said, rubbing her cheek with antibiotic ointment. "I haven't eaten or slept since this all happened. At least they left me alive. And you. You sure you're okay?"

"I'm okay. Are you?"

"No. I mean, yes. I mean, I won't be okay until Nora's safe."

"Me, too. I can't… If something happens to her…" Tears started to run down her face again. Wes handed her a tissue and kept working on her cheek.

"Nora's the toughest woman alive. I keep telling myself that," Wes said as he applied a pad of gauze to her cheek.

"She is. I believe in her. I know he'll do whatever he can to get her back."

"So will I."

He taped the gauze to her cheek and smoothed it down.

"I'll check it in a few hours."

"Thank you." She raised her hand and touched her face. She felt better already.

"Are you hurt anywhere else? I can get Grace. She's really nice. If you think, you know, you're hurt somewhere else…" His words were plain and simple but she could see the concern in his eyes, the searching look.

"I wasn't raped."

He stared at her as if trying to discern whether or not she was lying to him. No wonder he'd been so careful with her, not even touching her without warning her of his every move first.

"I work the E.R. a lot. I've seen women come in for sprained wrists and broken noses and stitches—they say the same thing. If you were, we need to get you checked out. You don't want to wait. If it happened, it's not your fault at all. But you have to tell somebody."

"I was conscious the whole time."

"Are you sure? It only takes a minute sometimes."

"I'm sure." She looked him in the eyes so he would believe her.

"Okay, I believe you."

"I promise, if that happened I would tell you."

"Good."

Wes put his arm around her and helped her down off the countertop. She took advantage of their proximity to smell his hair. He smelled like summer, like warm, clean towels drying in the sun. She wanted to stretch out in the warmth of him like a cat lying in the sun.

He bent over the sink and started washing the blood off his hands. Laila wondered if she should give him some privacy in the bathroom, but before she could go, he paused in his hand-washing and put his hands on the counter and closed his eyes.

"What's wrong?" She watched his face, the pained set to his mouth.

"I should eat something." She saw sweat break out on his face. His hands shook. Not eating for a day should only make him hungry. This was something more.

"You're…" She tried to remember the English word for it. *"Diabetisk?"* she said, recognizing the symptoms of a blood sugar crash.

"Yeah. How did you—"

"Even dogs have it. Sit down." She put an arm around his waist and helped lower him to the floor. Better get him on the floor now before he ended up there by fainting. "My turn to be the doctor."

# 13
# THE QUEEN

Nora had been allowed to take a shower. She'd been so shocked that Marie-Laure told her she could have one that Nora'd actually said, "Thank you." Thank you, she'd said to the woman who'd kidnapped her? Thank you? Fucking Stockholm syndrome. Nora turned on the water. No more thank-yous unless it was "Thank you for dying, bitch, and this time stay dead." One of the guards led her to a luxurious bathroom off the bedroom where they'd been talking and told her to clean up. She'd climbed into the shower fully clothed. No way would she strip in front of Marie-Laure's boys, who she had mentally dubbed Fat Man and Little Boy. Fat Man was Andrei, easily two hundred and fifty pounds of solid muscle. All muscle, no brain. Little Boy Damon with his coldly intelligent eyes and expensive shoes had to be the brains of the operation. Everything about him screamed "mercenary." Neither one of them seemed to have any amorous interest in her. Marie-Laure wasn't the type to allow the men in her life, hired thugs or not, to show interest in any woman beside herself, but that was no reason to tempt fate. Plus Marie-Laure hadn't been kidding. She did smell like piss and horse shit.

The hot water scalded and Nora let the heat seep into her skin. She took cold comfort from it. Too many thoughts of Wesley intruded. A few nights ago they'd been in his shower together, fully clothed and talking. What she wouldn't give to be back there now.... That night she'd been miserable, devastated that she'd beaten a newborn foal on the off-chance it would stir his mother from the exhaustion and stupor that threatened to kill her. Now that sort of misery seemed like paradise compared to this one. Trapped in a house with a madwoman and her two gun-toting bodyguards. And for what? Revenge against Søren? Against Kingsley? Against her? What was Marie-Laure's endgame in all this? That woman would never make it out of this alive. If Nora died, there'd be no reason to stop Kingsley from blowing them all away. If it meant Søren's happiness, there was nothing Kingsley wouldn't do.

Nora wrapped a bath towel around her as Damon led her back into the bedroom and pulled out ropes and handcuffs. Marie-Laure looked trussed up like a princess in her chic nightgown all cozy in the bed.

"I don't play with strangers on the first date," Nora said, eyeing the rope warily.

"We've met before. We'll call it our second date." Damon gripped her by the arm and pushed her. "On the bed. Back to the bedpost," he ordered, and Nora reluctantly obeyed. She would have tried to fight or run for it but Andrei, the Fat Man, stood at the door holding a gun in his hand as casually as a pinwheel.

"It's fine. It's late. Let's settle in for the night, shall we?" Marie-Laure spoke as if they were two girls at a slumber party and not one sociopathic murderer and one terrified and soaking-wet prisoner. Meanwhile, Damon clapped the cuffs on her wrists and started to thread the rope around her ankles.

"You're tying me to the bed?" Nora asked.

"You're my guest. If you wander in the night around the house, you might get hurt. We don't want that, do we?"

Nora heard the threat tucked inside the faux concern. If she wandered in the night, someone would blow her brains out.

"Fine. Whatever. Not the first night I spent tied to a bed." She sensed Damon behind her expertly threading the rope through the cuffs and the sturdy frame of the bed. The cool air in the room sent goose bumps all over her wet body. Cold, wet and terrified and sitting up with her back against the bed-post, she doubted she'd get any sleep at all. Good. She should stay awake, alert, and thinking. There had to be a way out of this. They'd let their guard down at some point. She could make a run for it.

"Nice," Nora said to Damon. "You do good rope work. You a Dom?"

"Headhunter," he said simply and without translating. Nora hadn't been around the mob since her father died but she hadn't forgotten the lingo. Headhunter—hired killer.

"Headhunter? You and Kingsley could talk shop." Nora looked at Marie-Laure again. "You know your brother is an ex-assassin, right? You sure you want to tangle with him?"

"I helped change his diapers. Forgive me if I can't see him as much of a threat."

"Helped change his diapers? Wow…you are old, aren't you?"

"Damon," Marie-Laure said.

Damon stepped forward, grabbed a handful of Nora's wet hair and pulled. He rested a sharp cold blade against her neck.

"You are here to amuse me," Marie-Laure said from the head of the bed. "Not insult me. I suggest you start being a bit more entertaining if you want to live a few hours more."

"Entertaining?" Nora repeated. "What do you want? A song and dance? Some stand-up? A bedtime story?"

Marie-Laure said nothing as she studied Nora's face. It might have only been seconds, but with the knife at her throat and Nora's life flashing in front of her eyes, it felt like hours. Damon let the knife dig a millimeter deeper into her skin and in that moment Nora regretted every last time she'd told Søren she hated him. Hopefully he knew she never meant it, that she only said it because she didn't know how else to tell him how annoying it was to be loved that much by someone who was so right all the damn time about everything.

"Damon." Marie-Laure spoke his name softly and the knife immediately disappeared. Nora breathed carefully as if the blade still waited at her neck.

"I'm sorry," Nora said. "I'm pretty sensitive about my age, too. Doesn't help when you're sleeping with a younger man."

"Yes, your younger man—fascinating."

"Wes? Is he alive?" Nora asked the question she'd been afraid to even utter in her own mind. But she had to know.

"Oh, *oui*. We barely touched him. Andrei is well-trained. He knows how to make someone unconscious without killing him. He doesn't like it—not killing them, I mean. But he follows orders well. You see, your fiancé is actually important."

"You got his attention, I promise." Nora offered a silent prayer of thanks to God that Marie-Laure hadn't killed Wesley. One thing to be grateful about today. Wes was alive and so was she…for now.

"Handsome boy, your younger man. Very handsome. But no one is as handsome as my husband."

"Blondie's a hottie," Nora agreed.

"Once I thought if my husband loved me, I'd never desire anyone else on earth. How could I when I had him? And yet, you have his love but have run off with another."

"It's complicated."

"I see that. Go on. I'm all ears."

"What? You want me to tell you about my love life?"

"Tell me about this fiancé of yours. That ring on your finger could feed a third-world country for a year."

"Only a very small country."

"You aren't impressed by the ring?"

"It's a rock," Nora said. "Literally. Diamonds are rocks. You dig them out of the ground with a shovel. Wes might as well have given me a bag of gravel."

"That's a rather rare and large bit of rock. And you must have liked it if you accepted it, *non?*"

Nora set her jaw tight and glared at Marie-Laure. Everything within her rebelled at talking about her Wesley with this woman. She didn't even deserve to say Wesley's name much less know all about their private life.

"Wes is a good friend."

"A good friend? That's how you describe your fiancé?"

No, it wasn't. In her heart Wesley was love and light and big brown eyes that made her thighs melt. He adored her and desired her and wanted to protect her even from Søren, who was the only man who she felt safer with than even Wesley.

"We're good friends, yes."

"A very good friend. You spent a week in his bed."

"Well…not the whole week. We did get out sometimes."

"You're trying to pretend you don't care about him. I don't believe it. You don't agree to marry someone you don't care about."

"Why not? Søren did."

Marie-Laure's eyes flashed.

"Damon?"

Damon stepped forward and grabbed Nora by the throat. Marie-Laure crawled forward across the covers and knelt primly in front of where Nora sat pinioned in place with Damon's hand squeezing her neck. She could breathe still, thank God, although his fingers gripped her tight enough to leave bruises. It's okay…she could take this and not panic. How many times had Søren held her against the wall, his fingers around her throat? A thousand times surely. Of course, with him, the hand on her throat had belonged to a man who loved her, who'd cut off his own hand before actually hurting her. And when he held her by the throat, it was to arouse her, to stir her hunger for him with his power and possessiveness. Damon did it to terrorize her into compliance, into defeat. She went silent and still. Let him think he won. She knew better.

"Listen to me," Marie-Laure began, her voice soft and sinister. "I'm going to tell you something very important so pay attention. I can't begin to tell you how entertaining it's been making my husband and my brother dance for me this past week, trying to discover who on earth it was who was tormenting them. I love this game and I'm not ready for it to be over yet. Right now my husband is experiencing real terror, terror so potent I can smell it on the air. For whatever reason, he loves you, whore and harlot that you are. And since he loves you and I have you, I can make him dance for me as long as I desire. Of course this can't go on indefinitely, can it? Even I get bored."

"What do you want?" Nora asked when Damon's fingers slackened enough to let her speak.

"I want someone to die," Marie-Laure said simply. "I have seen you all—you and my husband and my brother—you're like a fabric all woven together. I want to pull one thread and see you all unravel. If you die, my husband will be destroyed. If my husband dies trying to save you, my brother will be destroyed. To kill one of you will kill you all. I want to watch this happen. I want to see it unfold before my eyes. I want my husband and my brother and you to know that eventually we all must pay for our sins. That is why I have you now and why I'm going to keep you here a little while. I'm calling in their debts. It's time for someone to pay up."

Marie-Laure moved a little closer. She picked up the abandoned towel and wiped the dripping water from her shower off Nora's face. Nora cringed at the gentle gesture.

"If you keep taunting me like this, however," Marie-Laure continued, "then I'm going to lose my patience with you and let Damon and Andrei have you, and I'm quite certain you wouldn't survive playtime with them. So I will ask you very politely to keep your commentary to yourself. I would hate to see this game end prematurely. Do you understand me?"

Marie-Laure tossed the towel onto the floor and sat back on her legs.

"I understand," Nora said. Marie-Laure nodded at Damon, who let Nora go. He stepped back again, and Nora swallowed air with renewed gratitude for every unencumbered breath.

"Good. Now let's talk about this fiancé of yours." Marie-Laure returned to the head of the bed. She propped herself up on the pillows and let her diaphanous robe frame her like an unfurled fan. "And stop pretending that you don't care about him. I know otherwise. I've read your file. Kingsley described your young man as your only weakness. I would love to know what he meant by that. Especially since you seem comprised entirely of weaknesses."

"I don't know what he meant by that, either. Like you said, Wes is one of many weaknesses."

"Younger men are a weakness of yours?"

"Kind of. I have a little soft spot for virgin boys. All that untapped potential makes a girl want to, you know, tap that."

"So it's merely sexual?"

"Not entirely. Although that's a big part of it," Nora said without apology.

"Is it? Have you been with a lot of virgin boys?"

"A few."

"I'd love a number."

Nora clenched her jaw again but repressed the urge to say something which would no doubt get her in death's crosshairs again. Taking a deep breath, she reflected on her past as ghosts of long-ago nights flitted across her mind's eyes.

Bram...a seventeen-year-old male submissive who Kingsley had introduced her to.

Alex...age eighteen, barely eighteen.

Noah...one of Wes's friends from Yorke. She didn't know they were friends until after Wesley had moved in. She suffered a couple of sleepless nights wondering if Noah would tell Wes about the night he'd spent tied to her headboard.

And, of course, her angel, Michael. Age fifteen. A gift from Søren, who knew about her weakness and had decided to put it to better use than simply getting her off.

"Five, counting Wesley. Enough for a pattern, not enough for a fetish."

"Five. Impressive. Actual virgins?"

"Every last one of them. If we're talking kink virgins, you'd have to triple the number."

"No guilt at all?"

"None. Okay, maybe a little but only with Alex."

"Alex?"

"He was the son of this bitchy book reviewer. Totally blasted my first book. Called all my lovely kinksters 'sick' and 'abusive.' So I got my payback by sickly abusing her youngest all night long."

"And you felt guilty about that?"

"Not the sex. The note I sent Mom the next day."

"You sent his mother a note after you seduced her son? What did it say?"

"It said…" Nora began, and paused for a breath. Not one of her prouder moments. "It said, 'Your son gave me five stars last night. And five fingers.'"

"You're smiling."

"I'm trying so hard to feel bad about it. I swear to God I am."

"You amaze me. Why all the virgins? They have no idea what they're doing."

"I had such an amazing first time that I like giving that experience to other people. Better than five minutes in the back of a Buick, right?"

"How altruistic of you."

"I'm a giver."

"And my husband doesn't mind that? Doesn't mind you cuckolding him left and right with other men?"

"Did you say *cuckolding*? I didn't know people still said that."

"It sounded more polite than calling you a slut and whore who'll spread for anyone who pays you the slightest bit of attention."

"Look, in my world *slut* is a term of endearment. Why do I have to keep explaining this to people? You're going to have to find a new name if you want to actually hurt my feelings. Telling me I've had too much sex is about as insulting as telling me I'm too thin."

"I'm simply stating the facts, not trying to insult you."

"Fine, then. Here are the facts. The vanilla mind has a little trouble grasping these facts, but you're going to have to trust me that I know what I'm talking about. Søren loves me and he loves what I am. He takes pleasure in my pleasure. He no more begrudges me enjoying myself sexually with someone else than he'd begrudge me going out for a nice meal with a friend. Sex is sustenance to me. He'd rather I eat than starve."

"You say that and yet you lived with your young fiancé for over a year without…feeding on him."

"I'm capable of some self-control on rare occasion. Wesley wasn't a virgin because he hadn't gotten around to getting laid yet. He was a virgin because he wanted to wait for someone special. He has a different philosophy of sex than I do. I didn't share it, but I respected it."

Marie-Laure sighed and shook her head.

"Fascinating…" she said again.

"What is?"

"Your capacity for self-justification and rationalization."

"If it were an Olympic sport, I'd medal."

"No doubt. I have to say after that speech about my husband's love for you that I can't quite understand why you're so drawn to a young man with whom you have so little in common. Not only drawn to him, but you agreed to marry him."

"I saw a death threat carved into the barn wall that wasn't there before we went on our ride together. I saw a shadow moving in the background. I would have agreed to marry Satan himself if it meant getting Wes and me out of that barn safely."

"You don't actually love him at all, do you?"

"I didn't say that."

"Then what are you saying?"

"Not wanting to marry somebody doesn't mean you don't love them. Marriage and love are two very different things. Ask a married person. They'll tell you that themselves."

"So you do love him?"

"Yes. I love Wesley very much."

"Tell me why."

"I can't."

Marie-Laure glanced at Damon.

"Wait, whoa. I can," she said before Damon put her in a chokehold again. "I can and I will. Sorry. My editor kicks my ass when I tell and not show in a story. I'm out of practice with the telling."

"Show me, then. You did offer me a bedtime story earlier."

"I write erotica, not bedtime stories."

"Aren't they the same thing?"

"Touché."

Marie-Laure leaned forward in the bed. She put her chin on her hands and smiled angelically.

"Tell me a story."

"You're going to have to talk to my agent. She handles all book deals."

"Damon?"

Damon stepped forward again, knife at the ready.

"In the very olden times there lived a semi-barbaric king…" Nora began, and Marie-Laure sat back in the bed as she fluffed her pillows.

"Not that story. I want a story about you. Tell me a story about this younger man of yours. You have the love of my husband and yet you walk away from it for a boy. There must be a reason."

"Reasons aplenty."

"I'd love to know them. Tell me. Be my Scheherazade."

Nora's stomach tightened. She remembered Scheherazade's story, the bride of the sultan who told him a thousand and one stories simply to keep him from executing her. Nora took a deep breath. Damon watched her, his knife in hand. Andrei stood at the door, gun in hand. Marie-Laure watched her, madly grinning.

All she needed now was a story that explained why she loved Wesley. She had hundreds of them. Picking only one of them would be the hard part, but she'd have to pick one of them if she wanted to live to see her next birthday. And with that thought she knew exactly what story to tell.

"Once upon a time," Nora began again, "I was fucking my friend Griffin when the phone rang…"

# 14
# THE ROOK

Grace sat alone in one of Kingsley's guest bedrooms and stared at her phone. She should call Zachary and tell him what had happened. She knew she should. And yet something kept her from dialing his number, something much more than a long-distance bill to Australia. It would take days for Zachary to get to the States if he knew what was going on. The flight alone could be an entire day, and it would take him at least that long before he could even get to the airport. All that time he'd be in a panic. She imagined him sitting in the airplane seat with no ability to contact her and find out what was happening. It sounded like misery to her, the purest hell. He loved Nora and it gave her no grief to acknowledge that. He turned to her for advice, for laughs, or simply when he wanted to get in a good fight with someone who wouldn't back down. She never had to ask who he was on the phone with when she stumbled across him talking to her. No one else got under his skin like she did, got him so passionate, so annoyed.

Perhaps another wife would have been jealous of their friendship. But how could she be jealous when she reaped all the benefits? The minute he hung up, he'd grab Grace by the waist or the wrist and drag her off to the bedroom. Sometimes they didn't even make it to the bedroom. Married almost twelve years and he still loved bending her over the kitchen table, shoving her skirt to her hips and burying himself inside her. And always after he'd come inside her, he'd pull her close, whisper that he loved her. She knew he did love her. He'd crossed an ocean for her and left Nora behind on the other side.

No, she couldn't do this to him, bring him into this nightmare and force him to suffer through it in impotence. Ignorance was bliss, he'd reminded her. She'd tell him only if and when she had to. Until then...

After shoving her phone back down into her purse, Grace exhaled with some relief. To call Zachary or to not call Zachary had finally been decided. One less thing to worry about.

Now she only had everything else in the world to worry about. Foremost on her mind was Søren. The look Kingsley had given Søren after reading the note Laila had delivered had been a look she'd only seen once before. Twelve years ago, when the doctor had come into the hospital room to tell Grace and Zachary that there was no hope, their baby was gone, and they'd have to face the fact Grace might never get pregnant again—it had been *that* look.

Sympathy from the executioner.

The note contained a death sentence. She knew it in her soul.

She left the room in search of Søren or anyone else who would give her some company. She couldn't stand to be in the

presence of her own thoughts anymore. Wandering around
the house, Grace saw Griffin again, the young man who'd
first let her in the house. He paced by a large picture window, his ear glued to his phone. She stayed on the stairs and
out of his line of sight. She couldn't hear anything he said but
whatever he'd heard must not have pleased him very much
as he abruptly ended the call and threw his phone across the
room. He buried his face in his hands and only looked up
when a younger man with black hair pulled back in a low ponytail came up to him. The younger man, more a boy than
a man, took Griffin's wrists and gently pulled them away
from his face. For a moment they only looked at each other.
Grace couldn't blame either of them. Griffin was undeniably
attractive with his chiseled chin, his dark spiky hair, his tattooed biceps peeking out from the sleeves of his T-shirt. But
the boy had an ethereal beauty to him the likes she'd rarely
seen before. Only teenage boys could achieve that level of
lithe loveliness, that almost angelic air. Griffin grabbed the
young man by the back of the neck and pulled him into a kiss
so powerful, so passionate, that Grace almost gasped aloud.
They kissed like the world was about to end. Perhaps it was.
Perhaps they should all find someone to kiss like that if only
to remember they were still alive. Riveted by the display of
near-apocalyptic lust at the end of the hall, Grace didn't even
hear the footsteps behind her.

"New love," came Søren's voice from behind her.

"No wonder Kingsley works from home. I'd need twenty-
four-hour access to a bed, too, if I was surrounded by sights
like that all the time."

"Kingsley takes near-constant advantage of his twenty-
four-hour access to beds."

"I don't blame him." Grace turned away from the scene at
the end of the hall. "I don't blame any of you."

"Not even me?"

Grace sat down on the top step and put her back to the stair railing.

"Not even you, Father Stearns." She smiled as he sat down next to her on the step. "My grandfather was a minister in the Presbyterian church. He had a wife, children. Zachary's brother Aaron is a rabbi and has a wife and children, too. I've never understood the Catholic church's insistence on celibate priests."

"Celibacy wasn't always mandatory for the priesthood. New Testament church leaders were reported to have had wives. It wasn't until the eleventh century that it was spelled out as obligatory in the First Council of the Lateran. The Second Council of the Lateran banned jousting."

"Jousting?"

"Yes. They were apparently of equal theological weight."

"You don't joust, do you?"

"Only with Eleanor."

"I remember my European history. I don't think many of the popes even adhered to the vow of celibacy. Rather unfair to enforce it among the priests."

"It hasn't been enforced. Not consistently. Most African priests do get married and the bishops turn a blind eye. Eastern Rite priests are allowed to marry. Only the breaches that reach the public are punished."

"So what's the purpose of the vow? Psychological torture?"

"There are varying theories. When the church became rich, it had a vested interest in keeping itself rich. Married priests meant sons. Sons inherited money and land. The church wanted to keep that money and land in its own hands. Thus was born the vow of celibacy. Now, of course, most bishops knew the priests would still have lovers and mistresses. But if

they weren't allowed to marry, their children would all be illegitimate and couldn't inherit."

"That's the reason?"

"One of several. I would say it's the real reason, which is
why it's difficult for those of us who know church history to
take the vow as something God intended. The church's of-
ficial position is that priests are to be celibate because Christ
was celibate. It's also why women can't become priests."

"Christ was also Jewish and circumcised. Do they require
all priests to be of Jewish descent and circumcised, as well? If
that were true, then my husband would make a better priest
than you. And I promise, he wouldn't. It's ludicrous to draw
the line so fine."

"I won't argue with you. The Jesuits have always been more
liberal on these issues. A married Catholic woman on birth
control is considered unchaste even if she's faithful to her husband. We tend to overlook those types of glaring absurdities."

"And overlook the occasional lover?"

Søren started to smile at her question before composing his
face once more.

"I know a few Jesuits who also have lovers. Other men,
mostly."

"Do they know about you and Nora?"

"The only Jesuit who knows is the priest who hears my
confessions."

"And what does he say?"

Søren smiled and something in that smile made her toes
curl up inside her trainers.

"He says to send her his way when I'm done with her."

Grace only looked at him before bursting into laughter.

"I'm not joking, I promise."

"I believe you."

"He's in his seventies, my confessor. I've warned him a

night with Eleanor would mean the end of him. He said he was quite content to go out with a bang and meet Saint Peter with a smile on his face."

"I like him already."

"I asked him thirty years ago before I went to Rome if God would let someone like me be a priest."

"You told him what you were?"

"I did. It might have been one of the more awkward conversations of my life. But he listened, asked a few questions, asked if my needs could be met without intercourse, which they can. I never intended to break the vows of chastity and celibacy."

"So why did you?"

"Let's simply say that a young Eleanor Schreiber drove a hard bargain. Fifteen years old and she was already trying to get me into bed. I should have taken her up on it, not made her wait for four years for me. All that time we could have been together…and now time is running out."

His words, so simple, so sorrowful, hit her like a fist in her stomach.

"We can't think like that." Grace shook her head. "*You* can't think like that. We know where she is, don't we?"

"Yes, we do." He pulled Laila's necklace from his pocket and opened it. Grace leaned in close to look at the pictures inside.

"Your mother was beautiful." No one could doubt the young mother in the pictures had given birth to the man sitting next to her. They had the same intelligent eyes, the same complexion, the same coloring, the same Nordic beauty. He'd even inherited his mother's mouth…the lips sculpted and inviting.

"She was. Laila looks very much like her. My God, I can't

believe Marie-Laure stooped so low to make my niece a pawn in this."

"How did she get here?"

"Marie-Laure got into Eleanor's email somehow. Laila and Eleanor email each other all the time. Laila thought Eleanor was bringing her to the States to surprise me. Nasty surprise."

"That poor girl. Is she all right?"

"She will be. I made her call her mother and tell her she was visiting me. Laila refuses to go back until we find Nora, and I don't have the heart to make her. Laila...she's worked at a veterinary clinic after school every day for four years. My sister, Freyja, is very well-off." He smiled faintly and swallowed hard. Grace wanted to touch him for comfort but pulled her hand back at the last moment. "So Laila doesn't have to work. She was out walking one day and found a dog on the side of the road. He'd been hit by a car. That fourteen-year-old girl picked him up and carried him into town to the vet's office. That's how she got the after-school job. Because when the vet asked her why she'd carried this stray mutt so far Laila said that not even a dog deserved to die alone."

"My God, what a beautiful heart she has." No doubt Laila was distraught at this very moment, worried her own aunt might die alone.

"She does. She takes after my mother in more than her appearance. My mother survived a great deal of trauma and tragedy and went on to have a happy life."

"Is she still alive?" Grace asked before she let her mind wander any farther down any path that ended at Søren's mouth.

"No. She died a few years ago."

"You loved her very much. I can tell." His eyes softened when he spoke of her. She rather liked seeing that.

"I did. She..." He paused and closed the locket. "It's a long, ugly story. I won't bore you with it."

Grace nearly laughed at that.

"You couldn't bore me if you read me the phone book. Talk to me. I'd rather hear your words than the thoughts in my head."

He nodded sympathetically. He must have felt the same. Better to talk of anything except what was happening right now.

"My mother came to America on a music scholarship and took a job with my father and his wife as an au pair for my half sister Elizabeth."

"And he fell in love with her?"

"No. He raped her."

Grace covered her mouth with her hand.

"My father was a bitter man. A penniless English baron of all things."

"Are you serious?"

"Quite. His father squandered the family fortune. He came to America and leveraged his title to marry wealth. He tried to recapture the glory he thought should have been his. He made everyone call him Lord Stearns."

"I live in England where we still have a peerage, and I can't even imagine growing up in such an environment."

"He was an evil man, my father. Highly manipulative, charming. He commanded respect wherever he went. No one would cross him. No one would dare. They had no idea what kind of person he was."

"But you knew."

"I knew." He tightened his fingers around the locket. "I knew my mother feared him. I learned to fear him, too. Most mothers tucking their children in tell them bedtime stories. My mother recited her full name and address back in Copenhagen to me every night. That was my bedtime story. Her name, her address, her father's name, names of relatives. *Gisela*

*Magnussen, datter af Søren Niels Magnussen, 23 Halfdansgade 2300
København S...."*

Søren closed his eyes as he recited his mother's bedtime
story to him. Grace stopped breathing as his voice dropped
to a whisper. She saw the girl, only eighteen, pale hair, gray
eyes, sitting on the edge of a small boy's bed. She watched the
young, scared mother bring the covers to his chin as she whispered to him in a language no one else in the house spoke.
Did she tell her young son why she made him learn names
and addresses by rote? Or did she make a child's game of it?

"Every night she told me the same story. Every night I had
to repeat it all back to her. She knew it was only a matter of
time before he shipped me off to school and tired of her."

"She feared you two would be separated?"

"She thought he would kill her."

Søren met Grace's eyes a moment before looking away
again.

"Instead, he simply let her go and moved on to a new victim."

"My God, what your mother must have suffered...."

"It's unbearable to think about. She loved us, my half sister Elizabeth and me. That's why she stayed and didn't leave,
didn't run away. Love kept her a prisoner in that house. Love
for me."

"Were you separated?"

"When I was five. He sent me to an English boarding
school. My mother was summarily dismissed and returned to
Denmark. She married and had my other half sister Freyja. I
didn't see her again or meet my half sister until I was eighteen."

"What was it like when you saw her again?"

He paused and seemed to ponder the question.

"I can only answer your question by saying that I hope
heaven is full of half the joy our hearts were that day. Even

now that she's gone, I still hear the echoes of that joy, still feel the aftershocks."

Grace's throat tightened.

"I can't even imagine." Grace thought of the child she once carried. A child never meant to be and yet still a small part of her grieved for what could have been. "What she must have felt losing you and then finding you again...."

He fell silent and stared at the pictures in the locket. Grace ached to touch him—his hand, his face—but the priest's collar he wore around his neck and the wall he'd warned her to stay behind kept her from reaching out to him.

"And now the only other woman in the world I have ever loved is trapped in the very same house where my mother was trapped and raped and lived in fear. And for the same reason—for loving me. There is no way Marie-Laure did this on her own. She has help. She has... I can't even think about it."

"Then don't think about it," Grace said with more confidence than she felt. "Nora wouldn't want us to. She'd want us to get her the hell out of there. We know where she is, yes? What's the plan?"

"Kingsley will attempt to get her out. He begged me to let him try. I couldn't say no."

"Alone?"

"If anyone can rescue her without bloodshed, it's him."

"Without bloodshed?"

"He's lived with the guilt of his sister's death for thirty years. All this time he blamed himself, believing it was suicide. I can't ask him to kill her again. I won't."

"If that doesn't work, if he can't get her out, is there a plan B?"

Søren didn't answer.

Kingsley came up the stairs and faced them from the landing. "Daniel said to come anytime."

"Who's Daniel?" Grace asked.

Kingsley gave a cold sort of laugh. "He's an old…friend, I suppose. His late wife and I were lovers before they met and got married. When she died, Daniel holed up in his house for a few years. Took his pet to get him back out again." Kingsley pointed at Søren.

"You mean Nora?" Grace narrowed her eyes at Kingsley.

"The very same. He lent her to Daniel for a week."

"For what?" Grace wasn't sure if she wanted the answer.

A broad grin crossed Kingsley's face. Søren wouldn't meet her eyes.

"Our Nora has a magic pussy. It's the opposite of the Bermuda Triangle. Lost men sail into it and then find themselves."

"Kingsley, that's enough." Søren glared at him.

"You were her first Lost Boy," Kingsley said, entirely uncowed by Søren.

"Daniel's an old friend," Søren said to her, ignoring Kingsley. "His house is very close to my half sister Elizabeth's house. That's all that matters. Has Daniel warned Anya we're coming?" He turned back to Kingsley.

"He said Anya and the children are in Montreal for a few days."

"Good," Søren said. "We want as few people involved in this as possible."

"We'll leave the children here. And you, too, *madame*," Kingsley said, facing Grace.

"I'm going, too. Wherever it is, I'm going." No way in hell would she return to England until she saw Nora safe again.

"She's coming with us, Kingsley." Søren stood up so that he towered feet above Kingsley down on the landing. "So are Wesley and Laila. It's for the best and you know it."

Kingsley gave Søren a cold and bitter stare, a stare so hard and so sharp it could have cleaved a diamond in two.

"Goddamn you," Kingsley said, and Søren made no reply. The Frenchman turned on his heel and disappeared back down the stairs.

"What was that about?" Grace came back to her feet.

"Kingsley doesn't care for plan B."

# 15
# THE QUEEN

*Once upon a time…*

When Nora woke up that morning two and a half years ago, she knew exactly what she could do to make this fucking day bearable. She needed sex and lots of it. Luckily sex and lots of it was one naughty voice mail message away.

*Griffin…darling…this message is for your cock. I'd like to spend the day with it if it would be so obliging. Have it call me back if interested.*

At about noon, Griffin's usual waking hour, he called her back. She didn't even have to finish asking if he wanted to spend the day playing before he said, "Yes, yes and yes. Oh, and my cock says yes, too. And thanks for asking."

Once Wes left the house for school, Nora had dressed in her best fuck-me attire—thigh-high black boots, short, pleated black skirt, tight white blouse and panties that were designed to end up on the floor and stay there all night. She couldn't get to Griffin's fast enough. She and Wes had only been living together about two and a half months. She loved having him in the house. The house felt like home with him around, but the kid made it really fucking difficult to get laid these days. Today she would be proactive. Desperate times called for desperate orgasms.

When she arrived at his posh East Village apartment, Nora grabbed Griffin by the shirt and pushed him into the wall without him putting up anything remotely resembling a fight.

"Missed you, too," he said, his hands already sliding up the backs of her thighs and under her skirt.

"Behave yourself."

"Where's the fun in that?"

Nora pushed her tongue into his mouth, so warm and eager.

"Good question," she whispered into his lips.

She knew Griffin had hoped for sex and lots of it, and he would get it, most definitely. But she'd decided to make him work for it a little first. So she pulled out her favorite game, one Søren had taught her—the "pick a number" game. A wonderful game, especially since the person picking never knew what he or she was picking until after they'd made the choice. "Pick a number between one and four," she'd said after dragging Griffin by his shirt to the living room, pushing him down and straddling his hips on the floor.

"Two," he'd said.

"Spoilsport." He always did play it safe with her mind games. One to four could mean how many fingers she shoved inside him. One to four could mean how many times she'd let him fuck her. Today one to four meant how many hours she would tease him before they got down to the actual fucking. So for two hours, she slowly stripped him naked, kissed and nibbled on every inch of him—his tattooed biceps, his strong collarbone, his favorite inches—but never once did she let him come.

At one hour and forty-five minutes, she tied him to a chair. She'd seen Griffin put at least a dozen men and women into similar situations. Fucking the tied up and immobilized made the sexual violating so much easier.

Once she'd secured Griffin, she sat on the leather sofa opposite him. She pulled her panties down and draped them over his thighs. Then, throwing one leg over the arm of the sofa, she proceeded to pleasure herself in rather graphic fashion. She found it gratifying to tease him about how her underwear seemed to be rising off his lap.

"Nora…please," he begged, "you're killing me here."

"That's *Mistress* Nora to you."

"You shouldn't treat another Dominant like this."

"If you didn't want to be my man-whore today, you shouldn't have let me in your place."

"I'll never do it again."

"Really?" she asked, lifting her hips to give him a better view.

"Okay, I totally will. Please?"

"I am so wet right now. Can you tell?"

Nora spread herself as wide open as she could. To make the show a little better, she slowly slid a finger in and out of her vagina. Griffin moaned in the back of his throat.

"My clit's swollen, too. Wonder what I should do about that…"

"I have some suggestions."

Nora coughed.

"I have some suggestions, Mistress," Griffin said. Even a hard-core Dominant like Griffin knew better than to antagonize a horny Domme in the mood to top.

"I think my panties just saluted my vagina."

"My cock would love to salute your cervix."

"You have quite a way with the pickup lines, Griff. If you

beg some more, I might let you salute any part of me you want."

"Please, fuck me, Mistress. Or let me fuck you. Or grab someone off the street and let me fuck him or her while you watch. I don't care. I need my cock inside someone, you preferably, in the next five seconds or I will die in this chair, and you're going to have to answer to the law for that. And my parents."

"Oh, I'm so scared. Not your parents."

"Dad can get pissy."

"I'm still not scared. Let's try bribery. If I fuck you now, will you promise to give me a massage after?"

"I will massage anything and everything you want me to, Mistress. Especially your pussy with my entire hand."

"Will you take me out to dinner?"

"You pick the place. I'm buying."

"Of course you are. I think I could use a night in the city, too. I might want to ride your cock all night long."

"Anywhere. *Mi cock es su cock.*"

"Gansevoort penthouse."

"It's yours."

Nora rolled up off the couch and dug in her bag for the necessary items.

"Now I'm going to gag you. Don't take it personally. It's easier for me to orgasm if you aren't talking my ear off the entire time."

"Anything. Cut my tongue out. Just fuck me."

"Your desperation is very pleasing, Griffin. If you keep this up, I might even let you come, too."

"I'm keeping it up, I swear to God."

"I can tell," she said, eyeing his erection.

Nora ripped open the condom package and tossed her panties across the room. She took about one minute longer than necessary to roll the condom onto Griffin. Afterward, she grabbed a rubber ducky squeaky toy from her bag and shoved it into his bound hands. Once gagged Griffin wouldn't be able to safe out or tell her he needed to talk. Squeezing the duck would be his out. Not once in their years as fuck buddies had he ever squeezed the duck.

"By the way," Nora said as she slathered Griffin in lubricant, "if you come before I come, I'm leaving you tied to this chair for another hour while I fuck myself with the vibrator in my bag. Then I'll take pictures of you trapped like this and send them to Kingsley, who will show every single member of his household before putting them in your file."

"You're a sadistic bitch, Mistress."

"Flattery will get you everywhere."

"Will it get me laid? That's all I care about right now."

"It's about to."

For a moment Nora considered spending five minutes longer than she had to gagging Griffin to torture him a little further. But she was horny enough and she was in no mood to torture herself.

She straddled Griffin's legs but didn't let him inside her yet. As she hooked the heels of her boots onto the bottom chair rungs, she unbuttoned her blouse and unclasped her bra in the front. Pressing her bare breasts against his chest, she relished the warmth of his male body against her hardening nipples. Later she would make him suck and kiss them for a solid half hour while he engaged in some digital pussy worship. Griffin was fantastically good with his hands, after all. She had it all planned out. They'd get to the hotel and then she'd tell him exactly what he would be doing to her for the rest of the night. No reason to tell him now. Not like he was going to argue with her about any of it. And he certainly wouldn't be given a choice.

Nora reached down and grasped Griffin, guiding him to the entrance of her body. Slowly, one inch at a time, she sunk down onto him, taking him deep inside her.

"That's better, isn't it?" she asked, and the gagged Griffin mutely nodded. "I'm a big fan of your cock, my dear. I should spend more time with it."

Griffin's head fell back as Nora began to move on him, working her hips in a slow, undulating figure-eight motion. He filled her body so completely…she wanted to stay here all day and all night with him inside her. Everything disappeared during sex. Memories, dreams, all the ghosts of her past…gone. She became a being of pure sensation, pure desire. She loved sex for a thousand reasons, but these days she loved it mostly for the escape it gave her, the bliss of oblivion. And she needed that oblivion…especially today.

With one hand on the back of the chair and one hand between their bodies and against her clitoris, Nora brought herself to the edge of orgasm and stayed there. She kissed Griffin's neck, bit his shoulders, nipped at his ears. She loved his moans, his sharp breaths, his hard stomach tightening even more as he held off coming as he'd been ordered.

But in the back of her mind Nora heard something…a familiar sound.

"Fuck." She sighed as her phone began to vibrate from inside her toy bag. But the phone she'd brought with her was her private line. Only three people had the number to it—Kingsley, Søren and Wesley. She'd already gotten chewed out this week by Kingsley for not taking his calls. She always answered the phone when Søren called. And Wesley…he worried about her when she didn't answer, and she hated to make him worry.

"Hold that cock," she said as she raised up and off Griffin. She grabbed the phone out of her bag and answered without even checking the number.

"Hey, Nor," Wesley said over the line.

"What's up, kid?" she asked as she climbed onto Griffin again and pushed him once more inside her.

"You sound out of breath. You okay?"

"I was walking." It was only half a lie, she told herself. She *was* walking… At some point that day she definitely had been walking.

"Are you home again?"

"Yeah, of course." She winced a little at the outright lie. But she knew telling Wesley she was currently impaled on one of the sexiest men in New York wasn't an option, not unless she wanted him in a depressed funk for a week. Why he cared so much about who she fucked was beyond her, but he did care and that made *her* care.

"I need a favor. Me and Fitz are pulling an all-nighter at Josh's. Can you maybe bring me one of my insulin pens? I mean, only if you're not busy."

"It's fine. Not busy."

"If you're busy—"

"Not. Busy."

"Can you read my final paper, too? It's due tomorrow."

Nora almost groaned aloud, but not from pleasure. She'd painted herself into a corner with lies. She couldn't tell Wes no now that she said she was home and not busy. Now she had to drive back to Connecticut, drive to his school, read his twenty-page final and help him fix it. Wes was a math and science geek, not a writer. This would take all night. "Where are you?"

"Basketball court for the next hour or two. Can you come?"

"Oh, yeah. I'm definitely coming."

She hung up the phone and dropped it onto the carpet. With renewed determination, she rode Griffin harder, slamming her hips into his, grinding her clitoris into the base of his cock. With a lusty gasp, she came hard, squeezing him with her inner muscles so hard he flinched underneath her. She kept moving. He'd been such a good boy he deserved his orgasm.

"Come for me," she ordered. "Come now."

He didn't require any more encouragement. Nora dug her nails into his shoulders as he came with a shudder, the rubber duck falling from his fingers as he panted against her chest.

"Very nice," she said, pulling off him. She untied the gag and his hands.

"Nice? That's all I get is a 'nice'?" Griffin teased as he grabbed her and dragged her to him. "I'm going to spend all night showing you how not 'nice' I am."

"Can't. Change of plans." Nora found her panties and dragged them on under her skirt. She closed her bra again and buttoned up her blouse. "I'm needed."

"Needed?" Griffin yanked his long-abandoned boxer briefs back on. "What about the night in the city? Gansevoort? All night riding my cock? I think we had this discussion."

"Rain check?" she asked, a small pang of guilt stabbing her heart. "I have to do a favor for a friend."

"Nora…" Griffin gazed at her with a look of utter disappointment on his face.

"Griffin…" She tried to smile at him.

"He better be really fucking good in bed to dump me."

With a sigh, Nora put her arms around Griffin and kissed his chest. He made no move to return the embrace.

"It's not personal, and it's not about sex. Trust me, I'm not getting laid tonight. Come on, you know I'm crazy about you."

"You have a fan-fucking-tastic way of showing it."

"Please don't be mad. Seriously, I'm not leaving your bed for someone else's. I have to do a friend a favor. That's all."

He nodded and she rose up on her tiptoes to kiss him on the cheek.

"I'm serious about the rain check," she said as she gathered her toys and zipped up her bag. "I love fucking you."

"I love fucking you, too…and you'd love it if you let me."

"We've had this talk. I don't let anyone top me anymore."

"Except for Søren."

"Søren has needs." She hated having this conversation with Griffin. Griffin loved reminding her she was a switch, and as a switch, she should be a little more flexible in the bedroom, i.e., let him top her every now and then. As much as that fantasy appealed to her, she'd tried subbing with other men, and all she'd done during the sex was think of Søren the entire time. He was the only man she let top her these days and even then only on rare occasion. Griffin deserved better than that. He deserved better than this, too. But for Wes? Anything.

"I have needs, too. I need someone who isn't going to dump me for someone else after making plans with me."

Nora stood by the door and stared back at Griffin— gorgeous, kinky, rich, hilarious, sexy as fuck Griffin. And she did want to stay and have her wild night of sex and kink with Griffin. All she had to do was call Wes back and say, "Hey, something's up. I had to go. You'll have to get your own pen." And Wes would say, "Okay."

But she didn't.

"I hope you find her someday, then. Or him."

Nora turned to leave but a question from Griffin stopped her.

"Who is he?" Griffin asked.

Nora winced, not wanting to bring Wesley into this part of her world.

"No one you know."

"You like him?"

Nora gave him her best apologetic shrug.

"Enough to give up sex with you for."

Griffin laughed softly, laughed enough to tell her she was forgiven.

"Damn."

Damn indeed.

"So you left this man Griffin for your Wesley? I'm not impressed," Marie-Laure said, pulling Nora from her memory and out of her story.

"I'm not done yet," Nora reminded her testily. She hated being interrupted when she was on a roll. "Story's not over. Do you want to hear the ending or not?"

"I hope it's a happy ending. You paint quite a picture. Your Griffin sounds lovely. Another younger man of yours?"

"Not that much younger. He's twenty-nine."

"A very good age."

"It's a very good age to be Griffin. He's currently ass over ears in love with a teenage boy. I introduced them. One of my better matches."

"A teenager? You have no morals, do you?"

"If he's old enough to join the army, he's old enough to get it from Griffin. And you married an eighteen-year-old, Captain Morality. Oh, and you killed someone."

"I never said I had morals. I'm simply pleased to find that you don't, either."

"Let's be best friends," Nora said. "We can braid each other's hair and murder runaways together."

"Let's. After your story, *s'il vous plaît*. It's enjoyable but I still don't understand why you love this Wesley boy of yours so much. I certainly wouldn't have sacrificed a night with your friend Griffin for a night of editing a teenager's term paper."

"Some things are more important than sex. Wes...he was more important than sex."

"An interesting statement from a woman who used to sell her body."

"I never sold my body. I only sold my time and talents. And that's something any working woman can say—secretary or Dominatrix or both. And there's not a mother on the planet who hasn't had to say no to fun in order to help her kid with his homework."

"So that's why you loved your Wesley? He was like your son?"

Nora exhaled heavily. No, Wesley wasn't her son. He'd been her sun, but there was no explaining something like that to someone so deep in darkness.

"Do you want to hear the rest of the story or not?"

"By all means, carry on."

Nora left Griffin's and drove into the fading sunlight of evening. All the way there she plotted playful revenge on Wesley. She was going to have to do something to punish him for taking her away from a night of food, sex, massages, kink, more sex and the eight most impressive inches of manhood in the East Village. She'd come up with something good. She always did. She could put tampons on the next grocery list. That might be too cruel. After all, she didn't have periods anymore thanks to her IUD. Not that Wesley knew that. Tampons and yeast infection cream. That would do it. And condoms and lube, the flavored kind. That would stoke his virginal imagination, wouldn't it? She briefly considered putting Hershey bars on the grocery list, too, but that would be a bit too cruel even for her. Wes might be a virgin by choice, but he never asked to be a type 1 diabetic.

But seriously, he deserved a little torture for dragging her all the way back to Westport from the city just to bring him his insulin pen and read his midterm paper. She caught herself smiling as she contemplated the various tortures. Goddammit, why did doing things for him make her so happy? She pulled onto their street and furrowed her brow. There, in her damn driveway, sat Wes's yellow VW bug. What the hell? If he was home, why did he need her to get his pen for him? Did that little twerp actually make her abandon a night with Griffin for absolutely no reason whatsoever?

Ready for a fight, Nora stomped up to the front door, threw it open and was immediately besieged with confetti.

Confetti?

In the middle of the living room, hiding behind a bouquet of white roses, stood Wes, peeking at her over the top of the petals.

"Wesley…what the hell?"

"Happy birthday," he said, grinning broadly over the flowers before hiding his face behind them again.

"What…you…" Nora grabbed the flowers from his hands and stared at him.

"Don't look so surprised. I cleaned your office and found some insurance forms. I now know that you have low cholesterol and that your birthday is March 15 which happens to be—"

"Today, yes. Don't remind me."

"I'm reminding you. So are those." He nodded at the flowers.

"You're killing me, kid."

"Don't be depressed. You're only thirty—"

She covered his mouth to prevent him from announcing her age.

"Good boy." She removed her hand.

"Don't freak out, Nora. You've got at least a couple good years left."

Nora took the roses and smacked him on the ass with them.

"Ow. Those have thorns."

"I know. That's why I hit you with them."

Wes grabbed her by the shoulders and spun her toward the kitchen.

"I have presents for you."

"You shouldn't have done all this," Nora said. "I hate my birthday."

"Tough. We're celebrating whether you like it or not."

"I don't like it. Can I safe out?"

"Nope. Look."

On the kitchen table, Wes had arrayed a birthday cake with her name on it plus two wrapped presents.

"You got me a cake? You can't eat cake."

"I can eat, like, a *bite* of cake. But you can have it all. You can't open your presents until later, though. I'm taking you out to dinner first."

"You're trying to get me fat, aren't you?"

"I'm trying to get you not emaciated."

"It's working." She reached out and grabbed a corner of the cake with her bare hand and shoved it in her mouth. She had a little too much fun licking the icing off her fingers while Wes watched. "It's definitely working."

"Speaking of working…" Wes grazed her from head to boots and raised his eyebrow. "You said you were home."

"I lied."

"I know. I was here when I called. You were on a job, weren't you?"

"Something like that. A girl's gotta get paid." And laid.

"I didn't mean to trick you. I wanted to get you home in time so we could party."

"We're going to party?" Nora knew how to party. She could party with the best of them. Kingsley, his crew, a shit ton of money, too much alcohol, a dash of an illegal substance or two and waking up on top of Griffin or Kingsley or…

"Yes, party. We'll go to dinner and rent some movies."

"Are we doing another installment of 'Catch Nora Up on the Past Fifteen Years of the Vanilla World Theater'?"

"Yes, I got *The Matrix*."

"Never seen it."

"You'll love it. *Alice in Wonderland* references, secret societies, theology, people in leather and vinyl outfits…"

"Ninjas?"

"Sort of."

"I'm in. So presents? Yes? I see them. I'm opening them."

"No opening presents. Not yet."

"Wrong answer," Nora said, reaching for the first box.

"Those aren't your presents."

"They aren't? Then why are they on my table? If it's on my table, it's mine. So, you know, hop up."

She expected Wes to blush like he always did when she hit on him, but he didn't. Not this time. Instead, he did as she asked and sat on the edge of the table. She stood in front of him with her hands on his knees. Goddamn, this kid would be the death of her. That shaggy blond hair, that sweet face, those big brown eyes… Looking at that smile of his was like staring into the sun. She'd even started getting up earlier every day on the off chance she'd catch him walking out of the bathroom, towel around his waist, water dripping down his young, muscular back. If he only knew some of the fantasies she'd entertained about him…

*Look but don't touch,* she reminded herself.

"In honor of *The Matrix*…" he began, putting his hands over hers.

"Which I haven't even seen yet."

"I'm giving you a choice. This will make more sense after you see the movie."

"A choice of what?"

"You can have the presents in the boxes or…anything else you want. You can have the stuff on the table or what's down the rabbit hole."

Nora raised her eyebrow at him.

"I can have anything?"

"Anything," he said. "But only if you decide to go down the rabbit hole."

"Like a castle or a trip to Jamaica or a ten-carat emerald ring anything?"

"Any. Thing. Name it. Anything."

"Wes, darling, you're adorable. But you are a freshman in college. From Kentucky. You moved in with me—"

Wes raised his hand and covered her lips with one finger.

"If I told you that I could give you anything you wanted, would you believe me?"

Nora stared into his eyes and saw nothing but the truth in them. It was a beautiful truth, one she wanted to be a part of. Anything she wanted…from her Wesley…and she knew what her answer was. She wanted to take him into her bed tonight and make love to him. She wanted to teach him everything she knew about sex and how good it felt and how right it could be to join your body with someone else's and let the entire world fall away from you until there was nothing left but you and him and the new being the two created together. She wanted his virginity for her birthday and his heart and body every day after that. And she wanted that because she loved him and treasured him and didn't want anyone ever hurting him as he never wanted anyone hurting her, even though she loved that sort of thing, not that he would ever understand that. And she didn't care that he didn't understand. She cared that he loved her. Oh, yes, Nora knew exactly what she wanted from Wesley for her birthday. She wanted to look into his eyes the moment he entered her the first time, wanted to hear his breathing change with the first thrust, wanted to hold him before, during and after and let him tell her everything he felt and everything he wanted.

But she couldn't ask for that, could she? Wesley deserved a little bit better for his first time than a woman who was still wet from the last guy she'd fucked an hour ago. She still could feel Griffin's warm skin against her breasts, could still remember the press of him inside her. As cute as he was to offer, she knew Wes couldn't buy her emeralds and castles. Maybe he wanted to see if she'd believe him. Maybe he wanted to know what she'd wish for if she could have anything on earth.

"Anything, Nora," Wes whispered, and took both her hands in his. Nora smiled.

"I'll take the presents on the table, the dinner with you and the movie. And that's all I want," she said, reaching out to cup his face. She kissed him on the cheek and he gave her a smile. In his eyes she saw a flash of disappointment quickly hidden.

"Okay, but dinner first."

"We're getting Indian, right?" she asked. "The correct answer is yes."

"Yes."

"You must have read my mind. I'll go change out of the fetish-wear first."

"Thank you. And I'll change into mine."

"The assless chaps, please. It is my birthday, after all."

"Anything for you."

At the bottom of the stairs, Nora turned around and found Wes still looking at her and on his face she saw no subterfuge, no lies, no jokes, no tricks. When he said, "Anything for you," he meant it.

★ ★ ★

"Do you regret picking the birthday presents on the table?" Marie-Laure asked, dragging Nora out of the past again. It hurt leaving that memory of Wes, especially since returning to the present meant remembering she sat cuffed to the bed of a psychopath. While she dredged up her past, Marie-Laure sat on the bed four feet away, fluffing her goddamn pillows.

"No. Yes. Maybe." Nora exhaled heavily. "The only thing I wanted was him. And that I didn't feel right asking for. Castles are too much upkeep. Emeralds I could buy for myself. But I couldn't buy him. That kid tricked me into coming back home just so he could wish me happy birthday and take me to dinner. And he didn't even want to fuck me. And even if he did want to fuck me he didn't try. He didn't do anything that night but put his arm around me on the sofa and let me lean against him while we watched movies."

Nora remembered the peace she felt that night curled up with Wesley, eating cake, talking, being vanilla and boring and happy. She forgot all about sex with Griffin, the Gansevoort, even forgot about her birthday. She didn't even remember it again until she'd gone to bed that night and found a box from Søren on her bed. Kingsley had a key to her house. He must have had one of his underlings sneak it in while she and Wesley were gone. It took her a week to work up the courage to open the box and a week to recover from the gift inside—a handblown glass hart, tiny and exquisite, its antlered head held high proudly. When she was fifteen, she'd dug through boxes of her old toys until she'd found a little plastic hart that had been part of a set of toy animals her grandmother had given her. She'd given it to Søren after midnight mass on Christmas Eve. *A visual pun,* she'd explained to him. *My hart...my heart.* What the gift of the glass hart meant she didn't want to think about. Was Søren reminding her he still had her heart?

Or confessing she still had his? Both, most likely, because she knew both were true.

"You know your Wesley's truth now—his family, his fortune. Do you wish you'd chosen the rabbit hole?"

As much as Nora hated to admit it, Marie-Laure asked a good question.

"I faced that same choice with Søren once," Nora said, blinking back tears. "I could learn the truth about him and be changed forever. Or walk away from him, from the truth, and stay blissfully ignorant."

"You made a different choice with my husband."

"I did. I was seventeen years old and it was here in this house. His father had died and he finally felt safe enough to tell me what he was, what we could be. He warned me it would change everything and that once learned it couldn't be unlearned."

"What did you say to him?"

"Two words—*tell me.*"

*Tell me.*

And he had. And as he told her the truth of what he was, what she was, what they could be together if she chose, she felt like an amnesiac waking from the haze of forgetfulness and finally remembering herself. The only secrets he'd told her that night were the ones she already knew without knowing she knew them.

*If you choose, Little One...I can own you. You would be my property, mine alone.*

And her heart had answered before her mouth could find the words.

*Of course you own me. You always have....*

"But your Wesley, you didn't want him to tell you what was down the rabbit hole." Marie-Laure leaned forward and gave Nora a darkly amused grin.

"No, I didn't. I think instinctively I knew I would be lost down there. I was right. Thoroughbred royalty. Southern gentility. And God, the money everywhere. Old money, new money, mob money. I do my damnedest to avoid the mob. I'd rather not end up like my father did."

"Not your world?"

"Not at all. I like our version of royalty better than the vanilla version."

Money bought nothing in Kingsley's world but a key to the front door. Once inside, they built their own kingdoms. Dominants with boring day jobs earned respect with the power they created out of their own dignity and desires. Exquisite submissives—male and female—who laid themselves out on the altar of sacrifice and sexuality in order to find themselves at someone else's feet. Wesley always accused the people of her world of putting on costumes and playing dress-up. He had no idea that the suits and the ties and the beige pumps and navy slacks her people wore during the day were the real costumes that they shed when they came out after dark. Nora remembered that night of her birthday party, curled up on the couch in her ducky pajamas, which felt as much like a costume as her kink-wear. He didn't understand her world of role-play even as the woman he held in his arms played a role for him.

"But that's what you left Griffin for? A night of being boring and 'vanilla' as you call it with your Wesley?"

Nora nodded. "I liked it. No…I loved it. It was a role I was playing, but one I liked playing."

"Playing house?"

Nora smiled before she remembered she had a man with a knife at her side and was sitting on the bed of a sociopath.

"Exactly. Playing house. Husband. Wife. Home of our own. Dinner on the table. No kids, thank God, unless you count Wes. It was… Here's the thing," Nora said, shifting position as her foot had started to fall asleep. "That day, my birth-day, Wes and I went out to eat. He took me for Indian food at this great hole-in-the-wall place by his school. One of his friends he played basketball with was there. Someone from his church, too. And he introduced me to them like...nothing. I was Søren's property for ten years from age eighteen to about twenty-eight. I've been in love with him since I was fifteen and now I'm thirty-four. Almost twenty years. In twenty years, we've never done that, never gone out to dinner together just the two of us. Not around here. We can't. Too risky. Can't even go to a hole-in-the-wall Indian place. A shame, right? The man speaks Hindi, and he fucking loves Indian food."

"You wanted a different life than my husband could give you? That's why the boy?"

Nora swallowed.

"Maybe. I don't know. Wes is...he's so different from any-one I've ever known. Life is weird when you're a professional Dominatrix. One day I would have dinner with Ilsa Strix and I'd ask her questions like 'So when you put the three hundred and thirteen needles into that guy's dick, did you charge by the time or the needle?' Or you're hanging out at the club and the seventy-year-old age-play fetishist shuffles past you in his diaper and bonnet. You go a solid week and you real-ize you haven't had a single conversation or day that didn't have something to do with kink or sex or money. You have enough nights like that and you start to wonder if maybe, just maybe, on the subway ride of your life, you got off at the wrong stop. Wes was a different stop. A prettier neighbor-hood. Good schools. Nicer scenery."

"Did you belong there? With your Wesley in his world?"

"He thought I did, and since it's his world, it's his decision."

"That's a wonderful nonanswer."

"It's the truth."

"Tell me this truth. Your Wesley...would he have given you anything you asked for?"

"His family is richer than God, turns out. I guess he was ready to tell me that. Or was at least testing the waters to see if I was ready to hear that. But yes, I think he would have given me anything that night. Even his virginity if I'd asked for it, although I loved him too much to take it."

Marie-Laure tapped her chin and seemed to lose herself in thought for a moment. Nora stared at the woman who still retained the ghost of her former beauty. Who was this woman who thirty years later still hated Søren enough she would torture him like this? By stealing his heart from him? What did she want? Vengeance? Retribution? His body? His love?

"Would your Wesley have given you his life had you asked for it?"

Nora went still and cold at the question.

"I don't know. I would never ask him to give up his life for mine. I wouldn't let Søren leave the priesthood for me. I tried to get Wesley out of my world before he got even more hurt. I don't ask people to sacrifice themselves for me."

"I do."

"You ask people to sacrifice themselves for you?"

"No. I asked my husband to sacrifice himself for you."

# 16
# THE KNIGHT

Wes kept his eyes closed and breathed through his nose. The last thing he wanted to do was puke his guts out in front of Laila. She'd been through enough today. Dealing with him throwing up and passing out was about the last thing in the world she needed right now.

"Here. Drink."

He heard Laila's accented voice right next to him, sensed her presence.

"Don't. Let me," she said as he opened his eyes and reached for the small glass of orange juice she held in her hand. "Your hands are shaking. I'll hold it."

She brought the glass to his lips.

He drank rapidly and soon the orange juice was gone.

"Where's your kit?" Laila laid her hand on his forehead.

"Backpack. In the front room."

"I'll get it. Don't stand up."

Wesley knew he probably couldn't stand up even if he tried.

He cursed himself over his own stupidity. Driving for two days, panicking all the while, he'd barely eaten anything. No wonder he was crashing like this. Good thing Laila had recognized his symptoms before he'd simply fainted and gone into DKA. He would have woken up in the hospital and been useless to anyone, Nora especially, for days.

He heard Laila's footsteps on the tile bathroom floor and he managed to pry his eyes open.

"I'm sorry," he said. "I'm such an idiot. I know better than to skip meals."

"Don't apologize. It's not your fault."

"Didn't I say that to you like five minutes ago? 'Don't apologize, it's not your fault'?"

"It's a good line." He watched as Laila dug through his backpack and pulled out a small black leather bag. "This it?"

He nodded.

She unzipped the bag and took out his insulin meter.

"I think I can do this myself," Wes said as she took his hand in hers and swabbed his finger with an alcohol-soaked cotton ball.

"Sit. Breathe. I can do this. I do it all the time."

"On dogs."

"It's all the same to me." She grinned at him and he was suddenly struck by her beauty. How had he not noticed before that this girl who'd dropped out of nowhere into this nightmare was easily the prettiest thing he'd seen since…well, since Nora. Not that they looked anything alike. Laila had blond hair like her uncle and sky-blue eyes, high cheekbones and a dizzying smile. Even the nasty gash on her cheek couldn't mar her beauty.

"You're staring at me." She pricked his finger with the lancet. "Does my face look that bad?"

"What? No. I was just noticing the resemblance between you and your uncle."

"We both look like my grandmother."

"She must have been beautiful. I mean, since you are. He's not. I mean, he might be but he's not my type."

Laila grinned again as she slid the testing strip into Wes's blood sugar meter.

"Most women would tell you he's beautiful. My aunt especially."

"It's so weird that you call Nora your 'aunt.' I can't get used to it."

Laila shrugged. "I don't remember a time that she wasn't in his life. There are pictures of her holding me when I was only four or five years old."

"Did she visit you all a lot?"

"Once a year. Sometimes more, sometimes less. How did you meet her?"

Wesley stiffened. This conversation would be a lot easier if Laila didn't consider Nora part of the family. What was he going to say to her? Oh, your aunt and I have been sleeping together for the past week. Yes, your uncle knows. Long story.

"I worked for her," he said, deciding not to rock her world any more than it had been tonight. "She taught a class at my school, a writing class. We'd talk all the time after class. Theology, philosophy…sex, drugs, rock 'n' roll. We talked about everything. At the end of the semester, she asked me if I wanted to move in. She wanted an assistant."

"You lived with her?"

"It sounds bad, I guess." And it was bad. Oh, man, the constant shit he got from his friends when he moved out of the dorms and in with "smoking-hot Professor Nora" as they called her…he loved it. He might have pretended to be mad when they expressed their envy over all the things he and

Nora were no doubt doing under that roof of hers…yeah, he loved it. The guys were beyond jealous. Older woman, erotica writer—the Mrs. Robinson fantasies they had…he let them have them. *Wes Railey does not talk about his sex life,* was his answer to their interrogation. They'd have much more fun with their imaginations than they would with the truth.

"Sounds fun. I'd love to live with her."

"It was fun. She was a great roommate."

"Was? You moved out?"

"Yeah, last year. Things got…complicated."

He didn't know how else to explain it without going into all the awful details, but Laila didn't seem the least confused.

"I understand. When she went back to my uncle, he probably didn't want her having a roommate who looked like you."

Wes's eyes widened in surprise.

"I mean, a man," she said quickly. "He wouldn't want her living with another man."

"You knew they broke up?"

Laila blushed again, a guilty look in her bright blue eyes.

"Your blood sugar's still low."

"I have a glucose tablet in the bag. And you're blushing," Wes said, smiling at her.

She handed him one of his tablets.

"I hate being this pale."

"You're not pale right now. You're bright red."

"I should have let you pass out." Laila glared at him before smiling back.

"You should have," he said. "But I didn't so now you have to tell me why you're blushing."

"I'm blushing because…my uncle doesn't know that I know he and my aunt broke up."

"How did you find out? Did Nora tell you?"

"Their room is next to mine. I heard them talking."

"What did you overhear?"

"Just talking." He wasn't sure he believed her. That blush of hers was so bright he wanted to put his sunglasses on. "She came to visit once and I overheard her saying something about leaving him, about him not telling us. He seemed to know she would come back to him. That's why he didn't let us know she'd left him."

"She did go back to him." Wes closed his eyes again. "He was right."

"He's always right." Laila laughed a little. She had a good laugh—sweet and musical. "Wes? Are you awake?" Laila snapped her fingers by his ears.

"I'm awake. Dizzy. If Nora saw me now, she would kick my ass all the way back to Kentucky."

"I don't think she'd be mad at you."

He nodded with his eyes still closed. She would be mad at him. Furious. God, how much he wanted her here right now yelling at him, telling him how stupid it was of him not to take five fucking minutes to eat something. He wanted her back so badly he'd sell his own body for it. Kidneys, lungs, anything he had to spare to get her back. Thank God for this little bout of low blood sugar. At least everyone would blame his shaking on that and not the truth that he'd simply never been so scared in all his life.

"I went into DKA while living with her. As soon as I was out of the hospital, she lectured me for a solid hour about how much I'd scared her, how I was never allowed to do it again."

"It couldn't have been that bad. You're smiling."

"It's almost fun getting chewed out by Nora. I didn't realize she cared about me that much until...you know, she thought she'd lost me."

"They say you never know what you have until you've lost it."

He shook his head. "No, it's not true. I always knew what I had. I didn't need to lose it to know."

"What did you have?"

Nora, he thought but didn't say out loud. Laila seemed to take comfort in the idea that Nora and her uncle were in love and back together. For Laila's sake he'd keep the truth of his relationship with Nora to himself.

"I had my best friend, and I want to get her back again."

"And we'll get her back again." The voice came from the doorway to the bathroom. Wes opened his eyes and saw Søren looking in. "No matter what it takes."

"Are you sure?" Wes stared up at Søren from the floor.

"Yes."

"I hope you're right," Wes said as he started to drag himself off the floor.

Søren held out his hand to Wes. He only looked at it before standing up on his own even as a wave of dizziness nearly sent him back to the floor.

"I'm always right," Søren said. "When you're ready, we'll leave for the house."

"Who's we?"

"Me, Grace and you two." Søren nodded at him and Laila.

"Not Kingsley?" Wes asked as the dizziness passed and his vision cleared.

"No." Søren held out an arm and Laila tucked herself against his chest like a bird under a wing. "He's already gone."

# 17
# THE QUEEN

*I asked my husband to sacrifice himself for you.*

Those were the words Marie-Laure left with Nora after their little bedtime story. The French bitch had said a jaunty, *"Bonne nuit,"* before curling up into bed and falling fast asleep. Nora had considered screaming at Marie-Laure or kicking her or something, but Damon stood as a mute menace, watching her. So Nora got as comfortable as she could despite the bonds on her wrists and the awkward position and had prayed with all her heart and all her soul and all her might that no one would die because of this woman and her bitterness and her obsession. No amount of reasoning or rationalizing could make sense of this madness, so Nora prayed only for a miracle.

And at dawn, she finally slept. She woke up to her hands numb from the rope and in a world without miracles.

Alone in the bedroom Marie-Laure had commandeered, Nora assessed her situation as calmly and rationally as she could. Marie-Laure was clearly off her fucking rocker. That was the calmest and most rational judgment Nora could muster about Søren's ex-wife. No. *Current* wife. And to think Nora had been worried for the past eighteen years that the church would find out about her and she was nothing but a mistress. Wonder what they would do if they discovered he had a wife?

But…Nora tried to comfort herself as she watched the sun peeking over the windowsill. Søren hadn't been a priest when he'd gotten married. And all the world considered Marie-Laure a dead woman. The marriage had never been consummated despite Marie-Laure's attempts to seduce her husband. Surely Søren could get an annulment once all this was over. Or, even better, he'd be a widower.

Nora forced her mind away from all the vagaries of Søren's marital situation. It didn't matter. She was only thinking about that because it scared her a lot less than her real problem. She had to break that mindset. She couldn't give in already. Marie-Laure had no qualms about killing people. She pushed a teenage girl off a cliff once. Having one of her boys put a bullet in Nora's brain would be an even easier kill.

Luckily Marie-Laure seemed intent on toying with her first, toying with her and Søren and all of them. That took time and with enough time anything could happen. Marie-Laure clearly underestimated the people she'd chosen to fuck with. It had always amused her, when out on the town with Kingsley, how the two of them intimidated the innocents they'd mingled with. Kingsley Edge—King of Kink, King of the Underground—his bedroom exploits were the stuff of legend. That he openly admitted to a love of both men and women, of sex, of kink, of the darkest sorts of pleasure—blood-play, knife-play and, his personal favorite, rape-play—engendered fear in the hearts of the outsiders they encountered. The word *play* clearly didn't register with them. That Kingsley was kinky was the least of their worries. That Kingsley was an ex-spy and assassin who had spent his twenties killing enemies of the French government. Now that should make them nervous.

Oh, and on top of that, Søren, the man who loved her more than anyone else had ever loved her and would ever love her, was an unapologetic sadist who'd once hammered nails through the testicles of a Dominant at the Eighth Circle, a man who'd ignored his submissive lover's safe word and pleas for mercy and had beaten the boy unconscious. Nora smiled at the memory. After all, she'd passed Søren the nails while Kingsley had held the man down. They'd offered the Dominant two choices—King's justice or the courts. He'd picked King's justice and soon regretted it.

Marie-Laure would regret it, too, eventually. Hopefully Nora would live long enough to see that.

As visions of bloody retributions danced through her head, Nora ignored the quiet voice in the back of her head that warned her Søren would do nothing that put her life at risk. A rescue mission with doors kicked opened and guns blazing would only end up getting them all killed. Even now she heard the creak of hardwood outside the door—one of Marie-Laure's boys standing guard, ready to mow her down if she somehow managed to untie herself.

Worth a shot, anyway.

Nora twisted her arms slowly as she tried to get the feel of the ropes, the knots. She'd done her fair share of Shibari in her days as a pro. She loved it, especially for clients who'd paid for three- and four-hour sessions. Putting a client in a reverse shrimp tie could take an hour in itself. So she knew knots and she knew rope, and she knew there was no way in hell she would be able to wriggle her way out of these. He'd tied her wrists and her forearms. She'd have to dislocate her own shoulders to get to the knots.

Still, a little dislocated shoulder never killed anyone. Bullets, however, killed lots of people.

As Nora started to pull against the rope, the door opened.

She froze in place as Andrei stared at her. She didn't like the look on his face—one of utter disdain—but it was better than the alternative. At least she didn't see any violent or lascivious intent in his eyes. "May I help you?" Nora asked as Fat Man continued to stare at her in mute contempt.

"She wants you for breakfast."

"Is she a cannibal, too?"

"Probably," he said as he came to the bed and began untying Nora. Once her hands and legs were free, he nodded toward the bathroom. "One minute. Make it good."

She ran for the bathroom and pissed like a racehorse. She knew Doms and subs who played around with bathroom control. Thankfully Søren's kinks focused on a far narrower swath of tortures. Although every now and then he got a bit demonic with her while playing at the club. In the middle of a scene, she'd admitted to a desperate need to pee. He'd kicked a metal bucket into the middle of the room and said, "Go."

Andrei had given her one minute so she didn't waste it. While in the bathroom she looked around wildly, trying to find anything that she could use. Nothing. Jack-fucking-nothing unless she thought she could smother a man to death with a bath towel.

"Better?" he asked when she emerged.

"My bladder thanks you."

"Don't thank me. She doesn't want you pissing on yourself again."

"She seems kind of sensitive," Nora said as Andrei the Fat Man grabbed her by the arm and led her into the hall, his large gun strapped to his side. Briefly Nora regretted refusing Kingsley's offers to teach her to shoot. Søren had instilled his

Jesuit's pacifism in her at too young an age. That and a pre-teen crush on MacGyver had pretty much ruined any appeal guns might have held for her once. Kingsley taught her long ago that the main rule of self-defense was "Don't do anything stupid." Trying to steal a gun from a giant mercenary when she didn't even know how to take the safety off easily qualified as stupid. Fatally stupid.

Fat Man led her into the breakfast room where Marie-Laure sat at the table in her gown and robe, looking for all the world like a damned duchess at tea. Marie-Laure said nothing to her, didn't even glance at her as she picked up her cup of tea and sipped from it. Fat Man pushed Nora down to the floor and stood behind her. Nora waited in silence and made a surreptitious sweep of the room. When she'd been here for Søren's father's funeral, the family had gathered here for breakfast. Nora had been only seventeen then but she knew enough to keep her mouth shut and her head down and disappear into the background so no one would wonder who she was, what she was doing here. When anyone asked, she'd said she was a friend of Claire's, Søren's sixteen-year-old half sister from his father's second marriage. It wasn't entirely a lie. She and Claire had gotten along beautifully. And "friend of Claire's" sounded a hell of a lot better than "my priest who's in love with me brought me here so he could tell me all his secrets." Discretion had proved the better part of valor then. She decided it was the better part of valor again today.

"Hungry?" Marie-Laure asked after five minutes of silence.

"Me?" Nora asked.

Marie-Laure nodded.

"I wouldn't turn breakfast down if you offered."

"I'm offering."

Nora started to stand up but the guard pushed her back

down to the floor. Marie-Laure held out a plate, which Fat Man took and dropped on the floor in front of Nora.

"No butter?"

Andrei, the Fat Man, only glared at her.

"You don't mind eating on the floor, do you?" Marie-Laure asked as she finally turned to look at her.

"I've been subbing half my life. You think this is the first time I've had to eat off the floor?" She tore a bit off a piece of dry toast and popped it in her mouth.

"Subbing half your life? Interesting...tell me about it."

"About subbing? What do you want to know?"

"Why do you do it? Why do you like it?"

"The answers might take a little longer than breakfast."

"It's more brunch-time."

"Fine. Subbing. Some people, men and women, enjoy giving up control. Sometimes for short periods of time—during sexual encounters. Some like to do it all the time, 24/7. It turns me on giving my body and my will to Søren."

"You don't seem very submissive."

"What gave it away?"

Marie-Laure laughed softly.

"Someone not that long ago made a very poor decision to cross me in an important matter. Andrei brought him to me for a discussion."

Nora had a hunch that this meeting Marie-Laure alluded to was the sort of "discussion" that ended with someone bleeding to death on the floor.

"You two work things out?" Nora asked, trying to focus her energy on eating as quickly as possible in case Marie-Laure changed her mind and took the food away. She'd need to eat to keep up her strength.

"He and Andrei worked things out in such a way that this man will never breathe again. I wouldn't mourn him, though.

He was something of a demon, notorious for the sorts of things…well, that Andrei is notorious for."

"Mad fly fishing skills?"

Marie-Laure grinned. "You see, that's my point exactly. This man who had murdered for love, lust and money begged and cried and wept for mercy. You who are in an equally tenuous situation sit on my floor, insult me and crack jokes."

"I haven't insulted you all day."

"Oh, yes, that was last night. Do forgive me. But still… explain to me how a woman so…" Marie-Laure paused as if searching for the right word.

"Courageous? Brave? Badass?"

"Stupid," Marie-Laure corrected. "How a woman with such wanton disregard for her own safety could be happy as a simpering little pet sitting at a man's feet. Can you tell me that?"

"Well…first of all, I don't think I ever simpered. I'm not particularly coquettish. I'm not even sure I could spell *coquettish* if you held a gun to my head. Please don't," she said, looking up at Fat Man, who glowered at her. He wasn't the simpering type, either.

"But you were happy sitting at my husband's feet."

"He has nice feet."

"You're not answering my question. It's getting irritating."

"Okay, serious answer. Ready? Here we go." Nora took a deep breath. She didn't want to talk about this stuff with Marie-Laure, but as long as she stayed interesting, as long as she stayed entertaining, she stayed alive. "I get off on submitting to Søren. I don't know how or why. I can't explain any more than you can explain why you like Irish breakfast tea instead of English breakfast or whatever you're drinking. It's a personal taste. I liked it. He's the most beautiful man on earth, he's got an inner drive and power that I'm drawn to, he can scare the shit out of someone with a glance, he can put someone on their knees with a word, he can see into your soul if you make the mistake of looking into his eyes. And it is a mistake because you will never want to look away again no matter how bare and naked he lays your most private self. I knelt at his feet because I felt like that's where I belonged. And no, not because I was so unworthy of him, but because he was so utterly worthy of my devotion."

A noble speech and a true one, Nora decided as her words settled into the room. True, yes, but not the whole truth. Might as well spill it all.

"Oh," she added a moment later. "And me submitting to pain gets him rock hard and the man fucks like a freight train when in the right mood. Not that you would know anything about that."

Marie-Laure let her fork drop to her plate and the metallic clatter echoed throughout the room.

"I don't think I like you," Marie-Laure said.

"Join the club," Nora said. "There are many other members to keep you company."

"Is my brother in that club?"

Nora balked at the question. Trying to explain her relationship with Kingsley would be more fraught with peril than trying to explain her love of submitting to Søren.

"You don't want to talk about my brother?" Marie-Laure taunted. "Fascinating."

"We can talk about Kingsley. Whatever you like." Nora decided she'd probably pushed enough of Marie-Laure's buttons today. Morning had dawned bright and beautiful today. She would love to see another morning.

"Good. Let's talk. But work while you talk. Clear the dishes."

Nora glanced up at Fat Man, who nodded at her. With his permission, she pulled herself off the floor and started piling dishes in her arms.

"You can answer my question anytime now," Marie-Laure said, sipping her tea again.

"Um…Kingsley and I, we're complicated. No, some days he doesn't like me very much. Some days we're thick as thieves."

"Why is that? Because you aborted his child?"

Nora almost dropped the dishes on the floor. With only force of will did she manage to keep the dishes and herself from shattering.

"I did, yes," she admitted without shame. "But no, that's not why he doesn't like me sometimes. The pregnancy was an accident, his and mine. He'd never be petty enough to hate me because of that."

"Then why does he hate you?"

"He doesn't. Not all the time, anyway. If he's mad at Søren, I'm his partner-in-crime, the only person on the planet other than Kingsley who can get to Søren. If he's…if he's remembering what he and Søren used to be and missing it, he sees me as the enemy."

"Are you?"

Nora put the plates on the sideboard.

"No, I'm not the enemy. Even if I didn't exist, I doubt Søren would let them have the kind of relationship they had back when they were teenagers. Hard to tell that to someone still a little in love after thirty years. So yes, Kingsley might be in the 'I don't like Nora club' but you should know, he's very much in the 'I don't let bad things happen to my people' club. And I'm definitely one of his people."

"The threat is duly noted."

"Can I ask you a Kingsley question?" Nora picked up a napkin and started wiping at the crumbs on the table. Marie-Laure's dark eyes glinted with dark pleasure.

"Please do."

"Kingsley and Søren have been friends, for lack of a better word, for years. Barely a day passes without them talking to each other. And despite that, Kingsley's managed to move on more or less. He has someone he loves and shares his life with—"

"Oh, yes, that. I'm a little disgusted about her. The Haitian woman? My brother could do better."

Nora briefly envisioned stabbing Marie-Laure in the eye with a fork. She might have done it but didn't have a fork handy. She'd left them on the sideboard.

"There is no one better than Juliette. Besides, what do you care about Kingsley or Søren or anybody they fuck? That's my question. It's been thirty years. Of course, Kingsley still has feelings for Søren—they're together all the time. But you... you disappeared thirty years ago. Why are you back? Why now? Why not five years ago, ten years ago?"

"That's an interesting question, and I have a more interesting answer. You'll find it especially interesting considering your history with my brother." Marie-Laure sat her teacup down and adjusted her robe. "You see...a certain nostalgia overwhelmed me last year. I'd been living in Brazil on my estate and quite happy. And yet, I did miss France. Every August when we were children, my parents would take my brother and me to a lovely seaside town in the south of France. I adored those times in that tiny village. I decided to go back for a few days. Self-indulgent, I know...but I thought it would be nice to see some old ghosts."

"Did you see any?" Nora brushed her napkin off in a small trash can.

"I did. I walked the narrow winding streets, along the beach, down the dock. I stopped for coffee in an outdoor café. And there...I saw him..."

"Who?" Nora asked.

"I saw Kingsley."

Nora shook her head.

"No way. Couldn't be him. He never goes back to France anymore. He says he has too many people there who'd like to see him dead."

"But it was Kingsley. I promise you it was. I'd wondered for years how Kingsley grew up after I died. I wondered what he looked like at age twenty, twenty-five, thirty…and there was Kingsley walking down the street with a beautiful girl on his arm and secrets in his eyes. You see, I found out about my brother's true inclinations by accident. And by that I mean, I met one of his accidents."

"Accidents?" Nora wasn't quite sure she heard right. Kingsley…had a…

"I assume he wasn't planned. My brother's son, that is."

The entire room rattled with the sound of the dishes in Nora's hands clattering on the sideboard. Marie-Laure glared at her. Nora ignored it.

"Kingsley has a kid?"

"*Non,* not a kid, as you say. He looked to be in his twenties. A son he doesn't even know exists."

"Oh, my God. Kingsley has a son," Nora repeated. And for whatever reason, a reason she didn't want or need to think about, that knowledge gave her renewed hope. She would have wept for the joy of it had she learned this news in any other context. Kingsley had a son? A son in his twenties and handsome as his father? It seemed too good to be true, and yet she believed it. And once she believed, a wound she didn't know she'd had suddenly closed up and healed over.

"Are you sure he's Kingsley's? Completely certain?"

"I doubted it, too, at first," Marie-Laure said. "Although the resemblance was uncanny it was possible he was a distant relative…or merely a doppelgänger. So I had someone do some digging on him. Turns out my brother had been feeling nostalgic, too, about twenty-four years ago. He'd met a woman and spent a few days in her bed. A married woman whose husband had gone to Paris for a week of business. She kept the boy's parentage a secret even from his real father."

"Do you…" Nora paused for a breath. Tears lined her eyes. She knew then she had to survive this nightmare no matter what if only to find this young man, this child of Kingsley's. "Do you know his name?"

"Nicolas…a fine French name for my nephew." She said the name with relish and in the French pronunciation—Nee-coh-lah. "I'm still considering whether or not to make the acquaintance of my brother's bastard."

Rage surged within Nora. Kingsley's son… Nora had once carried Kingsley's child, and she'd chosen not to have it. To this day she never regretted that decision, but now she found motherly feelings she didn't think she possessed rising up in her heart like an army preparing for battle. She would live and she would find him and tell him where he came from and where he belonged. And perhaps she might even give him one chaste embrace and know all the while she was doing something she thought she would never do—hold Kingsley's child in her arms. She'd never even met him, met Nicolas, Kingsley's son. But she would fight to the death to protect him from this woman and whatever sick, sordid plans she had in mind.

"Do not go near Kingsley's son if you value your life," Nora said quietly and with menace. And something in her tone must have penetrated even Marie-Laure's madness and darkness.

"I don't care anything about him." Marie-Laure waved her hand dismissively. "Mere curiosity alone. Seeing him simply caused me to wonder about my brother for the first time in years. After all, I was under the impression that his interest in women had been feigned, a cover for his true inclinations. And yet, there was living proof that my brother, in his twenties, had bedded women. I had to wonder…what else had I been wrong about?"

"So you started investigating?"

Marie-Laure nodded as Fat Man pointed at the floor. Nora sank to her knees again, listening avidly. After the revelation about Nicolas, she knew she had to hear it all. What other secrets did Kingsley have? More secrets than he even knew he had?

"I did. I even came to New York, something I swore I would never do knowing this was his territory. I learned a great deal on that excursion. He had no idea I followed him, watched him, studied from a distance. Lovers…men and women. That Juliette most often, although he tries not to show anyone he cares for her."

"He has enemies. He protects her by not letting on how much she matters."

"I know he has enemies," Marie-Laure said with a smile. "I'm one of them. I had prepared myself for everything I knew I would see watching my brother come and go from his town house, in his box at the opera, playing football—I mean, soccer, excuse me—on the field of a school."

Nora's stomach clenched hard at Marie-Laure's words. Kingsley only ever played soccer these days with…

"You saw him with Søren."

"*Oui*. I saw him with my husband. My husband had become a Catholic priest, I learned, and my brother was still in love with him after all this time. But that merely seemed a tragedy to me, my brother lovelorn even thirty years later. Lovelorn for a man he couldn't have for so many reasons. For surely if he was a Catholic priest, he'd taken a vow of celibacy. It made so much sense to me then. My husband, not interested at all in women, had become a priest. From what I've heard, he would simply be one of a legion of priests entirely not interested in women."

Nora's hands started to shake as Marie-Laure continued her story. She didn't like where it was heading.

"Still…" Marie-Laure continued, "I couldn't stop watching him. A terrible itch, I had to keep scratching. And so I kept watching. I watched his home from the little copse of woods that shielded it."

Nora's breaths quickened.

"Lovely little rectory, so quiet and alone. He seemed so pathetic to me, my husband. A celibate priest who'd given up love and marriage and children to serve a God who couldn't care less what the little ants under His feet did with their days. I liked that he'd become a priest. It comforted me to know he slept alone in his bed with no one to touch him, to make love to him. I hoped that in the middle of his loneliest nights he thought of me and our marriage and how I lay next to him waiting to be touched by a man who cared as little for my love as God cared for him. Then I saw her."

Nora remained silent. She didn't have to ask who Marie-Laure saw.

"I saw a woman come to his home in the middle of the night, and walk to the side door and enter without knocking, enter as if she owned it. An hour later he and she emerged carrying blankets, a bottle of wine, a candle and—"

"Binoculars," Nora completed Marie-Laure's sentence for her. "It was the night of the meteor shower. We wanted to watch it."

"I watched you watch it. I watched you two lay down blankets and stare through the opening in the trees up at the heavens. I saw your head resting on the center of my husband's chest. I watched him run his fingers through your hair as you two talked and laughed for an hour as stars fell out of the sky. I watched you...."

Nora closed her eyes and one tear ran down her cheek. She remembered that night last summer. She'd only been back with Søren a few weeks, and yet already it felt as if she'd never left him. It had been his idea to watch the meteor shower. One of his old teachers at Saint Ignatius had been an astronomer and had instilled a love of the nighttime science in the boys. So they'd had a midnight picnic, the two of them in Søren's backyard where they could hide behind the trees. It was a risk for them to be together outdoors, but one Søren had been willing to take. After the last star had fallen from the sky, she'd turned over and kissed him long and deep, whispering against his lips the apologies she'd been hiding in her heart. *I'm sorry I left you. I'm sorry I had to. I'm sorry I hurt you. I'm sorry I lied about you. I'm sorry I tried to hate you all this time and blame you for everything. It was only because it made being apart from you easier....* He'd forgiven her with a kiss and the words, "I'll forgive because you've asked me to, not because you need my forgiveness. You did what you had to. You had to leave to become who you were meant to be. All that matters now is that you're here, Little One." And then he'd lit a candle and pushed her flowing summer skirt to her waist. He dripped the scalding wax over her thighs and hips and she'd submitted to the pain with peace and pleasure. How good it felt to surrender herself to him again, how safe, how right...and then with only the stars to witness, he'd made love to her until dawn.

But the stars hadn't been the only witness.

Marie-Laure sighed heavily, angrily.

"I knew then that I had been lied to, that I had been betrayed even worse than I'd thought. It should have been me underneath him that night, not you. I am his wife, not you."

"He thought you were dead. You can't blame him."

"He killed me," Marie-Laure said, her voice so flinty with bitterness Nora could swear she saw sparks coming off her words.

"You killed yourself. You ran away."

"I had no choice. I loved my brother. I wanted him to be happy. I was in the way of that happiness."

"You didn't want him to be happy. If you did, you would have gotten the marriage annulled or gotten divorced and gone back to France or even stayed married, taken the money and run. You had a thousand options that would have let Søren and Kingsley be together, be happy. You took the one option guaranteed to break them up. You wanted to punish Kingsley because he made the mistake of being the one Søren was in love with, not you. Don't act like you faked your death for some noble purpose. You wanted to destroy their relationship by making them think they killed you."

"I did destroy their relationship," Marie-Laure said with pride. There it was. Nora saw it. The real motive coming out. She'd been right and Marie-Laure wasn't going to deny it. She'd faked her death to punish Kingsley and Søren for daring to love each other. "I know what happened. Kingsley quit school and joined the French Foreign Legion right after I died. My husband went to Rome and began training for the priesthood. That kiss of theirs, the one I witnessed, it was their final kiss."

And Marie-Laure grinned so wildly Nora wanted to rip it off her face with her fingernails. And she'd do it, too, but not with her hands—she had a much better weapon at her disposal.

"You didn't destroy their relationship, though, despite a very good effort on your part."

"Don't lie to me. I know my husband. I read your file. You're the only person he's been with sexually since becoming a priest."

"Kingsley writes the files and he's a very unreliable narrator. He decides what goes in, what stays out."

Marie-Laure narrowed her eyes at Nora, and despite the fear in her heart, Nora refused to look away.

"What do you mean I didn't destroy them?"

Nora searched deep within herself for the courage she needed. She searched for it and she found it. She gave Marie-Laure a smile of her own.

"Let's just say that tonight, if you want it, I'll have one hell of a bedtime story for you."

# 18
# THE KING

Kingsley drove through the dark all the way to Elizabeth's house in New Hampshire. He drove alone and took no calls. He needed the company of his thoughts to plan his next step. Søren had forced a promise out of him. He could try to get Nora out of the house if Kingsley swore he would kill no one in the process. He knew Søren couldn't care less if Marie-Laure's compatriots ended up with their brains on the carpet. But the priest didn't want him killing his own sister. A nice thought but Kingsley had seen battlefields and bloodshed of the kind Søren had never even dreamed. He'd made the promise and had no intention of keeping it. No room for sentimentality on a battlefield, not if Søren wanted Nora back.

By dawn Kingsley arrived at the house and parked the car in the woods off the road. He slipped through the trees, a high-powered rifle strapped to his back. Would the children of his kingdom even recognize him now if they saw him? Gone were his Regency- and Victorian-era suits and military coats. Gone were his riding boots. Gone was the roguish smile that seduced all comers. He'd changed into jeans, a black T-shirt, pulled his hair back into a low ponytail to keep it out of his face. He left his shoes in the car, far preferring the sensitivity and silence of bare feet. And instead of a smile he wore a look of grim determination.

He saw the house through the trees. Ducking down behind thick branches, he pulled out a spyglass and studied the windows. Laila had said she and Nora were held in the library. With all the curtains closed he couldn't see anything, not even the hint of movement.

His sister…what the hell was she doing? She had to know taking Nora was simply a slower form of suicide. Did she think she would get her revenge against them and live to enjoy her victory? No, of course she didn't, and that's what scared him most. If Marie-Laure had no intention of surviving this gambit, then she had nothing to lose. If she wanted to die, planned to die, there would be no stopping her from taking Nora and anyone else with her to the grave.

If he tried to get Nora out and Marie-Laure caught him, there would be no more nights with his Juliette, no more days. He'd never see her again. And the last time he saw her, they'd fought over his insistence she leave him. Now he couldn't be more grateful for what seemed like paranoia at the time. And yet, what he wouldn't give to have another chance to look in her eyes and tell her how much he loved her.

"Ah, Jules…" he whispered to nothing and no one, a smile flitting across his face, "your timing is atrocious."

If only he could tell her how sorry he was that it had come to this. His Juliette, his Jules, his Jewel… He'd dreamed all his life that he would find someone like her, someone who understood who he was. Not only did she not judge him for

what he was, she loved him for it. What they had, he treasured it above all things and for that reason alone he'd sent her
away. A week ago she accused him of overreacting, of letting
his fears for her get the better of him. But still, she submitted
to his wishes and had flown to Haiti where she still had family, where she could disappear, blend in and be safe. Now he
thanked God he'd had the foresight to send her away. If Marie-
Laure had stolen Søren's most precious possession, no doubt she
considered stealing his, as well. Sister or not, if Marie-Laure
had laid a hand on his Juliette, his lover, his property, his…

Kingsley stopped his thoughts in their tracks. He couldn't
think about Juliette now, what she was to him, what the future held. He needed to stay calm, rational, if they were to
make it out of this alive, all of them. And they would survive
this. He would make sure of it no matter the price to his soul.

For two hours he sat and watched the house, waiting for a
curtain to move, a door to open. Nothing happened. Nothing
at all. A wasted trip. As Kingsley started to stand, to stretch
his legs, he saw something.

Ducking down again, he waited and watched.

At the front of the house on the second floor, a curtain
moved. It could have been nothing, the air-conditioning coming on. Or it could be something, someone… He brought the
spyglass up and stared.

The curtain parted and a woman stood at the window.
Thirty years disappeared in an instant. Long dark hair, bistre
eyes, a dancer's physique…

*"Ma soeur…"*

Marie-Laure stood staring out the window onto the long
driveway. She seemed to be waiting for someone. He knew
who she waited for, and as long as Kingsley had a breath left in
his body, he'd make sure the person she waited for never came.

He raised his rifle and peered through the sight.

Only Marie-Laure stood at the window, however. And surely she hadn't executed Nora's kidnapping alone. If he killed her now, what would stop her henchmen from killing Nora and making a run for it? Nothing.

Marie-Laure stepped away from the window and Kingsley lowered the rifle.

He had no choice. He would wait for tonight, for darkness, and he would go in.

Back through the woods he crept, careful to not be seen or heard. Once in his car he stopped to breathe. Until that moment he saw Marie-Laure in the window, he had cherished a shadow of a doubt that perhaps they'd been wrong, that it was someone pretending to be her to torture them. Now he had no doubts. It was her, his sister, still alive. But not for long.

He started the car and eased back onto the road. Although it had been years since he'd been to Daniel's house, he needed to consult no maps. He still remembered the way.

Funny how terribly, maddeningly small the world was they lived in. Kingsley had met a beautiful woman named Maggie back in his twenties during a brief trip to New York. Although wealthy and with a high-powered job as an attorney, she craved the domination of powerful men. He'd happily fed her hunger to submit until he had to return to France. Soon after she'd met a younger man named Daniel, a librarian without a penny to his name, and married him. Maggie and Daniel had a house in the country, a retreat a few hours from the city yet less than ten miles from the house Søren had grown up in. Ten miles—close enough to scout out the house easily, far enough away not to tip them off.

As he pulled into Daniel's driveway he saw Søren's motorcycle parked near the front door. Kingsley felt a momentary stab of sympathy for the man. He knew Søren hated being anywhere near this part of the world. Even Kingsley didn't know the extent of what had happened in that house, the house where Nora was being held. Not even to Nora had Søren shared all the horrors of his past. Not to Nora or to him, and for that Kingsley was grateful. He had enough skeletons of his own in his past. He'd run out of closet space for any more.

He glanced up at the colonial manor as he headed to the door. Lovely place—two stories, two hundred years old. Elegant. Tasteful. Stately. And home to one of the kinkier men of his acquaintance.

The door opened before Kingsley even knocked.

"Daniel, get out of this house right now," Kingsley said without any preamble.

"It's my house," Daniel reminded him as Kingsley pushed past him.

"Yes, and I'm commandeering it."

"You can't commandeer my house."

"Fine, then I'll commandeer your wife."

Daniel followed Kingsley down the hallway into the library where Kingsley deposited himself on top of Daniel's desk.

"Kingsley."

"Daniel."

Kingsley attempted to stare Daniel down. A bad idea. Daniel's ability to stare down people was notorious in the Underground. Only Søren had a more vicious glare than Daniel's infamous unyielding blue-eyed stare. Maggie called it the Ouch and the name had stuck. Anyone on the receiving end of the Ouch would likely be saying "ouch" for the next couple of days.

"Put the blue eyes away," Kingsley ordered.

"I can't very well take my eyes out." Daniel continued to glare. The years had been kind to Daniel. Marriage and children even kinder. In his day the man had been so handsome he'd even tempted Nora from Søren. For only about five seconds, she'd confessed to him, but still, something of a feat. Then again, Nora always did have a bit of a fetish for blonds.

"I'll do it for you if you don't stop glaring at me. I told you that I needed your house for a few days. And *non,* I'm not going to tell you why."

"I already told him why." Søren stood in the doorway. He, too, had gone for "business casual," as Griffin always called it. No collar, no clerics. Black pants, white shirt open at the neck. He never got used to seeing Søren in his collar and clerics. Yet, he never quite got used to seeing him without them on, either. "If we're stealing his house, he deserves to know why."

Kingsley sighed. It was for the best. Unless Daniel knew the real danger, he might put up more of a fight about leaving. Thankfully, Kingsley had four little trump cards he could use on Daniel.

"I know about Eleanor. I can't believe someone would kidnap her." Daniel glanced between them. "I wouldn't even borrow a teacup from you two."

"Is that so?" Søren asked, and gave Daniel the only glare more feared than the Ouch.

"You let me borrow her, remember?" Daniel asked.

"For one week. You're the one who attempted to convince her to stay."

Kingsley watched as Daniel walked across the room and met Søren in the doorway.

"Come on," Daniel said, looking up at Søren. "You would have tried to keep her, too."

"Yes," Søren agreed. "Only I would have succeeded."

"You get more arrogant with age. Aren't priests supposed to be humble?"

"We're also supposed to be celibate." Søren smiled at Daniel, and Daniel and Kingsley had to laugh. No need to fight an old battle when a new one was already brewing.

"Good point. Now someone tell me what I can do to help," Daniel said, turning back to Kingsley.

"You can leave," Kingsley said.

"I'm not leaving. I love Eleanor, too. You know she—"

"Tell me the names and ages of your children," Kingsley said.

"King, I know—"

"Tell me the names and ages of your children, Daniel," Kingsley repeated.

Daniel paused to glare at Kingsley again. "That's not fair."

"It was not my idea for you to get married again and have how many children?"

"Four," Daniel said almost apologetically.

"Right. Four children. And a wife. And your wife has how many siblings that you're taking care of?"

"Daniel…" Søren said as he came into the room. "He's right. This is dangerous. You should go."

"Your niece is here," Daniel countered.

"She has a purpose being here. You don't."

"Well, thank you very much for that."

"He means Laila was there," Kingsley added. Did Søren always have to be so *Søren* all the time? "She knows things."

"Who's the guy with her? Boyfriend?"

Kingsley nearly hurt himself trying not to smile. Søren turned his glare on Daniel up a notch.

"He most certainly is not," Søren said, his voice dangerously icy.

"Sorry. Jesus. I said 'boyfriend' not 'pimp.'"

"*Le prêtre* is annoyingly protective of his nieces," Kingsley explained.

"A product of spending too much time in your company," Søren said.

"And the young man to whom you're referring…I suppose

you could call him an interested party," Kingsley said, looking for the most tactful description of Wesley's presence. All of it was nonsense, lies and subterfuge. Neither he nor Søren wanted nor needed any of them here—not Wesley nor Laila, not Grace. He knew why Søren insisted that they be allowed to come. He knew and refused to accept that their presence here would ever be required.

"An interested party?" Daniel repeated, a slight smile on his lips. "So he's sleeping with Nora."

*"Précisément,"* Kingsley said.

Daniel only shrugged. "Figures."

"I'll let you two talk," Søren said from the doorway. "But, Daniel, for the sake of your family, you do need to go. You shouldn't be involved in any of this."

"I appreciate the concern," Daniel said, and Kingsley heard no sarcasm in his words. "I was prepared to die in this house after I lost Maggie. Eleanor saved me from that fate. I owe her…everything."

"Then do what she would want you to do," Søren said.

"She'd want me to take care of my family first," Daniel admitted with obvious reluctance.

"She would," Kingsley said.

"I'll go." Daniel raised his hands in surrender. "But I want to know everything. I want to know when she's safe."

"Thank you," Søren said with real sincerity in his voice.

"For leaving?" Daniel asked with a small laugh.

"For saying 'when she's safe' and not 'if.'"

Kingsley watched as Daniel's jaw clenched and his eyes darkened.

"You're welcome."

Søren merely nodded and walked away.

Daniel exhaled heavily as if he'd been holding his breath.

"I've been friends with him for decades, and he still scares the shit out of me sometimes," Daniel said.

Kingsley sat on Daniel's desk.

"He knows he does. You make it too much fun for him."

"I thought he was going to kill me for daring to suggest his niece had a boyfriend."

"He might have."

"So that boy…one of Nora's conquests?"

"Worse," Kingsley said, grimacing. "He's her fiancé. Supposedly. He asked her to marry him right before he was knocked unconscious and she was taken."

"Are we sure he asked her before he received the head injury?" Daniel winked at him.

"I knew I liked you for a reason." Kingsley hopped off the desk and clasped Daniel by the shoulder. "I'm taking care of this. You know that I can."

"I know you can. If anyone can work the necessary miracles it's you two."

"Good. *Bien*. Now get out of your house."

"I'm going."

Kingsley followed Daniel from the library. They passed the well-appointed but comfortable living room where Grace sat curled up on a couch. At the back of the room, Wesley stood staring out the window in the direction of Elizabeth's home. They couldn't see it from Daniel's house but perhaps it gave him some comfort to turn toward Nora like a faithful Muslim toward Mecca. Laila came up to him and offered him a cup of something—coffee or tea, Kingsley couldn't tell. Wesley thanked her and Laila's face lit up like a Christmas tree.

"So he's not Laila's boyfriend?" Daniel whispered to Kingsley.

"*Non.*"

"Has anyone told Laila that?"

"Not yet."

Kingsley followed Daniel all the way upstairs to his bedroom and supervised the packing. He knew Daniel would keep to his word and leave the house to them. But he couldn't stomach being in the presence of the grief-stricken huddled masses down in the living room, and he could barely look Søren in the eye for the pain and fear lurking behind his steady gray gaze.

"Do you know what you're going to do yet?" Daniel asked as soon as he'd packed the basics in his suitcase.

"*Oui,*" Kingsley said simply. Luckily Daniel was one of the more intelligent men he'd ever met, and he had to say nothing more than that.

"Be careful, okay?"

"You know, with my connections, I could assassinate the governor of New York in broad daylight and not get arrested."

"I know all about your connections. It's not the police I'm worried about. I don't want any more reasons to have to visit cemeteries. I'd much rather visit you in prison. In fact, I might have fantasized about it a time or two."

"No prisons, no cemeteries," Kingsley pledged.

"I'm holding you to that."

"Go, Daniel. Go and fuck your wife for me."

"Happily. After I fuck her for me. Try not to break anything while I'm gone. I kind of like my house."

"I'll only break the bed."

Daniel paused on the threshold of the door.

"I know you're terrified, King. I know you're pretending not to be for all our sakes."

Kingsley said nothing in reply. To deny would be a lie. To agree would be to admit weakness.

"And I know..." Daniel continued, "I know you and Eleanor have had your differences. I know you and him—"

"I love him," Kingsley said.

"I know you do. Please, don't let that cloud your judgment."

"I'm not going to let her die on the off chance he and I can be together. She's one of mine. I promised him when she started working for me that I would keep her safe. One promise I intend to keep."

"I didn't think you'd let her die to get him. I just…" Daniel paused and raised his hand. He started ticking off on his fingers. "She saved me."

"I'll save them," Kingsley pledged, and the use of "them" was no slip of the tongue. If she died, there would be no hole they could dig wide or deep enough to bury Søren's grief. He knew this for a fact. He knew this because he once overheard Søren saying it. That was the day they buried Maggie, Daniel's first wife.

"I know you will." Daniel turned again but immediately spun back around. "To answer your question from earlier, it's Marius, age nine. Byrony, age seven. Willa, age six, Archer, age four. Oh, and Leonard."

"Leonard?"

"The goddamn cat. The other baby in the family."

Kingsley laughed.

"You have to blame Anya if you don't like the names," Daniel continued. "Her rule—she has the babies, she names the babies."

Kingsley swallowed a sudden knot in his throat. It took all his strength to meet Daniel's eyes and speak in an unbroken voice.

"They're beautiful names."

"Thank you."

"You should be with them."

"I'm going. You'll call when this is over."

*"Non,"* Kingsley said. "She will call."

"She better."

"And knowing her, she'll demand phone sex."

"If she insists."

Daniel gave Kingsley a long searching look, one Kingsley tried to ignore. He turned and left Kingsley alone in the master bedroom. As soon as he was alone, Kingsley sank down onto the bed, letting his guard down finally. He couldn't let his fears overwhelm him, not when he had a job to do.

Closing his eyes, he tried running through what he remembered about Elizabeth's home—the layout, the rooms, possible places to hide, the trees—but instead he heard Daniel's voice. *Marius, Byrony, Willa, Archer...* Long ago he'd forgiven Nora for her choice not to have his child. His shock of the discovery had translated into horror to her. How many times on his bathroom floor that morning had she told him she was sorry...so fucking sorry...accident...had no intention, she swore to God. And no matter how much he tried to calm her down, she'd remained frantic, terrified, her entire life before her hanging in the balance. Every moment with Søren she had to steal. A child would steal the already too few hours he could make for her. So he let her make the choice and didn't try to sway her, didn't tell her the secret truth.

He'd wanted to keep it.

He pushed the thought away. The house...the hallways... the trees...the line of fire... He ran through various scenarios, visualizing the target, anticipating the worst, but it wasn't a target, was it? His sister had Nora and he'd seen her with his own eyes.

He stood at the window in Daniel's bedroom and stared in the direction of the house as Wesley was doing on the first floor. No doubt somewhere else Søren was staring in the same direction. "Please, Marie-Laure, don't make me do this...."

Kingsley turned around, putting his back to the window,

and noticed for the first time the rocking chair sitting in the shadows. He'd been in Daniel's bedroom before but had no memory of such a bourgeois bit of furniture in the otherwise elegantly decorated room. It must be Anya's doing. No doubt she had rocked the children to sleep many a night in that chair before carrying them off to the nursery and returning to her husband's bed as his own mother had with him and Marie-Laure.

Whatever Marie-Laure's crimes, she was still his sister. She'd even named him, his mother had told him long ago when he'd asked who was to blame for giving him such a decidedly un-French name. Marie-Laure, only three years old, had a set of paper dolls—knights and squires, lords and ladies, kings and queens. One day Marie-Laure took the king doll and placed it on top of his mother's pregnant stomach. His American mother, wanting her daughter to know French and English, had pointed at the doll on her stomach and said, "It's a king." For the next two months whenever curled up with her mother, Marie-Laure would pat the growing stomach and repeat, "It's a king. It's a king."

And so Kingsley was born.

How did it happen…how had it come to this? His sister had been a sweet child once, his mother's little angel… and then she'd become a teenager and her beauty had blossomed. More than blossomed, it had exploded, gone off like a bomb complete with mushroom cloud and utter devastation. *Mon Dieu,* the fallout—he'd never seen anything like it before or since. Nora had broken her fair share of hearts but she somehow always managed to leave the men better off than she found them—even Daniel, especially Daniel. But his sister… At the time he'd been too busy with his own conquests to pay much attention to her. Last thing he wanted to think about was who his sister was spreading for. Looking back, they should have seen the signs. One boyfriend had threatened suicide over her dismissal of him. When he ended up in the hospital after swallowing a bottle of pills, Marie-Laure had laughed and bragged about it to friends and said it could only have been better had he died. Perhaps that's where she'd gotten the idea—punishing someone who didn't love you by killing yourself. But for whatever reason she had come back and seen both him and Søren happy and in love.

Kingsley had wealth and power and the most beautiful, intelligent, understanding woman in the world in his bed. Søren had a peaceful life in his parish, and the respect and devotion of his entire congregation. And he had his Little One, whom he loved above all others and who loved him in return in her own beautiful if broken way. Marie-Laure's first attempt at revenge had failed. This was take two.

He would make sure her second attempt would fail like her first had.

And this time, Marie-Laure would stay dead.

# 19
# THE QUEEN

Nora lay on the floor and stared at the door. After her late breakfast with Marie-Laure, Andrei had escorted her to a room, locked her in and made casual mention that if she tried anything, Damon would be waiting right outside the door ready to shoot her—or worse. Death waited outside that door. She barely noticed the rest of the room. The footsteps in the hallway commanded her complete attention.

The footsteps faded and Nora forced herself to breathe, to relax. Carefully she got off the floor and tried the window. That was a waste of time, of course. Elizabeth, having had the childhood from hell, had taken childproofing her home to an absurd extreme. If Nora had a lead baseball and a cannon, she still couldn't have shattered the window glass. And someone, Damon or Andrei, had kindly nailed the wood to the frame. She was trapped. Nothing to do but wait and stare and pray the day away.

And plan.

After all, while she believed in the power of prayer, she also believed in having backup plans on the off chance God wanted her to get off her ass and do it herself. Escape plans... these were her specialty. The daughter of a man who ate his meals with the Mafia, she'd learned early on that the world was an ugly, dangerous place full of men with guns who'd pat you on the head, call you a good kid and then walk out the door and kill somebody who'd made the fatal mistake of crossing them. The lowlifes of the world had been her father's best friends, his worst enemies and all at the same time.

So even at the tender age of eleven she'd started to figure things out. A coat hanger bent the right way could unlatch a car door in under a second. A tiny ball bearing held between two fingers and aimed at the center of a pane of glass could shatter it into a thousand pieces. This wire to that wire and the car would start, no key necessary, no permission asked.

They hadn't tied her up before tossing her into the room. No reason to bother if she couldn't get away through door, window or ceiling. Trapped...she was trapped in this house that had been a house of horrors to Søren growing up. He'd almost died in this house the day his father had caught him with his sister in the library. He'd almost died and now she might, too.

No. She wouldn't give in to such apocalyptic thinking. She was a Dominatrix, after all, not some damsel in distress waiting for a prince on a white charger to ride in and save her. Søren had taught her to be strong. Any woman sharing the bed of a sadist had to be strong.

The thought stirred Nora and slowly she rolled up off the floor.

The bed of a sadist...

No bed sat in the room they'd thrown her into, but clearly once there had been a bed. She saw the piles of ash on the floor, the blackened walls and ceiling, smelled the scent of burned wood and fabric. And that's when she realized she'd been in this bedroom before. Standing up, Nora walked to the door. She didn't even bother touching the knob. One jiggle and Damon would probably start firing. No, she wasn't going to try to get out...she only needed to remember.

The night she first visited this room, she'd been seventeen. Two years she'd lusted after her priest, loved him, obeyed his every last command he'd given her under the auspices of supervising the community service Judge Harkness had imposed upon her. And all that time she'd known...something. She had no idea what she knew but she knew she knew it and she knew Søren knew it, too. It had been maddening, like living with a word on the tip of her tongue for years. Her gut had told her she belonged to Søren in some deep cosmic way she couldn't begin to comprehend. Even if he never laid a hand on her, never kissed her, never made love to her at all, that changed nothing. She was his. She knew it.

He knew it, too. But it wasn't until his father had died that he finally felt safe enough to tell her the truth. He'd told her... in this very room.

Nora stood by the door, closed her eyes, and when she opened them again she could see the chair by the window... and she saw Søren even younger than she was now, praying in his childhood bedroom, his blond hair like a halo in the moonlight. Walking across the floor, Nora inhaled the memories of that night—kneeling at Søren's feet, crawling into his lap, surrendering to his arms. He'd held her before—when her father had been sentenced to prison, when her mother had turned her back on her for the final time—but all those times before the embrace had been that of her priest, a caring friend comforting a troubled girl, and nothing more. That night he held her like a lover. He'd asked her if she wanted to know the truth about him, about them, and he'd given her the sternest of warnings that her life would never be the same again if she let him tell her the truth.

To that warning she'd simply answered, *Tell me.*

"Tell me..." she said to the empty room. But no, not entirely empty. The bed was gone. It appeared someone had set it on fire and let it burn down to the hardwood, leaving waste, burn marks and ashes behind. Yes, even the residue of the ashes snaked up the wall and onto the ceiling, and around the outline of words someone—Elizabeth most likely—had tried and failed to wipe clean.

*Love thy sister.*

"You sick bitch." Nora raised her hand and traced the outline of the words on the wall. How dare Marie-Laure mock Søren and Elizabeth for the sins of their childhood, sins no God in heaven or on earth would ever hold them accountable for?

The night of Søren's father's funeral, he'd confessed his darkest secrets to her, and she'd listened in silence and in horror—never horror at him for what he'd done, horror only at what this man she'd loved so completely had suffered. She would never forget him turning his face from her and meeting the gaze of the moon. The words he said...she wanted to take them into her hands and set them alight and watch them burn until they ceased echoing inside her ears.

*I am like him, like my father. I take the greatest of pleasures in inflicting pain. Eleanor, you cannot even imagine what I did to my sister...what she did to me. I never want you to imagine... Please,* Søren had begged of her, *please never imagine.* And for his sake and Elizabeth's sake she never tried to imagine.

But today she knew she needed to imagine.

"Søren," she whispered to his childhood bedroom. "Please... don't fail me. If I know you half as well as you know me..."

She started to look around the room where Søren had lost his virginity to Elizabeth, his own half sister, the room where he'd first begun to explore the strange dark desires he'd been born with. She knew herself. She knew her past. As a young teenager she'd often scald herself with candle wax, carve shallow patterns into her skin with needles—games, they were. Challenges. Dares. A game of chicken played with herself. All their kind started young. The sadists' first victims were their own bodies. The masochists' first sadists were themselves. Simone, one of Søren's favorite submissives, had once confessed that she'd play cowboys and Indians with her brothers only because they always tied her up during their role-play. The sexual thrill she'd experienced as her older brother lashed her to the foot of their parents' bed embarrassed her even to this day. When the game ended, she'd disappear into the privacy of her own bedroom, and tie herself up, leaving only one hand free to masturbate.

The innocent games children play...

Nora got on her hands and knees and swept along the edge of the baseboards looking for a loose board. Nothing. Over the top of the window frame she found only dust. Little furniture in the room but for the remnants of the bed and the bookcase.

The bookcase.

Kneeling in front of the shelves Nora ran her eyes over the books. They looked untouched, unread. Søren had spent almost his entire childhood from age five to ten away in England at boarding school. The books had been mere decoration in this house where every smile was nothing but show. Søren had come back to this house at age eleven after he'd killed the boy who'd attacked him in his bed.

As Nora studied the titles of the books, a memory stirred of a long-ago conversation between two people who'd not yet become lovers.

*You'll need a safe word, Eleanor.*

*I trust you.*

*That's all well and good but I don't entirely trust myself with you. Choose a word and I'll carve it onto my heart and when you say it, I'll know I have to stop. Otherwise, there is a very good chance I won't, not even if you struggle, especially if you struggle.*

She'd remembered the first poem she ever memorized as a child. The words had been all nonsense and yet they tripped easily off her tongue. "Twas brillig and the slithy toves..."

*Jabberwocky,* Nora, age eighteen, had answered on the day Søren started training her. *I always loved that monster.*

*He was always my favorite monster,* Søren had said.

And Nora, then still just Eleanor, remembered smiling at him, kissing him...

*You're my favorite monster,* she said against his lips.

Ignoring all the other books on the shelves, Nora carefully removed a gilt-edged hardbound copy of *Through the Looking-Glass* from the shelf and held it in her lap.

*I'll carve it into my heart...*

Nora closed her eyes and let the book fall open.

As she looked down into the book, a tear fell from her eyes and landed onto the paper monster.

"Oh, Søren," she whispered, love and anguish warring for possession of her heart. Love for the man and anguish for the boy. "You poor little boy, thank you."

The book had fallen open right to the Jabberwocky. And that reason was the razor blade a child had secreted between the pages thirty-six years ago. Nora took the blade from the book and held it into the light. The acid-free paper had kept it perfectly preserved—no rust, no decay. It was as sharp now as the day Søren had hidden it inside the book, hidden it away after using it on his sister...or perhaps, even worse, on himself.

She put the book back where she found it. Had she possessed a brick of solid gold it would feel less precious than this sliver of steel that could possibly cut her free from the ropes that would bind her to Marie-Laure's bed tonight, or perhaps even save her from an attack on her own body. Aimed just right she could slice the jugular artery wide open with it, the femoral vein in the thigh. If Fat Man or Little Boy got any ideas, she could slice their balls off and shove them in their mouths. That vision gave her a dark smile. No more defeatist thinking. She would survive this to see her kidnappers pay for their crimes. She would live to watch them die.

A new and precious hope had burrowed a hole into her heart. She tucked it in, let it get comfortable. Thirty-six years ago, a troubled little boy had hidden a razor blade inside this book and thirty-six years later the woman who'd grow up to love him would find it the moment she needed it most. The razor blade in her hand felt like a miracle, like a sign, like salvation. She tucked the blade into her back pocket where she could reach it even with her hands tied.

"Thank you, God," she prayed with the deepest, most profound gratitude she'd ever experienced in her life. Even the night her father had been killed and she'd realized she was free of him and his kind forever, she hadn't felt this unfathomably infinite gratefulness. "Thank you for making him like this…thank you."

How could she not thank God right now? Søren had confessed there were times as a child and teenager that he wondered why God had made him this way, made him so that he took the deepest of pleasures in causing the most brutal pain. Now she knew the reason why and she couldn't wait to see him again, couldn't wait to tell him.

God made Søren what he was so that he would leave this precious gift for her three years before she'd even been born.

# Part Three

# QUEEN'S GAMBIT

## 20
## THE PAWN

Evening came and Laila knew she would go mad from waiting. Her uncle and Kingsley had something planned but whatever their scheme, she wouldn't be allowed to take any part in it. She wandered the house they'd been brought to and found little in it to distract her. A beautiful house, well-decorated and clearly loved. She'd found one stray pink sock in the hallway outside the bedroom she'd been given. A little girl's sock… Laila had stared at it until finally picking it up and putting it in the laundry room. She felt like an intruder in this private home. She didn't belong here in these rooms and halls. Children did. Love should fill every room. Instead, Laila found only fear.

Knowing he'd discourage her from leaving the house, Laila didn't even tell her uncle she decided to go on a short walk. She left a note on her bed in case he came looking for her and set out on her own. But she hadn't made it to the end of the drive before she heard footsteps behind her.

"Your legs are too long." Wes jogged a little to catch up with her.

"I'm sorry," she said, smiling at him as he met her at the end of the long driveway. "I'll try to shorten them."

"I'm used to walking with Nora. I'd forgotten not every woman on the planet is a shrimp."

"She can walk really fast when she wants to." Laila set out again down the tree-lined road. "But don't ever ask her to—"

"Run. I know. Hates running. Told me she's allergic to it. She has a long list of allergies."

"Yes. Let's see, there's…cooking."

Wes nodded. "She's definitely allergic to cooking. Anything that required more than two ingredients—or, as she called them, the hard stuff and the chaser—she'd give up and order takeout."

"Cleaning," Laila thought of another.

"That was one. She had scared off six housekeepers by the time I moved in with her."

"Six?" Laila gazed around her at the beautiful August evening with the sun low through the trees and this man walking with her. She wished she could enjoy it even a little but the fear held her heart in its unforgiving grasp. "Why so many?"

"Um…" Wes winced and Laila knew she'd inadvertently stumbled into secret territory.

"Let me guess…I don't want to know."

"She had a bad habit of not picking up after herself."

Laila weighed whether or not to tell Wes what she wanted to tell him. Might as well. Her uncle tried to shield her from the truth about him and her, but her aunt never had.

"I have read her books. You don't have to pretend she's… you know…"

"Normal?" Wes supplied.

"Vanilla," Laila said. "You read even one of her books and you learn the words."

Wes exhaled with obvious and profound relief.

"Thank God. I wasn't sure what you knew and what you didn't."

"I know enough to know that I wouldn't go sneaking around in her bedroom without body armor on first."

"It's not that bad, I promise. I lived with her. She keeps most of the stuff in her closet. Sometimes I'd find snap hooks between the couch cushions. One time I accidentally sat on a Wartenburg wheel. That sucker hurt. And ripped a hole in my jeans."

Laila laughed and the sound bounced off the road and into the trees.

"And she had this big long bag," Wes said, stretching his arms three feet wide. "Kept it in her office most of the time. She told me not to open it unless I never wanted to look her in the eyes again."

"Did you open it?"

"Nope." He shook his head and Laila's heart jumped as a sliver of the day's last sunlight caught in Wes's hair. She felt the most overwhelming urge to run her fingers through it. But she restrained herself. He probably wouldn't like some girl he barely knew messing with his hair right now. "I liked looking her in the eyes."

"I think I could have, anyway, even after opening the bag. My uncle, on the other hand…" She let her voice trail off and Laila found herself blushing.

"I guess you know about him, too, then." Wes crossed his arms over his chest.

Laila nodded. "Well, if she is like that, then he is. Other-wise, they wouldn't have stayed together so long. I've even accidentally heard them." Accidentally? Not quite but he didn't need to know that.

"I overheard my parents once. Oh, my Lord, I thought I'd never be normal again."

"My parents got divorced when I was very young. I think I would have liked to have parents in love enough to sometimes overhear them in bed together."

"I'm sorry. Yeah, hearing your parents having sex is better than not hearing it, I guess. How old were you when they broke up?"

"Six. Gitte was two. It was a bad match, my mother said. Neither of them did anything wrong. They didn't have anything in common. She had the good job, and all the money, so we stayed in the house and he moved away. *Min onkel* Søren tried to step in, but it wasn't easy for him across an ocean. He called all the time to check on us."

*"Min onkel?"*

"My uncle Søren," she corrected herself. "Sorry."

Wes only smiled. "Don't apologize. Seriously. I like when you slip into Danish."

Laila blushed as if he'd complimented her breasts instead of her words. Maybe since they were outside in the sun he wouldn't notice how much talking to him made her turn so red.

"Happens when I'm tired. I slip in and out."

"We should go back if you're tired."

She shook her head. "No, not yet. I don't want to go back. It's too…"

"I know," he said quietly, staring into the sun for a moment before looking back at her. "Everyone's so scared and we make it worse being around one another, scaring one another even more."

"It's hard to be around him," she said. "My uncle. He loves

her so much, and I can't help him. I can't even look in his eyes…I hate seeing him so scared. I don't ever remember seeing him scared before." Laila stepped off the road and into the manicured woods.

"Never?"

Wes followed right behind her. Inside a clearing she found a downed tree and sat on it.

"I didn't think anything could scare him. Anything bad that happened, he was always so calm. Gitte fell once and hit her head on a rock. So much blood…I'd never seen so much. All of us were screaming and crying. He picked her up and carried her into the house and held her until help came. He made her tell him about her day at school and what she'd learned that week. Anything to keep her calm and awake. I realized that day that he was different from us."

"Different how?" Wes sat next to her on the tree trunk. As he lifted himself and settled in, Laila noticed the muscles flexing in his arms. She needed to stop noticing stuff like that.

"No one in Denmark is Catholic. It's a secular country. No one goes to church. I think that was the day I realized that him being Catholic and believing in God…he did believe there was some higher power taking care of people. He did have faith and it kept him calm when everyone else was afraid."

"Is it weird having a priest for an uncle?"

"Yes and no." Laila looked up at the darkening sky. "I'm so used to it now that it's only strange when I stop to think about it. I'll see something on television about the pope or Rome and I'll think, 'He's one of them….'"

"He's not one of them. Priests aren't supposed to have girl-friends."

"The girlfriend is the part that isn't weird. If he didn't have her, then that would be strange. What man would choose to be alone if he could have her?"

"No man in his right mind."

Laila tried to smile at him but Wes didn't meet her eyes. For some reason it seemed he was hiding something from her. But he glanced her way again.

"I don't blame him for being in love with her. I just wish, for her sake, she wasn't in love with him."

Wes said the words tentatively, as if he worried about giving offense.

"Don't tell him I said this," Laila found herself almost whispering, "but I've thought the same thing."

"You have?" Wes looked at her with new eyes and in shock. "I thought—"

"I love him. Completely. He was a father to me and Gitte after our father was gone. But I love my aunt, too, and I can't imagine how hard it is for her."

"Hard?"

"In our house in Copenhagen, she's his wife. We treat her like family because she is family. Everywhere else she goes, she's just…"

"The mistress," Wes finished the sentence for her, and she was glad he had. The word felt like treason to her.

"Yes, the mistress. She told me she fell in love with him when she was fifteen years old and loved him every day since the day they met. That's almost twenty years now. And not once has he been able to publicly say they're together. She's his dirty secret. She's something he has to hide. When I found out that she'd left him, I wasn't surprised and I wasn't angry. I was sad, but I understood why."

"I'm glad you get it," Wes said. "I didn't want her to go back to him. For a lot of reasons. I feel like she thinks I'm the bad guy because I don't want her in a relationship like that. She deserves better."

"She does," Laila agreed. "And he tried to give her more."

"What do you mean?"

"Tante Elle and I went for a walk together last time she came to visit. I asked her why she and my uncle never got married. I said I felt bad for her because she couldn't be his wife. I asked her if she was mad at him for not leaving his job and marrying her."

"What did she say?"

"She said being a priest was like being a writer or a healer or a parent. It was a calling, not a job. It wasn't something you did, it was who you are. And she would no more ask him to quit being a priest than he would ever ask her to quit being a writer, or ask my mother to quit being a mother. She said that for Catholics the priesthood was a sacrament. Being a priest was written into his very DNA. She loved him and he was a priest, and if he quit the priesthood, he wouldn't be him anymore. He'd give up so much of himself there would be nothing left of him to love. And then she told me something I'd never known...."

"What did she say?" Wes asked, seemingly clinging to every word she spoke. She'd never had anyone like him paying so much attention to her before.

"She said I shouldn't judge him for not leaving the church and marrying her. He'd offered once and she said no."

Wes went completely still. He didn't even seem to be breathing. Why her aunt and uncle's love life mattered to him so much, she couldn't guess and didn't want to. But she wasn't stupid. Obviously Wes had feelings for her aunt. But it seemed to go deeper than a crush.

"He asked her to marry him and she said no," Wes repeated.

"Yes, and that's when she left him. She said she was scared she'd change her mind and say yes and he would leave the church for her. She said it was like hearing someone offer to commit suicide to prove their love. She left so he wouldn't destroy the man she fell in love with."

For a few minutes they sat side by side in silence as the evening faded out and became night.

"It's crazy," Wes finally said. "All this time I thought she left him because he wouldn't stop being what he was for her."

"He offered. She refused. She said she'd rather be the mistress of a priest than the wife of the ghost of a priest."

Wes started to say something but she heard a woman's voice calling her name.

"We're here, Grace," Laila said as Wes jumped off the log. Laila started to jump down, too, but Wes stood in front of her and held out his hand. She took his hand in hers and let him help her down. She probably would have landed okay even in the dark but she couldn't turn down a chance to hold Wes's hand, could she?

"What's up?" Wes asked as Grace jogged into the clearing.

"Your uncle was wondering where you'd gone," Grace said as the three of them retook the road toward the house.

"I needed to walk," Laila said. "I was going crazy in that house."

"I don't blame you." Grace gave her hand a quick squeeze, a kind and affectionate gesture that Laila appreciated even as part of her wished to feel her hand in Wes's again. "But it's late and your uncle wants us all under the same roof tonight."

A car passed them and Wes watched as it drove away.

"Yeah? Well, then, where the hell is Kingsley going?"

# 21
# THE QUEEN

Nora spent the entire day in Søren's childhood bedroom, searching it for anything she could possibly use against her kidnappers. Apart from the razor blade she found nothing else hidden away and for that she was almost grateful. Søren had made her promise to not think about, not to imagine, what had transpired between him and his sister. She wanted no reason to break that promise to him. Hopefully the one razor blade would be enough if Nora could keep it, save it, use it, if and when the time came.

The hours ticked by with excruciating slowness. She knew Marie-Laure was waiting for…something. Some move to be made by Søren or Kingsley…or perhaps even Nora herself. Marie-Laure had put the pieces into play. Now she sat back and waited for someone else to take their turn. But who?

An hour after nightfall, Nora heard footsteps outside her room. She'd been hearing them all day…random squeaks of the hardwood, the slight creak of leather soles. She knew one of Marie-Laure's boys was out there making noise to scare her. It worked. With every sound she sat up straight as her heart hammered in her chest. She slept a little but not enough. Every sound the house made sent her into immediate fight or flight mode. The constant surges of adrenaline exhausted her. She wanted nothing more than to be at home in Søren's bed and to sleep for weeks, sleep until every moment in this house felt like it was nothing more than the absurdity of a dream, and when she woke up, she would tell Søren, "I had the craziest dream last night—your wife was still alive and she came for me…." And he would laugh and tell her to stop eating Cajun food before bed. By noon the last embers of the dream would have burned out entirely, and she'd remember nothing of the dream except that she'd had it.

Nora smiled at the thought as the door opened and Damon stood staring down at her on the floor.

This was no dream.

"Story time," he said. Nora stood up and reluctantly joined him in the hallway.

He followed behind her, his right hand in his pocket, his left hand resting like a silent threat on the back of her neck.

Deciding to test the waters, Nora cleared her throat and opened her mouth.

"Don't," he said before she could get a word out.

"Don't what?"

"Don't even bother. You can threaten me, flirt with me, bribe me all you want, it won't work."

"True love, then, is it? You and her?"

"Not even close."

"Do I get a hint?"

"Threaten me," Damon said, "and I'll laugh. Her dead husband made all his money smuggling drugs and guns. I used to work for him. He killed people for amusement when he got bored and he died a billionaire. No one you know is scarier than he was. No one you know is richer than she is. And as for the flirting, I've heard all about you. I've fucked Eastern European prostitutes with fewer miles on them than you. No thank you."

"I do have a lot of STDs. Most of them raging and fatal." Nora hoped she sounded slightly convincing with that. She didn't have anything but they didn't need to know that. She'd never been so grateful for her bad reputation in her life.

"I don't doubt it."

"What about the other guy? Any use bribing, fucking or threatening him?"

"No."

"Same reason as you?"

"You were right the first time."

Nora laughed mirthlessly.

"He's in love with her? Well, how sweet. I know a good priest if they decide to get married."

"I'm sure they'll send you the invite. It can be a double ceremony. Their wedding. Your funeral."

He pushed her hard through the door of Marie-Laure's bedroom, hard enough she almost hit the floor, but she managed a graceful recovery and remained on her feet, her back to the bed.

*"Très bien,"* Marie-Laure said from the bed. She sat in her nightgown and robe, her left foot propped up on a tissue as she painstakingly painted her toenails. "You're very graceful. Were you ever a dancer?"

"I can do a mean Davy Jones 'Daydream Believer' shimmy. But no formal training."

Marie-Laure shrugged. "Too bad. You're short and that's an asset for a ballerina. Not thin enough, though, and your breasts are too large."

"Mother Nature's a bitch."

Marie-Laure capped her polish and stretched her leg out on the bed. Even at fifty years old, she still retained her dancer's physique. She must work at it constantly to stay so lean and graceful. Marie-Laure might be thin and older than her, but Nora didn't doubt for one second that she was strong enough to seriously hurt her.

"Have a seat." Marie-Laure tapped the edge of the bed. She knew what was next and, sure enough, Damon brought out rope to bind her to the bedpost before leaving the two women alone in the room. "Did you have a nice day?"

Leaning back against the pillows, Marie-Laure gave her a broad innocent smile. One could almost believe they were nothing but two schoolgirls having a slumber party.

"Lovely day. Stared at the wall, stared at the ceiling, counted cobwebs." Nora pulled on her bonds—rope only. Thank God for small mercies.

"You've probably stared at a lot of ceilings in your life."

"Not too many. I like being on top. Except with Søren, and then it's a lot of floor staring. Unless I'm blindfolded."

"You have sex with my husband often?"

"I didn't know he was your husband at that time he and I were fucking. You're the one who faked your death. Can't blame me."

"I don't blame you. I blame him, and I blame my brother."

"They didn't know you were alive, either."

"I don't blame them for not knowing. That was the plan. I blame them for not caring."

Nora's blood momentarily turned to ice in her veins. She felt as though she was standing on the edge of a cliff, maybe even the very cliff Marie-Laure had supposedly fallen from. But this time it would be her who would fall off it if she wasn't careful.

"They did care," Nora said, weighing her words.

"That's not what you said earlier today. You said my revenge against them didn't work. And you promised me a story to prove it. I want this story of yours."

Fuck... Nora felt the wind rushing past her as the ground sped toward her. Marie-Laure had set a nice little trap and she'd fallen into it.

"I said your revenge didn't work because it didn't break up Kingsley and Søren. I never said they didn't care."

"It's the same thing to me. If my love for someone had killed my brother, I would never want to see that person again."

"Yes, I can tell how much you love Kingsley."

Marie-Laure leaned forward and rested her elbows on her legs. With her chin on her hand and a dangerous glint in her eyes, Marie-Laure only responded with four words.

"Tell me the story."

"You sure you want to hear a graphic narration of me having sex with your brother?"

"But of course. Leave us, Damon. She's shy."

Damon finished off Nora's knots and left them alone in the bedroom. Marie-Laure reached into the nightstand and pulled out a gun. She laid it by the lamp and leaned back against the pillows. A nice little taunt. The gun lay pointed at Nora. Nora ignored it.

"Get comfortable," Nora warned Marie-Laure. "This story, much like sex with Kingsley, takes a while."

Four years...that's how long Eleanor waited to have sex with Søren. Too long for her tastes but then again, knowing her, she would have let him have her the day they met. Stupid priest had scruples, however, and this weird idea that she should be fully mentally and emotionally prepared for what it meant to share his bed. He said it like that, too. *Share his bed*. So classy...respectful even. He never said anything about "fucking" her. He only swore when he wanted to deliberately provoke or shock someone. She, on the other hand, swore like a sailor with Tourette's syndrome. She never told Søren how much she liked the way he talked to her about their private life, how it made her feel like a lady to have sex discussed in such discreet civilized terms. Of course, it wasn't until they became lovers that she realized how much of a mindfuck that delicate talk of his was. Outside the bedroom, he was all euphemisms and elegance. Once she started "sharing his bed," she discovered the gentleman outside the bedroom turned almost savage inside it, inside her. Sex with Søren was raw, brutal and merciless, and she'd loved it, reveled in it, couldn't get enough of it, enough of him.

Three months after they'd become lovers, she lay across his strong stomach, spent from the beating he'd given her and bruised from the sex. She made the mistake of uttering a very dangerous sentence to a very dangerous man.

"I wish I had two of you," she said, dropping a kiss onto the center of his chest as she traced his rib cage with her fingertips. "I want this every night."

All she meant by it was that she loved him, that she loved being with him, submitting to him, seeing the real him that he kept hidden away from the world and who only came out at night.

But instead of laughing at her insatiable desire for him, teasing her about her libido that rivaled any teenage boy on earth, he simply said, "I'll speak to Kingsley."

Nora, then still Elle or Eleanor, sat up straight in bed and stared down at him.

"You're not kidding, are you, sir?"

"Of course I'm not."

She shook her head and tears filled her eyes.

"I belong to you," she whispered, and she put meaningful and desperate emphasis on the "you."

At that the hint of a smile appeared on the corner of Søren's perfect lips and within seconds she found herself flat on her back underneath him, her hands pinned over her head by his steel-strong arms.

"I'm a Jesuit," he reminded her. "We share everything in common."

Using his knees he pushed her thighs wide open and shoved two fingers inside her. As always her body responded to his touch even against her will.

"I don't want to be with anybody but you. I waited for you." She tried squirming away from him but he held her down hard and in place. There was nowhere to go.

"Kingsley's been waiting for you almost as long as I have." He lowered himself onto her and kissed her. At first she ignored the kiss, tried to pretend it wasn't happening, but his mouth was too insistent, her heart too willing. She gave into the kiss, gave into him. "Let's not keep him waiting."

So it was decided entirely without consulting her feelings on the matter that the two of them would spend an evening at Kingsley's the very next week. No amount of pouting and protesting would talk Søren out of it. Before they became lovers they'd talked at length about what her limits were. She had a hard time coming up with any. She knew he wouldn't shave her head or cut off her arms or stab her in the heart. So she'd told him that she trusted him, that she knew he would never push her past her breaking point.

"I will never take you anywhere you don't want to go," he promised, taking her hand in his, raising it to his lips to kiss her palm. "But there will be times you might not enjoy the trip there. Will you still go with me?"

She'd answered simply with "Anywhere." A mistake, possibly, because it appeared "anywhere" meant Kingsley's bedroom.

"You let him force you to have sex with my brother?" Marie-Laure interrupted, pulling Nora out of the past.

"Your use of 'let' and 'force' are a tiny bit contradictory," Nora reminded her. "Søren owned me. I was his property. I was his property because I let him own me. It was my choice to let him own me. Once he owned me, though, he *owned* me."

"You didn't want to be with Kingsley?"

"I didn't *want* to want to," she said, smiling. "I had this idea in my head that once you fell in love with someone and they loved you back, that was it. There was no one else, right? That's how it should be. Don't judge me. I was so young and foolish."

"You were in love."

"I am in love. Søren was kind enough to show me the folly of that sort of thinking early on. One person for your entire life? One? Ridiculous. Who needs that kind of pressure? Expecting someone to fulfill all your needs is blasphemy. You're expecting a human to be God for you."

"You have a strange theology. My husband let my brother rape you and you make it about love."

"Rape? Are you serious? Have you met your brother? I don't think he's physically capable of raping someone. He speaks and your panties spontaneously combust."

"You didn't want to be with him and my husband made you. That's not rape?"

"A rape victim can't say a single word to get her rapist to stop. I could have. I had my safe word, and I chose not to use it."

"Why not?"

"I didn't want to disappoint Søren."

"That's all?"

"Well…and admittedly, I'd always been attracted to King-sley."

"Was he attracted to you? My brother?"

"You sound skeptical." Nora raised her chin and stared down at Marie-Laure.

"I am. But I suppose I was wrong thinking my brother had good taste in women."

"He has amazing taste in women. He's probably fucked the thousand most beautiful women on earth."

"And you."

Nora laughed, low and throaty. Catfights…she didn't get into them often. The women in her world were usually too scared of her to even blink wrong in her direction. She might not play this game often but that didn't mean she didn't know how.

"You know what they used to call me in the Underground?"

"Tell me."

"The White Queen. The subs wore white. I wore it bet-ter than anyone. The other submissives were scared of me. They took orders from me like I was a Domme. Being Søren's property made me something special in that world. I was en-vied, feared and desired. And you better fucking believe your brother wanted me. And he wanted Søren. That night we went to his house…he got us both."

## 22
## THE ROOK

Grace didn't know the answer to Wesley's question. She was rather certain she didn't want to know the answer. Where was Kingsley going? Her heart tried to keep the answer a secret from her mind. If he was going where she thought there might be a chance he wouldn't come back. She hardly knew the man but it didn't matter. She didn't know how much more stress and fear she could live with before she simply broke down.

They returned to the house and Grace left Wesley and Laila talking in the living room. Lovely place, it reminded her of a small English manor she'd visited as a teenager on a school trip. She remembered wandering the halls of that elegant old mansion and thinking it was such a shame it had become a museum. It had been built for a family and a family should live in it.

Although she knew she shouldn't, Grace opened every door on the first and then the second floor. Her heart clenched when she saw a bedroom that obviously belonged to two little girls. Twin beds, side by side. Pale pink and white walls, everything the color of cotton candy. Over the left bed hung a painted sign. Byrony, it read in block letters. Over the right bed in cursive was the name Willa. On each bed sat a mountain of stuffed animals—lions and wolves, sock monkeys and smiling dolphins. Grace picked up a small brown dog and held him to her chest. She'd had one just like this as a child. Still had it somewhere in her parents' attic. She'd named him Bernard, "although he isn't a saint," she'd tell people, proud of her joke. How she wanted to have a room like this in her house someday—a tiny bed piled with toys with Zachary on story patrol every night. Knowing her husband, he'd read their son or daughter adult novels—Thomas Hardy or Virginia Woolf. At least they'd work to put their little one to sleep.

Grace ran a hand over her stomach and hated its flatness. She ran five miles four days a week, ate right, took her vitamins…and yet every month she failed to conceive. She'd prayed for a miracle, that God would heal the scar tissue inside her enough that she could have a baby. Now that prayer seemed so small, so selfish. Nora was trapped by a madwoman intent on revenge. She could only pray now that God was in the miracle-making mood today.

With reluctance, Grace put the dog back on the pile, and left the bedroom. She noticed a door at the end of the hall now open that she could have sworn was closed when she'd come into the girls' room. Grace walked to the door and saw that it didn't lead to a room but a staircase going up. She saw no light switch so in total darkness she ascended the stairs until she could go no farther. Running her hand over the dark door, she found a knob, opened it and discovered she'd come up to the roof of the house.

She stepped out from the landing and looked around. At

the farthest corner of the roof stood Søren, staring out into the nighttime forest that surrounded the property. Grace froze at the sight of him so silent and solemn. She should go back and leave him alone with his thoughts. But she'd been alone all day and knew she'd go out of her mind if she didn't get away from her own voice in her head.

Summoning her courage, she walked toward him and came to stand at his side. He held a steep glass of red wine in his hand, raised it to his lips and drank.

"Do you mind if I join you for a while?" Grace asked, suddenly fearful. Fearful of what, though? That he wouldn't want her company or that he would?

"Please stay. Your company would be most welcome."

"I don't know about that," she said with a sigh. "I can't stand to be around myself right now."

He turned his head from the dark forest before them and studied her face. His gaze felt intimate and penetrating, like he was trying to understand her more than simply see her.

"You've been crying."

Grace raised her hand to her face and ran her fingers under her eyes to wipe away the traces of tears mingled with mascara.

"Sorry. I must look a mess."

"No, you look beautiful. And troubled."

"Thank you," she said with a low and weary laugh. "You aren't put off by a woman's tears?"

"Hardly," he said, raising the glass to his lips and drinking. "I rather enjoy them under the right circumstances. I'm guessing, however, yours weren't of the variety I'm referring to."

"No, sadly," she said, almost blushing at the thought of how Søren would bring a woman to tears. "I made the foolish mistake of wandering into one of the children's rooms."

"You and Zachary are still trying to conceive?"

"Yes, actually. How did you know?" Had she been speaking to anyone else, Grace might have been embarrassed at broaching such a personal topic. For some reason she seemed like she could talk to him about anything and it would go no further than his own ears. Priest, she remembered. Of course.

"Eleanor told me. She wasn't spreading gossip, you should know. She asked me to pray a novena for you."

"She did?" Grace's heart clenched at the kindness.

"Eleanor is convinced I make God nervous and that He's more likely to take my calls than hers, as she says."

"So…you've prayed for me to conceive?"

"Novena. I've prayed for you to conceive nine times."

"Thank you." Grace nearly whispered the words. "Zachary wants to give up trying for a biological child. Says it's too hard on me. He's fine adopting, but I want to keep trying. But now that dream seems so selfish and small with Nora out there—"

"Don't, Grace. Don't think God isn't capable of giving you a child and bringing Eleanor back to us. He is infinitely powerful, after all. He can handle more than one item on His to-do list."

"I'll remember that." The night air ran its hands over her skin and Grace moved closer to Søren, instinctively seeking shelter. He didn't move away when her shoulder met his arm. "Although…something like this happens and I can't help but be a little grateful I'm childless. No child means no child for someone to take. People seem awfully fragile right now to me, the world terribly unsafe. Nora is someone's daughter and there she is out there somewhere and scared…she must be so scared."

Søren put an arm around her shoulders as the tears started to fall again. She huddled close to him, resting her head on his chest. She felt like a child now seeking the comfort of a father's arms.

"Eleanor," he began as he wrapped both his arms around

her, "is the bravest woman I know. She wasn't even afraid of me when she was only fifteen. And believe me, I did try to scare her."

"I would have been terrified of you. I *am* terrified of you."

"She wasn't. You know her first words she ever said to me...I remember them like yesterday. She said, 'You're kind of an idiot, you know that, right?'"

Grace laughed out loud and pulled back from his embrace.

"She said that to you?"

"She took exception to the fact that I didn't put a lock on my motorcycle. She said I was asking for someone to steal it. Considering that a week after that conversation she was arrested for stealing cars, she did know what she was talking about."

"Arrested for car theft? That naughty girl. I had no idea she'd been in that kind of trouble. I thought teenage girls got arrested for shoplifting purses and makeup."

"Eleanor does not do anything the normal way."

"And you loved her for it." Grace smiled up at him.

"I did. Utterly and unrepentantly. My heart was so torn after meeting her. Rent in two. I knew I should only love her like a father to a daughter, but her wildness and her beauty made it nearly impossible. I protected her, though, like a father. I always tried to protect her. And I always did. Until now."

Grace took another step back. She needed some space between her and Søren. Being in his arms felt preternaturally good, unreasonably safe. She wondered if this is what Zachary had felt with Nora—this strange pull toward someone she couldn't understand, who seemed almost alien. They had some kind of secret knowledge, both of them. Secret insight. They had seen things she couldn't imagine, Søren and Nora, knew things she would never understand. But how she wanted to see, wanted to understand....

"My heart is outside myself tonight and far away," Søren said, staring into the darkness.

"How far away?"

"Ten miles between here and Elizabeth's house. I could run it in an hour."

"I could run it in fifty-five minutes," she said, grinning up at him.

"Behave yourself. You're seventeen years younger than I am. Respect your elders," he said, clearly trying not to smile at her.

"If I don't will you turn me over your knee?"

Søren raised his eyebrow, and Grace blushed ear to ear.

"Good God, now you've got me doing it." She buried her face in her hands.

"Be glad Kingsley didn't hear that. He'd take you up on that offer."

He smiled as he spoke but she saw sorrow in his eyes, sorrow and fear.

"Where is Kingsley?"

"The last place I want him to be."

"He's trying to get Nora back."

Søren nodded.

"Both Kingsley and Eleanor are out there facing unknown terrors. I'm most content when they're both near to me."

"You love Kingsley?"

"I do. Does that shock you?"

"Not at all. He reminds me of Nora. Arrogant, cocky, dangerous, beautiful."

"Those two—they've twin spirits, although they'd deny it with their last breaths. Kingsley's parents died when he was fourteen. Eleanor's parents were beyond useless to her as a teenager."

"You were a father figure to both of them."

"In a way. And now I'm a father who'd give everything to have them both back safely."

"They will come back. You have faith I'll have my child someday. I have faith you'll have yours."

"Thank you. Until then…" He raised the glass and took another drink.

"I should have thought of that," she said, nodding at the wine. "Better than crying over a stuffed dog."

Søren smiled subtly and held out the glass to her.

"Take it. I shouldn't have any more."

Grace hesitated a moment before taking the wine from his hand. It seemed an unbearably intimate thing to drink after him. Still, she took a sip.

"Merlot. Very nice."

"Daniel has a decent cellar. His late wife, Maggie, was something of an oenophile."

"Then I'll drink it in memory of Maggie." She raised the glass for another drink.

"*Sláinte mhaith,*" Søren said, his pronunciation of the Celtic words so perfect even her Irish mother would have been impressed.

"Sure you don't want it? Happy to share."

"I've already had five glasses tonight."

"Five?" Grace repeated, aghast. "I'd be underneath a table in a coma after five glasses of Merlot." Four glasses equaled an entire bottle.

"I rarely drink this much. One glass a day at most."

"It's wonderful for occasional stress relief. If it was Zachary trapped in that house, I'd have to have an alcohol IV inserted in my arm."

"I usually find far pleasanter means to reduce my stress than alcohol."

Grace laughed as she took another deep drink of wine, willing it to go to her head as quickly as possible.

"I'm sure you can. A night with Nora must make for excellent therapy."

"You have no idea…." The smile that crossed his face was so amorous that Grace felt her knees nearly buckle. Potent wine. Must be the wine.

"I am a very happily married woman with a husband who's a spectacular lover. *And* I've read all of Nora's books. I think I have some idea."

"I've read her books, too."

"Scandalous," she teased. "A priest who reads erotica."

"Only Eleanor's."

"She's certainly my favorite author."

She sat on the ledge of the roof and put the forest to her back. She'd much rather look at Søren, anyway. Never in her life has she been attracted to blond men but something about him was so utterly arresting. Even at night he cast a shadow. Strange to see him like this—a white shirt and no Roman collar and yet still he seemed priestly to her, sacred.

"May I ask you a question?" Søren gazed down at her.

"Of course. Anything."

"Why don't you hate Eleanor?"

"I might need a lot more wine to answer that." She tried to laugh but it didn't quite come out. Søren waited, his eyebrow raised. "All right… My marital problems with Zachary began long before he met her."

"But they were lovers," he reminded her.

"I'm well aware of that. She hits on him every time they talk. I know this because she tells me my husband is being mean and won't put out for her anymore."

"And that's not infuriating?"

"It would be if I genuinely thought she was a threat. I think she would be heartbroken if Zachary and I broke up."

"She would be. She loves you both."

"She flirts with him and she flirts with me, and if given the chance I think she wouldn't say no to another night with him but it's only a game with her, it's play." Grace stopped talking when she realized what she'd said and to whom she said it. "I'm sorry. I'm sure the last thing you want to hear is about Nora flirting with—"

"Don't be sorry. I have never begrudged Eleanor her dalliances. The sacrifices she's made to be with me are so profound that I would be the worst of men if I demanded complete fidelity from her."

"I wish more people were as open-minded as you and Nora. A few of Zachary's friends, well, ex-friends now, hate me because I dated someone while we were separated. No matter how many times he tells them he was involved with someone else, too…boys will be boys but a woman who has sex with anyone other than her husband, that's an unforgivable sin."

"Not to me. And not to God, either. Eleanor and I have always had an open relationship, and it was entirely at my instigation. Because of what I am—"

"And what are you?"

He crossed his arms over his chest and stared down at her. She suddenly felt like a naughty schoolgirl about to get scolded.

"You know what I am, Grace."

"I know you're a sadist. That's what Nora says. And I also know you're a good man and a wonderful priest. Which she also told me."

Søren sighed and sat next to her on the roof ledge. She studied his profile as he weighed his words. It had been years since she'd taken pen to paper and written a poem. She'd been quite a good poet in her university days and had dreamed of making poetry her life's work. But marriage, her career, the real world, had taken that dream from her. Now she suddenly felt inspired to try to write again. She knew she would remember this quiet moment on this roof with this priest for the rest of her life. The still-forming memory fluttered about her head like a moth. She would net this night with words and pin it to paper so it would stay in place forever.

"There are those of our kind who play at sadism like a game. That might sound crass and sordid to you."

"My brother plays rugby. I'm familiar with the concept of inflicting pain as a game."

"They're the lucky ones. The ones who can play at it. The whistle blows, the game ends, they walk away. But for me… it's not a game. I can't walk away from it."

"Nora explained it to me a little. She said it's like being gay or straight. It's what you are instead of what you do."

"I'm glad she helped you understand. Not everyone does. It scares people. As it should. I would worry about someone who was blasé about the concept of hurting another person for pleasure."

"It must be terrifying, doing what you do."

"It can be. The greater the pain I inflict on someone, the greater my pleasure. It's a tightrope walk, a balancing act. There's always the fear of going too far, of falling off. And in such a situation, you don't fall off alone. You take the other person down with you."

"But that's what the safe words are for, right? To stop the fall?"

Søren nodded. "They help, the little safeguards we have. Eleanor and I have been together for so long she knows how far she can take me without me losing myself."

"Have you ever—" Grace tried to find the right words "—lost yourself?"

"Yes. Once with Eleanor shortly after we became lovers. She taunted me in play. I retaliated in earnest. In her shock she forgot that she had her safe word to stop me. I didn't stop."

Grace shivered as his voice dropped to not much more than a whisper. *I didn't stop...* She didn't want to know what he didn't stop doing. That was a secret she would let him keep.

"Any other times?" Grace brought the glass to her lips.

"Several. All with Kingsley."

Grace nearly choked on the wine. She swallowed hard and took a deep breath.

"With Kingsley? Really?"

"You seem surprised." She wasn't surprised. She was shocked and Søren seemed entirely amused by her shock.

"I thought you two were teenagers when you were together."

"We were. Although there have been a few occasions since then. Rare ones. They have to be rare."

"Why?"

Søren stopped speaking for a moment. He held out his hand. Grace laughed, handed him the wineglass and watched him drink. He returned the glass to her, slightly less full than it was before.

"Kingsley Edge...not his real name. Would you like to know his real name?"

"Very much."

"Kingsley Théophile Boissonneault."

Grace blinked.

"Can you spell that for me?"

"B-o-i-s-s-o-n-n-e-a-u-l-t." Søren spoke each letter with the French pronunciation. "As you can imagine, he was rather keen to divest himself of such a name when he settled in America."

"That is quite a mouthful."

"Not unlike the man himself."

Grace nearly dropped the glass, but she saw the glint of wicked amusement in Søren's eyes.

"You're doing it again." She pointed at him. "You're trying to play with my mind."

"I am and entirely without remorse."

"You're the one who's half-drunk. I'm the one who should be in control of this conversation."

"You've already forgotten what we were talking about."

"That is not true. You were…" She paused and retraced their conversational steps. The "mouthful" remark had blown her far off course. She would get back on it. "Kingsley. You were telling me why your *encounters,*" she said, trying for the most tactful word possible, "with Kingsley are rare."

"Good girl."

"Thank you," she said, basking in the praise. "And…?"

"Kingsley didn't choose the last name Edge at random. It wasn't an affectation. It wasn't a joke. It wasn't even a nickname. The choice of the last name 'Edge' is a warning."

"Warning of what?"

"Kingsley is a connoisseur of a certain style of BDSM known as edge-play. Eleanor keeps a running list of what she calls 'The lies kinky people tell vanilla people.' On that list are things like 'All scenes are prenegotiated.' And 'No, of course the floggers and singletails never break the skin.' And 'Yes, we all use safe words and the submissive is the one truly in control.'"

"None of that is true?"

"It is true…for some of us. For others, we play by different rules. With his clients and in his clubs, Kingsley is a great enforcer of the rules of safe play. Kingsley, the man in private, he prefers more dangerous games. No safe words, no safeguards. He is particularly fond of breath-play and rape-play."

Another chill passed through Grace, a chill that had nothing to do with the night air.

"Rape-play…that seems self-explanatory. Breath-play?"

"Choking," Søren said simply. "Erotic asphyxiation. I'll admit I've enjoyed the same activities but under much more tightly controlled circumstances. Blood-play for instance. It's by far my favorite form of sadism. And yet, Eleanor and I engage in it no more than once a year. She bathes before the cutting and we clean her wounds and mine thoroughly after. No safe words necessary during because if she says stop, I stop. With Kingsley…you can beat him bloody, brutalize him, violate him in every way, and he won't try to stop you. He has no limits. I gave him a safe word to use when we were teenagers. He never once uttered it, and I broke him into a thousand pieces simply for the pleasure of putting him back together just to break him apart again."

Grace inhaled deeply and let the words sink in. She knew she should be horrified, disgusted…but nothing about this man or his confession created any reaction in her other than fascination and compassion. Even desire, if she dared admit that to herself.

"You see," Søren continued, "everyone instinctively understands that the submissive partner in the scene should feel safe and be safe. But it's often forgotten that the Dominant should also feel safe and secure. When I'm intimate with Eleanor, it's difficult to remain self-aware, but I can. If I start to forget myself she reminds me who I am."

"How so?"

"She's rarely used her safe word with me. Almost never. But if she needs me to stop for a moment she'll tell me. If something is starting to go too far, she'll pull me, pull us both, back from the edge. But not Kingsley. It's far too easy to forget myself with Kingsley, far too easy to go to the edge with him and fall over. And since I love him and would rather not be the architect of his destruction and therefore mine..."

"You don't touch him because you love him."

"The self-control required to hold back and not cause harm is often exhausting, especially when losing control is so intoxicating—far more so than even five glasses of wine. That's why Eleanor and I have had an open relationship from the beginning. Sometimes a few days or a week is necessary to recover from a night with me."

"So if she wants sex without welts and bruises, she goes to someone else."

"And if I want to paint a fresh canvas with welts and bruises, I go to someone else."

"You have other lovers?" Grace asked, utterly shocked. She knew Nora did, but from what she'd said, Søren was faithful to her alone.

"Eleanor and Kingsley are the only two lovers I've had since becoming a priest. But there are several other women who submit to me when Eleanor's out of town or needs a few days to heal."

"Only women?"

"Yes. I'm more careful with women than I would be with a man. And quite frankly, Kingsley is the only man who I've ever been attracted to."

"So she sleeps with others and you beat others?"

"An arrangement that works beautifully for us. Or did."

"She loves you. Whatever she had to work out with Wesley, it doesn't change that fact. Any more than me sleeping with Ian or Zachary sleeping with Nora didn't change the fact that he and I were married, that we loved each other and that we belong together."

"That's why you don't hate Eleanor?"

"Exactly. Because I hated Zachary like I was supposed to."

She took another drink of the wine. If she was going to talk about her separation from Zachary, she'd need all the liquid courage she could get. "That's why the wife always hates the other woman. It's good for her to hate the other woman. The other woman—" Grace stretched her arm far out in front of her "—is other. She's not even a person. We can heap all our hatred, all our disdain, on her even though deep down we know she's not the one to blame. She's the scapegoat."

"Did you know the scapegoat is an Old Testament concept?"

"I had no idea."

"From Leviticus. The sins of the Israelites were symbolically placed onto the head of a goat and then the goat was driven into the wilderness never to be seen again. It was a form of atonement."

"That's what it is exactly. You put all the sins of the husband and wife, of the marriage, onto the head of the other woman. You pray she will go away forever and take all that misery with her and leave your husband behind."

"You wanted to reconcile with Zachary?"

"Yes. So much. Which is why, at first, I was angry with everyone but him. There were dozens of other women. The job was another woman I blamed. Zachary's boss, John-Paul Bonner. I blamed him. He knew we were having problems and he took advantage of that. America…she was the trollop that had seduced my husband away from me."

"The whole country?"

Grace grinned. "Yes. I blamed the entire country. Typical bitter wife behavior. And then he mentioned Nora Sutherlin on the phone, one of his writers, he said. But he said it with heat. I looked her up, saw a picture of that beautiful woman. Then I hated her. But that didn't work for me, the scapegoat game. The sins were still there in the marriage. They couldn't be driven out so easily simply by blaming J. P. Bonner or Nora or the entire bloody country. I knew that if I wanted Zachary back, and I did, I couldn't blame anyone but us. Our problems were my fault. Our problems were his fault. Our problems were our fault, not hers."

"It takes a wise person to realize this. I've counseled many married couples who never see the truth of that. They blame everyone but the real culprit."

"I didn't want to see the truth of it. But I had to. Made a fatal mistake when I came rushing to New York."

"You met Eleanor."

Grace raised the glass in a salute.

"I met Eleanor. And instead of the 'other woman,' she was Nora to me. Beautiful, intelligent, compassionate, understanding Nora. She's impossible to hate. My God, I showed up at her house like a madwoman hunting down my husband, and she gave me tea and told me Zachary was still in love with me. You asked me why I don't hate her. All I wanted was my husband back. I got him back. That's all any wife wants."

Søren stood up and looked away from her, looked into the darkening woods around them. And as if someone else had said them, Grace heard her own words.

*She's the scapegoat… We know she's not the one to blame… All I wanted was my husband back…that's all any wife wants.*

"Marie-Laure," Grace said as a terrible realization dawned on her. "She doesn't want Nora at all, does she?"

At first Søren said nothing to her question.

"No," he finally answered.

"She would have kept Laila if Nora hadn't volunteered to stay. She didn't care if it was your lover or your niece she had as long as it was someone you loved."

Søren's mouth tightened into a hard line.

"What did the note say?"

"It doesn't matter."

"It does. What did it say? Tell me, please."

"It said something to the effect of 'Dear Husband, Have you missed me? I've certainly missed you. I have someone here you love. If you want this loved one of yours to keep breathing, I would highly suggest you and I mend this rift between us. It's a big decision. Take your time. But don't take too long. You have until noon on Friday. Love always, Your devoted wife. P.S. Tell my brother, Love thy sister.'"

Grace couldn't speak for a moment. She had to let his words sink in.

"She wants you," Grace said at last.

"She does."

"How were you supposed to find her? I know Laila told us but what if she didn't recognize the room?"

"'Love thy sister…' Last week someone broke into my sister Elizabeth's house and wrote those words on my childhood bedroom wall in ashes."

"You knew from the note where Nora was, not from Laila and her locket. Marie-Laure wanted you to know."

"She wants me to come to her. If anyone but me goes, she'll kill Eleanor."

"You can't go. This woman has killed before. Wesley told me she murdered a teenage girl. She'll kill you, too."

"Or worse."

"What's worse than being killed?"

Søren held out his hand and Grace gave him the glass of wine. He raised it to his lips and drank it down in one swallow.

Grace waited. Søren never answered the question.

# 23
# THE QUEEN

In all her twenty years on God's green earth, Eleanor had never been so nervous. Not even waiting for the judge to hand down a sentence on her for five counts of grand theft auto had been as terrifying as the prospect of sex with someone other than Søren. She'd met Søren, and her teenage plan to lose her virginity as soon as humanly possible hit a six-foot-four, blond wall of celibacy. No amount of flirting, begging or attempted seduction could entice Søren into divesting her of her virginity at age fifteen or sixteen, seventeen…eighteen. She had high hopes for nineteen but even then he held back. Years later she finally realized what he'd been doing by making her wait so long. He'd given her a reason to leave him. A very good reason. He loved her enough to let her go even before he'd had her. And she'd loved him enough to wait for him.

Waited for him she had, and now she wasn't a virgin anymore. Her first night with Søren felt as natural as breathing, so natural that she couldn't imagine that she'd ever feel comfortable being with anyone else. His hands belonged on her, his mouth on her mouth. He was the only man she wanted inside her...but Søren was adamant, unyielding.

"Fine, I'll do it," she'd finally said after arguing with him about it for an hour that night.

"Of course you will."

"But I won't like it."

At that Søren had laughed and such a laugh that goose bumps had risen on her arms.

"This is Kingsley we're talking about, Eleanor. You'll like it whether you want to or not."

With those ominous words ringing in her ears, Eleanor entered Kingsley's town house behind Søren. Always she walked behind him when in submission. She walked behind him, she would speak only when spoken to, she wore her hair up as requested, wore white whenever they were together as a couple in Kingsley's world. For all the restrictions on her, she loved those moments most—the evenings at Kingsley's or the club, the few safe places she could be seen with Søren and know that everyone knew she was his property.

They found Kingsley in the front parlor sitting in an armchair wearing a black suit vaguely reminiscent of the Regency era and his black riding boots. He had a book in one hand and a glass of wine in the other. She couldn't remember if she'd ever seen Kingsley simply sitting and reading before. Kingsley was the King of the Underground. He never simply sat and did nothing. If he wasn't on the phone he was in a meeting. If he wasn't in a meeting he was in a beating. Strange that she'd seen the man top and fuck a woman before but seeing him with a book on his knee and silver-rimmed eyeglasses on seemed more intimate, more revealing. Kingsley Edge, the man of secrets and mysteries, wore reading glasses.

He looked up from his book—*Les Trois Mousquetaires*—
and met her eyes from across the room. His dark, shoulder-
length hair had a bit of a wave to it, and every time she saw it
unbound, she fought the urge to run her fingers through it.

"So glad you could make it," Kingsley said, casual and deb-
onair as ever. "Wine?"

He spoke only to Søren, who poured himself a glass and sat
on the chaise longue. He tapped his thigh and Eleanor knelt
on the floor and waited at his feet. Resting her chin on his
knee, she listened in silence as the two men exchanged pleasantries. They spoke in French to each other most of the time,
even in front of her. They'd always done that from the very
first day she'd been in their presence. They rattled on and on
in French while she sat there not understanding a word they
said. Funny how hard it was to distinguish "Dominant" behavior from "asshole" behavior most of the time.

"Is your Little One in a mood to play tonight?" Kingsley
switched back into English. Eleanor didn't even look at him.
If she looked at him, she might smile and that would ruin
everything.

"No, she's in a mood to play martyr tonight."

"No martyrs allowed in my bed. Only satyrs."

"Try telling her that."

"May I speak to her alone for a moment?"

"Of course. I'll see you upstairs." Søren tapped the end of
her nose lightly. Always he reserved his most affectionate advances when she was least in the mood to enjoy them. Again…
Dominant and asshole… She was starting to think those two
words should be in the thesaurus together.

Søren left the room and Eleanor remained on the floor
awaiting orders.

"You may sit," Kingsley said as he took off his glasses and
set them on the side table.

"I am sitting, *monsieur.*"

"On the chair."

Eleanor moved from the floor to the chair and crossed her legs at the ankles. The heels of her shoes reverberated off the marble floor.

"You're nervous."

"What gave it away?" Eleanor forced her feet to rest firmly on the floor. The shaking continued but only inside her.

"You don't have to be nervous, *ma chérie.*"

"You're going to fuck me tonight."

"More than once."

"And that shouldn't make me nervous?"

"You've been fucked before."

"Only by him."

"If letting him fuck you doesn't make you nervous, nothing should."

"So—" she paused to laugh "—you might have a point there."

Kingsley set his book aside, stood up and joined her on the sofa. He took her hand in his and rubbed her fingers.

"Your fingers are like ice."

"I'm terrified."

"No need for terror. All stops with a word. You know that."

"I know but still…I don't know."

He gave her a smile and it felt like a gift. She saw a person in the smile, a person with a heart even if he tried to hide it.

"He was destined for the Jesuits, you know. Even in school, I saw it. I didn't want to see it but I did. You like his motorcycle? The Jesuits, they hold all in common. He had to beg permission to keep his motorcycle otherwise he'd have to give it to the order to be sold. Everything he owns, he doesn't. It's the order's or the church's. You, *chérie, you* are the only thing he owns. You understand?"

"Then why does he want to give me away?"

"Because you he can take back."

He raised his hand to her face to wipe off a tear she hadn't noticed falling.

"Elle, I know you understand what he is. We both know being with him exacts a certain toll on a person."

"He has to play hard to get hard, I know that. I'm okay with that. More than okay."

"But will you always be? Sometimes you might want the pleasantries of sex without the associated pain that comes from spending a night with him."

"I have no interest in having vanilla sex with anybody," she said, meaning every word. One night with Søren had ruined the idea of vanilla sex for her forever. How could she ever enjoy something so banal after discovering the primal, fearsome power of kink?

"I am certainly not talking about vanilla sex." He brought her hand to his lips and kissed her fingertips. "But rest assured, there are other games to be played, ones equally savage and sensual but without the aftermath. He can't show you that world, but I can…if you'll allow it."

Eleanor had looked at him then, looked at him for a long time. And she looked at him because she realized in that moment, even though she'd known him for years and considered him a friend, she didn't know who he was.

"What are you?" she asked, not sure she knew what she meant. "To him, I mean. I know you're friends, and I know you've known each other a long time and I know about *her*… but there's more, isn't there?"

Kingsley gave a soft chuckle, one that made the hair on her arms stand up.

"You're smart," he said, and although it was a compliment, it didn't sound like one.

"I'm more than smart. I'm not stupid."

"You're standing at the edge of a rabbit hole. Are you sure you want to fall down it?"

"I'll trade you my hole for your hole."

Kingsley laughed then, a laugh of pure surprise.

"You…" He pointed his finger at her. "You are more than you seem."

"I could say the same about you."

She held out her hand and he pulled her off the sofa and straight into his arms. In seconds he had her back to the wall, his thigh pushing between her legs, and his mouth at her mouth.

With a dark-eyed smile he looked at her a moment before meeting her lips with his. The kiss started off slowly…gently… even carefully, as if Kingsley knew she teetered on the verge of spooking like a startled horse. She enjoyed the kiss, the skill of the lips, the taste of his wine-tinged tongue on hers. But still…this wasn't Søren kissing her, but Kingsley. She'd kissed others and felt terrible about it. How was this okay? Kissing another man? How was this not cheating? As if reading her worries, Kingsley pulled back long enough to whisper, "He wants this for both of us…."

"Why?"

Kingsley gave her a seductive grin, one that nearly set her to shivering again.

"What father doesn't want his children to play nice together? Come…let's go play nice."

She took his proffered arm like a lady being led to a waltz, and they said nothing on their way to Kingsley's bedroom.

Play nice, Kingsley said. Play… Nothing to be afraid of… It's only a game, she told herself over and over again.

Kingsley opened the door to his bedroom and she saw the dark red room illuminated by dozens of pale yellow taper candles. At the end of the bed stood Søren holding something wrapped around his hand. Tonight he'd dressed incognito—black pants, black shirt open at the neck. When he opened his fingers a dozen leather tongues of the flogger lapped at his leg.

Only a game.

Game on.

Kingsley left her side and walked to Søren.

"She's in a better mood now," Kingsley said, divesting himself of his jacket. Underneath the jacket he wore a white shirt and a black vest, intricately embroidered with silver thread. "She'll be in an even better mood once we're done with her."

"Kingsley, remind me…didn't we have a dream like this once," Søren said as he raised his hand and crooked a finger at her. As slowly as she could without getting scolded, she came to stand in front of him. Her white collar sat on the end of the bed. Søren picked it up and buckled it around her neck without even looking in her eyes. He acknowledged only Kingsley's presence as Kingsley only acknowledged his.

"Black hair and green eyes…pale like you, dark hair like me…"

"And wilder than the both of us together," Søren finished. "How nice when dreams come true."

"*Oui, mon ami.* Although she doesn't seem particularly wild at the moment."

"Wait and see. She might surprise you."

Eleanor came this close to screaming at them both. Had no one ever told them it was rude to talk about someone in third person as if she wasn't standing right in front of them? But she remembered her training and kept her mouth shut… at least for the moment.

"Let's begin, then, *oui?* Who first?"

"You can decide," he said to Kingsley, so nonchalant as if they were simply picking a wine for dinner.

"Ahh...better idea." Kingsley reached into the pocket of his trousers and pulled out a coin. "We'll let the coin decide tonight. Heads or tails."

"We win both ways." Søren ran a hand from her lips to her hips where he lingered long enough to give her an insinuating slap on the bottom. Heads or tails indeed. Staring at these two beautiful condescending, infuriating men who talked about her like she wasn't even in the room made her want to...something. Scream? Cry? Slap them both? What was it she wanted to do to them?

Kingsley gave Søren a wink before he flipped the coin. The coin came down and Eleanor snatched it out of the air before it landed on Kingsley's palm. The act had been unpremeditated, unplanned, and she saw from the looks on their faces, she'd managed to surprise them both.

"Heads," she said without even looking at the coin. She tossed it over her shoulder and dropped to her knees in front of Kingsley. He opened his pants and Eleanor took him deep into her mouth.

Now she knew exactly what she wanted to do to those two beautiful condescending, infuriating men....

She wanted to fuck their brains out. Both of them.

*"Mon Dieu,"* she heard Kingsley saying from above her.

"I told you so," was Søren's only reply.

Eleanor had only ever done this to Søren but he'd called her a natural. More than a natural, he'd even once joked she was something of a siren—the things she could do with her mouth would blow any man off course. The soft gasps escaping Kingsley's lips and his hand clinging to the bedpost for support seemed to reinforce that assessment of her skills and her enthusiasm for the task.

It wasn't as bad as she thought it would be. She had always been attracted to Kingsley, fascinated by him, feared and desired him. And he tasted amazing in her mouth. It was strange, though, going down on someone other than Søren. When she did this to him, he always held her so hard she'd have a bruise on her back at the nape of her neck the next morning. She thought of those bruises as her souvenirs, a little black-and-blue reminder of the previous evening's pleasures. But Kingsley had threaded his fingers through her hair and cupped her head, giving only the gentlest of encouragements. Strange, definitely. Not what she was used to. But definitely not bad. Not bad at all.

After a few minutes, Kingsley snapped his fingers in her ear and Eleanor pulled away and rested back on her hands.

"Now do you understand?" Søren asked over Kingsley's shoulder as they both looked down at her waiting on the floor.

"If I didn't before, I do now." Kingsley gave her his hand and helped her to her feet. But the chivalry ended there. Kingsley pushed her over the end of the bed and yanked her skirt to her hips. Per Søren's instructions, she'd worn no underwear. With her face buried in the red silk sheets, she couldn't tell whose fingers entered her from behind. "She's wet."

"Of course she is," Søren said.

"Of course I am," Eleanor said from the bed. *"Monsieur."*

"She's rather...what is the word I'm looking for? Enthusiastic? Ardent?"

"Horny," Eleanor supplied.

"And talkative, too." Kingsley sounded annoyed but annoyed in that way only a Frenchman could be annoyed. Annoyed and aroused at the same time. "We'll have to gag her if she keeps this up."

Eleanor fell silent immediately. She hated being gagged, hated being blindfolded. When gagged she couldn't crack jokes to annoy Søren like she loved to do. And what woman spending the night with two such beautiful men would ever want to be blindfolded?

"That's better. Good girl," Søren said as he ran his hand over her bare thighs. "Less talking. More moaning."

"Moaning...I like that sound of that." Kingsley dug his fingers deeper into her. "Let's see how much we can make her moan, shall we?"

"After you."

Something hit her hard across the backs of her thighs. Long and thin—a crop or a cane. Didn't matter, they both hurt like fuck. Again and again it came down and set the back of her body on fire.

Finally it stopped and she sagged in relief against the bed.

"You were right," Kingsley said, running his hand over her burning skin. "She can take pain."

"I've only known one person who could take more."

Kingsley laughed then, a warm intimate laugh that told her Søren hadn't merely told a joke, he'd told an inside joke, one only Kingsley understood.

She wasn't given much time to recover. Kingsley gripped her by her white leather collar and yanked her to her feet. He grasped her by the back of her neck and brought his mouth down onto hers for a bruising kiss.

She kissed back just as hard, feeling her hunger rising with each liberty Kingsley took with her. She'd never dreamed it would be so erotic to be used by another man while her own lover watched and helped. But Søren knew...he knew she would love this. That's why he'd ordered it, why he had ignored her protests and her objections. The man knew her better than she knew herself. One of these days she'd learn to trust him.

As they kissed, Kingsley unbuttoned her blouse and pulled it out of her tight white skirt. He unhooked her bra and dragged it down her arms, letting it drop to the floor. He cupped her breasts, caressed them and toyed with her nipples. He pinched one hard and she retaliated by biting down onto his bottom lip.

*"Merde,"* he cried, pulling back. He wiped his bottom lip and blood came off on his hand. Eleanor braced herself for his anger, but anger wasn't what she saw in his eyes…not at all.

"I knew you two would get along," Søren said.

Kingsley looked at Søren as Eleanor waited, half-naked and nervous. Something seemed to pass between them as Søren studied the blood on Kingsley's bottom lip.

"I told you that's no submissive you found for yourself," Kingsley said. "Your little kitten is going to grow up to be a tiger."

"Even more reason to tame her now." Søren winked at Kingsley and Eleanor saw something in that wink she didn't quite understand, but whatever it was, the way Kingsley and Søren looked at each other made her body temperature shoot up about ten degrees.

Kingsley came up to her again and faced her. Only a single drop of blood still remained on his lip.

"Lick it off," he ordered. Eleanor stood on her toes to reach him. With a flick of her tongue she lapped off the blood. Kingsley's eyes half-closed with naked desire. "Keep kissing."

He raised his hand and opened his collar more. Eleanor kissed his chin, his neck, under his ear, his neck and throat.

"Bite."

She dug her teeth into the graceful tendon between neck and shoulder.

"Harder."

She dug her teeth in hard enough he flinched. After the flinch came a groan, barely restrained. Not of pain nor of pleasure but pain in the pleasure, pleasure in the pain.

As she kissed and bit her way slowly across his neck and

shoulders, Kingsley ran his hands possessively over her back, her breasts and her arms.

"We will both be inside you tonight," he whispered as he raised her chin with one finger.

"I know. That's the plan, right? Wouldn't be a threesome if you didn't both fuck me?"

He gave her one last kiss, this one almost tender. He followed up the kiss with a smile, one utterly terrifying.

"You misunderstand. I mean we'll both be inside you tonight...at the same time."

All gentleness and tenderness ended at that moment. He grabbed her by the back of the neck and steered her to the bed. Søren waited with rope cuffs in his hands. He wrapped the cuffs around one wrist and threw the end over the wrought-iron bar of Kingsley's canopy-style bed. He cuffed her other wrist and pulled the rope tight. Now she stood facing the bed, the front of her thighs pressing against the mattress, her arms tied high over her head.

She watched as Kingsley walked to the opposite side of the bed and pulled off his shoes and socks. He unbuttoned his vest and shirt before crawling across the sea of red silk toward her. He straddled her thighs so that she stood trapped between his open legs. With both hands he stroked her breasts, her chest and stomach.

"He's going to beat you now," Kingsley said before pausing to give each nipple a long, slow, deep kiss.

"You did say you wanted me to moan, *monsieur.*"

"That's not why you're going to moan. He's going to beat you...I'm going to eat you."

At that she felt the first lash of the flogger onto her back. She gasped from the sudden shock of pain even as the things Kingsley did to her nipples sent shock waves spiraling deep into her core. The flogger came down again and again. It bit at her back with a dozen fangs while Kingsley kissed and licked every inch of her chest. Søren paused only long enough to switch to a harder flogger and, in that moment, Kingsley rolled onto his back, spun around so that his head lay off the end of the bed at her hips, lifted her knee onto the bed and buried his tongue inside her.

Eleanor's body went to war with itself. Pleasure versus pain…with every passing moment, one would top the other. Pain dominated the pleasure until the pleasure threatened to take over her whole being. She knew she moaned and moaned loudly as they'd predicted. In the back of her mind she could even hear herself. Witty, articulate, intelligent—all words that had been used to describe her a thousand times. Now these two men and their desires had reduced her to a cat in heat moaning for relief.

"Please…" She panted the word and didn't know what she pleaded for. Relief…release…

The flogging stopped even as Kingsley continued to lap between her legs, licking and teasing her with his lips and tongue. She felt like every drop of blood in her body had pooled in her clitoris. She would die if she didn't come soon.

Søren pressed his naked chest into her back.

"Not yet," he whispered in her ear. "Not quite yet."

She could have cried from disappointment but for the erotic torture Kingsley continued to inflict on her.

"If you don't mind, Kingsley," Søren said with an air of the nonplussed gentleman.

*"Pas de tout,"* he said as he pulled away from Eleanor and resumed his prior seated position in front of her. "Allow me."

Eleanor whimpered as Kingsley raised the front of her skirt and tucked the hem into the waistband. He slipped a hand between her legs and penetrated her with his middle finger. He wore a silver ring with a fleur-de-lis signet on that hand. She could feel the cold metal pressing against her burning clitoris. She waited for another finger or even two…the more the merrier. She was so wet she could have taken his whole hand with a little patience. But no…only the one finger. He pulled his hand toward him and Eleanor cried out as her inner muscles spasmed hard as he stretched her open. Then she felt something else…Søren opening his pants. And then he started to enter her from behind. Slowly, inch by inch, he filled her… they filled her, both of them—Søren sharing her body with Kingsley's finger.

She'd never felt so filled before, so open. Søren thrust into her with torturous slowness as Kingsley moved his finger in tandem. She couldn't say what aroused her more—that Kingsley and Søren were both inside her at once, or that Kingsley was touching Søren.

She might have taken a few seconds to decide the answer to that question but Kingsley then decided to bring his other hand to her, and start stroking her clitoris.

"Now you can come, Little One," Søren whispered into her ear. "Come for Kingsley. Come for me."

When she came she came hard, her vaginal muscles contracting wildly around both Søren and Kingsley. As the spasms fluttered and faded, she leaned back against Søren's chest and sighed.

"Don't be mad, sir," she said to Søren, "but I totally came for me."

He laughed then, a deep pure laugh of utter happiness. A beautiful wide-open laugh. She wanted to hear it every day of her life.

"Oh, very well," he said, kissing her as he cupped her breasts from behind, "but the next one is for us."

"Promise."

"She might not have come for me…" Kingsley said as he

pulled his finger out of her. "But she did come *on* me." He raised his arm and, in the candlelight, Eleanor could see a wet stain on Kingsley's cuff.

"Very nice," Søren said, impressed.

"I'll pay for the dry cleaning," Eleanor promised.

"Never. I'm never washing this shirt again." He sounded like he meant it.

Søren untied her from the bed, and her arms fell heavy to her sides. She wobbled a little on her heels, light-headed from the orgasm and the restraints. Søren caught her up in his arms. Kingsley pulled back the covers and Søren laid her down. He unzipped her skirt and pulled it off her hips. As he undressed her, Eleanor watched Kingsley. His eyes moved from her to Søren and back to her. She saw desire in his dark eyes but not only for her.

When he'd stripped her of everything but her white high heels, Søren pulled her into the bed. She lay on top of him, her back to his chest. He draped her legs over his thighs and held her arms down by her sides. With his body alone he held her in bondage as Kingsley crawled between her knees and kissed her from her hips to her breasts to her mouth. When their lips met he pushed inside her. She'd had to fight one moment of panic when she looked up and saw Kingsley's face over her and not Søren's. But the pleasure consumed her. This wasn't making love or even sex. Kneeling between her legs, Kingsley fucked her and he fucked her harder than she'd ever been fucked. She came with her eyes closed and only after, when she opened them again, did she see Kingsley staring down, but not at her.

Slowly, Kingsley pulled out of her and started to undress. Søren left her on the bed while he undressed, then lay next to her left side. Kingsley was at her right. Søren brought her leg over his hip and entered her. Face-to-face, no restraints tying her down... Had they ever had sex like this before? Not that she remembered. Usually he put her on her stomach or bent her over the bed if no bondage was involved. During face-to-face sex, her hands were almost always tied to the bed. The beating had even been mild compared to their usual level of pain he brought her to. Something about Kingsley being with them heightened Søren's arousal as much or more than sadism did. Did Søren enjoy seeing her with another man that much? Or was there something else?

As he moved in her, Eleanor let herself simply enjoy the presence of him inside her, the taste of his mouth on her lips, the scent of skin—winter, always winter. She'd almost forgotten Kingsley was there until she felt a hand that didn't belong to Søren roving over her side, sliding over her hips and down her thighs.

"Thank you." Søren kissed her neck right under her ear.

"For what?"

"Trusting me."

"I do trust you, sir."

"How much?" he asked, a dark glint of amusement shining in his eyes.

"Try me," she challenged.

"Dangerous words."

"That's why I said them, sir."

Søren answered her challenge by rolling them both onto their sides. He dragged her leg over his hip and kept moving in her. She felt Kingsley's hand caressing her from her neck to the small of her back. She relaxed into the touch and the hypnotic rhythm of Søren moving inside her. When she stiffened at the cold liquid on her and started to protest, Søren shushed her with a kiss and a hand on her face tracing her cheekbone.

"For me?" he asked.

She answered with a nod and buried her head against his

chest as Kingsley began to push inside her. Eleanor whimpered in the back of her throat as both men pushed into her at once. Her first experience with anal had been horrific, but since then she'd come to love it. It was the height of sexual intimacy to her and Søren seemed to love it almost as much as she did. Maybe even more. But she'd never been penetrated anally and vaginally at the same time. She clung to Søren in need and fear. She felt filled beyond belief with both of them inside her. Her fingernails dug deep into Søren's back. Søren took her hand from around his neck and pushed it onto Kingsley's thigh.

"Him," he breathed against her lips, and Eleanor scratched hard into Kingsley's leg, hard enough she knew she broke the skin. Kingsley gasped as the pace of his thrusts increased. Receiving pain seemed to turn Kingsley on as much as it turned Søren on to give it.

Eleanor breathed deep as her climax built again. Kingsley's hand wrapped around her hip and found her clitoris. She'd never known pleasure like this before. It consumed her, devoured her, swallowed her whole. She gave in to it, surrendering herself entirely. Never in her life had she felt so wanton, so shameless. She was nothing but a body that existed solely to be used for the pleasures of men. In that moment she embraced that purpose like the temple prostitutes of ancient times, spreading for the gods, men and beasts alike, for inside her body the three became one.

When she came, the climax gripped her stomach with iron claws and she shuddered for what felt like an eternity in Søren's arms. She didn't even notice either of them coming inside her, so lost as she was in her own ecstasy. Only when she lay on her back in the bed, emptied out, did she feel the wetness pouring out of her and dripping onto her thighs and the sheets.

Eyes were on her then and she knew both of them waited

for her reaction. At first she only breathed, her eyes half-closed. But something welled up inside her, a powerful wave of emotion, and for whatever reason, whatever wonderful strange unnamable reason, she started to laugh. It bubbled up to the surface, lifting her heart so high she felt that she'd come off the bed. And two other laughs joined her own until a symphony of laughter filled the room to bursting. Søren pulled her close and kissed her deep.

*"Jeg elsker dig, min lille en,"* he said into her lips.

"You have no idea how much it turns me on when you speak Danish," she answered, still laughing.

"Of course I do. Sleep now for a while."

"Where are you going?"

Søren looked over her shoulder and she turned to see him meeting Kingsley's eyes.

"Wine," Kingsley said. "We're going for wine."

Wine…of course. They both loved their wine. A glass of red, no doubt. Or two. Wouldn't take them long to drink it; she might as well sleep as ordered.

She settled into the bed. Kingsley and Søren pulled on their pants and shirts, not bothering to tuck anything in. They both looked so roguish, so dashing, in their disheveled clothes.

Hurry back, she thought but didn't say aloud. Hurry back could be construed as an order. They gave the orders. She took them. Oh, how she took them.

They'd arrived at Kingsley's house at midnight. Always safer to travel at night when the likelihood of an evening emergency call had passed. More than a few evenings had been lost by Søren being called away to attend to one of his parishioners. Every hour they spent together they stole. No wonder Søren had wanted her and Kingsley to share this night together. Perhaps in the future, when the church called Søren away from her, she could come here and not have to sleep alone.

But now she slept alone as Kingsley and Søren went to drink their wine.

They never got the wine.

"So what happened?" Marie-Laure interrupted. "No wine in the house?"

Nora sighed as Marie-Laure's question ripped her out of the story. How she longed to stay in that memory of the night the seeds of the woman who would become Nora Sutherlin were sown in Kingsley's bed.

"Oh, plenty of wine in the house. Kingsley has a well-endowed cellar."

"What happened then, after my brother and my husband had both violated you?"

"I don't know," Nora admitted, hating her ignorance on the matter. "Not everything, anyway."

"But you know something."

"I know something."

"Tell me what you know."

Nora looked Marie-Laure dead in the eyes. This woman didn't deserve these stories she told her, and for no reason other than to save her own life would Nora reveal such beautiful secrets that rightly belonged only to Kingsley, Søren and her. She'd never told Wesley any of this. She'd told Michael about Søren and Kingsley, because she understood the boy needed to know he wasn't alone. Wesley would have been horrified by it all, by the thought of Nora getting fucked by two men at once. He would have considered it, as Marie-Laure said, a violation, something disgusting and vile that only women in pornos allowed men to do to them. But that wasn't why she hadn't told him any of these stories. They were too private, too special, too sacred, to share even with him.

Nora sighed heavily and silently prayed Kingsley and Søren would forgive her.

"Søren and Kingsley didn't get the wine. They had gone to another room and fucked. I knew it when they came back to bed."

"My brother told you?"

"No."

"My husband told you?"

"No."

"Who told you, then?"

"The bruises told me."

## 24

# THE KNIGHT

Wesley would have rather died than do what he was about to do. But spending a day with Laila made it impossible to ignore for one minute longer the nagging of his conscience. Kingsley was gone, thank God, and so he wouldn't have to deal with that guy hanging around making snide comments the entire time Wes was attempting to do the hardest thing he'd ever done in his life.

Laila had gone to her room as soon as they'd arrived back at the house. He should probably check on her later. The cut on her face might need to be cleaned again, and in this house with a married Welsh woman, a French pimp and a sadist priest, Laila was like a gift from God sent to keep him sane and focused on something other than all the horrible scenarios running through his mind: Nora tied up in that house, a madwoman keeping her captive, men with guns who would do anything they were ordered to. Wes buried the thoughts under other concerns. They all needed to eat. He could cook something. That was something he could actually do. He could call his parents and let them know everything was fine. Lie, in other words. He could pray like he'd been praying since the moment he'd woken up on the stable floor and found Nora gone.

He wandered through the second floor of the house and didn't find what he was looking for. As he descended the stairs, he heard strains of music coming from a room he hadn't entered before. Wes followed the music to a door. Opening it, he saw Søren sitting at a baby grand piano. Only a few candles illuminated the music room. No way was there even enough light for Søren to see the sheet music. But still he played with incredible ease, each note flawless. The sound hit the walls and echoed back, amplifying itself into infinity.

The piece ended and Søren closed the fallboard and picked up a wineglass from atop the piano.

"I won't insult you by asking you how you are, Wesley."

"Thank you," Wes said, taking a seat in the window of the music room a few feet from where Søren sat on the piano bench. "But I don't mind telling you, I'm scared out of my mind and trying not to be. I'm not succeeding at that."

"None of us are. Myself included, if that gives you any comfort."

"It does. A little."

"There's no shame in being afraid. Even Christ was afraid in the Garden of Gethsemene. He prayed that the cup of his crucifixion would be taken from him. And he was so scared he sweat blood. I keep checking my forehead."

Wesley half laughed.

"She'd love this, you know. You and me alone in a room together talking," Wes said, wishing Nora could be here to see this.

"She would certainly enjoy seeing both of us so discomfited."

"When she's back, we'll all go out for a nice dinner together and she can watch us be all awkward and uncomfortable while she sits back and eats up every second."

"A lovely thought…her being back. Dinner notwithstanding."

"Kingsley…he's going after her now, isn't he?"

Søren nodded. "If he can. I told him that under no circumstances is he to do anything to risk his own life. If he can get her out without risking himself, he will try. Otherwise, I'm afraid he'll come back empty-handed."

"Are you more worried about him than her?"

"I am equally terrified for the both of them. Eleanor is a symbol of something Marie-Laure hates, a symbol that I moved on and found happiness with someone else. But Kingsley is her own brother, who she thinks betrayed her. She would be merciless to him if he were caught."

"What's she doing with Nora, then?"

"Marie-Laure is being merciless to me."

"You're not the only one who loves her, you know. I love her, too."

"I know you do. And she loves you."

Wesley's eyes widened in the shock of hearing those words from Søren's mouth.

"Don't look so surprised, young man," Søren said, almost smiling. "I've known how much she loves you for well over a year now."

"And that doesn't bother you?"

He inhaled and didn't answer at first.

"Does it bother me that she loves you? No. God is love. I'm sure you've heard that somewhere. When someone loves someone else, they are acknowledging the God inside that person. It's a spiritual act, loving someone. She sees God in you. So do I."

Wesley raised his hands and rubbed at the headache blossoming behind his eyes. He breathed through his hands to center himself before dropping them to his thighs and meeting Søren's gaze.

"How are you like this?" he demanded, the questions pouring out of him like wine into a glass. "How are you a priest and a sadist? How can you say you love God and yet you sleep with Nora? How can you hit women and still claim to be a man of the cloth? How are you…you? I can't figure you out, not to save my life."

Søren paused again. Wesley had never known anyone to do that—to stop and think before speaking.

"You might be surprised that I've asked that of myself many a time. When I was a child especially, I had these thoughts… desires… I didn't understand them. I saw what my father was, how he was with my stepmother. Brutal, violent, dangerous, merciless."

"Your father was abusive?"

"Yes, he was a monster. He did horrible things to his wife and my sister, to my own mother. I was only five when I was sent to school in England. I withdrew as much as I could there into my schoolwork. I feared I'd been tainted by my father, feared I was like him."

"You are, though, aren't you? I mean, you enjoy hurting people."

"I do, yes. It is different, however. My stepmother was powerless to stop my father from grabbing her by the hair and dragging her into the bedroom. She had no recourse, no safe word, nothing. Whenever Eleanor and I are together, anything I'm doing to her she can stop with a single word. I know she's told you all of this. Why do you need to hear from me?"

"I want to get what she sees in you. Other than the obvious."

Søren laughed softly. "The obvious? I suppose that's your tactful way of saying I'm not horrific to look at."

"I've seen worse," Wes conceded.

"I'm going to tell you something private, something I never imagined I would talk about with anyone other than Eleanor."

Wesley crossed his arms over his chest. He wasn't quite sure he wanted to hear anything private from Søren, but he knew he couldn't leave, not yet, not when he still hadn't done what he needed to.

"Okay...tell me."

"Eleanor and I met when she was fifteen. She was seventeen before I told her what I was. I waited until after my father died to tell her. It wasn't a conscious choice. Looking back I think I feared Eleanor would attempt to exact some sort of vengeance on my father for what he did to my sister."

"I don't doubt it."

"After he remarried and fathered my younger sister Claire, I made certain he could inflict himself on no other woman again."

Wesley shivered at the cold tone of Søren's voice.

"What did you do?"

"Let's just say I made certain he could never father children again."

Wesley's stomach plummeted through the floor.

"But...you're a Jesuit. Nora said you're a pacifist."

"I was eighteen when I castrated my father. Not a Jesuit yet. I was halfway to Europe by the time he woke. He assumed my sister Elizabeth had done it although he could prove nothing."

Søren smiled and it was the most chilling smile Wesley had ever seen in his life.

"You look horrified," Søren said.

"I am horrified."

"I told that same story to Eleanor the night of my father's funeral. She wasn't horrified. She was proud of me."

"No...Nora wouldn't..."

"Eleanor can be a bit barbaric herself. One of her more attractive traits. One of millions."

One of millions... The words reminded Wesley of what he'd come to say, but he couldn't quite say it yet.

"I wouldn't want to get on her bad side," Wesley admitted.

"You couldn't if you tried."

"That's good to know."

Søren took a sip of his wine and turned on the piano bench so that he and Wesley sat facing each other.

"Telling Eleanor about my father, what he did to my sister, what I did to him in return, that wasn't all I told Eleanor that night. I asked first if she was certain she wanted to know the entire truth about me. I warned her it would change how she saw me, how she saw us, possibly even how she saw the world. I'd long suspected Eleanor was of our ilk. The first time I met her she had self-inflicted burns on her arms. Teenagers inflict harm on themselves for only two reasons—either they're in pain or they love pain. Eleanor was of the latter variety."

"So you told her what you are?"

"I did. I told her all my secrets that night, all the ones that mattered. I told her I was a sadist who could only become aroused by inflicting pain, mental or physical, on another person, and if we were to be lovers someday, I would hurt her. I would have to. I told it all to her, and I did not spare her the gruesome details. When she was fifteen she made it abundantly clear she desired me. When she was sixteen she made it even more abundantly clear that she was in love with me and she knew, despite my best efforts to hide my feelings, that I was in love with her, too. I dropped all pretense, all subterfuge, and I laid out all the dark, stark truth before her."

"What did she do?"

"She said the three most beautiful words I'd ever heard in my life."

"I love you?" Wesley guessed.

Søren emptied his wineglass with one swallow and sat it back on top of the piano.

"'Is that all?'" Søren said the words so casually Wesley wasn't sure he'd even heard him right.

"What?"

"That's what Eleanor said to me when I told her the sort of horrific stories that would send anyone else running for their life. She said, *'Is that all?'* I didn't even know how to answer at first. I'm not sure I remember what I said. But I do remember her laughing, and breathing a sigh of relief. She said she'd been worried something was actually wrong with me. Perhaps terminal cancer or that I was a serial killer. Or even worse, she said, I could be impotent."

Wesley laughed. He couldn't stop himself. So Nora.

"Sounds just like her."

"That seventeen-year-old girl was braver than I was that night. I'd been anticipating shock and disgust from her, and I prayed with time she would understand and accept or at least forgive me for being what I was. Telling her the truth seemed like the greatest of risks, and yet I loved her too much to keep her in the dark any longer. I'd feared she would spurn me. Instead, she said she belonged to me and knew she belonged to me from the moment we met, and her body was mine to do with what I wanted. She loved me. She trusted me. She knew I wouldn't hurt her even if I hurt her. And we kissed for the first time, and I felt something I never dreamed I'd feel."

"Happy?"

"Normal. I felt normal. I'd felt loved in the past, and I'd certainly felt happy. But never normal. She so readily accepted everything about me that I'd worried she would fear or despise, I felt almost foolish. When Kingsley and I were teenagers at school, we often congratulated ourselves on what beautiful freaks we were. Typical teenagers thinking we were so different from the rest of the world. We were two lost souls who'd found each other in a wasteland. But with Eleanor, I didn't feel lost anymore. She simply saw nothing wrong at all with what I was. I might as well have told her that I had a bad habit of drumming my fingers on the desk, and I would have gotten the same reaction. The same patronizing, 'Is that all?' My God, I thought I loved her before that. After…you have no idea."

"I think I do have an idea."

"Yes…" he said, resting his elbow on the piano fallboard. "Of course you do. I apologize. I've loved Eleanor as long as you've been alive but it's wrong of me to dismiss your feelings for her simply because they're younger than mine."

Wesley winced at the words, visibly. Søren clearly noticed because the priest laughed at him.

"Do I even want to know what that expression was indicative of?" Søren asked.

"No. Maybe…" Wesley sighed heavily. "I need to tell you something and I don't want to say it, but I try very hard not to be an ass most of the time. My father can be an ass, and I've spent my whole life trying not to turn into him. But every now and then I say stuff and I hear it in his voice."

"Terrifying thought that one can so easily turn into one's parents."

"My father's no monster, though. He's a good man. He's just…an ass. I think the word Nora used was *imperious*. He's old money, at least for this country. I think he thinks he's kind of a king. He does nice things for people because he's…what's the word I'm looking for? Nora would know."

"Magnanimous?" Søren offered.

"That's it. Magnanimous. It's not normal charity or kindness. It's 'Here, let me show you how rich and powerful I am by paying for your son's surgery or buying your farm that's going into foreclosure and allowing you to stay on it.' He loves the gratitude, the homage from the peasantry. He does the right things, but not always for the right reasons."

"Better than doing the wrong things. Trust me, I have seen that side, as well."

Wesley rubbed the back of his neck, still sore from where he'd been knocked out.

"I used to try to understand what it was about my father that bugged me. And it wasn't the magnanimous gestures. He's got the money to spend, he's helping people, go for it. Great. He dotes on my mom, he's fair with people. He was never abusive or violent. If anyone ever tried to hurt me or Mom, he'd destroy them. No doubt. He's a good father, and I do love him."

"But?"

"But I don't think I've ever once heard him say, 'I'm sorry, I was wrong.' I told that to Nora and she said, 'Being a rich white son of a bitch means never having to say you're sorry.' She said that and I decided I'd be the kind of man who would say it, who would apologize when I said or did the wrong thing. I would admit it if I got something wrong. So…" He paused.

"Take your time," Søren said, almost smiling. Wesley appreciated that Søren was at least trying not to laugh at him.

Wesley took a deep breath. Like a Band-Aid, he told himself. Rip it off.

"I'm sorry," Wesley said. "I was wrong about you."

Søren said nothing for a minute, a minute that lasted an eternity. The silence felt like torture as the words hung in the air between them and taunted Wesley with the truth.

"Thank you, Wesley. I'm weighing whether or not to ask you what specifically you're apologizing for or to simply accept the apology as a gift of grace."

"I'll tell you. I should tell you. I don't want you thinking I like you or anything. I'm not saying I like you. You did shove me into a wall and hold me there by my throat, after all."

"Yes, after you rushed at me fully intent on causing me bodily harm," Søren reminded him. "Yes?"

"Okay, yes. You called me her puppy."

"I'm a sadist, young man. You're lucky I only put you into the wall. Anyone else I would have put in the hospital."

"And that's the reason," Wesley conceded. "You didn't put me in the hospital that day. And you didn't put Nora in the hospital that day she went back to you."

"Oh, I see..." Søren reached for his wineglass and seemed to notice it was empty. He put it back down again on the piano and stared at the empty cup a moment. "She told you what happened?"

Wesley slowly nodded. "She told me."

"Eleanor, she plays dangerous games sometimes. She gets that from Kingsley. A few years ago she spent the night with him and they engaged in some breath-play. Erotic choking."

"I know what it is. I lived with Nora." Wesley felt his jaw tighten. The thought of Kingsley with his hands around Nora's neck...

"Kingsley's very good at this game. So is Eleanor. It's not one I play often. A bit too dangerous even for me, especially for me. The temptation to go too far is ever-present. Not surprisingly that act can cause some light-headedness. She stood up too quickly after and fainted. She landed on her side on the hardwood floor. Only minor injuries resulted, thank God. A black eye, a bleeding lip, a bruised rib. Kingsley was deeply apologetic, although I wasn't angry at him. It's simply the risk we take."

Wesley swallowed hard and kept his mouth shut, his lips a thin tight line. He didn't trust himself to speak yet.

"That was the night she learned if she fell the right way she could give herself minor but visible injuries. The night she came back to me..."

"She hurt herself," Wesley finally said.

"She did."

"And you knew it wasn't an accident?"

Søren nodded. "Eleanor is one of the most naturally grace-ful women on earth. I've known clumsier cats. It takes alcohol or exhaustion to make any sort of dent in that grace. We were doing nothing that night but the usual pain-play we both find enjoyable. I stepped away and she fell. And I knew the moment I looked at her exactly why she'd done it. She wanted to scare you away from her for *your* own good."

"I wish she hadn't done that." Wesley rubbed at his face.

"You and I are in agreement. Let us pause and enjoy this rare moment of concord between us, Wesley."

Wesley's head throbbed, his eyes burned. He'd never felt so raw and wounded in his life.

"Do you have any idea," Søren began, picking up the empty wineglass once more, "how hard it is to overcome one's own sense of self-preservation? Try it. Try falling face-first into hardwood and see if you don't catch yourself. You think you can do it, but I promise you, at the last second you'll put your hands out and catch yourself every single time. She didn't that night. Her love for you outweighed her love for herself. The least I could do is let her have her way. She wanted you to think I was a brutal monster? Fine. It's not far from the truth. I've certainly been brutal in the past. Even to her."

"But not like that."

"No. Not like that. The one time Eleanor ended up in the hospital because of me was…" Søren stopped and ran a hand through his hair. It was such a human gesture of nervous en-ergy that Wesley almost didn't believe his eyes at first. Søren was human—who would ever have guessed? "I'm sorry. I'm sure you don't want to hear this."

"I think after all I've been through I can take it."

"The one time she had to go to the hospital because of me—I

had her tied to the bed, only her wrists to the bedposts by leather cuffs, and I was inflicting one of the worst forms of torture you can inflict on Eleanor...tickling. She has the most raucous laugh when she's being tickled. Infectious. God can hear it in heaven when she laughs like that. She flinched wildly and twisted too hard in the restraints. She sprained her wrist. She screamed in pain and then, because she's Eleanor, she kept laughing."

Wesley stood up and turned his back to Søren. He couldn't even look at the man anymore.

"She does have an amazing laugh."

"That she does. It's my favorite music."

"I'm going to miss hating you," Wesley said, staring into the shadows between the trees that surrounded the house.

"You're most welcome to keep despising me if you need to. I'm no saint. When Kingsley and I were at school together..." Søren's voice trailed off and Wesley said a silent prayer of gratitude that the priest chose to go into no further detail. "That he enjoyed it is no excuse for my savagery. When I put him in the infirmary it was no laughing matter. I've hurt Eleanor, too, very badly. Not necessarily physically, although she has been the primary target of my sadism for the past fifteen years. I have bruised her, beaten her, cut her, burned her...all for pleasure. I know that turns your stomach, and I certainly won't attempt to defend myself. But I also know I don't have to remind you that Eleanor was an adult who chose to submit to me and to pain of her own free will and that all she ever had to do was utter a single word to stop me, and I would have stopped."

"You're trying to make me feel better about hating you." Wesley turned back around. "You are the weirdest man on the planet."

Søren paused, glanced at the ceiling and seemed to mull the words over.

"You only say that because you haven't gotten to know Griffin yet."

"I know she consents to what you do to her. That's the only reason I never called the cops on you, and you better believe I seriously considered it a time or two. I even told her I was going to one night, that night of your…anniversary. She said it would be as stupid as calling the cops on two boxers fighting it out in the ring. Kink is a blood sport, she said."

"A not entirely inaccurate description."

"I hate blood sports. Hunting, cockfighting, dogfighting, all that horrible stuff people do to animals. Our horses, they run to run. They don't run because they're after a tiny fox that's about to get torn apart by a pack of dogs."

"Eleanor is no fox being chased by dogs. She's as much hunter as hunted. And if she runs it's because she wants to be chased. When she's caught it's because she wants to be caught. And when she's tired of being chased, she mounts her horse and she finds a fox of her own."

Wesley shook his head.

"You say you regret some of the stuff you did to Kingsley. Do you regret anything you did to Nora? I manned up and apologized to you for thinking you beat her into the E.R. At least you can admit you're sorry about something you did to her."

Søren laughed a little. "Very well. If you insist."

Søren stood up and took his empty wineglass over to the fireplace hearth. He uncorked another bottle of wine and poured a new glass. Wesley never imagined Søren would be this open, this talkative. Was it the fear over Nora's fate? Or the wine? Whatever, it didn't matter. Maybe he'd finally get some of the answers he needed.

"This house," Søren said, raising his glass to indicate the room, "belongs to a man named Daniel Caldwell. You met him briefly."

"Yeah, seems like a nice guy."

"He's more than that. He's an intelligent and honorable man. I've always respected him. He had a wife named Maggie. Older than him by over a decade when they met and married. She and Kingsley had been lovers once. They stayed friends after she married Daniel. Daniel is of the Dominant variety. We were friends, all of us—Daniel and Maggie, Kingsley and I."

"I saw the pictures in the house—him and his wife and kids. She looks a lot younger than him."

"That is Anya, his second wife. Maggie died of cancer a few years after they married. Daniel was even younger than Eleanor is now and already a widower."

"Shit. That's horrible."

"It was. He was bereft. It's difficult for those of our kind to find someone we're compatible with, to find someone who understands our desires and even shares them. He was not only a man without a wife, he was a Dominant without a submissive, a master without his slave. And he was lost. He'd gone into such deep mourning after the funeral he stepped into this house and didn't leave the property again for years."

"Years?"

"Years. Maggie died and he decided he wanted to die, too. He buried himself alive in this house. The thought of someone so young and vital giving up offended me to my core. Catholics abhor suicide not for the death but for the despair. I couldn't allow it to go on any longer. I believed Daniel simply needed reminding that there was something out there in the world worth living for. And if he had a reminder of what he was missing by staying in this beautiful coffin, he might come back to life again. So I lent him Eleanor."

"You what?"

Søren took a deep drink of the wine. Wesley was about ready to start chugging the stuff himself.

"I allowed Daniel to keep Eleanor with him in this house for one week. He was allowed any liberty with her he desired—sex, dominance, the infliction of pain and punishments to a certain degree. I told him Eleanor's limits and preferences, and as long as he didn't violate them, she was his for seven days while I went to my conference in Rome."

"And Nora was okay with this...why?" Wesley raised his hands in utter bafflement.

"I ordered her to submit to me by submitting to him. She did as she was ordered. She was not happy about it at first, to say the least."

"Can't imagine why."

"Don't misunderstand me. I'm not apologizing for lending her to Daniel for a week. She was my property and she knew she need only say her safe word, and I would have taken her back home again. I knew she would like it here. I knew she would be good for him. As you can tell from all the photographs of Daniel with his wife and children, it's safe to say I was right."

"So if giving Nora to some guy to screw for a week isn't what you regret, what do you regret?"

"I had an ulterior motive for lending Eleanor to Daniel. You may not know this, but when Eleanor was nineteen years old, there was someone else in her life."

"Someone else?" Wesley asked. Nora had never told him about another guy before.

"Yes. You weren't her first brush with a vanilla sort of romance. I was away at the time, working on my dissertation when she and this young man struck up a friendship. It quickly became something more. They were the same age, had much in common, and he adored her as well he should have. Still, she chose me. Hardly a fair fight—I was 32 years old, he nineteen. But Daniel—now he could give me a fair fight. And I assure you he did. I never quite trusted Eleanor's love for me only because it seemed far too good to be true. I could give her so little compared to what other men could. Our time together was and is limited by my calling. She and I could never be seen in public together. The simplest things you take for granted—going for a walk down the street holding hands, stealing a kiss under a streetlamp, being able to marry and have children—I could give none of that to her unless I left my life in the church. She claimed she didn't want that, didn't miss it, didn't want me giving up who I was for her. I feared that she said that only to be kind. If given the chance to take it, I thought she would. I feared she would. But because I loved her and prized her happiness more than my own, I gave her a chance to be with someone who could give her all that I couldn't. I loaned Eleanor to Daniel. I gave Daniel to Eleanor."

"That sounds...*nice* is not the word. Hard," Wesley said, finally finding the word he needed. "That sounds hard."

"It was very hard letting her come here to be with him. It's hard coming anywhere near that house I grew up in. I didn't want to come here. She certainly didn't. She was angry, petulant. I was cruel to her in response. Cruel on purpose. I wanted to give her ample reason to leave me. When I left her in this house, I didn't even kiss her goodbye."

"You were stacking the deck," Wesley said, understanding immediately.

"Stacking it against myself. And, of course, Eleanor surprised me. Daniel asked her to stay. What man wouldn't? Although tempted to stay with him, she came back to me. And when I told her that I was surprised she'd come back, she looked at me with so much hurt in her eyes..." Søren paused, lifted the wineglass but couldn't seem to bring himself to drink from it. "She said, 'I love you, you stupid man. Don't ever fucking forget that.' And that's what I regret, putting her through a vain and cruel test of her love for no reason. There were other ways to help Daniel. I didn't have to use her like I did. That I doubted her love…I regret that. I regret it enough that I went to confession over it. When I told Eleanor, she absolved me, too."

"So that's why you knew—when Nora fell that night she went back to you, when she fell on purpose—you knew she was doing it because she loved me."

"Exactly. She pushed you away for the same reason I pushed her away. That deliberate act of cruelty, like my deliberate act of cruelty to her, was born of love."

Søren stared into the wineglass, the liquid lapping the sides of the cup like blood.

"I only hated you because I wanted her to be safe," Wes explained. "I don't want you to think I hated you for any other reason. And I don't want her with me because I think you're evil or something. Not anymore. I don't like you. But I have to admit I don't know if I'd like anyone Nora was in love with. No one's good enough for her, you know? Not even me."

"I can empathize. I have trouble imagining finding anyone good enough for Laila."

"I'm glad you get it. It's not personal. I'm protective, I guess. The way you're protective of Laila."

"Protective is one word for it. Paternalistic might be another." Søren gave him a pointed look.

"Yeah, it might be," Wes reluctantly admitted.

"I only want Eleanor to be safe, as well. We want the same thing for her."

"Thank you. I mean, for not putting me in the hospital that day." Tonight he'd apologized to Søren and even said thank you to the man. He better get the hell out of here before he converted to Catholicism next.

"Eleanor would never forgive me if I broke one of her favorite toys."

Wesley started to argue but he saw the glint of amusement in his eyes.

"You do that on purpose, don't you?" Wesley asked. "Goad people?"

"Only worthy adversaries."

"Then I'll take it as a compliment." Wesley paused to yawn into his hands.

"Go, Wesley. You should sleep. It's late."

"I don't know if I can. I see too much when I close my eyes."

"Eleanor would want you to take care of yourself."

"She'd want the same for you."

Søren didn't answer. He opened the fallboard of the piano again. A few stray and beautiful notes wandered about the room—Brahms's famous lullaby. Wesley had never heard anyone play piano sarcastically before.

Wesley started for the door. Sleeping…that did sound like a good idea. Maybe he'd go to sleep and when he woke up it would all be over. Kingsley would have gotten Nora out of the house and he'd find her sitting on the edge of his bed when he opened his eyes.

"Wesley?" Søren's voice stopped him at the threshold.

"Yeah?"

Søren laid his fingers on the keys but played no notes.

"This past week when she was with you at your home… was she happy?"

The question came so out of left field, Wesley couldn't even answer it at first. Was Nora happy with him? The entire week he'd spent with Nora flashed across his mind's eye like a movie played at top speed. The nights together, the mornings, the sexual discoveries… Then voices intruded into his memories. He heard his father calling her a "whore." He heard his own angry voice demanding to know why she pulled back from him every time they got close to sleeping together. He saw Talel's horse dead on the stable floor and the heartbreak in Nora's eyes. The fight about how he couldn't do the things to her in bed that she needed. But the makeup sex had been amazing. Then Track Beauty going down and only Nora could get her back up again…and Nora's sobs in the shower when she realized what she'd done.

"Yes. She was happy with me."

Søren stared at his own hands resting on the keys.

"Good."

"Kingsley…you trust him, right?" Wesley asked, not sure he trusted the man at all.

"With my life," Søren said, still not looking at him.

"Do you trust him with hers?"

"Same answer," Søren said. "Same question."

Without another word, Wesley left Søren alone with his wine and his music. He trudged up the stairs feeling so much older than his twenty years. The past two days had taken years off his life. How did people do this—survive hostage crises and wars without losing their minds? Everything felt off, felt foreign, the sky had turned the wrong color. Even sleep seemed like the enemy. But maybe if he slept he would wake up and discover it had all been a dream. He'd wake up and Nora would be there in his bed, alive and beautiful. What he wouldn't give to have a beautiful woman lying in his bed when he opened the door. Would God judge him for praying for that? He didn't care. He prayed for it, anyway.

He opened the door to the bedroom he'd been given and switched on the lamp. He saw the two longest, shapeliest legs he'd ever seen in his life peeking out from a pair of short white shorts.

God was in a prayer-answering mood tonight.

# 25
# THE QUEEN

By the time Kingsley and Søren returned to the room, Eleanor had fallen asleep on her stomach. She awoke to the sensation of someone sliding inside her from behind. A hand covering her wrist held her down. She didn't speak, didn't protest, didn't care if it was Kingsley or Søren inside her. It gave her the greatest pleasure to lie there, to feign sleep, and let whomever it was take her. Unable to resist peeking, Eleanor finally opened her eyes and saw a glimpse of olive-skinned forearm marred by old scars and fresh bruises. With one glance it all made sense, everything fell into place, all questions were answered. She knew none of the details and all of the truth. Kingsley and Søren had never gotten the wine.

She buried her face deep into the pillow to silence herself. They'd certainly be suspicious if they heard her laughing. No wonder Søren had been so easy to arouse tonight. And no wonder Kingsley, although ceaselessly charming and seductive with her from day one, had always watched her with suspicious, wary eyes. They'd talk tomorrow and she'd tell him she didn't care, didn't mind, wouldn't stand in their way. She thought it was funny, thought it was sexy. Goddamn, she couldn't stop looking at the bright blue bruise on Kingsley's wrist, the twin to the bruise on her own arm. Søren and Kingsley? Lovers? Maybe if she asked nicely, they'd let her watch next time.

When Kingsley had finished with her, finished *in* her, Søren took his turn. He brought her to orgasm with his mouth and fingers before biting his way up her body and sliding into her. When he kissed her she tasted both her and Kingsley on Søren's lips.

An hour passed, maybe two—she didn't speak, not once. She gave herself over to them in total surrender, becoming nothing but a vessel to be used for their desires. She slept again and woke up in the final minutes of night right before it surrendered to dawn. It took a moment for her eyes to adjust to the darkness but when they did she saw the outline of Søren's naked back. He sat at the edge of the bed, one hand behind him to steady himself, the other hand… She saw another hand, not Søren's, clinging to the edge of the bed. Søren's head fell back in obvious pleasure and a soft sigh escaped his lips.

She closed her eyes and went back to sleep.

Not long after, she felt a hand on her shoulder and awoke to Søren at eye level.

"Time to go, Little One."

She dressed by dawn light and kissed a sleeping Kingsley goodbye.

On the way from the room she glanced over her shoulder and saw Kingsley lying on his side, the sheets around his hips, his naked back on display. On his shoulder she saw a black-and-blue bruise the size of Søren's hand and another mark that looked like a bite. She met Søren's eyes and he brought a finger to his lips.

"Why?" she whispered.

"For his sake, not mine."

Once safely ensconced in the back of the Rolls Royce, Eleanor curled up on Søren's lap. He ran his fingers through her hair, traced the outline of her lips with his fingertips.

"So you and Kingsley?" She laughed as she rolled onto her back and looked up at him.

"Kingsley and I," he said. "It's a very long story, Little One."

"We've got an hour. How about the CliffsNotes version?" He smiled at her, tapped her nose.

"Tonight," he began, "that was the first night we've touched each other in sixteen years. It may be that long before it happens again, if it ever happens again."

"Why not? I don't care. I mean, I do care but not that way."

"It's for the best," he said, and the smile left his eyes. "Trust me, it is for the best."

"What did he mean, it's for the best?" Marie-Laure asked, her eyes blazing with old hatred.

"Because of what Kingsley is, it was for the best he and Søren didn't sleep together. Or play together. Not alone."

"And what is Kingsley? What is my brother?"

Nora exhaled through her nose. For all their difficulties she loved Kingsley and hated betraying him to this madwoman. But perhaps if she knew about them, maybe she would understand and hate them all a little less.

"I was a professional Dominatrix for years so you have to believe I know what I'm talking about here. I've seen it all. And I mean *all*. So when I say this you should know it's not an exaggeration. Your brother is an extreme masochist. He doesn't want to get hurt. He wants to be destroyed. Søren told me that in the car ride back home that morning. I'll admit I thought it might be a little self-serving. How convenient for a sadist to say that the partner he brutalized was even more into receiving the pain than he was into giving it? Then I became a Dominatrix, Kingsley's Dominatrix, and I realized that Søren hadn't been exaggerating at all."

Marie-Laure got out of bed and stood at the window. As soon as her back was turned, Nora worked the razor blade out of her back pocket. Damon had tied her only with rope tonight. She couldn't waste this chance. Energy surged through her, adrenaline. She had a chance. Finally.

"An extreme masochist...poor dear," Marie-Laure said, her voice far away. "If only he were here, I would give him all the pain he wanted."

"Then I'm glad he's not here right now."

Nora remembered that early-morning ride back to Connecticut, Søren's voice soft and solemn as he recounted the story of his nights with Kingsley when they were teenagers...

"We can't be together anymore, Little One—an extreme masochist with an extreme sadist? We were like a two-headed ouroboros devouring each other. I know our encounters scared him. They must have. They terrified me."

"You? Scared?"

"You can't even imagine what it's like to have someone's life in your hands. Especially the most precious life, the life of the one person in the world you've ever loved...until you, of course."

Søren's voice trailed off and her heart had broken for him.

"You still love him, don't you?"

Søren paused before answering. He stared into the morning light of the city.

"Yes."

She'd shivered a little at the simple honesty in the one single word.

"But you must know it takes nothing away from us, away from my love for you, any more than my love for you takes anything away from what I feel for him. Not that he understands that."

"I get it. I do. Does Kingsley know how you still feel?"

"No. It's for the best."

"You don't want him to know, do you?"

"Telling him that I still love him and then refusing to be with him? That's a sort of sadism even I won't touch. Please don't tell him. Even tonight I went too far." She heard a strange new note in his voice, something she didn't recognize. Regret, perhaps? Repentance?

"I won't tell. I'll never tell."

"It's better he and I...we should be friends only. It hurts him but it would hurt worse to tell him I love him and still keep myself from him. At least this way perhaps he'll feel free to find another."

And then Søren had thanked her. She didn't even know what to say to that other than, "What for?"

"For not being angry that I love someone else."

She could only stare at him a moment, utterly baffled.

"Of course you love Kingsley. Who wouldn't?"

After all, she loved him, too, in a different sort of way. Especially after tonight she loved him. He and Søren had given her pleasures she'd never even dreamed of. She felt a deep kinship with Kingsley, like they were the same person or at least had the same nature. She couldn't quite understand, didn't have the words for it, but someday she would know.

"And what is it? What secret nature did you two share?" Marie-Laure asked.

"We're switches. There aren't that many of us around. Others don't trust us, don't get us. Only we get us."

"A switch?" Marie-Laure pressed her face closer to the glass of the window. "I thought he was of the Dominant persuasion, to use the terminology of your world."

"He is, definitely. Most of the time he is a Dom. But that's not all he is. He's a Dominant *and* a submissive, a sadist *and* a masochist. You can be all of the above. It's rare but it exists, especially in those of us who have incredibly strong libidos. We want it all and we want it all the time."

"Sluts, in other words," Marie-Laure taunted.

"And proud of it," Nora said entirely without shame or remorse. "You see, Kingsley loves topping, loves inflicting pain. But every now and then, when he gets the itch to be on the receiving end, you simply cannot hurt him enough. If I had tied him to the floor and kicked him with steel-toed boots, he wouldn't have tried to stop me. I did more damage to Kingsley in one night than Søren would do to me in a month. Thank God Kingsley doesn't get into that mood very often. The kind of pain he likes, it takes weeks to recover from. Søren loved Kingsley...loves Kingsley," she corrected. There was no past tense with Søren. When he loved, what he loved, who he loved, he loved eternally. "Sometimes the only way to show someone you love them is to let them go. It's hard, though. It's so fucking hard."

Nora closed her eyes as Wesley's face came back to her, the vision of him the day she went back to Søren. Kicking Wes out of her house was worse than any pain Søren had ever inflicted on her, any pain she'd ever inflicted upon herself. She wished Wes knew the same.

"So you saw your lover with another...and it didn't infuriate you?"

"No," Nora said simply. "Why would it bother me? It didn't bother him to see me with Kingsley. It was sexy."

"It's perverse."

"Don't knock it till you've tried it."

Marie-Laure narrowed her eyes at Nora and studied her as if an alien sat tied at the end of her bed. Nora stared back, unflinching, unashamed.

"You sit there and you tell me that my husband ordered you to have sex with another man...and after you do, you find out he's fucking him, too. They used you for their perverse pleasures, beating you and passing you between them like a whore...and you defend them?"

"No, I don't defend them. I fucked them, and I enjoyed it."

"They fucked you."

"Semantics."

Nora felt one of the ropes snap behind her wrist. Her heart punched the insides of her ribs. She had to stay calm. Now might finally be her chance. She had no plan, none at all. If she could knock Marie-Laure unconscious, she might be able to get out the window. Surely not every window in the house had been nailed shut.

"Marie-Laure, sweetheart, kitten, come here. I'm going to tell you another story. And I want you to look me in the eyes while I tell it so you know I'm telling you the truth."

"Oh, good. I do love your stories. Sounds as if I should be grateful that my husband didn't want me. Otherwise, I might have been subjected to your fate."

"Oh, yes, poor little me. Had to have sex with the two most beautiful men on the planet in the same night. It was torture by orgasm. All, I don't know, five or six of them."

"You were how old when you met my husband?"

"Fifteen."

"No wonder you turned out like this. And my brother."

"You know Søren's not a vampire, right? He's a sadist. You don't turn kinky just because he bites you."

"You make a joke of everything."

"Only the shit that's funny. And you thinking Søren made me kinky? Now that's funny."

"You deny it?"

Marie-Laure left her post at the window and walked over to stand next to Nora. Nora kept her wrists tight together and prayed Marie-Laure wouldn't notice the cut ropes or the razor blade she clutched in the palm of her hand.

"I do, actually. Here's the thing, and pay attention. I'll say this slowly so you can understand every word."

Marie-Laure stood by Nora, her arms crossing and her face a mask of pure condescension.

"Søren," Nora began, "is a sadist and a Dominant and that's it. That's all. He's not into pony-play or age-play. He doesn't cross-dress or want foot worship and he doesn't feel any need to make me iron his shirts while wearing nothing but an apron and high heels. He doesn't fetishize hair or feet or shoes or balloons or bestiality or anything other than pain. He doesn't want to play doctor. He doesn't want me to be his puppy on a leash. He doesn't want a harem. He doesn't want a man in a gimp suit following him around on his hands and knees. His desires are pure and simple. He wants to inflict pain on a submissive partner who enjoys accepting that pain. His needs are few and pure. But me…"

"You what?"

"Three years before I met Søren, I started burning myself with my curling iron. I would thread needles though my skin for fun. After I left Søren and became a Dominatrix, I started playing with Kingsley. Off the clock and without getting paid, I played. And I played hard. I had a whole stable of pony-boys, I did medical play with the sexiest little girl sub you've ever dreamed of, I adored having my feet worshipped. I did every kind of edge-play you can name and then I even invented a few of my own. I had a harem, I had orgies. I did the sort of shit Søren never even dreamed of. I fantasized about kink before I met him. I still did it after I left him. I did with him, without him, by land and by sea and by air. I did it every chance I got and with everyone I could. I did it for money, for pleasure, for pain and for the pain of pleasure. He does kink because he has to. I do it because I want to. And every time I did it I did it for me. You think Søren turned me into this?"

Nora shot her hand out as fast as a striking cobra and grabbed Marie-Laure by the neck.

"Bitch, please—I'm kinkier than he is."

She dug her fingers in hard and deep and pushed the woman onto the floor. In the struggle to take Marie-Laure down, the razor blade was knocked away. Didn't matter. She could kill her with her bare hands. Nora held Marie-Laure down by the throat, squeezing as tight as she could. She'd be unconscious in seconds. Nora couldn't—wouldn't—let go…all the while praying that neither of the boys had heard them hitting the carpet.

Marie-Laure's face turned red and her squirming quieted.

"Kingsley's file…" Marie-Laure managed to croak the words out.

"What about it?" Nora demanded in a harsh whisper.

"He said don't underestimate you."

"Good advice."

"We took it."

The world went black.

# 26
# THE KING

Kingsley parked the car far from the house and walked silently through the woods, moving in a different direction than he'd gone before. They had come this way, Marie-Laure and whatever crew she'd brought with her. He saw the troubled earth beneath his feet, the footprints in the marshy soil. She would have two men with her at least. Maybe three. Not much more. She'd need to pack light and take as few risks as possible. The more people involved, the more danger of one fucking something up or turning on her. Less was more in certain operations. Back in his days working for the government, when he was sent on a mission alone, he knew that was when the stakes were the highest. And they couldn't get any higher than this.

So he went alone.

Upon reaching the edge of the woods he paused. He'd have to cross an acre of open lawn to get to the house. Best to stay back and avoid detection. He waited for a wind to come through. When it did and the trees rustled, he slung his rifle across his back, climbed a tree and perched on a heavy branch. With binoculars he surveyed the house. One window and one window alone was illuminated from within—a bedroom on the second floor. Marie-Laure could have been a world-class sadist herself. She certainly had the mindfuck mastered. She taunted them by giving a hint to her location and yet demanded they not come unless they wanted to die.

No one seemed to be outside. He surveyed every inch of ground and saw no one on patrol. They were inside, all of them. Though God only knew where in that massive house. Nora had been the target, the one taken. Wherever Nora was, that's where Marie-Laure would be. There would be a guard inside the room most likely, but there was no way he could get a shot off from here. Not unless they all conveniently showed up in one room and decided to stand at the window. He had to go in.

The wind rustled again and Kingsley dropped back to the ground. On the darkest edge of the woods, he took a deep breath, and jogged across the open field to the house. He didn't sprint—too dangerous. He had to at least go slow enough to see where he stepped. He reached the house and pressed his back to the outer wall under the west side where he could remain hidden even from moonlight. Had this been his mission, Kingsley would have contracted a thief to disable all the alarms, the motion-sensor lights. Seems he and Marie-Laure thought alike.

Now at the house, Kingsley remembered Søren's instructions.

*There's a window by the servants' entrance. It will probably be the safest way in. Once through the window you'll be in a butler's pantry that no one uses anymore. The entrance to the servants' hallway is outside the pantry. It runs behind the bedrooms on the second floor.*

*There aren't entrances into every room but most of them. At the very least you should be able to hear them, hear where they're hiding her.*

Kingsley had asked him if he was sure. A servants' hallway could be the miracle they needed. If he could even hear into the rooms without them knowing he was there, he'd have the advantage.

*I'm certain. The servants never used the halls. But Elizabeth and I did. We hid in those hallways when the servants were about.*

Kingsley had left his rifle in the woods. It would be useless at close quarters. He'd strapped several handguns to himself when he'd left the car. He prayed he wouldn't have to use them. The first shot fired would kill one of them. The second shot fired would kill Nora.

Kingsley used a corner of his shirt and brute force to break the lock on the window. Without hesitating or pausing to look around, Kingsley dropped into the butler's pantry. The stairway was not much wider than the span of his shoulders and the hall only wide enough for one adult at a time. One adult or two children.

Kingsley pulled a penlight from his pocket and flashed it at his feet. He didn't need to see, only to hear, but if there were rats in the hall, he wanted to be prepared. One stray sound could mean the death of him and Nora both.

No rats in the hall, only dust. He covered his nose and mouth with his hand, trying not to breathe the decaying air.

Every few feet was a narrow door, back entrances into the larger bedrooms. Søren's father had been some sort of minor aristocracy back in England—a baron with no money and a useless title. But his marriage to millions of American dollars had given him the arrogance of a king. He couldn't live in a normal mansion. No, he had to have a manor house like the ones he'd coveted in England, complete with servants and their hidden passageways.

Kingsley paused when he saw the floor change color from dark wood to dingy white. He stopped and studied. Nothing but a sheet on the floor. Where had it come from? Then he saw the rust-colored stains on the white sheet—old blood. Kingsley stood up again and stepped over the sheet, leaving it on the floor, the forgotten shadow of a secret game two broken children had once played.

As he moved toward the end of the hall, Kingsley started to hear voices. His heart quickened at the sound even as his feet slowed. When the voices reached the highest volume, he stopped, pressed his ear to the wall and listened.

"I knew immediately. I knew Søren had given him those bruises. They looked like mine. I had to bury my face in the pillow to keep from laughing. And then not long after Kingsley fucked me, Søren kissed me. They had gone to get wine, they'd said. But I didn't taste wine on Søren's lips. I tasted Kingsley. I tasted blood."

Kingsley closed his eyes and listened harder. He knew this story that Nora told—the first night all three of them had spent together. Why was she telling it? And to whom?

"Whose blood was it?" came a voice Kingsley hadn't heard in thirty years but he still knew as well as his own. Light, feminine, forever flirtatious…the accent was mostly gone, however. She'd been living elsewhere for decades. Where? Australia possibly, the perfect place for a fugitive to flee and start a new life. Perhaps South America. With her olive skin she could blend in easily with the Latin population. She could have gone anywhere but France, where Kingsley had fled to, or Italy, where Søren had gone to school after Saint Ignatius.

"Kingsley's, I assume. I didn't see a bite mark on Søren's lip but there was one on Kingsley's back."

"My brother's blood on my husband's lips…fitting. And my blood on their hands."

"Are you going to keep interrupting or are you going to let me finish the story? You're the one making me tell them. So do you want to hear it or not?"

"Carry on…by all means, please."

So that was it. Marie-Laure was forcing Nora to tell stories of their life. At least that was a game Nora could play and win. She could stay alive a thousand nights from the power of her stories alone.

He closed his eyes and listened to Nora's story, to Marie-Laure's questions that interrupted her at every turn. Strange to hear about that night in Nora's voice. He and she never spoke of it. After all, she belonged to Søren and it was Søren who controlled the flow of information, what secrets his Little One was allowed to know and not know. Kingsley had known a secret about Eleanor that he kept from her, as well. Even as young as fifteen, sixteen, he'd seen the signs of it. He tried to tell Søren but Søren would have nothing of it. He'd forbidden Kingsley from telling Eleanor what he suspected.

*If she is, she'll figure it out for herself,* Søren had said, putting his foot down.

*There is no "if,"* mon ami. *It does take one to know one, and I know what she is. Your pet is no submissive, and you're lying to yourself if you think she is.*

*You're trying to define the indefinable. She is who she is.*

*You're trying to put a collar on a tiger. It won't turn it into a house cat.*

*Why do you think I love her so much?*

*And you call me a masochist.*

*If she is what you say she is…we'll cross the bridge when we come to it.*

*She'll cross that bridge when she runs from you. Then she'll burn the bridge behind her and leave you on the other side.*

*Then it's a good thing I know how to swim.*

*Swim? As far as she'll run from you and as fast, pray you learn to fly.*

It had been a dream of theirs when they were boys in school. A dream to find a girl wilder than the two of them together. But had it been a dream? Or a nightmare? No true Dominant could submit forever to chains. Kingsley knew a Dominant when he saw one, and he saw one the second he saw young Eleanor Schreiber for the first time. A sixteen-year-old girl who'd made even him nervous? At age eighteen he'd taken her to her first S&M club. Now that had been true love. He'd never seen anyone's pupils dilate like that, with such intense immediate desire. Before them a woman stood strapped to a Saint Andrew's Cross. Behind her a man whipped her with a singletail, a flogger, a cane.

*I want to do that, Kingsley,* Eleanor had said, a wild-eyed Cheshire cat smile spreading across her face.

*But which one? The girl on the cross, or the man with the whip? All of it.*

No submissive, that one. A switch, perhaps. Maybe something more.

He kept listening to the story Nora told. She remembered the night as well as he did. It had been such a relief to finally get his hands on her. Søren had kept her to himself for months and Kingsley had started to fear the worst—that he would lose Søren to her completely. Monogamy was the enemy of their kind. He'd seen it over and over again, a Dominant and his submissive falling in love, getting married, falling prey to the pressures of society to give up the lifestyle that had brought them together. Søren couldn't give it up, thankfully. He needed to give pain like he needed air to breathe. But Kingsley couldn't bear the thought of Søren loving her so much that he kept her to himself. Kingsley devoured Eleanor that first night she spent in his bed. He'd rejoiced every time he fucked her. That Søren allowed Kingsley to be with her meant something, meant Søren deemed him worthy. It wasn't the love that he craved, but it was enough. And truth be told, he'd never had more fun bedding a woman in his life. Not until Juliette.

"Almost nothing scares Søren," Nora continued. "Only the people he loves being in danger, which is why he let Kingsley go. Being with Kingsley scared even Søren. The last thing he wants is for anything bad to happen to me or King."

"How convenient, then. I hope he's terrified right now."

"I can guarantee he's never been this scared in his life."

"Good," Marie-Laure said, laughing. Kingsley closed his eyes tight. His sister's laugh…it hadn't changed at all.

"And he loves Kingsley. Deeply. More than even Kingsley realizes, more than Søren will ever tell him."

Kingsley's eyes shot wide open.

"My husband has an interesting way of showing it."

"It's the only way he can show it. After our night together, I curled up in Søren's lap in the back of Kingsley's Rolls Royce. I asked Søren if he still loved Kingsley. He said yes."

*You still love him, don't you?*

*Yes. But you must know it takes nothing away from us, away from my love for you, any more than my love for you takes anything away from what I feel for him. Not that he understands that.*

*I get it. I do. Does Kingsley know how you still feel?*

*No. It's for the best.*

*You don't want him to know, do you?*

*Telling him that I still love him and then refusing to be with him? That's a sort of sadism even I won't touch. Please don't tell him. Even tonight…I went too far.*

*I won't tell. I'll never tell.*

*It's better he and I…we should be friends only. It hurts him but*

*it would hurt worse to tell him I love him and still keep myself from*
*him. At least this way perhaps he'll feel free to find another.*

So that was it. The truth. The dark and beautiful truth. Søren still loved him, had always loved him, would always love him. But he'd feared inflicting irreparable harm and so had kept Kingsley at arm's length all this time. It hurt to know the truth and yet it was the sort of pain he most relished— pain inflicted by love. Now he had the truth in his heart, he'd never felt so free.

"You can't imagine how hard it is to be a sadist with a conscience," Nora continued. "Søren worries if he's with Kingsley he'll hurt Kingsley. He worries that if he's with Kingsley he'll hurt me."

"He should worry. I'm living proof of that." Marie-Laure laughed, a cold mocking laugh. He hoped she laughed like that when he put a bullet in her heart. And he would put a bullet in her. All this time he'd known Søren still desired him, still longed to use him as he had during their days in school. He thought the priest held back out of love and loyalty to his Little One. Kingsley never considered Søren didn't touch him out of love for him, out of fear of harming him beyond what even he could take.

He couldn't quite believe it and yet he knew Nora didn't lie. She had no reason to lie and every reason to tell the truth.

Søren loved him. Still loved him. And had loved him all this time. His heart reeled, his head spun. Dreams he thought dead and long-buried came back to life again. Hope resurrected itself. He knew he had to do something, anything, to honor this knowledge.

He'd get Søren's property back to him. That's what he would do.

Marie-Laure had chosen her room well. No door from the servants' passageway led into it.

He retreated down the servants' hallway and entered the kitchen through the pantry. Upon reaching the hallway, he peered down it, waiting for the right moment to proceed. He pulled his gun from his shoulder holster and checked the clip one last time. Søren had said to do nothing that would put himself into mortal danger, do nothing that would put her into mortal danger. A nice thought but being born gave everyone a death sentence. Why fear the inevitable?

From the end of the hallway he heard a commotion. One man and then another disappeared into the room. Quickly and silently he sprinted down the hall and hid himself outside the door in the shadows. There she was, his sister standing with her back to him. After all this time, she still had the same graceful neck, the same thin dancer's build. On the floor lay someone, a body. A man stood next to Marie-Laure, his back also to the door, blocking Kingsley's view.

"Feisty bitch," the man said. "She's stronger than she looks."

Another man knelt on the floor at Nora's head and checked her neck for a pulse. She apparently still had one.

"It took you two long enough to get in here," Marie-Laure said, her voice raspy and strained. She held a gun in her hand. So did the man. A Taser lay on the bed. Both of them had their weapons pointed at an unconscious Nora on the floor.

"You wanted to be alone with her."

"I thought she was tied up. How did she cut through the ropes?"

"No idea. We checked her for everything."

Kingsley glanced down and saw a glint of silver on the floor—a simple razor blade. So that's what Nora had used to cut through the ropes. It must have gotten knocked from her hand during the struggle and landed by the door. He crouched down and picked it up, slipping it into his back pocket. From his low post on the floor he watched and listened.

"When will she wake up?"

"Soon."

"Tie her up. And do it right this time."

Three shots would be all Kingsley needed. The back of the guards' heads. The back of Marie-Laure's head. The men, whoever they were, had the look of mercenaries about them— hired killers, completely disposable. But there…there she was, his sister, only ten feet away from him, and she had no idea he stood looking at her back.

"Any idea how much longer we have to keep her here? We shouldn't stay much longer. The family could be back any day."

Kingsley started to raise his gun.

"One more day, then we're gone."

"What are we waiting on?"

"Him."

"Your brother?"

Kingsley froze.

"Of course not. My brother doesn't care if I live or die. He didn't then. He doesn't now."

"You sure he even knows we're here?"

"He knows."

"You want to kill her now? We'll get it over with and leave the body on his doorstep."

Kingsley held the gun steady. The men first, then Marie-Laure. He could do this, had done this a thousand times. Strangers, though, all of them. Enemies of the state. Monsters who made Søren's own father look like a candidate for saint-hood. The mercenaries, he could kill them easily. But Marie-Laure…she was his sister, no matter what had happened. They were blood. He'd spent thirty years drowning in guilt because he thought he'd killed her the first time. He wouldn't survive killing her again, not in cold blood with her back to him. But he had to, he had to for Søren. He could do this. Three shots. That's all it would take. Nothing to it...only three bullets.

He stared down the gun and saw the end of the barrel shiver.

"*Non*. I don't want to kill her. I have a better idea. We wait."

The man on the floor by Nora's head started to rise up. The second he stepped from the room, they would find Kingsley outside the door hiding in the shadows. He had only a split second to decide. He could make a noise, cause them to turn around and see him. They'd fire at him first, then he could fire back without remorse.

How strange...for the first time he realized Marie-Laure had grown up to look so much like their mother.

He lowered the gun and disappeared into the room across the hall. Could he go back out, try again? But it was too late. He'd lost his chance, lost his nerve. Kingsley stayed crouched in the room, in the dark. When the silence settled on the house again, he opened a window and dropped to the ground. He ran through the woods and to the car. Once inside he picked up his phone and dialed.

"Kingsley." Søren's voice sounded so relieved Kingsley had to blink back tears.

"I don't have her," Kingsley confessed.

"She's alive?"

"*Oui*. She's alive. But...I couldn't take the shot. I couldn't kill my sister. She had her back to me. I would have had to shoot her in the back. And she said she doesn't want Nora dead. So I couldn't... I killed her before. I couldn't do it again." He leaned his head against the steering wheel. "Forgive me."

He heard silence on the other end of the line. He died in that silence, died a thousand deaths.

"Come back. It's late. She's alive. There's nothing to forgive."

"I'll get her back. I'll find a way. There's two of them at least but there might be more. I can wait it out and—"

"Kingsley...listen to me. Come back. Do as I say."

Kingsley could only nod first before he could speak.

"Yes, sir."

# Part Four

# CASTLING

# 27
## THE PAWN

Laila felt the bed shift. Her eyes flew open and she rolled up immediately. Wes sat at the end of the bed, his back to the bedpost, watching her.

"Hello?" Wes said, laughing at her sudden alertness. "You get lost?"

"Oh, no, I'm sorry." She grabbed a pillow and pulled it to her chest. "Grace and I are sharing a room. She was crying. I wanted to give her some privacy. I only meant to hide in here a few minutes."

"You fell asleep. It's okay. You can stay. I'll sleep somewhere else."

She started to stand up, but Wes waved his hand at her.

"Stay. Seriously," Wes said. "There's a bunch of bedrooms in this house. I'll grab my stuff."

"No, I'll stay with Grace. I doubt she wants to sleep alone tonight, either. It must be hard for her, being apart from her husband."

Wes kicked his shoes off and sat back down on the bed cross-legged.

"Yeah, I'm sure it is. They've been married like twelve years."

"But she's so young." Laila thought Grace looked no more than thirty.

"She got married at your age. Seemed to work out. They're still together."

"You have a girlfriend?" Laila asked. She wished she had more clothes on than the white T-shirt and boxer shorts she'd put on to sleep in. The last thing she'd planned on was falling asleep on Wes's bed.

Wes came up on his hands and knees and reached across her to switch on the bedside lamp. For a second he was so close to her she could have kissed his arm. She gave herself two seconds to imagine kissing his arm, the ridges of muscle leading from his elbow up to his shoulder.

"Not exactly," he said, sitting back on the bed. He couldn't seem to meet her eyes. "Or boyfriend. I feel I need to clarify that."

"Why?"

"I got a few jokes in school. Side effect of not having a girlfriend and not sleeping around."

"I get some jokes, too."

Wes reached into the bedside table and pulled out a small leather case.

"No boyfriend?"

"Never."

"Don't feel bad. Trust me. I know the feeling."

"I don't feel bad," Laila said.

"You blushed so bright they saw it on the space station."

Laila buried her face in the pillow.

"I can still see you." Wes narrowed his eyes at her. "And the blush."

"I give up." She turned her head and faced him.

"If it makes you feel any better, I was still a virgin when I was your age. God, I sound like Nora. She was an 'old virgin,' too. Her words, not mine." He unzipped the leather bag and pulled out a blood-testing meter.

"You don't feel well?" she asked, the blush fading.

"A little light-headed. I don't know if it's my blood sugar or talking to your uncle, though."

"He has that effect on people."

Grinning, she scooted closer to him on the bed and picked up an alcohol swab.

She took his hand in hers and swabbed the pad of his middle finger.

"Do you mind? I never get to play with humans."

"No, go for it. You'd probably have better aim than I do right now."

Laila took Wes's hand in hers and pushed up his finger, forcing the blood to pool at the tip.

"Why don't you use a pump?" Laila picked up the lancet and pierced Wes's finger. He didn't even flinch.

"Tried it for a while. Didn't work. I ride horses, go running, swimming. I can't deal with something being stuck on me all the time."

"You ride horses?"

"All the time."

"I love horses. We sometimes get to treat them on house calls. But not many horses in Copenhagen."

"Come visit me in Kentucky. I'll show you horses like you wouldn't believe."

Laila put the strip in the meter and waited for the beep.

"You're okay," she said. "One hundred five."

"Good. Thank you."

She took the bag and packed up the supplies neatly.

"So, no boyfriend?" Wes asked, and she noticed him staring at her hands. "Really?"

"None. It's his fault."

"Your uncle?"

"He keeps telling me I'm joining a convent. He has one picked out for me already."

"How nice of him. You want to be a nun?"

"No." She laughed a little. "I don't think he wants me to be a nun, either. He just doesn't want me to date. He takes sex very seriously. He considers it sacred."

"Do you?"

Laila scooted back on the bed, needing a little breathing room. She was on a bed with the most attractive guy she'd ever seen in her entire life, and they were talking about sex. Someone needed to check her blood sugar right now. And her vital signs. Heart attack seemed imminent.

"Yes, but not in the same way as him. Tante Elle and I talked about it. She believes sex is sacred, too, but in a different way. He says that the only people he's ever been with, he loved them. Tante Elle thinks sex is like…" She unzipped Wes's bag of testing supplies and held up a bottle of insulin.

"Insulin?" Wes asked.

"Medicine. She thinks it can help heal people."

"It can hurt people, too."

Laila nodded as she zipped closed Wes's bag of supplies and put it back in the nightstand for him.

"She knows that. She told me that all she hoped for me was that my first time would be as special as hers. And that I would only have sex when I wanted to and for the right reasons."

"And what are the right reasons?"

"When I wanted to."

Wes laughed and rolled onto his back.

"Of course. That's Nora for you."

Laila stretched out on her side and propped herself up on her elbow.

"You don't like her reasons?"

"I think 'wanting to' is maybe not the best reason to do something. Sounds like a recipe for chaos."

"Chaos sounds like a good description of her life sometimes."

"Can't argue with that," Wes said, and she saw a flash of bitterness in his eyes. Bitterness and fear. He might smile and chat with her, but she could see the fear there hiding behind it all. What else was he hiding? She'd give anything to know. Even her body. Especially her body.

"I don't know if I agree with my uncle that you should wait for true love to have sex with someone. I don't even know if true love exists, although he believes it does. And I don't think you should have sex just because you want to. I think it should at least mean something."

"What do you mean by 'mean something'?" Wes rolled onto his side to face her.

"It's hard to explain. When my grandmother died, my aunt and uncle came for the funeral. I could hear them in the guest bedroom."

"What did you hear?"

"Talking. Only talking," she lied.

"Sure. Right. I totally believe you. Go on."

"First, I have to ask you where you usually take all your insulin shots."

"My stomach. Why?"

"So I know the best place to punch you when you tease me."

"Stomach. Definitely the best place to hurt me."

"Thank you." She shot her hand out and pretended to punch him in the stomach. He flinched and pulled tight into the fetal position.

"Faker," she said.

"You're stronger than you look."

"You have to be to wrestle with Scottish deerhounds."

"Those dogs are horses."

"They aren't nearly as easy to saddle and ride."

Wes started to say something but closed his mouth when they heard Søren's voice in the hallway.

*"Nesichah?"*

Laila sat up immediately and raced to the door.

"I'm here," she said, rushing out into the hall. "Wes was checking my face."

Her uncle cupped her chin and turned her face toward the hall light.

"It's healing well. You should go to bed. Wesley needs his sleep, too."

"I will. Promise."

He kissed her on the forehead and walked down the hall. Laila went back into Wes's room.

"What was that he called you?" Wes asked. *"Nesichah?"*

"It's Hebrew. It means 'princess.' He's always called me that."

"Princess? Nice." He laughed at a joke only he seemed to get.

"When Gitte's good he calls her *Malcah*. That means 'queen.' When she's being wild he calls her *Behemah*."

*"Behemah?"*

"Hebrew for 'animal.'"

Wes laughed as Laila laid back down on the bed. He didn't seem in any hurry to get rid of her, and for her part she kind of wanted to stay in bed with him forever. A bad idea. She'd get muscle atrophy in only a few weeks. They'd probably need to work out in bed if they stayed here. She had a few ideas for some exercises they could do.

"Gitte's a little hyperactive. We're hoping she grows out of it."

"I would have loved some siblings. Brothers or sisters."

"You're alone?"

"Yeah. Lots of cousins. Tons of cousins but no siblings. Mom was six months pregnant and miscarried when I was four. Took her a long time to get over it. And I don't think she ever did. She didn't want to try again."

"I love Gitte when I don't want to kill her. You could get married and have kids."

"That's the plan. Fill up the house with them. You want kids?"

"Kids, animals, all of it. No one has big families in Denmark anymore. Small country, small houses, small families. It's why I've always wanted to come to America. Big country, big houses. I have big dreams."

"You have good dreams. I need some good dreams."

"Is that a hint I should go and let you sleep?"

Wes shook his head. "You can stay. I should sleep but I don't want to. I feel better talking to you."

"I like talking to you, too. Although we keep getting off the subject."

"I don't even remember the subject."

"Sex," Laila reminded him. Wes laughed again.

"How could I forget? I'm twenty and male. That's usually a safe guess for what's on my mind."

"I'm eighteen and female."

"I'm not buying it. What goes on in your head can't even begin to compare to what goes on in mine."

"That's not fair. There's no way we can compare without switching brains."

"That's not going to happen. No one is allowed inside my brain. It is not pretty in there. All sex all the time. Most of the time, anyway."

"That must be exhausting."

"You have no idea."

"At least you've had it. It's all theory for me."

"I've had it. But you've heard it," he teased again. Laila raised her fist and Wes covered his stomach.

"I didn't mean to hear it."

"Did you cover your ears? Leave your bedroom? Start listening to music? Knock on the wall and tell them to keep it down?"

"No."

"Then you meant to hear it."

"I didn't want to hear them having sex, I promise. I wanted to know what was going on. Tante Elle was acting strange when she came for the funeral. I heard them talking about how she left him."

"Did she say why?"

"I know why she did. I don't know how she does it, stays with him. I love him more than any other man on earth and even I would have a hard time being with him."

"She deserves better than to be a secret."

"He thinks so, too. That night, he said the same thing."

"What did he say?"

Laila sighed as she pulled her knees to her chest. It had started to cool off in the room, but it didn't seem right to get under the covers. They were only talking, not sleeping together.

"He said he was sorry that the only time she and he could

be together out in the open like this was in Denmark. And that he wished it was under better circumstances than a funeral."

Wes rolled off the bed and opened the closet door. He pulled down a blanket and came back to the bed.

"What did Nora say?"

"She said…" Laila paused as Wes laid the blanket over her before stretching out on the bed once more. He must have noticed her starting to shiver. "She said that her feelings right now were the last thing he needed to worry about. His mother had died. He was here for the funeral, and she was here for him."

"Thank you," Laila heard her uncle say through the wall. "Thank you for coming. I know how busy you are. I know you have other—"

"Nothing. I have nothing more important than you," Tante Elle said, and Laila had imagined her aunt covering his lips with her hand to playfully shut him up. She did that to him as often as he did it to her.

"Eleanor, please, let me thank you for doing this for me. I'll feel better."

"There's nothing to thank me for. Not coming wasn't even an option. You should know that by now."

A long pause followed, a long and painful silence. Laila had to cover her mouth to silence her crying.

"She loved you, Little One. You know that, don't you?"

"I know. I loved her, too. I think she even liked me. More than my own mother does, anyway, which isn't saying much."

"She certainly liked me more than your mother does."

"Again, not saying much."

Tante Elle laughed then and it heartened Laila. Such a laugh…it woke the angels up.

"My mother has terrible taste in men. She loved my father. She hates you."

"You left me. What does that say about your taste in men?"

"It could use some work."

"Come back to me," he said, and Laila heard the agony in his voice. "You don't have to stay away anymore. You never did."

"It's such a risk, Søren. Any second now we could get caught. The stories are in the newspapers every day, some priest falling from grace."

"You're worth the risk, and you are my grace."

"I can't be responsible for ruining your life. I won't be."

"Even if they did find out about us and excommunicated me, my life could never be a ruin, not with you in it."

"I can't come back...I just can't. I worked so hard for what I have."

"You wouldn't have to give it up, any of it."

"You say that and I want to believe you. But I remember how it was. I couldn't even cut my hair without getting your permission. I don't know if I could go back to that."

"You miss it."

"I miss *you*."

"You promised me forever."

"I was fifteen when I promised you forever. And you promised me everything the same day. I can no more keep my promise than you can keep yours."

"You won't let me keep it."

"Because I love you too much. You stupid, infuriating man, why do I love you this much?"

Silence followed again. What could they be doing in there? Laila hoped it was kissing or hugging or something. Anything. Their pain hurt so much worse than her own. For years she longed to join the Enchanted Kingdom of Adulthood, that world where people like her aunt and uncle lived and loved and no one told them what to do. But here they were, two people madly in love with each other and they couldn't be together. The unfairness of it felt like a bruise on her heart. He could no more leave the church than her aunt could quit writing or breathing. It would be suicide for a man who'd found his true calling. She couldn't ask him to leave it. But unless he left it, she couldn't go back. Why…why did anyone think there was any sin in the two of them loving each other? How could anyone who saw them together think they did anything wrong? How could God create two people so perfect for each other and then force them to stay apart? God was a sadist. No doubt in her mind.

No wonder her uncle loved Him so much.

"We're a mess," her aunt finally said, breaking the silence. "Look at us. Your mother is being buried tomorrow, and all we can do is fight the same old fight."

"I'd rather fight with you than bury her."

"Me, too. But I'm sure we can find something better to do than fight."

"It's hard to stay calm right now, Little One. Help me."

"That's why I'm here. I came here for you. Come to bed now. Hurt me. I want you to."

"I don't know if I can control myself enough tonight."

Laila remembered holding her breath during the silence that followed before her aunt started to speak again.

"Then don't. I know you're hurting. Don't be afraid to hurt me, too. I know you want to let go. Let go with me. You need comfort. Let me comfort you with my body. Lose yourself inside me. Forget what you've lost, forget what you can't have. There's no shame in trying to forget for a night even if you know you'll remember in the morning."

Laila blinked and tears fell onto the sheets. Wesley reached out and wiped them off her cheek with his thumb.

"I think I learned what sex was that night," Laila said. "I mean, I learned what it should be."

"And what is that?" Wes asked, his fingers lingering on her face.

"A gift. A gift you give someone you care about. A consolation, a comfort, even a distraction, but always a gift. I didn't listen after that. I made sure I didn't hear any more. I read her books. I know what happens with people like them in private. I didn't need to hear. But I'm glad I heard that much so I know...I know that love is giving yourself to someone else. Giving yourself to someone without losing yourself."

Laila knew she'd remember those words all her life. *Let go with me. Let me comfort you with my body...there's no shame in forgetting for a night even if you know you'll remember in the morning.*

They sounded like a poem to her, like a vow.

"No one loves like Nora loves," Wes said. "I wish I knew how she did it, how she could love so hard and still stay sane."

"Are you sure she is?"

Wes grinned. "Not entirely."

"You know, you have a big smile." She spread her hands out a foot apart.

"I do?"

"I think they can see it on the space station."

"Why are those astronauts so freaking obsessed with us? It's creepy."

"They get bored up there, maybe," Laila suggested.

"Then they should watch porn."

"Space porn?"

"What other kind is there?"

They laughed together and Laila felt human for the first time since arriving at her uncle's house two days ago. Had it only been two days? It felt like two years. Even Wes, this complete stranger...she felt like she'd known him all her life.

The tail end of Wes's laugh turned into a yawn.

"Sorry," he said. "You didn't need to see my molars."

"It's fine. Here's mine." She opened her mouth wide and Wes peered at her teeth.

"Good molars."

"They work out." She smiled at him once more before sitting up.

"Where are you going?" Wes sounded almost distressed.

"You're yawning. I'll let you go to sleep."

"You don't have to go," Wes said as Laila crawled off the bed and started folding the blanket. "It was just a yawn. You can stay if you want."

"It's not a good idea." She put the blanket in the top of the closet.

"Let me guess, you grope in your sleep. Should have known."

"Not that I know of." Although if she slept with Wes, she probably would grope him in her sleep. And she'd grope him while awake, too. She'd grope him every chance she got. "No, it's just that if you and I slept in the same room…"

"What?"

Laila opened the door and cast one last longing look at Wes. She wanted to go back to the bed, kiss him, stretch out on top of him and sleep on his chest all night long. A nice dream. But only a dream.

"My uncle would kill you."

# 28
## THE QUEEN

Nora's eyes fluttered open and in an effort to stave off the panic she knew would descend on her like a ravenous vulture, she started an inventory of her body. She knew she'd been tased as soon as she came to. But not just tased—drugged, as well. Tased and drugged—she was almost flattered. Now she made them nervous. Everything still seemed to be in place—all the body parts, anyway. Although they weren't feeling all that fabulous at the moment. Everything hurt from her head to her heels.

"How are you feeling?"

"I'm in agony," she said simply as she opened her eyes and looked up at Marie-Laure. She must have hit the ground hard when she blacked out. Her entire body felt like one solid bruise. "Typical morning after for me. It is morning, right?"

"Dawn."

"Dawn and I have never gotten along. We try to avoid each other."

"Try to enjoy it. This will be your last one unless someone shows up."

"Might help if you told them where I was."

"Oh, they know," Marie-Laure said, kneeling down at Nora's side. Nora wriggled in the ropes but this was some hard-
core bondage going on here. Handcuffs, rope and duct tape.
No way could she cut or squirm her way out of this mess.
"They've known from the beginning. I made sure they knew."

"Then they're coming."

"I don't see anyone yet...."

"Don't try to mindfuck a mindfucker. Either they don't
know where I am and you're lying, or they do and they're
coming. Two and two is four. I know Søren."

"You're so certain of his love?"

"Two and two is four."

"Harder question," Marie-Laure said. Nora glanced around.
She still lay on the floor of Marie-Laure's room. Damon
watched her from the bed, a gun in his hand, no emotion in
his eyes. "Is he certain of your love?"

"Do I have to do the math again? Yes, I love him. Yes, he
knows I do."

"You love him, you say. Strange answer for a woman wearing another man's engagement ring."

"I love Wesley, too. You can love more than one person."

"You're not supposed to. That's not how it works."

"Maybe your heart's just a few sizes too small, Mrs. Grinch.
Some of us are capable of loving more than one person."

"Who do you love more?"

"That is a stupid question."

"That is deflection. Don't want to answer? I would guess
you love your fiancé more. You turned my husband down
when he proposed. You said yes when your Wesley asked."

"I don't want to get married to anybody. I love Wes, but I

said yes to get him out of the stables. I saw the writing on the wall, someone in the shadows. I couldn't get him to shut up and move any other way."

"Still...you have the ring on."

"What was I going to do—swallow it?"

"You could have tried to bargain with it. I know diamonds. That one is easily worth seven figures."

"It's not mine to bargain with. It belongs to the Raileys."

"It belongs to you if you're his fiancée."

Nora winced. Wesley's fiancée? Next, someone would be calling her the Queen of England.

"It belongs to whomever Wes marries someday."

"Not you?"

"Not... Jesus, can you flip me on my back or something? I'm going to suffocate on this damn carpet."

"Of course." Marie-Laure stood up, put her foot on Nora's hip and pushed.

"Better." Nora scooted into a sitting position. Her hands were cuffed in front but the ropes encircled her arms and ankles. She felt half-mummified. She started to stretch out her legs but another rope tightened around her neck. "Oh, that's lovely. Choke collar. I'm good at those, too."

In addition to the rope, the tape and the cuffs, someone, Damon probably, had tied the rope around her neck. If she stretched out her legs, she'd choke herself.

"So am I," Damon said. "I also have very good aim."

"So does Søren. Oh, you were talking guns."

Marie-Laure knelt down again.

"You...I'm starting to think you aren't even a person. Just an animal with an animal's appetites."

"At least I'm housebroken. Usually."

"At the very least. I can't believe someone like you who makes these kinds of disgusting jokes all the time is even capable of something as complicated as love. You seem like some kind of rutting beast."

"You say that like it's a bad thing." Nora knew she was asking for it. But if she died today, she would at least die with her sense of humor intact. She would try to die with her dignity intact but she wasn't entirely sure she ever had any.

"I want to find out something. Indulge me."

"Milk bath? Chocolates? Massage?"

"Another story. A short story this time."

Nora sighed heavily. "Fine. Whatever. What do you want? I can tell you about the time Søren and I spent two nights at this great B & B owned by one of our freak friends. Søren beat me, he fucked me, we went for long walks on the beach in the middle of the night. The end."

"Not good enough."

"Yeah, it needs more sex, doesn't it? Story of my life."

"What I want is a very specific story...about this."

Marie-Laure reached into the pocket of her black robe and pulled out a square of white linen. Nora recognized it immediately.

"No...no. Fuck, you were in my house, weren't you?" She stared at the linen, aching at the very sight of it.

"I was. Spent a little time in your closet. We made a wonderful mess. It was a bit silly and melodramatic of us. I couldn't help myself. My only real interest was in seeing the things you hide, the things you cherish. I found this scrap of linen in a locked metal box. When I saw the box I thought, Oh this is where she keeps her most precious possessions—diamonds, pearls, secret papers.... But no. Only this. Tell me what it is. Tell me a story."

Nora couldn't even look at Marie-Laure, only at the white linen cloth in her hand.

"Once upon a time..." Nora began, her voice quivering

under the words. "A great and fair lady whose heart was made of music and who had given birth to a great and fair son... died."

The phone call came late at night and from her hotline. Not even Kingsley called that late, not unless it was an emergency. When Nora answered and heard Søren's voice saying her name, she already knew what happened.

"Your mom?"

"An hour ago," he said. "Freyja called."

"Call your sister back," Nora said. "I'll make the flights. I'll handle it all."

"Flights? You're coming?"

"I'm going to pretend you didn't ask me that."

"Thank you, Little One."

Nora hadn't even been able to speak at that point. She nodded even though he couldn't see her, wiped the tears off her face and managed only to choke out the words, "I'll be right over."

She'd packed in a hurry, focusing on the little mundane tasks one always focused on in times of grief. She'd need clothes for the funeral, for the wake afterward. She needed to call Kingsley and tell him to cancel her appointments this week. She'd call her editor from the airport and let her know that the book would be a week late due to a family emergency that would take her out of the country.

Into her suitcase went her shoes, clothes, makeup, toothbrush, the full-length, rather conservative gray silk robe she wore only when staying with Søren's family in Denmark. When alone with Søren, she always slept naked so she needed something to put on for nighttime trips to the bathroom. Right before she left the house to go to the rectory, she stopped, remembering something she knew she shouldn't forget. For almost a full minute she stood at the front door debating whether or not to take it with her. Had she not left Søren three years ago, it wouldn't have even crossed her mind. But she had left him and ever since the square of linen in the closet had taunted her, whispered at her, told her that it didn't belong to her anymore.

She decided to take it with her and let Søren decide.

When she arrived at the rectory, she found Søren sitting in the armchair by the fireplace staring into the fire. He had on pants and a shirt. He hadn't buttoned the shirt yet and his bare chest glowed in the firelight as if it burned from within him. She came to him and knelt at his feet, resting her head on his lap. The moment she felt his fingers twining through her hair, the tears started to flow.

"Her heart gave out," he said, his voice quiet and steady. "She's only eighteen years older than I am, and she's gone."

"She was sick for a long time. And her heart was never strong." In fact, it was a miracle she'd survived as long as she had. A congenital heart problem had plagued Søren's mother her entire life. A blessing in disguise, Gisela had always called it. Had she been a healthier child, she never would have had the patience to stay inside and learn the piano.

"I know, Little One. It's only...I thought I would have her a few more years. The women I adore always leave me before I'm ready to let them go."

She laughed and buried her face against his thigh.

"That is not fair." She smiled up again. "I am here, after all. When you need me, I'm always here."

He cupped her face in both hands and brought his lips to her forehead.

"I always need you."

She raised her head and kissed him. Even in their shared

grief there could be no denying the passion. He pulled her off the floor and into his arms.

"When does our flight leave?" he whispered against her lips.

"We have time." That was all he needed to know, all that mattered.

He laid her on the rug in front of the fireplace and stripped her of her clothes. They had no time for equipment, for cuts or candle wax, whips or floggers. But they didn't need them. Søren knew her body better than even she knew it, knew how to bring it to the extreme edge of pleasure and down into the depths of pain...all with his bare hands.

Gently he ran his fingers all over her naked body and desire quickened at the lightest of his touches. He didn't meet her eyes, merely stared at her body that she'd given up to him. She was glad he didn't look at her face since it gave her the freedom to study him. He'd no doubt been asleep when his sister in Denmark had called. Only in sleep did his perfect blond hair ever get mussed. It fell over his forehead, almost into his eyes. His eyes, how she loved looking at his eyes. She'd never known a more intelligent man with such perceptive eyes. And how strange that someone with such pale hair had such long dark eyelashes. She and Kingsley had gotten stoned together one night and spent an hour sitting in Kingsley's bathtub waxing poetic about those damn eyelashes. If she remembered correctly, they never even turned on the water. Or taken their clothes off, for that matter.

"Are you ready?" he asked, running a finger over her lips.

"Always, sir." She nodded, and tried to steady her breathing.

Søren slid his hand from her shoulder down to her wrist and back up again. He pressed his thumb hard into the top of the muscle where her forearm met her elbow. She gasped with a sudden pain she felt even in her legs. He pressed again and her back arched off the rug. If she'd been standing her legs would have involuntarily collapsed under her.

He moved his attention from her arm to her leg. Søren raised her ankle to his legs and kissed the soft spot above the outer heel. She braced herself for what was next. When Søren covered her mouth with his other hand, she made no protest.

With two fingers and two fingers only he dug deep into the cavity under her ankle bone. The pain came so sharp and sudden she screamed against his palm.

For what felt like an hour he traversed her body with his hands, finding all the pressure points on her that when touched the right way would send acute agony flashing through her body like lightning. By the time he stopped, she lay panting and sweating on the rug. She had not a single mark on her body, not a single bruise. A flogging would have hurt less.

Søren licked his fingertips and pressed them into her clitoris as he pushed her thighs wide open with his knees.

Pleasure pooled between her legs and radiated out through her entire body. He kissed her mouth, her neck, her nipples, and she raised her hips into his hand.

"Please..." she whispered, desperate to have him inside her. Making her wait was always the cruelest of his tortures.

Tonight he didn't make her wait. He moved her onto her stomach and raised her knee to her chest to open her more for him. He pushed inside her, releasing the slightest of groans as she raised her hips to take him deeper. As he thrust into her, he kissed the back of her neck, her shoulders. He pressed her wrists into the floor, holding her arms immobile.

*"Jeg elsker deg, min lille en,"* he breathed into her skin. *"Du tilhører mig."*

I love you, Little One. You belong to me.

"Tonight, I do," she whispered back in English.

He lingered inside her, not rushing, not hurrying to the

end. She relaxed underneath him and cherished each moment of their joined bodies. She felt pleasure with other men, ecstasy even sometimes...but only when Søren was inside her did she feel whole.

Søren came with his hand digging into the back of her neck and his teeth in her shoulder. She turned her head and kissed his upper arm before he let her go.

They rarely traveled together—it was far too great a risk. Tonight she threw caution to the wind and had booked the same flight but seats on opposite ends of the plane. She'd give her grieving priest the first-class seat. She'd hide out in coach. They wouldn't even get to speak to each other for the entire trip, but even apart for the eight-hour flight, she would keep something of him inside her.

Once in Denmark they could relax. A wonderful thing to come to a country so secular where no one knew him or her. When Søren told her years earlier that less than one percent of the Danish population was Catholic, she asked if they could move here. He'd laughed but she hadn't been joking. Once at his sister's house, the peace she felt being in such a safe and secular country evaporated. At the door she felt a sudden fearfulness, a sense of not belonging here anymore. Søren seemed to sense her fears for he took her hand in his, kissed it and whispered, "This is your home, too."

The girls broke her heart—Laila and Gitte. They'd worshipped their grandmother as much as they worshipped her son. Nora spent all evening with Gitte on her lap and Laila at her side. By nightfall Søren had to pry both unconscious girls off her. They'd fallen asleep after wearing themselves out with tears. Gitte she carried to bed. Laila had gotten so tall only her uncle could lift her. She woke up as he'd started to gather her in his arms.

"I can walk, you know," she said into his shoulder.

"Are you going to?" he asked when she leaned her head sleepily against his chest.

"No."

He laughed as he hefted the almost six-foot-tall girl off the sofa and into his arms.

"Want to trade?" Nora asked Søren. "This one's a little more manageable." Gitte was getting tall, too, but she still didn't weigh much.

"Yes. I'll toss you Laila. You throw me Gitte."

"Terrible idea," a half-asleep Laila murmured when they reached her bedroom. "Throw Gitte first."

Søren tossed Laila onto her bed and ordered her to go to sleep immediately. She shut her eyes and started to feign snores.

"Good girl," he said, pinching her nose before turning the lights off and shutting her door behind him. Nora watched from the door and smiled at them through her tears. In Gitte's room, Søren pulled the covers down and left Nora alone with the little girl as she helped her into her pajamas.

"Mormor's not coming back, is she?" Gitte asked, half in English, half in Danish.

"No, baby, she's not. She's in heaven with her *mor* and *far*. You'll see her again someday."

Gitte had nodded, taking comfort in the promises of grown-ups even if she didn't understand them.

"Are you coming back?"

Nora had swallowed hard against the rock in her throat.

"I never left," she said, kissing the girl good-night and fleeing before more tears could fall.

Alone at last with Søren in the small but elegantly furnished guest room, Nora collapsed into his arms and set her tears free. It should be a simple thing to let go of someone so good. She believed in God, trusted Him…why was it so hard to let Him have Søren's mother? She wanted Gisela back for her sake, for Søren's sake. Her own mother didn't understand her, didn't trust her judgment, didn't believe her when she said, despite appearances, Søren was the best man alive and that he would never hurt her, not in the way that mattered. But Søren's mother had loved them together. From day one when Eleanor Schreiber had first set foot in this house, Gisela had embraced her, called her a daughter, told her she was happy her son had someone who loved him so much.

Every year, sometimes twice a year, she and Søren would sneak away to Denmark for a week. The church knew he had family in Europe and one of the priests at Saint Peter's loved taking over Søren's masses at Sacred Heart. No other congregation in the diocese was so devoted, so devout, so respectful of the priesthood as Søren's. For her twenty-third birthday, Søren had brought her home again. Nowhere else had Nora ever felt such love, such ready acceptance. The family loved not only her and not only him, they loved them, loved her and Søren together. She'd carried Laila on her back and when Gitte was born carried her in her arms. She taught the girls songs she remembered from her own childhood days in Sunday school. She showered them with gifts of books.

Nora remembered standing in the doorway of the nursery and watching in awe as Søren paced back and forth with a colicky six-month-old Gitte on his shoulder, letting her cry it out for an hour until she finally slept. Even then he still held her, worried putting her in her crib would wake her back up again. It had hurt to see that, hurt more than she ever wanted to admit to. Most of the time, having children wasn't even a blip on her radar. Her heart yearned for other types of creation than motherhood. Søren, though, would have been the best of fathers. Patient, fearless, kind and terrifyingly protective. She'd been afraid to ask him back then if he wanted her to have his children. He wouldn't have been the first priest with a shadow family, after all. But she hadn't asked because she feared the answer. A "yes" would have broken her spirit of independence. A "no" would have broken her heart.

This was her family, Søren's family. They knew she and Søren weren't allowed to be together. They no more cared what the pope said about their relationship than they cared what the weatherman said about a rainstorm in China. And so on her twenty-third birthday, after Freyja had put Gitte to bed and Søren had left with Laila for a bedtime story, Gisela had given her the white cloth.

Without explanation, Nora had known what the square of linen meant, where Gisela had gotten it.

"I can't take this," she said. "This belongs to you."

"And I am giving it to you," Gisela said, laying her hand gently on Nora's face. "I know you and he can never marry. I would have loved to have seen that wedding, watched the church bless you both...but it's only a dream. I want you to have it. Please do me the honor of letting me give it to the woman who should be my daughter-in-law. Even if the church can't bless you, I can. This is my blessing."

She'd taken the linen cloth and held it to her heart. She'd said nothing, could say nothing. There were no words.

"But what is it?" Marie-Laure interrupted. She held up the square of linen. "Why does it even matter? It's linen. It's nothing."

"It's not nothing," Nora said, anger creeping into her voice. "That's a maniturgium."

"Speak English. Not Catholic."

"When a priest is ordained, his hands are blessed with holy oils. The maniturgium is a linen hand towel that's used to wipe his hands of those oils. It's a tradition that the priest..." Nora paused and swallowed. "The priest gives the maniturgium to his mother. She is to be buried with it, holding it in her hands, so that when she goes to heaven the angels will see that she gave birth to a priest. And they will open the gates at once and let her into God's presence."

Nora shut her eyes tight. Tears escaped and rolled down her cheeks.

"And Søren's mother gave it to me. She wanted me to have it because she said that with or without the church's blessing or understanding or acknowledgment, I was the wife of a priest. I took it with me to her funeral. I'd left Søren, and I didn't feel right about keeping it. I wanted his mother to be buried with it if that's what he wanted. But it wasn't. He wanted me to keep it. He wanted me to be buried with it someday. And I wanted to keep it. Forever."

Marie-Laure stared at Nora, who sat on the floor tied up and weeping. She'd never felt so helpless, so hopeless, so broken.

"If you kill me," Nora said between tears, "please let me die holding it. Please."

Marie-Laure looked at Damon, who sat and simply waited.

"Cut her loose," she ordered. Damon raised an eyebrow. "Do it."

He came to Nora and pulled out a knife. He cut the ropes, cut the duct tape and left her sitting with only the handcuffs on her wrists.

"Give me the ring," Marie-Laure said, "and I'll give the cloth to you."

Nora shook her head. "I can't. It's not mine to give."

Marie-Laure reached in her pocket and pulled out a long wooden match. She struck it and brought the flame to the cloth.

The next sound anyone heard was the sound of a ten-carat diamond ring striking the floor at Marie-Laure's feet. Marie-

Laure blew out the match and handed the cloth to Nora, who clutched it to her chest.

"You should thank me, you know," Marie-Laure said, picking up the diamond ring and placing it on her hand. "You're one of those people who doesn't know what she wants until she's got a gun to her head and a match poised ready to burn her whole world down. The day I realized my husband was in love with my brother was the best day of my life. I learned what mattered that day. Me. Only me."

"Thank you," Nora said, grateful that she held the cloth in her hand again. It gave her peace, hope, although she didn't know why.

"He loves you...my God, he does love you, doesn't he?"

"Yes, he does."

"And you left him. Why?"

Nora turned her head and smiled at the last morning she might ever see.

"I was so young..." Nora could barely speak through the tears. "I fell in love with him when I was fifteen. And he loved me, too. Even a palace starts to feel like a prison if you've been in it since you were fifteen years old."

"But it was a palace."

"It was paradise..." She smiled through her tears. "And paradise had a wall around it."

"You don't like walls, do you?"

"This was a big wall. When I was a teenager, Søren made me water a stick in the ground every day for six months. A goddamn fucking dead stick. A test of obedience. Jesuits are into obedience."

"You didn't like that?"

Nora glared at her through narrowed eyes.

"Do I seem like the obedient type to you?"

"But you did obey him."

"As long as I could. As much as I could. Those were the old marriage vows, right? Love, honor, obey? I did all three."

"Marriage vows? You compare your sick little world of collars to marriage? To a sacrament? No matter what blessing his mother gave you, you aren't his wife, you never were, not in any way. He married me, not you. And he's still married to me. I'm the wife. You're the mistress. But don't feel bad. I remarried when I was twenty-five to a powerful man. I didn't love him but I respected him. And I hated that I wasn't truly his wife because I had married another years before. Your priest—he made a mistress of both of us."

"I don't care what I am. I never have. It's everyone else who cares. Not me. I don't care if I'm his mistress or his wife. I only wanted Søren. People tell me to get married, settle down, have kids. Fuck them. They don't know me. You know who never told me how to live my life? Søren. He asked me to obey him, not to change for him. That's why I could never ask him to leave the priesthood, never let him marry me, because he never asked me to be somebody else so I won't ask him to be somebody else. And I left Søren the day he asked me to marry him, because that was the one day he asked me to change who I was and that was the one day he tried to change for me. He'll never make that mistake again. Look, I don't give a damn about being a wife or a mistress. I am who I am. I don't need paperwork to prove Søren loves me. I don't need paperwork to prove anything."

"Paperwork…good word. It's the only thing that separates you from me. A wife is nothing but a mistress with paperwork. At least he loved you. He never even gave a damn about me."

"He did, though. He did. He was in love with Kingsley, but he never wanted anything bad to happen to you. He never wanted to hurt you."

"But I know what he is now. Him not wanting to hurt me? That's the final proof he didn't care about me at all."

Nora couldn't argue with that. The two people he loved the most, her and Kingsley, were the two people Søren hurt the most.

"I lost face because of him." Marie-Laure knelt down in front of Nora. "It's a fine funny phrase—'lost face.' It means to lose honor, to be humiliated. A whole school of boys who worshipped me and the one who should have, my own husband, cared nothing."

"He tried to care."

"Only for Kingsley's sake. And now, thirty years later, I have lost face again. Look at me. Look." Marie-Laure grabbed Nora by the chin and held her with bruising strength. "I'm old now. I'm not beautiful anymore. My face...I've lost it. And he, he's still so...fucking...beautiful." With those words Marie-Laure's face contorted into true ugliness.

"You'll die," Nora said, and meant it. "If you kill me, or you kill him, you'll die. You know it. Kingsley will hunt you down to the ends of the earth if you hurt one of his own."

"Maybe that's what I want. Maybe I don't want to live anymore."

"Because you're not as pretty as you were when you were twenty-one? Is that all you have? Is there nothing else to you but your beauty? You lose your beauty and what's left?"

Marie-Laure let go of Nora's chin and stood up.

"Only my hate."

## 29

## THE ROOK

Grace woke at dawn and knew something wasn't right. Laila slept next to her in the bed. Usually Grace woke up gradually, downing cup after cup of coffee or black tea before coming fully to herself in the mornings. But now she vibrated like a live wire, alert and scared, although she didn't know why.

She left Laila sleeping in the bed. Footsteps...she'd heard footsteps in the hall lingering outside the half-open door. That's what had woken her. She entered the hall and followed the sound of the footsteps, her heart gripped in a panic she couldn't explain, not even to herself.

At the top of the stairs she paused. Søren stood at the front door in his black clerics and white collar. Something about seeing him in his collar... She knew...she knew exactly why she'd woken and she knew exactly where he was going.

"No." Grace raced down the stairs, her heart in her hands. "No...no, don't go. Don't."

He turned around and came to her at the bottom of the stairway.

"It's fine. It's all right, Grace."

She shook her head. "No, it's not. You can't go. Don't…" And she wrapped her arms around him and held him tight to her, so tight it almost hurt her.

"I'm touched." He laughed a little in her ear.

"Don't." She couldn't get any other word past her throat. Let him laugh at her. She would hold him and keep him here if it killed her.

"I have to go," he whispered, returning the embrace much more gently before pulling back and meeting her eyes. "It's the only thing I can do."

"But Kingsley…he was—"

"Kingsley went to Elizabeth's house, and there was no way to get her out without killing his sister. I can't ask him to do that, not even for me or Eleanor. I love him as much as I do her. I have to help them both now."

"There has to be another way. I can't…" She held his face in her hands. Never in her life had she felt such fear, such grief. Irrational, unreasonable…she barely knew the man and yet she felt to lose him would be to lose herself, to lose something priceless. She wouldn't have begged for her own life this fervently. "Please…"

"I have to go. I have to get my Little One back. No matter the cost."

"It's too high. She killed that poor girl, that runaway. She'll…you know she will."

"It doesn't matter. If it's me she wants, then she'll have me. She'll have her vengeance. If there's any chance at all Eleanor can come out of this alive, I have to take it."

"There has to be a way, a plan. Something."

"Grace…" Søren touched her cheek, wiped away a tear.

"This was always the plan. I promised Kingsley a day to try. I knew he wouldn't be able to go through with it. He's grieved his whole life for the imagined crime of killing his sister. I can't let him go through that again. Last time all he did was kiss me and he's blamed himself thirty years for her death. How much will he suffer if he actually pulls the trigger this time?"

"You can't save everyone. You can save yourself."

"This is how I save myself."

Grace shook her head, desperately seeking arguments, answers, anything she could say or do to convince him not to run off on this suicide mission.

"But Nora...she won't want to live without you."

"She already has. She left me years ago and made a life for herself. She'll do it again. I've never known anyone as strong as she."

"And she went back. She loves you. She told me how much she loves you."

"She loves Wesley, too. They can be together. He can give her everything. She'll want for nothing."

"She'll want for you."

Grace broke on the last word and the tears poured from her like wine from a broken cask. Søren held her again, held her close.

"Listen to me," he said into her ear. "I need you to be strong for her. I'm not sure what will have happened to her while they had her. Make her tell you, make her take care of herself. She hates going to the doctor. Take her even if it's against her will. Promise me you'll do that for her, for me."

"I will," she pledged. How could she ever say no to him?

"Laila's here for a reason. For Laila, Eleanor will stay strong. She'll take care of Laila so you have to take care of Eleanor for me."

Grace nodded, her face buried against his shoulder. Now

she knew why Søren had insisted Wesley and Laila and even she should come along with him and Kingsley. Søren had known he would do this, known all along. He wanted Nora to be surrounded by love after Søren had died for her. They were plan B.

"When the time comes, tell her that she and Wesley…they have my blessing. He's a good man, a good person, and he'll love her. That's all that matters…that he loves her."

Grace clung to Søren's shoulders, felt the smoothness of the black fabric under her fingers, the muscle in his arms under the fabric. She wanted to tell him something, wanted to tell him that she loved him, too, although it made no sense, none at all. This love went deeper than affection or attraction or romance or family. Something stranger, stronger, wilder… It felt like faith.

"I have to go."

"I'll go with you. Let me walk with you, please. At least a little while."

Søren said nothing at first. He closed his eyes and Grace could do nothing but cling to his hand.

"Would you? I would like that."

They left the house and stepped out into the newborn morning. They walked along the road and no cars passed them. At first Grace tried not to cry, tried to stay strong for him as he'd asked. But she couldn't stop the tears.

"I've always wondered if it would come to this," Søren said after twenty or thirty minutes of walking. "When I was in seminary in Rome, I had a friend. She taught me every-thing I know."

"Everything?" Grace tried to smile, tried and failed.

"She could kill a fly with the tip of a whip. After a few months under her tutelage, so could I."

"Who was she?"

"She ran an order of women."

"A convent?"

He smiled.

"A brothel."

Grace laughed. It hurt to laugh.

"Her name was Magdalena. That's what she said it was. I didn't believe her. I never asked her real name, never told her mine. I would run away to her house of ill repute at least once a week. Can you imagine? A young seminarian, a Jesuit-in-training, spending his evenings surrounded by the most notorious prostitutes in Rome. Her young ladies catered to a very specific clientele. I received quite an education in that house."

"I'm sure you did."

"When it was time for me to leave Rome and come to America, Magdalena took me aside. She always claimed to be part-Gypsy. It might have been true, not that it mattered. She got paid to tell lies to men. She said she would miss me, although she would be glad to see me go. Apparently some of her clients were not pleased to have a Jesuit hanging about."

"Can't imagine why."

"But Magdalena, she wanted to tell me my fortune before I left."

"What did she tell you?" Grace tightened her grip on his hand, knowing the moment she let him go would be the moment she let him go forever.

"She said that I would go to America and I would be sent somewhere I didn't want to go. But there I would meet a queen in disguise. And it would be a very good disguise, so good only I would recognize her. And she said this queen would be two things to me. She would be my heart. And she would be my penance."

He stopped walking and Grace knew this was where he would leave her. She wanted to speak, wanted to tell him everything in her heart. But she had no words, none for him. She would have rather seen every stained-glass window in the world shatter into shards, every church, every cathedral, fall into ruin, and see every holy book in the world dissolve into dust, than see any harm come to this man. As long as he lived there would be God in the world even if all the temples burned.

"I left a note for Kingsley in the library," Søren said as casually as if he'd said he needed his dry cleaning picked up. "Please see that he gets it. Don't tell them where I've gone. I don't want Laila…" He paused then, as if he couldn't bring himself to speak the next words.

"I'll take care of your girl…both of your girls."

Søren nodded and whispered, "Thank you."

He started to pull away but Grace couldn't quite let go yet. She grabbed his hand again and held it to her heart.

"I have to tell you something," she said, and he met her eyes.

"Last call for confessions."

"I love my husband more than life itself. And there's no one in the world other than Zachary who I want to grow old with. I want to have his children and be his wife and stay with him for the rest of my days. But the truth is…" She paused for courage and found it in him. "I would have sold my soul for one night with you."

She spoke the words and gave him a smile, gave it like a gift. He would die today. At least she could give him that one act of kindness, of letting him see a woman who loved him smiling at him on the last morning of his life.

"Beautiful Grace," he said, taking her hand and kissing the center of her palm, "I wouldn't have charged you nearly so much."

She laughed and the laughter shattered into tears as he let

her go and started to walk away into the woods. As he reached the tree line, Grace called out after him.

"She said you were the best man on earth."

Søren turned around.

"She says that all the time. No one ever believes her."

He turned again and was gone.

Grace spoke two words that only she and God would ever hear.

"I did."

Standing in the middle of the road she held her stomach. The pain...she'd never known such pain. She could have screamed so that every devil in hell heard her cry and it wouldn't relieve the pain, the betrayal, she felt. She would not live in a world where someone thought they had the right to hurt him, to hurt the woman he loved, the woman he would die for. She wouldn't do it. She wouldn't stand for it.

So instead she ran for it.

# 30
# THE QUEEN

Nora lay on her side on the floor. She'd been left alone in Marie-Laure's room. It seemed that they'd lost interest in her now. They'd expected something, something that hadn't happened. It scared her, this sudden lack of loathing, lack of fascination with her. Marie-Laure's obsession with Nora's stories had kept her alive for a couple of days. Now she wanted no more stories.

No more stories, no more Nora.

Alone on the floor Nora prayed her last prayers. If she did die today she prayed it would be clean and quick. She hated the thought of dying screaming and shitting herself. At least if they'd gotten bored with her, then they might simply put a bullet in her brain. One blink and she'd be gone.

She prayed for her mother, too, prayed she would be okay, wouldn't be broken by losing her only child like this. She prayed for Wesley, that he would find someone else to love, someone who would give him everything he wanted and deserved—marriage, children, an equal partner and an undivided heart. For Kingsley she prayed, too. She prayed he'd understand that she never wanted to steal Søren from him, that she never begrudged Søren's love for him, their friendship. She prayed he'd forgive her for not having his child and not asking what he wanted. She'd been so afraid of the answer she hadn't dared ask the question. She prayed he would find peace with Juliette and everything else he needed.

For Søren she prayed that he would survive losing her, that he would remember his faith and know that he'd only lost her a little while, and she would be with him again someday.

Her final prayer she devoted to Grace and Zach, who ached so badly to have a child. Maybe the final prayer of a condemned woman might get God's attention.

As the sun finally showed itself over the edge of the horizon, Nora finished her prayers and closed her eyes.

Even when she heard footsteps coming her way only minutes later Nora kept her eyes closed. She had no desire to look death in the face. She stayed safe behind her eyes, hiding in her heart where she kept all her most beautiful memories of Søren.

"Wake up," came Damon's voice from above her.

"Five more minutes, Mom," Nora said from the floor.

Nora cried out as her side exploded in pain. She curled into the fetal position and choked on her own tears.

"I said 'wake up.' I'll kick you again if you want me to."

She opened her eyes and painfully sat up. Every breath hurt. He'd cracked a rib kicking her so hard.

"I'm awake." She looked up at Damon and met his eyes. She saw a delighted fire burning in them.

"Good. He's here."

# 31
# THE KNIGHT

Wesley woke up early. Too early. The sun hadn't even quite clawed its way up into the sky yet. But now that he was awake he knew he wouldn't be able to sleep again until complete exhaustion overtook him. He crawled out of bed and pulled on jeans and a T-shirt. He forced himself to focus on the basics. He needed to eat something, check his blood sugar, take a shower. He shouldn't make things worse for everyone by going into DKA again. Nora needed to be the only thing anyone worried about. Saving Nora…getting her back, getting her safe.

Alone in his room Wesley checked his blood sugar and took his insulin. As he put away his supplies he noticed what was beneath his feet for the first time. An Oriental rug covered the floor. Peeking out from the edges of the rug, Wesley noticed darkly stained hardwood flooring. He walked to the edge of the rug and kicked it back, baring the floor beneath.

He could do this. Of course he could. If Nora did it, so

could he. Bumps and bruises…nothing bad. At worst he might get a shiner and a headache. With one deep breath Wesley let himself fall forward, barreling face-first toward the floor.

In an instant and only an inch from the floor, Wesley's hands shot out and caught himself. He rose up in a high push-up. Maybe from here, from a mere two feet from the floor, he could drop down and let himself hit the floor. For a solid five minutes he held that pose, daring himself to let go.

He couldn't. He couldn't let himself fall.

"Dammit, Nora," he said to himself as he stood up. Wesley left the room and his failed experiment behind him. Across the hall was Laila and Grace's room. Grace was already up but Laila still lay in bed, her body bowed into the fetal position. Did she always sleep like that? Curled up tight into a ball? Or was she cold and that's why she had her legs pulled into her chest? Without waking her, Wesley grabbed the spare blanket from the closet and covered Laila with it. She looked so pretty in her sleep, so calm and peaceful, with her long, dark eyelashes resting on her cheeks. Weird a girl so blonde would have such dark eyelashes. Hard to believe a girl this gorgeous had made it to eighteen still a virgin. Then again, he wasn't hideous, as Nora always said, and he'd made it to eighteen, nineteen, twenty even. Must be hard having such an intimidating priest for an uncle. Even if she liked a guy, no way would he be able to meet her uncle's exacting standards. And Laila seemed so smart, so sweet, and she wasn't even freaked out by the needles and the shots. No, a girl like Laila definitely deserved the best. Something else he and Søren agreed on.

God, he missed hating that man.

Wesley left Laila sleeping in her bed. He didn't want to be the weirdo creeper caught staring at an unconscious girl. Especially not by Søren, who would probably kill him as Laila had warned last night.

After eating his low-carb and no-taste breakfast, Wesley went in search of Søren. He needed updates, information, any news anyone had about Nora. He didn't find Søren anywhere downstairs. But in the library he found Kingsley sitting behind a big desk, a book across his stomach, his eyes closed.

"Any news?" Wesley asked without preamble.

Kingsley slowly opened his eyes.

"Shall I get you the *Sunday Times?*"

"About Nora."

*"Non."* Kingsley sat up in the chair and faced Wesley over the desk. "No news."

"You went there last night. What happened?"

He shook his head.

*"Rien."*

"Please. English."

"Nothing. Nothing happened."

"You went there and what? Had a picnic?"

*"Oui,* I had a picnic. Then I broke into the house, hid in the servants' halls, listened to your fiancée speaking—"

"You heard her?" Wesley's heart leaped with hope.

"And saw her."

"She's alive. Oh…thank God." He collapsed into the chair in front of the desk, his head in his hands. "Was she okay?"

"Okay is a relative term. She was alive, she looked uninjured. Her clothes were on and, although soiled, did not appear torn."

Wesley breathed through his hands.

"Then what? You saw her. You couldn't get her out."

"Not without shooting my own sister in the back."

Kingsley stared at him full in the face. A hard, cold stare that Kingsley wielded like a weapon. Wesley stared back and didn't look away. Kingsley seemed to be challenging him, daring him to question his choices.

"I couldn't do that, either," Wesley finally said. "Kill someone. Not in the back, anyway. Self-defense, maybe, but no, not in cold blood."

Kingsley narrowed his eyes as if not trusting Wesley's words.

"I left her there in the house. I couldn't get her out."

"So what's next, then? What's the plan? You say there are people there with your sister. People can be bought, bribed."

"Would you like to go to the house now and write them a check?"

"If I thought it would work, I would. Jesus, we can't just sit here and wait. We have to do something."

"I am doing something. I've made some calls. I have some help coming. When they get here, we'll try again. Don't worry. We'll get your fiancée back and you two can get married. Please don't forget to invite me to the divorce."

"Are you ever going to explain to me why you hate me so much?"

"You're not interesting enough to hate."

Wesley shook his head in disgust.

"God, I thought Søren was bad. Could Nora have worse taste in men?"

"I believe you're the answer to that question."

Wesley leaned forward in his chair.

"Tell me. Why do you hate me? I want to know."

Kingsley slammed the book in front of him shut and stood up. He came around the desk and sat on the edge.

"You want to know why? I'll tell you why, *mon petit prince*. You have never suffered. And don't tell me you have. I have shoes that have suffered worse tortures than you."

"You're right," Wesley agreed readily. "I haven't suffered. I'll be the first to admit I won some kind of cosmic lottery with my family."

"You have. And yet you think you deserve someone like her. And worse, you think she's better off with someone like you. You are a child. You are the child who wakes up from a nightmare and stumbles into his parents' bedroom and sees Daddy on top of Mommy and thinks, 'Why is he hurting her?' That's what you are. An ignorant child who has not lived, has not struggled, has not suffered, has not hurt, and yet presumes to tell his parents that what they're doing is wrong."

"And that's why you hate me so much? Because I'm not kinky?"

"I couldn't care less if you're kinky or not. You might as well ask me if I care what sort of car you drive, Ponyboy."

Wesley glared at Kingsley. He started to protest but Kingsley snapped his fingers in his face, cutting him off.

"I don't like you because you sit there in judgment of us. I have seen real evil. I have seen the horrors of this world and even committed a few myself. You look at *le prêtre* and you see some kind of monster. If there is anyone on earth who has the right to hate him or to judge him, it is me. And do you know who I see? I see God."

"Søren is not God."

"He's the closest thing to God I've ever found. He let his lover leave him and he took her back. She left him again and he would take her back again. He forgives and forgives and forgives. *Mon Dieu,* forgiveness is in his job description. It's what he does for a living. He forgave her for spurning his love and welcomed her back with open arms. No punishment, no questions asked. When he metes out his punishments, they are deserved and they are fair. His acts of mercy are legendary. His capacity for love is never-ending. And you come along and see him putting a knife in someone's chest and you scream, 'Murderer!' while the rest of us see a heart surgeon."

"Nice words but you're the one who choked Nora so hard

one night she passed out and hit the floor and had to go to the hospital."

"Oh, yes, that night. You mean the night she came to me and asked me to teach her how to do breath-play? The night we took turns on each other? I demonstrated on her. She practiced on me. That night between equals, you mean?"

"I'm sorry. I can't accept that hurting another person is ever okay."

Kingsley lowered his head until they looked at each other eye to eye.

"You apologize for not wanting to hurt another person? Little Prince, I think perhaps you've lingered in our world far too long. There is no honor in what we do. There is no evil, either. You think you know better about what your fiancée wants than she does. You insult her intelligence and maturity and ability to make her own decisions. You insult her, you insult us all."

"I want her to be safe."

"You don't want her to be safe. She is safe with us. You want her to be saved. You can't save someone—"

"I know. I know…I can't save someone who doesn't want to be saved."

"No. You can't save someone who doesn't *need* to be saved."

They locked eyes and Wesley knew Kingsley wanted to stare him down, make him blink first. Fine. He stood up and let Kingsley win. He'd go hang out with Laila or Grace, with anyone who didn't loathe him. Even Søren made for better company.

At the door Wesley turned around.

"I want to help get Nora back. I will help if you'll let me."

"Your hands are clean," Kingsley said, sitting back down behind the desk. "Keep them clean."

"I know you think I don't deserve her. Fine, I don't. No

one's good enough for Nora. But at least…give me a chance to try to deserve her."

Kingsley sighed and sat down in the chair behind the desk again.

"Sit down, Wesley."

Wesley paused in the doorway and gazed at Kingsley suspiciously. Kingsley pointed at the chair and Wesley returned and sat down.

"What?"

"I want to tell you a story. A short one."

"Fine. Okay. Tell me."

"I have loved two women in my life. Only two." He held up two fingers. "A thousand lovers but only two loves apart from him. The first was a woman named Charlotte. I called her Charlie."

"Why?"

"I prefer women with men's names. Satisfies a certain deviant side to me."

"Of course. Sure."

"Charlie, beautiful Charlie. One of the more sexually open-minded women I'd ever met. Anything I proposed she was more than willing to try. She was kind, too, caring, treated my staff well, adored me. But after a few months, I could tell she was restless. She wanted more than I could give her. She wanted to travel the world, have grand adventures, while I had to stay in the city and mind the Empire. Before me she'd been tied down to her job, her brother. Living with me in my world gave her wings. And so she flew away."

"I'm sorry," Wes said with genuine sympathy. Losing Nora that first time had almost killed him, had killed him for a few months.

"I'm not. I wanted something different than what Charlie wanted. As much as we adored each other, we were not a good match. While grieving over my lost love, I went to Haiti. I met my Juliette and in her I found the other half of myself, the half I thought I'd long ago lost and had learned to live without. Had I never met, loved and lost Charlie, I never would have met, loved and kept Juliette. My loss was the key to my greatest gain."

"Yeah, when God closes a door He opens a window. I've heard it."

"God or no God, it's true. Welcome to the real world. Shit happens. You get over it. I don't even miss Charlie and in my more honest moments I know she doesn't miss me, either. You grow up. You move on. You find someone new. And for God's sake, you don't ask the first woman who lets you fuck her to marry you."

"Shit happens? Move on? This is your big life advice?"

"It's good advice. I take it myself. I suffered for years before I found real love with Jules."

"Real love? If it's real love, then where is she? I don't see her anywhere."

"She would be with me if I allowed it. I sent her away."

"Romantic."

"I sent her away for her own good. That should sound familiar."

"Sounds familiar and stupid," Wes said, his anger rising. Søren lent Nora to Daniel for a week. He shared her with Kingsley. Kingsley sent his Juliette away for God knows what reason.

"It wasn't stupid to send Juliette away."

"Why? Why is it right for you to send away someone you love? Trust me, I've been sent away. I know what bullshit that is. Søren tells me I'm paternalistic with Nora because I want to protect her. You act like I've committed some capital offense because I want her safe. Why do you get to decide what's good for Juliette if I can't decide what's good for Nora?"

"It's an entirely different situation. Worlds apart."

"How is it any different? Why do you get to be paternalistic and I don't?"

"*Paternalistic* is the right word for it. Juliette is pregnant. And yes, in case you were wondering, it's mine."

Wesley couldn't speak. He just sat and stared at Kingsley. And Kingsley didn't speak, either. He rubbed his chin with two long and elegant fingers, lines of worry crossing his brow.

"She told me after you and your fiancée ran off together. I received a threatening piece of mail. I couldn't take any risks with Juliette. I sent her away to keep her safe. That is the one regret I do not have about this situation."

Wesley struggled to find the words, any words, right or wrong to say. He could only come up with one.

"Congratulations."

Kingsley gave him a look of profoundest shock.

"Congratulations? That's what you have to say?"

"Well…yeah…kids are great. What do you want me to say? You're going to be a father. Congratulations."

"You aren't horrified at the prospect of a man like me being a father?"

"I have a little trouble imagining you changing diapers. But you have money. You can hire someone to do that part, I guess. No, not horrified. Why would I be?"

"Because of what I am…what I do…"

"Nora's like you," Wesley said, hating to admit it but knowing it would be a lie to pretend she was anything other than what she was. "I don't think her being kinky means she'd be a bad mom. She's great with kids. She'll be an amazing mother someday."

"She does not want children."

"She might change her mind. Once things settle down, once we're married and—"

"Trust me on this…she does not want children. She had her chance once. She didn't take it."

Wesley's eyes bored into Kingsley.

"What are you saying?"

"I am saying…" Kingsley leaned forward and spoke slowly. "She had her chance. I know she had her chance because that child was also mine. Your fiancée got pregnant, she realized she was pregnant and, within two days, she wasn't pregnant anymore. So before you entertain another fantasy about nurseries and nannies and a glowing Nora Sutherlin swelling with your child, know this—she does not want children. And if you do, then you should very much reconsider your choice for *chatelaine*."

Wesley felt something break—something light and small, no bigger than a soap bubble. It burst in the air in front of him and evaporated into the ether. He didn't know what it was—a hope or a dream or perhaps merely a wish—but it was gone now, gone forever.

"She told me…" Wesley began, and stopped, waiting for his voice to steady itself. "She told me once why she trusted you. I didn't trust you. You sent her on all those jobs. Sent this five-foot-three woman to strange houses and hotels with nothing but a riding crop to protect her. You sent her into the bedrooms of these rich and dangerous men. I told her she shouldn't do it, it was dangerous, she could get killed. You two fought on the phone all the time. Fought and flirted and plotted and schemed. I asked her why she trusted you. You know what she said?"

"Enlighten me."

"She said that you were like the brother she never had. She said that yes, you two fought all the time, but only in the way siblings fight. She said that at the end of the day she knew you would never put her into real danger. You could punch her in the arm and pull her hair because you were her big brother but if anyone else tried it—"

"I would destroy them."

"Yeah. And then she said that she knew you were family because only family forgave each other like you had to forgive her. I asked her what she did to you that was so awful. She said she took something from you, something you wanted, and you forgave her for it, anyway. Now, I don't trust you, and I don't trust Søren, but I'm trying to trust Nora. So I'm going to trust that she was right about you when she said that even when you two didn't like each other, you still loved each other. Every now and then my father and I get into nasty fights. Usually on days ending in Y. But at the end of that day, he's still my father and he'd still burn the world down to save my life if he had to. Nora says it's the same with you."

Kingsley didn't speak and for that Wesley could have kissed the man. He'd had enough of that suave French accent and that patronizing tone.

"I'm sorry for what happened with you and Nora. I wished she'd told me the whole truth. Then I could have told her that I don't hate her for it, that I don't judge her," Wes said, wishing he could have been there for her back then. Maybe he could have talked her out of it.

"She'll never be the wife you want her to be," Kingsley said.

"You know what, I don't give a fuck about that right now. I just want her safe. You get that?"

"More than you can possibly imagine."

"Are you going to get her back? Or are you going to make a liar out of Nora for saying she trusted you like family?"

"I will get her back even if it kills me."

Wesley started to say something but heard the front door slamming and feet running.

Grace appeared in the doorway out of breath and shaking.

"He's gone," she panted. "He left you a note in the desk, but he's gone."

Kingsley nearly ripped the desk drawer opening it. He pulled out a white sheet of paper, barely glanced at it and dropped it on the desk.

He raced from the room. Wes stared at Grace in shock, in horror, in confusion. In the distance he heard a car starting.

"Søren…he went to give himself up," Grace said, still gasping for air. "He's going to let her kill him."

# 32
# THE QUEEN

"He? He who?" Nora asked.

Damon grasped Nora by the upper arm and yanked her off the floor so hard he nearly dislocated her shoulder.

"You get one guess."

Nora knew but she didn't want to know, didn't want to guess, didn't want to make it real.

"I'll give you a hint. She's already planning the honeymoon."

"Oh, God," Nora whispered, bringing her cuffed hands to her face. "What's she going to do to him?"

"I think she's going to leave that up to you." He pulled her into the hall and dragged her toward some destination unknown.

"Up to me? What do you mean?"

Damon didn't answer, he only laughed, and the laugh was so cold and evil she would have clawed his eyes out if she could.

He threw open the door to the library and Nora gasped at the sight before her.

Søren knelt on the floor in the middle of the library. Andrei stood at Søren's back. And from the serene look on Søren's face, one would think he was a pious man kneeling for his morning prayers instead of a man with a gun to the back of his head.

"Søren!" Nora wanted to scream his name but it came out hoarse and broken. He opened his eyes and looked at her and she saw nothing in the gaze but love.

She started to run to him but Damon held her struggling in his arms. Squirming and writhing, she desperately tried to wrench herself from his iron grasp.

"Eleanor, calm down," Søren ordered. "Don't give them any excuse to hurt you."

Everything within her rebelled but she did as Søren told her and forced herself to stop struggling.

"Damon, you can let her go," came Marie-Laure's voice from behind them. "She's not the one who matters anymore."

She sensed Damon hesitating but he released her. As soon as his arms left her, Nora raced forward and dropped, almost skidding on her knees to get to Søren as fast as she could. She raised her hands to his face, kissed his lips, leaned into him and breathed in the scent of him—winter even in summer.

"You lunatic," she whispered, caressing his face, his mouth, with her still-bound hands, "why are you smiling?"

He gazed at her with new eyes, with eyes of almost-innocent wonder.

"It's good to see you again, Little One. I missed you."

"I missed you, too. God, I missed you so much. You shouldn't have come."

"I had to."

"He didn't have to," Marie-Laure said as she walked to them

and started to circle them on the floor like a shark. "I would have killed you and then disappeared again. He loves you for whatever reason so I would have had all the vengeance I desired. But this…killing him? This is better."

"You fucking b—"

"Eleanor, look at me," Søren said, his voice calm but insistent. She did as he told her. There was no one else in the world she wanted to look at more, anyway.

She nodded and rested her head against his chest.

"You shouldn't have come." Nora wanted so badly to wrap her arms around him but the handcuffs held her wrists tight. "You should have let them kill me."

"You know I couldn't do that," he chided. "I told you there was nothing I wouldn't do to protect you."

"Goddammit," she said, resting her forehead briefly against the center of his chest before looking up at him. "Why do you love me so much, you stupid man?"

He smiled down at her.

"Because I met you."

"This is all very sweet," Marie-Laure said, still circling them. "But we do need to get this over with. I'm sick of this house, tired of this game. The boys are getting bored, too. They get restless when bored."

"What do you want?" Nora asked. "We'll give it to you. Money, apologies, firstborn children…anything."

Marie-Laure stopped and gazed down at Nora.

"I want you to make a choice. It seems you have a pathological fear of making any definitive choices in your life. You flit from man to man and never completely commit to anyone. Once you make a decision, you don't stick with it. You promised yourself to him," she said, pointing at Søren, "and then you left him. You had another man in your life and you sent him away. Then you went back to my husband but you didn't stay with him, either. Back and forth, back and forth. You make my head spin."

"Imagine how I feel," Nora said.

"I can't. I can't imagine you feel anything. If you did, you wouldn't spend your entire life fucking men over."

"Marie-Laure, that's enough," Søren said, giving her the barest glance before looking back at Nora again. "Your argument is with me and Kingsley. Eleanor was only a child when you and I married."

"Oh, yes, defend her. The woman who spread for half the country while you stay locked up in your church praying for her soul."

"I've never prayed for her soul," Søren said. "Only for her happiness."

"Doesn't she look happy now?" Marie-Laure grabbed Nora by the chin and squeezed viciously hard before letting her go.

"I am happy," Nora said, refusing to be cowed. "Of course I'm happy."

"Why?" Marie-Laure asked.

Nora looked at Søren. "Because he's here."

"*Mon Dieu,* if this is what love is, I'm rather glad I was spared it. You two turn my stomach with your little show."

"We should go," Damon said, coming closer to them, a gun held in his hand. "If he's here, then…"

"They're afraid of Kingsley," Marie-Laure explained. "I, however, am not. If he was going to try something he would have by now. He'll let you two suffer and die while he's off somewhere else not caring. I suffered for months right under his nose and he didn't care, wouldn't care."

"He suffered, too," Søren interjected. "I told you before we married that ours would be a marriage in name only. You agreed to it. You knew I didn't love you."

"You should have loved me." Marie-Laure glared at

him with the fires of hell burning in her eyes. "Everyone loved me."

"And you loved no one," Søren said without the slightest tinge of rancor in his voice. "You didn't even love me. You were merely insulted that someone you desired didn't desire you back. Kingsley knew what love was. You mistook desire and jealousy for love. You didn't want a husband. You wanted a conquest. I only fascinated you because I wouldn't give in."

Marie-Laure said nothing for a moment. Nora shivered as a little smile danced across her lips.

"You're right, my husband. I tried to seduce you and failed. I tried to woo you and failed. I tried to conquer you and failed. I will not fail again."

"There is nothing to be gained by this," Søren said. "If you kill me, what will you achieve? I'll die still in love with her and never having loved you."

"That's true." She nodded her agreement. "Too true. But perhaps you would be a bit easier to seduce now than you were all those years ago. Damon?"

Damon stepped forward and put his gun to the back of Nora's head. Her heart stopped the second the cold, heavy metal touched her hair.

"Now…" Marie-Laure knelt on the floor next to them. Søren had seemingly stopped breathing the moment Damon pointed the gun at Nora. "Kiss me."

"Søren, don't," Nora begged. "Not even to save my life. Don't."

But Søren ignored her. He turned his head and Marie-Laure rested her hand against his cheek. Nora's stomach churned in revulsion as Marie-Laure pressed her lips to Søren's with terrible ardor. Nora had seen Søren with Kingsley, seen him with submissives at the club, and never had she felt disgust or even the slightest shred of jealousy. In fact, she enjoyed watching him play with others, enjoyed watching others adore him. Seeing him forced to kiss Marie-Laure, seeing the tightness in his face that signaled his own disgust, his own revulsion, at being forced to do something so intimate with someone so foul, sent bile into the back of her throat. It was like watching someone piss on the *Mona Lisa*. It was like watching a rape.

Marie-Laure kissed Søren with endless passion and all Nora could do was watch.

*"Merde…"* Marie-Laure yanked back from the kiss and stared wide-eyed at Søren. Blood streamed from her lip.

Søren glanced at Nora and winked.

"Oh, no," Nora taunted. "He bit you. Now you'll turn kinky, too."

Marie-Laure's hand snaked out and slapped Nora viciously hard on the face, so hard she felt blood escape her nose.

When her vision cleared, Nora smiled at Marie-Laure.

"See? Told you so. You're one of us," Nora said.

Marie-Laure stood up and reached into Damon's jacket pocket. From it she pulled out a black-handled dagger, sleek and lethal. She laid it on the floor between Nora and Søren.

"Let's get this over with, then," Marie-Laure said to Nora. "Time to decide, and this time, whatever decision you make will be quite permanent. You have a choice…you can walk out of this room right now and leave him with me. He'll become my husband, my real husband, no pretense this time, and we'll fly away together to my beautiful home far from here. And Damon and Andrei and a few of my other boys will make sure he stays inside and does every little thing I want him to like a good and attentive husband."

"Or?" Nora asked. Whatever the other option was she'd already decided to choose. Søren forced into slavery, forced to service his madwoman sexually, forced to perform for her? Never. "I can already tell you I'm taking door number two."

"Is that so? Well, let me tell you the other choice. It's quite simple. You can take that dagger and you can shove it into his heart and let him bleed to death on this floor in front of your eyes, in front of mine. And while he's bleeding to death, you walk away. By the time you reach the end of the driveway, I'll already be on my way out of this ugly country."

Nora let the words sink into her. She could let Søren live out the rest of his life a slave to this woman...

Or she could kill him with her own hands.

"Eleanor," Søren whispered, giving her the most desperate and imploring look she'd ever seen on his face. No...the *only* desperate and imploring look she'd ever seen on his face.

"No helping." Marie-Laure snapped her fingers in his face. "She decides, not you."

But Nora had already decided. The choice was no choice at all.

Nora picked up the dagger. Søren sagged with relief.

"I want to say goodbye, first." Nora clutched the knife tight to her chest. "I won't do anything without saying goodbye."

"You can say your goodbyes. I'd rather like to hear this. Go on."

Marie-Laure crossed her arms over her chest and smiled. Nora ignored her, ignored the dagger in her hand, ignored the entire world around her. No one existed but Søren, and once he was gone, there would be nothing left.

She turned her eyes up to him.

"Søren...I'm so sorry—"

"Don't you dare. We only have a few minutes left on this earth together and do not waste a moment of this time apologizing to me for your imagined sins."

"You know I didn't imagine them."

"You have nothing to apologize for. You've lived your life

without fear and without regrets and without giving a damn what anyone thought of you. Don't start that nonsense now."

"I left you."

"You had every right to leave me. My God, Eleanor, the tests I put you through, the trials..."

"Don't forget that stick you made me water for six months."

"I remember. I was never shocked that you left me. Only shocked you didn't leave me sooner."

"You were kind of a hard-ass," she said, grinning at the memories that barreled through her mind with the force and speed of a runaway train. Watering that damn dead stick in the ground as if it were a living plant...changing her clothes seven times in a row because Søren had a specific ensemble in mind he wanted her to wear and they wouldn't leave Kingsley's house until she guessed what it was and put it on...lying curled up on the floor of the Eighth Circle, his shod feet resting on her back as he used her that night as a footstool and nothing more—he didn't even beat her or fuck her or even kiss her. She'd been nothing but furniture.

"You're being too kind."

"Okay, you were an *unbelievable* hard-ass."

"That's better."

"I loved it, though. I loved being yours. Even when I carried that stupid watering can out to water that fucking stick, I loved it. I knew you tortured me like that because you loved me, because you wanted me to be strong."

"You were always strong, Little One. I only ever wanted you to be mine."

Nora leaned against his chest again and he bent to kiss her forehead.

"I am yours," she whispered. "I always was. Even when I was with someone else...I was always yours."

"I know," he said with utter arrogance.

She growled in frustration and fury. The unfairness, the absolute unfairness, that this injustice, this travesty, was happening to Søren of all people…she could have screamed, could have cried all the way to heaven.

"It's not fair, it's not. This isn't how it's supposed to happen. This isn't how it's supposed to end." Nora felt the dagger in her hand and wanted to plunge it into her own heart to give it respite from all the pain. Maybe she would.

"It's not?" Søren asked, his voice tinged with amusement. "You've already decided how we're supposed to die?"

"I have. I've given it a lot of thought."

"That's very…Catholic of you," he said.

"I've even seen it." She closed her eyes for a moment. "You're going to be one of those men who gets more handsome with every passing year. You'll be like Christopher Plummer—handsome even when you're eighty."

"I've been meaning to talk with you about your unhealthy level of interest in him."

"He'll return my emails eventually, I know he will."

"Or file a restraining order."

Nora laughed as the vision danced across her mind's eye.

"It'll be peaceful, quiet…" she said. "You're fourteen years older than me. I've had to face that fact since the day we met. Barring a bus hitting me in downtown Manhattan, you'll go first."

"Something I'm profoundly grateful for."

"You'll be in the rectory reading the Bible in your favorite chair by the fireplace and you'll…you'll fall asleep." She saw it all in her mind's eye. The hand holding the Bible…the Bible slipping from his fingers and fluttering to the floor. "That's where I'll find you when I sneak in that night. In that chair asleep. And I'll know…I'll know you're gone. And I'll kiss your beautiful hand and put the Bible on the bookshelf. I'll take your collar and I'll go away. I'll disappear."

"Into thin air?"

"Almost. I'll go north to my mother's convent. I'll bribe them if I have to, and they'll let me in. And that's where I'll stay the rest of my life."

"Giving up? That's not like you, Little One."

"Not giving up at all. I'll be so busy I'll need the quiet of a convent and no distractions. I'm going to write books about us, you and me. And Kingsley and Juliette and Griffin and Michael and Zach and Grace. That's what I'll do with my last years."

"I told you that you weren't allowed to write about me."

"You'll be dead. What do you care?"

"My ghost will be most put out with you."

"But will your ghost put out?" she teased.

"If you're good."

"I won't be good." She opened her eyes and smiled at him. "I'll be wicked until my last day. I'll write one wild, wicked book after the next. I'll change our names, change the locations, change the dates, the details. But it'll be us, our story. I'll write the books in third person so Zach won't kill me. He hates first-person novels. Plus if it's third person I can write about how beautiful and sexy I am and it won't sound arrogant."

"Good plan. Will these books be comedies or tragedies?"

"Both. Just like life."

"Will I be a hero in your stories? Or the villain?"

"Haven't decided yet," Nora confessed. "But I promise you this...I will give you the last laugh."

"Then that's all I can ask."

"And after I give you the last laugh, I'll put my pen away and I'll fall asleep. And when I wake up, you and I will be back together. I'll be fifteen again and you'll be twenty-nine and it will all start over again—you and I. That's how I'll know I'm in heaven."

"My Little One..."

"I love you," she said, not able to go on any longer without him hearing those words, without her saying them. "I always loved you. I never once stopped loving you. All those times I said I hated you, I never meant them, not once. I loved every part of you, every secret, every sin. I love what you are and what you do and how you make me feel so scared and so safe all at the same time. God, I wish I had my collar."

"You don't need it. I know who you are, who you belong to."

"I promised you forever." Nora remembered that day in the police station when it seemed her life would end at age fifteen, and this man, this priest, who said he would save her if she promised to do everything he told her to do forever. Forever, she had said. "Forever isn't long enough."

"And I promised you everything in return," Søren said. Nora looked at the dagger in her hand, the gun at Søren's head. "I meant it."

"Enough," Marie-Laure said. "My feet are getting tired and you're both starting to bore me. Damon, if she doesn't kill him in one minute, kill her."

Nora kissed Søren and he returned the kiss ardently, long-ingly, deeply, with such love it felt as if he kissed the very heart of her.

"Don't be afraid," he whispered against her lips. "This life is nothing but one blink of God's eyes. He'll blink again, and we'll be back together."

"Are you sure I'll go to heaven?"

"Of course. It wouldn't be heaven without you."

Marie-Laure reached down and pulled out Søren's white

Roman collar. Brusquely she unbuttoned his shirt and pulled it open. Seeing her touching him, baring his chest to the entire room, Nora felt the rightness in what she was about to do. To let any hands other than hands of adoration, devotion and love touch Søren's body seemed the greatest abomination, the deepest blasphemy, the unforgivable sin. Better to see him die than suffer that indignity. Better for them both to die.

"Now." Marie-Laure was still standing so close she would feel Søren's last breath on her feet when he fell.

Nora heard Damon checking his clip.

"Now," Søren said. "Don't hesitate, Eleanor. Do it because you love me, as you love me."

"I do love you," she said, and knew it might be the last words he ever heard from her. "Forever."

Nora gripped the handle of the dagger and started to raise it. She prayed a final prayer.

*God…give me good aim and the strength to use it.*

In less than the time it took God to blink, it was over.

# 33
# THE KING

The words on the note Søren left him told Kingsley everything he needed to know.

*I would have done the same for you.*

Kingsley saw the words and believed in them, which is why, even with the woman he loved thousands of miles away and carrying his child, he knew he would have to risk death, risk anything, to save this man who would have risked all to save him.

He drove to Elizabeth's house at breakneck speed, cursing Søren's noble, foolish heart the entire way there. He couldn't waste a moment coming up with a plan or a strategy. He'd either save Søren and Nora or he would die with them.

Once at the house he willed himself to stay calm, stay quiet. He went through the window again but instead of hiding in the pantry, he raced around the house until he found them. At the library door he paused and took a deep breath. He had two guns fully loaded and cocked. He prayed it would be enough.

Peering in the door he saw he wasn't too late. Nora and Søren were still alive, still breathing, but they both had guns aimed at their heads. And Marie-Laure stood close, staring at them and smiling, smiling and waiting.

Waiting for what?

Kingsley saw it, the knife in Nora's hand. Marie-Laure was making Nora kill Søren. But Nora wouldn't do that…not even with a gun to her head. She'd die first before she hurt him. And yet the knife rose higher and higher.

Her hand trembled only a moment before it steadied and she took a quick breath in.

Kingsley raised his gun. The first shot would start the war. If he shot the man at Nora's back, the man behind Søren could shoot him. Shoot Søren's guard and Nora would die. Shoot Marie-Laure and they all could die.

He made up his mind in an instant. He had no other choice.

He aimed his gun at Nora.

# Part Five

# CHECK

# 34
# THE QUEEN

Nora brought the dagger down and at the last moment turned and plunged it deep into Marie-Laure's thigh. Her scream of shock and pain momentarily confused both Damon and Andrei into inaction. Bullets whirled all around her, bullying the air. Where did they come from? What was happening? She could see nothing. Someone had her trapped, pinned down. She could barely breathe.

Then the guns went silent as death, and she smelled death in the room. Copper and smoke.

But whose death? She feared opening her eyes. If she kept them closed, then she would never know the answer to her question. If she opened her eyes she would see who had died and she couldn't face that, not yet. Someone held her in his arms, held her tight. She decided to keep her eyes closed and stay there.

Forever.

# 35
## THE KING

The men shot wildly in their confusion and Kingsley killed the guards before they even saw who it was who brought death to their doorstep. Kingsley rushed toward Søren and Nora but soon had reason to regret that choice.

Marie-Laure wrenched the dagger from her leg and came at Kingsley with it. She thrust it through his side. He grabbed her, trying to restrain her. In such close quarters he couldn't get a shot off without hitting himself. The gun clattered to the floor. She clawed at his face, fighting him like a wild animal. She managed to fight her way out of his arms. Dropping to the floor she grabbed the gun and aimed it at the corner of the room—right at Søren's back.

From his pocket, Kingsley pulled out the razor blade. When she tried to kick Kingsley away, he sliced through Marie-Laure's hamstring. She howled in agony and the gun fell from her fingers.

Panting and bleeding, she lay coughing on the floor.

Kingsley brought his hand to his side.

Blood…so much blood. He'd been hit. No matter. *Pas de problème*. One more wound. He'd add it to his collection.

Gazing around the room he saw the carnage. One man dead on the floor.

Two men dead on the floor.

One woman on the floor…still breathing.

Kingsley knelt at Marie-Laure's side.

"You always were one for temper tantrums," he whispered in French as his sister lay on the ground twitching, blood pouring from her thigh. "One tantrum too many."

He laid his hand on her forehead, wiped a drop of blood off her face. After all these years she was still beautiful, his sister.

"We should have died," Marie-Laure whispered, "you and I. We should have died on that train when Maman and Papa died. We should have died together…."

"We did. The whole Boissonneault family died that day. I'm only the ghost of Kingsley Boissonneault. You're only the ghost of Marie-Laure."

"I don't want to be a ghost anymore."

Her back arched, her face contorted in agony. Kingsley shushed her gently and pulled her close. Her hand gripped his arm hard and she dug her nails into his skin.

"He didn't love me…" she whispered. "My own husband."

"But I loved you."

She nodded and breathed in deeply. It was her last breath.

*"Merci."* She whispered that final word and left Kingsley behind a second time.

# 36
# THE KNIGHT

The moment Wesley realized where Søren had gone and where Kingsley was going, he knew he couldn't stay in the house and wait for the world to end. He raced after Kingsley, knowing he would be putting himself in the gravest of danger. But that didn't matter anymore. Nothing mattered anymore. Only saving Nora mattered.

He parked the car almost at the front door of the house and ran inside. Not knowing the layout at all, he could do nothing but run everywhere, searching every room. Finally he found the room, the library, and the bloodbath that it had become.

Kingsley knelt at a woman's side. Blood seeped through his shirt. But he was vertical, breathing, alive.

One miracle.

"Nora!" Wes shouted. He called her name again. And a third time. Louder every time.

A large man with a gun lay on the floor, obviously dead. A few feet away lay another, smaller man—also dead.

Two miracles.

At last he saw something, someone, lurking in the corner of the room. A man dressed entirely in black.

Søren. Alive. Unharmed from what Wesley could tell.

Søren knelt facing the wall, his back to the room. As the guns had fired, as the bullets had flown, Søren had ducked and covered out of harm's way. But he wasn't out of harm's way. He would kill the man himself for his cowardice, for letting Nora—

"I'm here, Wes," came Nora's voice, still and small and coming from seemingly nowhere and everywhere at once.

"Where are you?" he called, rushing around, looking for her. Had she been shot? Was she hiding somewhere?

Slowly Søren started to turn and Wesley rushed toward him.

"Søren, where the fuck is Nora?" Wesley demanded, more furious than he'd ever been in his life. If he'd hidden while Nora had gotten hurt, he'd kill the priest with his own bare hands.

"I said I'm here, Wes." Now he saw her.

She lay curled in the corner of the room, tucked tight into the fetal position, entirely unexposed to the battlefield all around them. Søren had shielded her from the bullets with his own body. With her head against his chest, with her eyes closed, Nora had never looked so alive, so beautiful.

So safe.

# 37
# THE ROOK

Grace stood at the window of the house and prayed. She hadn't done this in years, hadn't given her faith any thoughts at all. Two days in Søren's presence had turned her devout as a nun. She had no thoughts anymore, no fears. Her mind had turned into nothing but one prayer that she repeated over and over again until it became like the chant of the medieval monks.

*Deliver us from evil...deliver us from evil...deliver us from evil...*

She started as she heard the sound of a car coming up the road. It turned into the driveway and crawled toward the house, another car behind it. Grace couldn't speak, couldn't breathe, could do nothing but clutch her hands at her heart and stare.

The first car stopped and Kingsley stepped out from the driver's side. Kingsley...bloodied but alive. He laid his hand on the hood and breathed, clearly in agony.

Another car door opened and Søren emerged, something

in his arms. Not something…someone. He carried Nora to the house. But was she alive? Grace couldn't tell.

From the second car emerged Wesley. He looked shell-shocked, pale as a ghost, but alive. Alive was all she cared about. Alive was all that mattered.

Wesley went to Kingsley and took his arm and put it around his own shoulders. Kingsley let his weight fall onto Wesley and Wesley half walked, half carried Kingsley toward the house. Towels, bandages…she'd find them and see to Kingsley's wounds.

Grace ran to the door and opened it. Søren came in first.

Nora's head lay on Søren's shoulder. Grace gasped as two bright green eyes met her own.

"Grace? What the hell are you doing here?" Nora asked, as if they'd met at a party in Manhattan and not a house in the middle of nowhere.

"It's a long story. Are you all right?"

"Oh…I'm fine," she said as Søren carried her up the stairs and Grace waited at the bottom. "Is Zach here?"

"He's in Australia." Grace laughed the words. How absurd it was for her to be here—she wanted to be nowhere else in the entire world.

"Can you tell him something for me?"

"Anything," Grace promised.

"Tell him my edits are going to be a little late. I have a good excuse, I promise."

# 38
# THE PAWN

Laila awoke to silence. Silence, yes, but not stillness. The air buzzed around her as if something great and terrible had happened and the whole world still shuddered from the aftershock.

She threw off the blankets and raced into the hallway. She saw her uncle and her aunt disappear into a bedroom at the end of the hall. At the bottom of the stairs Grace stood with Kingsley, helping him take off his bloody shirt. And Wes, he stood in the middle of the foyer, leaning against the wall, taking short, shallow breaths like he was trying to stop himself from throwing up.

"She's alive…" Laila looked at Wesley and started to head to her uncle's door. He grabbed her hand and pulled her back to him.

"We should give them some time."

Laila nodded and tried to calm herself, although everything in her wanted to run to her aunt, embrace her, cling to her, weep in her arms for unparalleled joy. But something told her Wes was right, she should stay here. She should stay with him. He'd taken her hand and hadn't let it go.

She looked down at their hands and then back up at Wes. He stared down the hall, stared at the closed door behind which her aunt and uncle had their reunion. On Wes's face she saw grief and relief wrestling with each other. The relief she understood. The grief...

It came to her then. Wes wasn't merely a close friend of her aunt's. His feelings went far deeper than a crush. He loved her. He was in love with her. And in her moment of greatest crisis, her aunt had clung to her uncle and not him.

It seemed such a travesty...such a waste. Here stood this beautiful young man who had everything to give and no one to give it to.

"I shouldn't say this," Laila said, summoning all her courage. When all her own courage wasn't enough, she summoned some of her aunt's and then some of her uncle's. Finally it was enough. "But I will."

"Say anything you want, Laila." Wes still held her hand. She took that as a sign to say the words her heart demanded of her.

"If I were her..." she began before leaning forward and giving him the quickest of kisses on the cheek, "I would have picked you."

# 39
# THE QUEEN

Nora clung to Søren as he carried her up the stairs. They didn't speak. What was there to say? Everything they needed to say to each other they'd said in that room where they knelt facing each other with death at their backs. They needed no words, needed nothing but each other, and since they had each other, they wanted for nothing.

Søren sat her gently on the edge of the bed while he went into the bathroom and turned on the bathtub faucet. She was covered in blood, in dirt, in two days of sweat and fear. She couldn't wait to get clean again, to get out of these clothes she'd been wearing for what felt like a year now. A long hot bath sounded like heaven and she knew it would be heaven because Søren was there.

As the water filled the bathtub, Søren came back to her and helped her undress. He didn't wrinkle his nose at how badly she smelled. He didn't comment on her wounds, even the huge blackening bruise on her side from where she'd been brutally kicked. To talk about it would make it matter and now nothing mattered except the beautiful truth that she was alive and safe, he was alive and safe and they were together.

He led her to the bathtub and she sank into the water slowly, gingerly, and winced as the heat seeped into her wounded skin.

Søren knelt at the side of the bathtub and pulled her hair loose and helped her lay back into the water. When she rose up again she saw water on his face.

"Sorry, sir," she said, picking up a towel. "I didn't mean to splash you."

He rested his forehead against hers.

"You didn't."

Part Six

# PROMOTION

# 40
# THE QUEEN

The day Søren and Kingsley saved her was the best day of her life. And like all her best days, Nora spent it entirely in bed. The day after she woke up to an empty bed and a note from Søren on his pillow that simply read "Running."

She smiled at the note. Running. Of course he was. Grace brought her breakfast and they spent a good hour catching up. She'd liked Grace from the moment she'd met her all those months ago at her house—liked her so much that it made it impossible for Nora to put up any kind of fight for Zach. Of course he belonged with Grace. She knew it the second she saw that beautiful scared, brave Welsh redhead standing on her porch. Nora offered to help Grace with the breakfast dishes but Grace told her to stay in bed—Søren's orders.

A few hours later Søren returned from his long run and brought her lunch. He spent a good hour after lunch massaging the unbruised parts of her body. Two days cuffed and tied up in weird positions had left her more sore than she'd ever been in her life. And for a woman like her, who'd lived the life she'd lived, that was saying something.

At dinnertime, Grace showed up again with more food.

"I'm loving this room service," Nora said as Grace handed her a mug of tea. "But I feel like I'm being quarantined. I don't think 'kidnap victim' is an illness that's catching."

"Your priest has ordered all of us to leave you alone." Grace blushed a little and Nora narrowed her eyes at her. "I don't think any of us are brave enough to countermand his orders."

"Countermand away. He went for another run."

Grace sat on the bed next to Nora's hip.

"Another one? Didn't he go running this morning?"

Nora nodded. "Yeah. He's feeling a bit pent-up."

"Pent-up?"

As she sipped at her tea, Nora tried to figure out a way of putting the matter to Grace delicately. Then she remembered she was Nora Sutherlin and didn't ever put anything delicately.

"I mean, he's horny."

Grace nearly choked on her tea. She coughed to clear her throat.

"What? Priests get horny, too," Nora reminded her. "He's a sadist so that complicates the whole sex thing. I'm a wreck. He'll be giving me the kid glove treatment for weeks. Kingsley's a wreck. He needs stitches, but Søren says he won't hold still long enough to let anyone take care of him. When Søren gets like this, and he can't punish someone else, he punishes himself. Hence the running. We need to get him a sub."

"A sub? You mean—"

"A submissive. Kink is like Søren's lithium. It's a mood stabilizer for a lot of people. Half my clients came to me for medical reasons—not sexual. Without kink Søren gets...difficult."

"Difficult?"

"Cranky. Grumpy. Surly. Pick a synonym for *bitchy*."

"Fascinating. So he needs a submissive to play with?"

"If by 'play with' you mean 'beat the shit out of,' yes. Wish you could order a sub and get one delivered. The people, not the sandwiches."

"I can't imagine anyone would charge him a single pence for the privilege of spending the night with him."

"Not for him, no. Søren practically has to beat the subs off with a stick. And he does sometimes."

"I can certainly see why."

Nora narrowed her eyes at Grace. Grace seemed to notice the scrutiny as a blush started on the center of her pale, freckled cheeks and spread to her ears.

"You have a crush on my priest," Nora said.

"What? No. Of course not."

"You totally do."

"Nora, I'm married."

"You're human. Don't deny it. I'm not the jealous type. Kind of the opposite actually. More the 'either let me watch or give me all the details after' type."

Nora fell silent as Grace looked away and stared out the window and down the road. Was she waiting for Søren to return? Probably.

"He got to you, didn't he?"

Grace shook her head. "I told you—I'm happily married and that's the end of the discussion."

"Grace, I was kidnapped and held at gunpoint. I could have died. You can at least answer my question."

"You're playing the 'I was kidnapped' card?"

"Yes, and I will keep playing it as long as I can."

"That's not fair."

"Do you want to see the soccer-ball-size bruise on my side from where I got kicked?"

Nora raised her eyebrow at Grace and waited.

"Spit it out, Red."

"Your priest is magnificent beyond words and I'm a poet. I should have the words. I...*rejoice* is the only word I can come up with, knowing he's real and he's on this earth. He has a holiness to him that I feel in my spirit, in my soul. He went to die for you, and that is a great and mighty thing. I feel scattered around him and yet blessed. If he sat on a throne, I would sit at his feet. This feeling isn't even romantic or sexual. It's simply..." She paused and raised her empty hands. She'd run out of words. Nora knew the feeling. "And, Nora...I don't even like blonds."

"Really? I love me some blonds."

"You must think I'm mad."

"Believe it or not, I completely understand."

"I'll never hear the end of this from Zachary. I'll be teased for this crush until the day I die."

"You're going to tell Zach?"

"We try to tell each other everything. In fact...he told me while I was in the States I could be as wild as I wanted to be as long as I was careful and didn't give him any details the next day. I told him I was jealous of all the fun he got to have in your world. He said I could have my turn."

"Oh, you're having your turn all right before Zach knocks you up and you get boring again."

"I don't think—"

Nora started to shush Grace's objections but a soft knock on the door interrupted her train of thought.

"This conversation isn't over." Nora pointed at Grace. "You wait right here. I've only just begun to interrogate you about what sick sordid things you and Blondie have been up to while I was languishing in captivity. If there're no pics, I'm going to be pissed."

Nora opened the door and saw Wesley standing across the

threshold. Her heart plummeted just at the sight of him looking so humble and nervous.

"Hey, stranger," she said, closing the door behind her and
slipping into the hall. She couldn't stop herself from wrapping
her arms around him. He held her close, held her tight, and
when she winced from the pain she whispered, "Don't let go."

"I'll hold you as long as you want me to."

*Forever.* She only thought the word and didn't say it. She'd
missed these arms, this comfort.

"I've been going crazy waiting for a chance to talk to you.
Søren—"

"I know." Nora sighed as she pulled back to look at him.
"He's keeping everybody away so I can rest. But you're you
so you get to skip the rope line."

"That's good to know. I'm feeling a little shut out here, and
then I remember what you went through—"

"Wes, you're allowed to have feelings about this situation.
Just the same way as I'm allowed to milk it for all it's worth
for sympathy points and cookies and stuff."

"You want cookies?"

"I think they would help with the healing process."

"I'll bake you some cookies."

"Please don't. I feel shitty enough about you as it is."

"Why?"

"The ring?" Nora crossed her arms across her chest. "The
engagement ring...I lost it."

"I don't think you lost it." Did he know she'd traded his
priceless family heirloom for a square of white linen? "I think
she took it. Didn't she?"

Nora swallowed hard. She couldn't tell him the truth. A
lie was far more merciful.

"Something like that."

"It's okay." Wesley dug into the pocket of his jeans and pulled the ring out. "We took it back."

"Holy shit." Nora stared at the diamond glinting on the palm of his hand.

She'd been in such shock after Søren and Kingsley had come for her that she hadn't even thought to try to find Wesley's ring. She had the maniturgium tucked inside her shirt. The ring she'd given up as dead and buried with Marie-Laure.

Wesley raised his hand and rubbed his forehead ruefully.

"Kingsley brought it to me. I don't like having a reason to like that man. Now I have tons of them."

"Tons?"

"Yeah. Tons. The ring, you being alive and standing in front of me—that's pretty much all the reasons I need. The ring made us even. You being safe sent us into infinity."

"I can't believe…" Her voice trailed off. Yes, she could believe. From out of so much hell had emerged so much heaven. She could believe anything right now. "I'm so glad King got it back to you."

"He's an interesting guy, that Kingsley. Going to make an interesting father."

"Wait…you know?"

"Yeah. He told me his girlfriend is pregnant."

"What?" Nora almost fainted. "Juliette's pregnant?"

"Yeah, wasn't that what you were talking about?"

Nora shook her head, struck utterly dumb. Marie-Laure had told her about Kingsley's bastard, who was in his twenties and living somewhere in France. And now Juliette was pregnant? Something welled up in Nora, a fearful sort of joy. It rose in her high and fast and came bubbling out of her in holy laughter.

"Nora?"

"I'm sorry," she said, holding on to her bruised and battered side. Laughing was excruciating but she couldn't stop doing it. It would hurt worse not to laugh. "Kingsley...everything...life is good. Life is weird and wonderful and terrifying and good."

"You're alive. It doesn't get better than that."

Her laughter finally died and she stepped forward to rest her head on the center of Wesley's chest. She raised her head and rose on her toes, intending to kiss him. But he moved his head and her lips met only his cheek.

"Wes?"

"Nora...we should talk. I've been thinking about things, about this ring, about us—you know, since we got you back. Kingsley gave it back to me, and I'll admit I was relieved. Didn't know how to explain to Mom and Dad we'd lost the family's most precious heirloom. Then I thought, why am I happy he gave it back to me? Why am I not pissed that he gave it to me instead of you?"

"That's a good question."

"I'd hated Søren for a long time, hated that world you lived in. And now that I've gotten to know him, and I know you're safe with him, and I don't hate him anymore..."

"What are you saying?"

"I think half of me being in love with you came from how much I wanted to keep you from him. The thing is...I think S&M is weird. I don't get it and I never will. I don't know why the hell I would ever want to tie up a woman in bed. How is she going to touch me if her hands are tied up?"

"That's a fair question."

"And I don't want to share the woman in my life with another guy. I don't. I want to love her completely and I want her to love me completely."

"I don't blame you. Lot of people feel that way."

"And I want kids."

"There's nothing wrong with that."

"And I'd like to sleep with a woman who wasn't comparing me to all the other older and more experienced guys she's been with so I'm not thinking the entire time that I'm not measuring up. I think I deserve that."

"All that and more."

"My point is…I don't understand your world, and I never will. But you're happy there. You're safe. And the more I think about it the more I realize that you and I are too different to be together forever. I do love you and you're my best friend but—"

"Wes…" Nora took a step back. Then another. She stared at Wesley with wide eyes. "You're dumping me, aren't you?"

"It's not that." Wes put his hand on his chest.

He seemed to lose the ability to speak for a moment. Nora felt something in her throat, something like a rock, and she couldn't seem to swallow it.

"I love you," he whispered. "You have no idea how much. And I love you enough to know you'll be happier with him. As much as that hurts to admit, it would hurt worse keeping you and knowing the whole time you belong somewhere else. I was…" He stopped and raised his hand and closed his eyes. "I was going to pay every penny I had to get you back. Every penny my parents had. Every penny I could beg, borrow or steal. And he…he went to pay with his life."

Nora couldn't speak at all. She could do nothing but wrap her arms around Wesley and hold him tight to her, hold him one more time.

"I know you love him," he whispered into her hair, "and you always will."

"I know I love you…and I always will."

"I love you, too. You crazy, weird, wild woman, I love you. But…"

"I know. I do know. It's the right thing. You're absolutely right."

"He'll be good to you."

"He always has been."

"And you're safe with him."

"I always have been."

"I get that now."

Nora pulled Wesley even closer. It hurt her bruised body to cling to him so hard but she had to. She had no choice, and by now, she was used to this kind of pain.

"You're going to find the most amazing girl," Nora said as she leaned her head against his heart. "A girl who adores you and loves you and sees all the good I see in you. And she'll be as vanilla as the day is long."

"God, I hope so."

"And she'll be your best friend and your partner and she'll help you run that big damn farm of yours."

"I like this girl already."

"And she'll be smart and strong, but sweet, too. She won't have my rough edges. She won't keep riding crops in her closet."

"Just in the stables."

"And she'll be so beautiful…"

"Crazy long legs?"

"If you want."

"I want."

"Long legs, it is, then. You and Legs will be so damn happy together it'll hurt to look at you."

"I don't want you to hurt," Wesley said, his voice breaking a little as he buried his head into her shoulder. "Never again."

"A little pain never killed anybody," she said. "And you know me, I only like it when it hurts a little."

"Right. It is you, after all."

"So what now?" She looked up at him, at those big brown eyes with the flecks of gold around the irises and all the innocence that even a week with her in his bed hadn't made a dent in.

"We let go," he said. "And we get on with our lives."

She nodded and took a hard breath.

"You let go first." She inhaled deeply, wanting to take in as much of his scent as she could. Summer. Warmth. Clean laundry hanging out to dry. Wesley.

"I can't."

"I can't either."

"Same time, then?"

"Okay. On the count of three. Ready?" Nora asked, trying to steel herself.

"No, but we better do it, anyway."

"All right. One…" she said.

"Two," whispered Wesley.

The met each other's eyes and together spoke the final count.

"Three."

They let each other go.

Nora forced herself to stand there in the hall and not move. After all she'd put Wesley through he deserved this much from her. He deserved to be the one who walked away first.

He took a step back and turned around. As he neared the end of the hall Nora called out to him.

"We can still be friends, right?"

Wesley didn't turn around to answer but the word was all she needed.

"Forever."

Nora laid a hand against the wall to steady herself. Wesley… her Wesley… This time she knew he was gone for good. It was okay. It was all right. As much as she loved him she knew she never intended to marry him. She knew he wanted things she would never give him—children, monogamy, an undivided heart. He deserved all that and she prayed he would get it someday. Sooner rather than later, she hoped for his sake. For all their sakes.

After a minute Nora felt strong enough to go open the door to her bedroom. Grace was there. She would talk to Grace about it all. That would be nice, wouldn't it? Talk about man troubles to a woman? What a novel concept…a female friend who wasn't in the Underground. She could get used to that, maybe. More women in her life, less men. More stability, fewer adventures. Maybe she could get used to a quieter life, less kink, less craziness…

Worth thinking about. Settling down with Søren a little. Might be all right. People did that. They got older, they calmed down, they stopped sowing wild oats and started sowing…what? Domesticated oats? Something like that.

Nora started to back into her room but paused with her hand on the doorknob when she saw someone slipping into the darkening hallway.

Laila…she'd know those long legs anywhere. Instead of her usual jeans and tee, Laila had on a little slip of a white nightgown, girlish and innocent. She must have stolen it from Anya's closet. Perfect fit. And Laila didn't even look her way. She seemed a girl on a mission and that mission involved leaving one room and going into another room.

Wesley's room.

Nora couldn't help but smile, proud of Søren's niece for doing something so foolhardy as to attempt to seduce the almost unseduceable Wes Railey. She must get that from Tante Elle.

"Good girl," she said to no one. Nora walked to the end of the hall and listened a moment at the door. She heard nothing, no voices. Hopefully Wes would let her down easy and not hurt her feelings. Hopefully Laila would take the rejection well and get back into her room before her overprotective uncle discovered what she'd been doing…or attempting to do. The only man who'd sleep with Søren's virginal eighteen-year-old niece was a man with a death wish. Crazy kids.

Nora heard the front door open and close and she peered around the corner of the stairway. Søren had returned from his run.

"Hello down there," she called from the top of the stairs. "I snuck out of my room."

"I see that." He stood at the bottom of the steps looking sweaty and sexy and absolutely overjoyed to see her standing up and smiling down at him. "I think I ordered you to get your rest, didn't I?"

"You did."

"You think I won't punish you because you're already bruised?"

"I'm willing to take that risk. Speaking of risks…"

"Eleanor…"

"Catch me."

She swung her bottom up onto the banister and without any further warning slid down it toward Søren. He caught her with far more grace than her awkward dismount warranted, and she wrapped her arms and legs around him.

"Eleanor, how old are you?" He sounded utterly disgusted by her childish behavior.

"Fifteen."

Søren shook his head.

"You're too young for me," and he moved as if he would drop her.

"I'm thirty-four, I'm thirty-four, I swear." She clung to him and he pulled her back up.

"Are you going to act like it?"

"Do I have to?"

"No."

"Then no."

"Could you at least try to behave yourself for a week or two? My heart could use the rest."

"I am. I'm going to be a saint from now on. No more wild partying, no more drinking too much, no more running off with younger men, no more wild craziness."

"A miracle has been wrought today. And I'll believe it when I see it."

"Of course if I stop sleeping with other guys...and gals, that means you can't play with other submissives anymore."

"Well..." he said as he hoisted her into his arms and started up the stairs with her, "let's not get carried away here."

# 41
# THE PAWN

Laila knew she would fail even before she slipped into Wes's room. She also knew she'd never forgive herself if she didn't try. Her mother was frantic on the phone, wanted her back home immediately. She'd talked Freyja off the ceiling, reminded her that she and her uncle had discussed a short trip to the States earlier that summer. But her mother was adamant. She had to come home as soon as possible. So tomorrow she flew back to Denmark. Everything that had happened had been hushed up, hidden, swept away. No reason to get the police involved or freak out her mother any more than she already was. The people who'd kidnapped her and her aunt were all dead and gone. Kingsley's people had "cleaned up" the mess. At least that was all he said about it, and she certainly didn't want to know any more.

She didn't want to know anything tonight, didn't want to think about anything. She only wanted to be with Wesley in every way he would let her before she returned home and probably never saw him again.

When she entered his room, she heard water running from the bathroom. He was in the shower. Good. That gave her a few minutes to collect herself. She sat on the edge of the bed facing the window. The sun had set and night was rising and taking over the sky. A few stars peeked over the tops of the trees. The world seemed to be waiting for something wonderful to happen. She hadn't felt this way since she was a child, resting her head against the wall and listening to her aunt and uncle tell secrets to each other in the dark and feeling that she would die, absolutely die, if she couldn't be part of that enchanted world they seemed to inhabit.

Now she sensed the enchantment tiptoeing in through the window and spreading its tendrils through the room. They danced over the Persian rug that lay atop the gleaming hardwood. They whispered across the white linens on the bed. They spiraled up and down the black bedposts of the old sturdy New England bed.

A summer breeze tickled her bare ankles.

Laila had never felt more calm in her life.

The water stopped in the bathroom and she closed her eyes. She heard movement and a door opening. Footsteps...and then the footsteps faltered.

"Laila?"

She didn't speak, not a word. She only waited.

Wes came around the bed and stood in front of her. He wore nothing but jeans and the water that dripped from his hair onto his strong and sturdy shoulders. He had such a beautiful body—his flat stomach, his muscular arms, his chest she wanted to kiss so badly she could taste his skin on her tongue....

She met his eyes and saw that he looked at her with more than just confusion. The confusion was there, the question, but also desire. She saw it and knew it the moment she saw it. She'd been waiting to see that look all her life.

"This isn't a good idea," he said.

"I know that."

"You've never done this before."

"I don't care."

"This is such a big deal. We have to talk about birth control—"

"I'm on it."

"And what this means for us."

"We can answer that question later."

"Laila…I don't want to hurt you."

"You're hurting," she said.

"That's why it isn't a good idea. I'm not strong enough to say no to you tonight."

"It's not weak to say yes."

Wesley heaved a breath. Laila gathered her words and put them in order. She wanted to get them just right.

"Wes, I know you're hurting," she repeated, her voice tremulous and low. "Don't be afraid to hurt me, too. I know you want to let go. Let go with me. You need comfort. Let me comfort you with my body. Lose yourself inside me. Forget what you've lost, forget what you can't have. There's no shame in trying to forget for a night even if you know you'll remember in the morning."

The words hung in the air and vibrated like the final notes of a symphony.

Wes raised a hand and gently cupped her neck. He bent his head and kissed her.

At first Laila couldn't even believe it was happening. What she wanted and what she believed would actually happen were two opposite things. But no, his mouth was on her mouth and she opened to him and gave herself over to the kiss.

She rose off the bed, wanting to press her body to his but not quite ready to drag him down on top of her yet. When she wrapped her arms around his shoulders, he pulled her close and hard against him. Warm…so warm… She almost groaned as the heat of his body seeped into her skin. His lips moved against hers in gentle, seeking waves. She thought she'd be terrified at this moment, on this night, but every kiss, every touch, felt so natural, so right.

Her lips moved down to his neck and she kissed the water drops off his shoulders.

"Laila…"

"What?" She pulled back immediately. "Did I do something wrong?"

"No." He took a ragged breath. "Not wrong at all."

"Something right?"

He nodded. She stepped forward again and dropped another kiss on his right shoulder, a second slow kiss onto his left. She feathered more soft kisses over his neck and chest and to each end of his collarbone and back again.

"I love how tall you are," he said, dipping his head to kiss under her ear. He brushed her hair off her shoulder and she shivered at the light tickling sensation of his fingertips touching such delicate skin. "Not used to that."

"I like looking you right in your eyes." She met his eyes then and saw desire and concern in his gaze. She ached for the desire. She adored him for the concern. "I never liked being this tall before. I do now."

Laila ran her hands up and down Wes's arms and then over his chest and stomach. When her hand came to the waistband of his jeans, she hesitated.

"It's okay," he whispered, kissing her again. "You can touch me."

With shaking hands, she unbuttoned his jeans and unzipped

them. Straight from the shower he had on nothing under his pants. She tried not to stare or gape but she'd never seen a naked man like this so close before, so close she could touch him. She wrapped her hand around him and stroked upward.

"You're big," she said, blushing against her will.

"And you're a virgin."

She shook her head as she continued to trace the length of him with her fingertips.

"Don't. Don't think of that. I want to take care of you tonight. That's why I'm here."

"I'm not going to forget that you're a virgin, and you better believe I'm going to try to take care of you, too."

"We'll take care of each other."

"I like that idea."

Wes reached past her and yanked the covers down on the bed. She sat down and scooted back as he crawled in and on top of her.

They kissed again for a long time, long enough for Laila to truly start to relax underneath him. Everything he did to her sent reverberations through her whole body. The kiss he placed on the center of her chest she felt in the backs of her thighs. His hand sliding from her knee to her hip caused her lower back to tighten.

"Anytime you need me to stop or slow down, tell me," Wes said as he came up on his knees and looked down at her.

"I will. But I don't want you to stop. Not now or ever."

"Good." He gave her a wide grin before raising his hand and crooking a finger at her. She sat up and waited. He gathered the edge of her nightgown in his hands and started to pull it upward. For a split second, Laila froze in a moment of sudden self-consciousness. But she forced herself to raise her arms and let Wes undress her.

Now wearing nothing but her panties, she laid back down on the bed and looked at anything and everything but Wes.

"You have amazing breasts," he said. Laughing, she crossed her arms over her chest. "Don't you dare."

He took her wrists in his hands and forced them to the sides of her head.

"Wes…"

"I let you see me and touch me. My turn."

He let go of her wrists and she kept them at her sides as he brought his mouth down to her chest. He kissed her over her pounding heart.

"You're beautiful, Laila."

She shook her head. "You're the pretty one."

"English lesson, little Danish girl. I'm a guy." He looked down at her. "Guys aren't pretty. *I* am not pretty."

"So my English isn't perfect. What are you, then?"

"I'm stunning." He winked at her and she burst into laughter, laughter that turned to a gasp as he dropped his head and took a nipple into his mouth. The heat from his mouth on her breast caused her entire body to tense. She felt like a knot inside her was tightening with every kiss, every touch, every new intimacy. How did people get anything done when they could be doing this instead? She wanted to do this for the rest of her life, lay in bed with Wes and touch him and be touched by him, kiss him and be kissed by him, give herself to him and take everything he had to give her.

She closed her eyes and let herself drift into the pleasure of his hands and his mouth on her. He stayed at her breasts for what felt like an hour—kissing, sucking, teasing her nipples in such a way her hips lifted and a muscle deep inside her twitched with need.

When Wes finally pulled away from her swollen breasts, her nipples ached and a light sheen of sweat covered her body.

"Please…" she whispered, not even knowing quite what she begged for, only knowing that whatever it was, no one could give it to her but him.

Some part of her felt a woman's pride when she felt Wes shaking under her hands, panting with his own need.

"Are you sure?" He pulled her close and she melted against his body. She couldn't get enough of his skin, his warmth, his touch, couldn't get enough of him.

"Yes."

With a ragged breath, Wes rolled back onto his knees again and slowly dragged her panties down her thighs. Laila stared up at the ceiling and tried to stay calm even as Wes stood up and stripped out of his jeans. With every moment that passed it become more and more certain, more real, more irrevocable… they'd gone too far. They couldn't, they wouldn't, go back.

Wes lay with her again, this time at her side. He slipped his hand between her legs and nudged her thighs apart.

"It's okay," he whispered. "I'm going to use my fingers first."

Laila nodded as she opened her legs more for him.

"I want this so much," she said as he traced the curve of her hip with his hand. "I'm nervous. That's all. Please don't think I want you to stop."

"I understand nervous. And I won't stop unless you tell me to stop."

He cupped her between her thighs and she pressed into the heel of his hand.

"Is there a way you like to be touched?" Wes asked as he made slow circles against her with his palm.

"I don't know…I've never done this with anybody before."

"With yourself?"

Laila laughed and stared at him.

"Don't laugh. I lived with Nora for a year and a half. Trust me. I know what you women do in the privacy of your own bedrooms."

"Okay...so we do. Sometimes. I'm not saying, I do, but..."

"You do. I do it, too."

"Fine. I do."

"Good. Then show me."

"Show you?"

"Show..." Wes kissed her quick on the mouth. "Me."

Laila sighed.

"Please," he said. "Use my hand. Teach me how you like to be touched."

Tentatively she covered his right hand with hers. His hand became her hand's shadow as she guided his two fingers to her clitoris.

"Does that feel good?" Wes kissed her neck, nipped at her shoulder.

"Yes...so good."

"Good," he said, and slipped a finger inside her.

Laila arched her back as his touch sent a wave of pleasure through her entire body. She opened her legs a little wider, inviting more of him. He responded with a second finger.

"Too much?"

"No, I want more."

"Greedy," he teased, kissing her on the mouth again. He slowly moved his fingers in and out of her. She'd grown so wet she could hear her own fluid on his hand. But Wes didn't seem to mind, didn't seem disgusted or even amused. She'd fantasized about this night as long as she could remember and she felt nothing but gratitude she'd chosen to do this with someone who knew what he was doing.

He pushed his fingertip into a spot inside her and her vagina twitched around his hand.

God, did he know what he was doing.

He rubbed her clitoris with his thumb. Rising up on her elbows, she stared down the length of her body and watched his hand moving inside her. She'd never seen anything so erotic, so beautiful, as Wes's fingers disappearing into her and pulling back out again, shining with her own wetness.

He took her nipple in his mouth again and sucked deep as he pushed a third finger into her. This time she felt her body's resistance. Still she breathed through the slight pain and in a few minutes the pleasure, all of it, had come back.

His hand moved faster inside her and her hips pushed in time with his hand. She'd come whether he wanted her to or not if he kept this up. Closing her eyes she relaxed against the pillow and let the sensations wash over her. Something built inside her. It felt like a river pushing against a dam and any minute the dam would break. She wanted it to break, needed it to break.

She panted as her fingers dug into Wes's back and the sheets. So close…almost there…

Abruptly Wes pulled his fingers out of her and covered her body with his.

"Laila?"

She opened her eyes and gazed up at him.

"Ready," she whispered.

He reached between her legs, parted her folds with his fingers and kissed her mouth. Her last kiss as a virgin…she almost didn't want it to end.

"Do you want me to stop?" he asked, and she shook her head.

"Never."

With arduous slowness, Wes started to push into her. She wanted it so much, wanted to feel him filling her, but she couldn't stop herself from flinching as her body protested against him.

Wes kissed her again, kissed her cheek, kissed her forehead, all the while barely moving inside her. She breathed because she forced herself to breathe. It burned inside her and part of her wanted to push him out of her, anything for relief from the pain. A cry of pain escaped her lips.

"I'm sorry," he said. "Do you need to stop?"

"No…don't stop." She wrapped her legs around his back, desperate to keep him close, keep him in her. As much as it hurt she didn't want to let him go.

He pushed in and she inhaled sharply as she felt something tearing.

"Breathe," he ordered as he pulled out of her.

"Wes?" She immediately felt empty the moment he left her.

"We're not done, I promise." He smiled down at her and wiped her hair off her forehead. When she'd entered his room she'd almost felt chilly. Now sweat covered her body and she burned from within. "But you're in agony. I don't like agony. Maybe this will help."

"What will help? Anything. I don't want to stop."

Wes kissed her chest and her stomach. She twined her hands in his hair as his lips feathered delicately over her hips. When he pushed her legs open wide she almost stopped, but his mouth upon her silenced any protest. Carefully he spread her wide and licked her clitoris. He teased it with his tongue until she started panting again from the pleasure. He moved lower and licked her aching lips, even pushing his tongue all the way into her. Moans, deep and guttural, escaped the back of her throat. She felt wanton, beautiful, erotic, even womanly, as he opened her up with his mouth. He lavished her with his lips and tongue. Her moans turned to pleas, begging him to enter her again.

He covered her again with his body. Hooking his hands under each of her knees, he forced her legs wide open as he sat between her thighs. With short thrusts of his hips he worked himself into her again, this time with much less pain and almost no resistance. Laila reached out her arms and Wes fell into them as he pushed all the way into her. She needed to hold him, needed to touch him, needed to have as much of him as possible in her and against her and on top of her. She couldn't quite believe it…Wes was inside her. They were joined, their two bodies moving as one. She might love him… she did love him. Even if it wasn't forever, she did love him tonight. This was love, what they did together. Two people saving each other from a night spent alone and lonely. They brought their pain to each other and each accepted the gift. This was love, keeping watch together until dawn. This was love, not letting the people who hurt them win. This was love, taking a risk for someone else.

Whatever anyone said or thought, Laila didn't care.

Wes was inside her because he wanted to be, needed to be. This was no sin.

This was love.

# 42
## THE ROOK

Grace stared down at her wedding ring and smiled. How far she and Zachary had come since the day he'd slipped this ring onto her trembling hand. They'd married in fear and desperation, not knowing what else to do. She'd been barely nineteen then and pregnant with her university professor's child. Nothing good would come of this, she'd feared. Nothing but heartache and disappointment for Zachary.

The night she'd woken up hemorrhaging in their bed, she wondered a moment if God was punishing her for seducing her teacher, or punishing Zachary for succumbing to a student. Only now did she realize how foolish she'd been to think of God as some cosmic dean of academics who'd slap their hands with a ruler for breaking some ordinance of the honor code. Terrible and beautiful things happened to everyone. That was life. Simply life. And now she understood...now she felt the method behind all the madness that had brought her to this moment. She didn't quite know the meaning yet, couldn't see the plan, but she felt it, sensed it, trusted it like a pilgrim walking a labyrinth blindfolded with her hand on the wall knowing she'd find the answer at the center and yet not hurrying her steps. The answer would wait. The journey was what mattered.

And tonight the journey brought her here.

She raised her hand to her lips and kissed her wedding band. Although still thousands of miles apart, she'd never felt closer to Zachary. He'd given her a promise, given her a night of freedom, given her his trust that she could wander the labyrinth a little and would still find him at the center.

When Søren entered the room, Grace smiled.

He locked the door behind him. In his hand he carried a long back bag. When he dropped it, she heard the distinctive and unnerving sound of metal clicking against metal.

She wanted to ask about the bag, what was inside it, but she decided to enjoy the mystery.

Søren came to where she stood at the end of the bed. She wore nothing but a white Oxford shirt, one of Zachary's she'd packed. She'd asked Nora what she should wear for such a night. Nora's answer was both elucidating and terrifying.

*Doesn't matter. You'll be naked five minutes after he shows up, anyway.*

"Nora said I wasn't supposed to speak until you spoke to me."

He crossed his arms over his chest, leaned against the bedpost and smiled.

"You're doing a wonderful job at it."

Grace burst into nervous laughter.

"I have no idea what I'm doing," she admitted.

"Obviously."

"That obvious?"

"Well…you are standing."

"I'm…of course, I'm sorry." She knelt on the floor and Søren stepped so close she could have rested her cheek against his thigh. She rather liked that image.

Søren snapped his fingers in her face and she started and looked up at him.

He crooked his finger and she stood up again, feeling both awkward and foolish.

"Grace…" Søren laid his hands on either side of her neck and caressed the line of her jaw with his thumbs. Relaxing into his touch, she closed her eyes. "You don't have to do this."

"I know. But I want to." She opened her eyes and looked at him. "Please."

"Saying 'please' is a good start." He smiled and laughed a little. "Are you sure?"

"Absolutely. Are you?"

"Not even remotely."

"Thank God." She collapsed against his chest like she had that night on the roof. Only two nights ago she reminded herself. Seemed like a lifetime had passed between then and now. "I can't recall ever being so nervous or wanting something so much."

"I won't even charge you your soul for it."

"Good. I'm a poet. I need my soul."

Søren held her close and massaged her back while she got used to being in such close and intimate proximity to him.

"It's very kind of you to offer yourself," he said, kissing the top of her head. She wasn't short, not at all, but with him she felt tiny. Nora must feel like a little girl whenever around him. No wonder she adored him like a father while she rebelled like a child.

"It's not kindness, I promise you. I feel this…I don't even know the word. It's not desire, not quite. Attraction? Definitely. I need to do this with you." She looked up at him. "If it helps you, wonderful. It's my honor. But please don't think I'm doing it for you. I only know that if I don't do this to-night, I will regret it for the rest of my life."

"And Zachary?"

"I told him how I've envied him the adventure Nora took him on. He said I could have my own. I could do whatever I wanted, although he preferred to not know any details after."

"A wise man in many respects."

"I know my husband. I know my marriage. This won't harm it. If one night with your Nora could change everything for him, then maybe a night with you…"

"It might change things, yes." He slid his hand under her shirt and rubbed the small of her back. She'd prepared herself for pain tonight. She hadn't expected such simple, gentle pleasures like this one. "I know these past few days you and I have gotten close. Tragedy and adversity can make best friends of even strangers. But you've only seen one side of me…and you seem to rather like that side of me. This…this would be a very different side of me."

"Are you afraid I won't respect you in the morning?" She grinned up at him.

"Morning?" He laughed as if she'd told the most hilarious joke. "You'll be lucky to last an hour."

"Is that a challenge?"

"Are you accepting?"

"I'm here. I've already accepted."

He raised his hands to the back of her hair and pulled out the ponytail holder that tied the end of her French braid. Slowly he worked his fingers through her hair, freeing it from its confines. She almost always wore her hair up, wore it back, wore it in a braid or a ponytail. Only in the shower, only in bed, did she take her hair down. She always knew Zachary was in the mood for sex when he took her hair down and ran his fingers through it.

"What do you want to do?" Søren asked, his voice almost a whisper.

"I don't know. Like I said, I've never done this before. I don't know what the protocol is."

"We should talk about your limits."

She shrugged and smiled.

"Limits?"

"Limits. What you don't want me to do. The lines that you don't want crossed, what are they?"

She stared at him like he'd started to speak a foreign language or had broken into song. Her lines she wouldn't let him cross?

"I walked with you to your death. You knew you were going to have to die for Nora and you went, anyway. I saw you do it. There is nothing I wouldn't trust you to do to me. I don't care if that's the wrong answer. It's the truth. And it's the only answer I have."

Søren sighed and took her by the shoulders.

"If you won't tell me what you don't want, perhaps you could tell me what you do want."

His hands moved from her shoulders to the front of her shirt. He unbuttoned the top button. Grace stiffened but made no protest. Nora had warned her, after all.

"What I want...that might be a loaded question."

"I'm not saying I'll give you everything you want. But I might let you try to earn it."

He smiled at her, a smile so arrogant and dominant she felt her knees weakening.

Another button came undone, then another.

She'd asked Nora about how it would all proceed once things started.

*He'll beat you with various toys probably,* Nora had said, as if getting beaten were nothing more than a game. *Anywhere from a few minutes to a couple hours, whatever you can take.*

Nervously Grace posed one final question.

*And how do we…I mean, how does he…finish?*

*Grace, my dear, God created the female back and made it such an easy target for one very good reason.*

"Tell me something you want, Grace," he said as he reached the bottom button, "or the night ends here."

"I want you to kiss me," she said, surprised by her boldness.

"Is that so?" He undid the last button and opened her shirt. With torturous slowness he dragged it over her shoulders and down her arms.

"Yes."

"Do you want to guess how many people I've kissed on the mouth in my life?" He ran his hand up and down her side, barely grazing her breast with his thumb.

"Probably as few as I have."

He laid his hand in the center of her chest. She couldn't believe she stood naked in front of this man, this priest. Even in the black jeans and black T-shirt he still seemed like a priest to her. He had a holiness about him, a sacred quality. No matter what happened between them tonight, she knew nothing could change the way she saw him. His sanctity was immutable as truth or beauty.

"Tell me how to earn it, and I will."

"Ten minutes."

"Ten minutes?" she repeated. "Of what?"

Søren stepped away, squatted down to the black bag and unzipped it.

"You have your…equipment with you?" she asked.

"I'm a man. I always have my equipment with me."

She blushed.

"You know what I mean."

"I didn't pack any 'equipment,' as you call it, before coming here. This is some of Kingsley's gear he keeps in the car. Thankfully Kingsley has flawless taste."

"In what?"

"Floggers. Canes. Singletails. Massive toy collection."

Søren stood up and she saw floggers in his hands, several of them.

"Floggers? Do those hurt?"

"Very much so," he said, laying them out on the bed. "My niece is in this house so try not to scream please."

"I'll try. But…" She looked at him and saw the hint of a smile on his lips. "You're doing it again. You're playing with my mind."

"Foreplay, Grace." He came back to her and lightly bit her shoulder. "Mind-play first. Then body."

He brushed her hair off her back and swept it over her shoulder. When he laid a hand on her back at the base of her neck, Grace inhaled and closed her eyes. So strange to have another man's hands on her body. Ian had barely touched her those three awful nights they spent together. It was nothing but tab A into slot B. That had been actual sex and it had felt less intimate than Søren's hand on such a vulnerable part of her.

"I'm not going to tie you up, not yet, anyway. Cross your arms in front of your face and lean forward against the bedpost. Rest your forehead on your arms. Don't forget to breathe."

She did as instructed and took comfort in the calm authority in his voice.

"A flogging will not injure you." He lightly stroked her back from neck to hip. "At worst I might break the skin a little. The pain is sharp and flat at the same time as opposed to the pain from a singletail, which is sharp and pointed. Nothing I do to you tonight will debilitate you or leave you scarred.

But it will hurt and it will hurt very much. Do you understand that, Grace?"

"Yes."

"I'll start when you tell me you're ready."

"I'm ready," she breathed, a tremor in her voice.

"Good. We won't bother with safe words. Eleanor and I have them because she enjoys being overpowered during sex and we often play hard. She likes to say 'no' and 'stop' for the pleasure of having me ignore her protests. Only when she says her safe word, do I actually stop. For you, if you say 'stop' or 'no' I will honor your wishes."

"Thank you."

"And if you last ten minutes," he said, and she turned her head and saw him glance at the clock on the fireplace mantel, "I'll give you what you want."

Ten minutes of pain? For a kiss from him? She would have traded an entire hour of pain for a kiss. Who was she kidding? She would have traded all night.

"Ready," she said, and before she could prepare herself, the first blow landed on the center of her back. She gasped from the sudden shock of pain.

From behind her she heard Søren laughing.

"I told you so," he taunted.

"I didn't say 'stop.'" Let him tease and taunt. She could do this.

"No. No, you did not."

Grace braced herself but the second blow hurt even worse than first. The third came fast after that. She flinched with each strike but managed to do no more than gasp or wince. Not once did she cry out. Not once did she scream. After a few more strikes she found herself zoning out. The pain didn't fade. On the contrary it built as the flogger landed again and again on her raw back. But she stopped caring about the pain, stopped counting the minutes until it would end. The most enigmatic man she'd ever met desired to give her this pain, needed to give her pain, and so she accepted the pain as a gift and offered him her body for his use as a gift in return.

When the flogging finally ceased, Grace sagged against the bedpost and swallowed large gulps of air.

Søren came to her and laid the flogger back on the bed. He reached up and took her by the wrist, turning her to face him.

He cupped her chin, forcing her to meet his eyes.

"Good girl," he whispered. "I'm proud of you."

"You are?"

He nodded. "For someone who has never done this before, you take pain beautifully."

She beamed with pride. Praise from him was worth all the pain.

"Thank you. I want to please you."

"You do." He raised her hand to his lips and kissed the center of her palm. Still holding her hand he brought his mouth to hers. At first he kissed her so gently she barely felt it. Then she realized he was waiting, waiting for her to kiss him back, to take what she wanted, what she'd asked for, what she'd earned. And since she had earned it, she pressed her lips to his, opened her mouth and let him have at her. She tasted his tongue, the hint of wine, tasted his hunger or perhaps it was hers. She wrapped her arms around his neck and pressed her naked body into him. An ache unlike any she'd ever felt before coalesced within her like a storm cloud forming. With each passing moment the storm intensified as her desire for him thundered through her.

Finally he pulled back and looked down at her with something akin to surprise in his eyes. Had the ferocity of the kiss shocked him as much as it shocked her?

"Tell me what you want, Grace," he said again, this time slightly breathless. "And I'll tell you how to earn it."

"I want you to touch me...all of me."

"It will cost you."

"I'll pay any price."

"Stand in your place."

She turned her back to him, crossed her arms and rested her forehead against her wrists. He didn't pick up the flogger this time. He'd gone back into the bag for something else. She didn't see it, but she heard it. When he whipped the air it made a whistling sound.

"You recall how much the flogger hurt?"

"Yes. A lot."

"Good," he said. "This is a cane. It will hurt worse."

"Ten more minutes?"

"Oh, I won't cane you for ten minutes. You'd end up in the hospital. I'll cane you for one minute."

"Thank God..."

"I'll whip you for the other nine."

The cane landed in the center of the backs of her thighs. The impact felt like a line of fire erupted on her skin. The next blow moved up higher. The third higher still. But the fourth moved lower so she quit guessing where the next would land. Her bottom, her upper thighs, her lower thighs...they burned with a pain she'd never experienced before. And as quickly as it started, it was over. But only the caning. Something bit at her back with tiny, tearing teeth. She heard a snap, something cutting the air, something stinging her skin. As before she lost herself after a few moments. The pain became a fact of life, as much a part of her as breathing. She didn't seek to stop it. She didn't even endure it. She received it, accepted it, even enjoyed it for the fact that the man who gave it to her needed to give it to her. The gods of old had demanded blood sacrifices from their people—a dove slain on an altar, a rook or a sheep. For some gods, even a person. The blood atoned for the sins of the people, bent the ears of god toward the supplicant. But Grace felt nothing like a dove laid out upon an altar. Giving herself to Søren for a night? This was no sacrifice.

When the pain stopped, Grace did nothing but stand and wait. When the pain stopped, Søren was at her back, turning her toward him again. His mouth found hers and she returned the kiss as ardently as he gave it. As they kissed he pushed her onto the bed and held himself over her. She lay underneath him as his hands traversed the full plane of her body, over her breasts and down her stomach, down her legs and across her hips. He had such graceful hands, such knowing fingers, and when she opened her thighs and he slipped his fingers into her, she accepted them like a gift. She gloried in every touch, every sensation, even the discomfort of her battered back on the sheets.

"Tell me what you want," he ordered, and she knew the answer before he'd even asked.

"You," she said. "All of you. Whatever the price."

Søren brought his hand to her chest again.

"Grace…"

She met his eyes, gray and burning. She'd never seen gray fire before. She memorized the color because she knew she would never see it again for the rest of her life. But she saw it tonight and that would be enough.

"Please."

He pressed his hand into her throat. The world turned white as the morning.

"Tell me what you want," he whispered once more in her ear.

She told him.

Then she earned it.

# 43
## THE KNIGHT

Wesley moved carefully inside Laila. As much as he wanted to let go, he remembered her soft whimpers of pain, remembered she'd never done this before, remembered that, this time, he was the experienced one who had to take the lead.

"You okay?" He kissed her neck and shoulder.

"More than okay." She moved her leg higher up his back. "Are you okay?"

He laughed as he nuzzled the side of her neck. She smelled so good, like a warm kitchen, vanilla and strawberries.

"Beyond okay." He pushed in again, a little harder this time, a little deeper. Laila rewarded him with a moan of pleasure, low and hungry. "How's that for okay?"

Closing his eyes tight, Wesley focused on his breathing and tried to ignore that wet heat wrapped tightly around him. Looking at Laila was also too much of a temptation. Her lips red with kisses, her pink-tipped nipples, her smooth skin he wanted to lick and nibble… And God, those long legs of hers. He could die with them wrapped around his back like that.

Wesley took slow, calming breaths. He knew where he wanted to go, but he refused to go there without her. Reaching out, he grabbed the bottom bar of the headboard and pushed himself up, putting room between him and Laila. Now only their hips met.

"Wes?" Laila's confused tone brought him back to himself.

"I'm here. Changing position a little." He pulled her down the bed a little as he rose up even more. Sliding a hand between their bodies, he found her clitoris and kneaded it. Laila gasped and clung to the sheets with desperate fingers.

He slowed his thrusts and concentrated instead on Laila's pleasure. He could come any second now but he refused to do it until she did. He might never see her again after tonight, although his gut told him this was only the beginning of something, not the end. But whatever happened, nothing could change the fact that this was her first time and he'd make it good for her if it killed him.

And considering she was Søren's niece, it might just kill him.

"Is that good?" He touched her the way she'd showed him she liked. And as swollen as her clitoris was, she clearly liked something he was doing to her.

"More than good," she said, grinning and gasping for air.

Her breathing quickened even more and her hips moved in tight pulses against his hand. He took her by the wrist and brought her arm around his shoulder.

"Hold my neck," he said, wanting her hands on him when she came, needing her touch as much as she needed his.

She dug her hands in the back of his hair and held tight to him. Her grip was nearly painful. He didn't mind it at all.

He moved his fingers harder against her and her breaths stopped in the back of her throat. He felt her tightening around him, so tight even he winced from it. With a final near-silent whimper, Laila came, her inner muscles spasming around him. As much as he wanted to relish the victory of bringing her to climax, his body demanded its own release. He pushed back in, stretched out on top of her and rode her with long, full thrusts that left Laila writhing underneath him.

With a few short, sharp and final pushes into her he came, emptying himself out with more force than he'd ever felt in his life. The orgasm hit him behind his eyes and in the pit of his stomach. Even as he came, he knew he'd never come this hard in his entire life.

He collapsed on top of Laila and once more she wrapped herself around him—this time with both arms and both legs.

They breathed together and said nothing. He felt no guilt, no shame, no awkwardness. Carefully he pulled out of her and noted that Laila barely winced.

Rolling onto his side, he brought her with him, her back to his chest, his arms around her.

"Thank you," she whispered, dropping her head to kiss the arm that encircled her.

"My pleasure. Literally."

"And mine."

"I was wrong," Wes admitted. "That was a seriously good idea."

Laila laughed and the sound filled the air like music.

"It will be a terrible idea if my uncle catches us," she said, settling in against him. He kissed her shoulder, the back of her neck, kissed every part of her he could reach. "I hadn't planned this far ahead."

"It's fine. He'll only kill me. He'll let you live."

"And that's fine with you?"

"Oh, yeah. Sex with you?" Wesley rolled her onto her back and covered her with his body again. "Worth dying for."

# 44
# THE KING

Kingsley stood shirtless in front of the cheval mirror in Daniel's bedroom and examined the damage. After Nora had stabbed Marie-Laure in the thigh, his sister had pulled out the dagger and used it on him as he tried to take her down. He'd lied and said he'd shot Marie-Laure when she'd sliced his side open. He hadn't needed to shoot her. Mistress Nora had paid attention during all those self-defense lessons he'd given her years ago. She went right for the femoral artery and had struck it clean. Marie-Laure had bled to death. He would never tell Nora that. She'd earned her clean hands. He would keep his bloody.

Luckily for him, Marie-Laure didn't have the good aim Nora did. The blade left a flesh wound on his side, a deep one, but nothing fatal. Only painful and now...

"Fuck..." He sighed as he pulled off the gauze. The wound had opened again. No more denying the obvious. He needed real medical attention, not his own feeble field efforts.

"Oh, good," came a voice from the doorway. "Someone in this house is in worse shape than I am."

"I don't know about that, *Maîtresse*," he said as Nora came up to him and examined the damage on his side. "You look like *merde* yourself."

"I know you said I look like shit but it still sounded sexy. Why does everything sound better in French?" She carefully ran her finger along the outside of the injury. "You want some help?"

*"S'il vous plaît."*

"On the bed, slut," she said. "If I hurt you enough, I'm going to expect payment."

"We'll put it on my tab."

Kingsley laid on the bed on his uninjured side. Nora returned in a few minutes with rubbing alcohol, a towel and a needle and thread.

"Good thing Anya's a sewing freak. She's got every kind of thread in existence in this house."

"You're going to stitch me up?"

"I am. Either you let me do it now, or I'm taking you to the hospital."

"No hospitals," he said, recalling his last hospital stay that would have been his last stay anywhere had it not been for a priest showing up and scaring the *merde* out of the doctors.

"Thought so. Now hold still."

Kingsley winced as Nora cleaned the wound. The alcohol burned deep and he breathed through the pain.

"Want some real alcohol? The drinking kind?" Nora threaded the needle with black thread and soaked the thread in the alcohol. "This is gonna hurt like a motherfucker."

"You remember who you're talking to?"

Nora laughed as she bent over his wound.

"Good point. Speaking of points…" She pushed the needle

into his skin and Kingsley closed his eyes, fighting the urge to wince or flinch. "Jesus, King, you got beat to hell. Some of these bruises look old."

He raised an eyebrow at her. Nora rolled her eyes.

"That horny priest. I leave to go fuck somebody else for one week, and he jumps you the second my back is turned."

"Not true. I seduced him, *and* he did make me wait a few days."

"He's such a sadist."

"He almost killed me, if that makes you feel any better."

"It does." She pulled the thread through his skin and brought the needle back down. "But we both know that's how you like it."

"I wasn't complaining, I promise."

She worked in concentrated silence for a few minutes as Kingsley clung to the rung of the headboard to steady himself.

"Where did you learn how to do sutures?"

"Mistress Irina."

"Ahh…yes, my Russian. She was quite the good sadist, too."

"That client of mine with the medical fetish…what was his name? Rhymed with Fucker."

"Tucker."

"Him. He liked having his lips sutured. Paid me five hundred per stitch."

"I don't recall you making nearly that much off him."

"It was off the books." She winked at him.

He started to laugh but stopped himself. No laughing during stitches. He learned that the hard way once.

"I knew you were skimming."

"You were, too."

"It wasn't skimming," he protested. "It was creative arithmetic."

"Times like this," she said, tying the end of the thread, "I miss working for you."

"We were a good team, you and I, *Maîtresse*."

"We were. Especially when we teamed up on Blondie."

"He's his own army. We needed a unified force to defeat him."

"He still always won."

"Only because we let him," Kingsley said, and Nora grinned broadly. She wore nothing right now but black panties and a black tank top so all her bruises were on open display. But even with the bruises, the cracked and healing lip, she was still a thing of beauty any man would lay down his life for. Even a priest. Even a king. "At least, that's what we told ourselves."

"You think we could do that again?" Nora asked, pausing to dab an alcohol-soaked cotton ball over the bleeding stitches.

"Do what? Gang up on him?"

"Be a team again." She looked at him without smiling. "Friends, maybe? Or maybe at least you could stop hating me?"

"I never hated you."

Nora flicked his open wound with her fingers. Kingsley gasped in pain.

"Liar."

"Fine. I did hate you. A little."

"Why? We were good once, King. You and me. When I worked for you, we were almost even friends."

He exhaled heavily.

"When you left him the first time, I knew why. I understood, and as much as it hurt me to see him so broken, I didn't even blame you. Quite honestly, I was shocked you lasted as long as you did in his collar."

"I took great pleasure in imagining creative ways of murdering him."

"This does not surprise me. Any true slave or submissive

wouldn't have minded his tests. But I knew what you were and I knew how hard it must have been for you to deny that half of yourself that wanted to be the master."

"The Mistress," she corrected him.

*"Oui, la Maîtresse."*

She worked in silence through a difficult patch of especially torn skin. Without a word, Nora handed him a pillow and Kingsley bit down on it.

"You need to start taking better care of yourself," she said, eyeing his battered body after a few more stitches.

"I'm fine."

"Fine? Let's not even talk about the six-inch gash I'm sewing up right now. You're covered in welts and bruises and it even looks like that big blond fucker tiger-striped you."

"He did," Kingsley said with some pride.

"Have you possibly maybe once considered using, I don't know, a safe word or something?"

"Don't insult me."

"Or maybe the green light, yellow light, red light system?" Nora dug her needle into him again and Kingsley bit down into the pillow.

"You might as well turn me vanilla."

"Kingsley, you stubborn ass, you have a child on the way."

He stopped biting the pillow long enough to bury his face in it for a moment and mumble something.

Nora pulled the pillow back.

"What was that?"

"I said, 'Do not remind me.'"

She nodded her head knowingly.

"Terrifying as fuck, isn't it?"

"You have no idea."

Nora glared at him.

"Forgive me," he whispered. "You did have an idea."

"Yeah, I do. I'm so happy for you I could cry. I probably will when I remember how."

"I'm trying not to think about it."

Nora sighed heavily as she continued to stitch him up.

"Don't sigh at me," Kingsley ordered. "I'd much prefer you hit me than sigh at me."

"I'm sighing because Juliette's pregnant, and you're obsessing over Søren again. Any possibility those two things are related?"

"Don't analyze me. I'm still sore from the last time I was analyzed."

"Kingsley Théophile Boissonneault, talk to me or I'm going to suture your eyelids shut."

"Very well. It is terrifying. I feel everything starting to change. I don't want to lose him. I don't want to love someone more than I love him, more than I love Juliette. My heart's divided enough as it is. I'm not sure it will survive another cut."

"I know it's scary. But you're not going to lose Søren because you have Juliette and Junior now. What you two have, it's something even I can't touch."

"Funny…I've always thought the same about what you and he have. I've envied it."

"Envied it? I have to obey him. That's how it works. How many orders has he given you this week?"

"Dozens."

"How many have you disobeyed?"

"All but one."

"You want to take my place? You want to sit at his feet and water sticks and do everything he tells you?"

"He'd be dead in a week."

"Thought so."

"He saved me." Kingsley closed his eyes and he remembered waking in the hospital and knowing his superiors would let him die and take their dirty little secrets with him. Søren had come and made sure he walked out on his feet instead of being carried out in a bag. That was only the first time Søren had saved his life. God knows who or what would have killed him if Søren hadn't come back into his life at the right time. "I can't let him go."

"You don't have to let him go. His heart is strong enough to put up with you and me. And that's saying something."

*"C'est vrai,"* Kingsley agreed as she resumed her stitching. "But I envied you. I envied how much he loved you and how freely. That's why I was so angry with you for throwing that away for your pet. The only reason I was so angry."

"His name is Wesley, thank you very much. And he was never my pet."

"Keep telling yourself that. You might believe it someday." She flicked him again before picking up the tape and finishing her bandaging. "Your Wesley...he wasn't one of us. I knew he would never be. When you fell in love with him, it was like you were leaving us all, throwing away everything *le prêtre* gave you and everything I worked so hard for. Denying yourself, what you are, it was like denying us."

"I never threw it away. I never denied you or him. I cherished it always even when Søren and I were apart, when you and I were apart. Especially then. I loved Søren when I was with Wes the same as Søren loved you when he and I were together."

"But you chose *le prêtre,* didn't you? In the end you loved him more. The same way he loves you more than me."

Nora sighed again, heavier this time. Kingsley almost laughed at her disgust. He did love to torment her.

"Love versus love. King, you're comparing infinities. There is no 'more.' That's not how love works. If it's love, it's infinite. You can't count it. I can't line up my love for Søren and my love for Wes side by side and see which one is longer. I'll never reach the end of either. Søren will no more reach the end of his love for you than he'll reach the end of it for me. He let you go because he loves you, because he knew you needed your freedom. He keeps me close for the same reason. Because he loves me and that's what I need. Him."

Nora tied off her thread and taped a gauze pad over the stitches.

"See? That wasn't so bad, was it?"

"I think I almost enjoyed it," he admitted, rolling onto his back.

Nora laid a hand on his inner thigh and slid it up to his crotch.

"I don't think 'almost' is the right word. Fucking masochists."

"If I didn't think you'd tear my stitches, I'd insist upon it."

She raised her eyebrow and started opening his pants.

"I won't tear a thing," she promised as she pulled her top and panties off. He'd never seen a blacker, uglier bruise than the one on her side. And yet she still seemed uncrushed to him, unbroken. "I can be gentle, believe it or not."

"Where did you learn how to be gentle?"

"Where else?" she asked, the shadow of sadness briefly crossing her face. "Wesley."

The sadness disappeared as the Nora he knew and loved and hated and loved again reappeared in her wild green eyes.

"Now stay still while I blow you. Doctor's orders."

*"Mon Dieu…"* He gripped the bar of the headboard as she worked her siren's spell on him with her lips and tongue, with her hand that knew his hungers as well as he did. She pulled up and straddled him before sinking down onto him an inch at a time.

He started to raise his arms to touch her, but she grabbed his wrists and pinned them to either side of his head.

"Behave yourself," she said, narrowing her eyes at him. Slowly she began to move on him. "We're both wrecks. If we're going to survive this fucking, we have to be careful."

"If you insist…"

He relaxed underneath her, surrendered to her will, her body.

"You would have died," Kingsley said as she bent over and kissed him on the mouth, the neck, the chest. "You know that? Stabbing her instead of him—they would have killed you both. You committed suicide yesterday."

Nora looked up and grinned.

"More like martyrdom. I'm working on my bid for sainthood."

He glanced down at their joined bodies, indicating their current erotic position.

"Work harder."

She worked her hips harder against him and when they both came, it was with as much pain as pleasure. It didn't matter. To those of their kind, it was one and the same.

After one round of sex they both collapsed into bed, too sore and too tired to do anything but sleep. Long day. He'd called Griffin to tell him the good news about Nora. Then called Juliette and told her to come home to him. Then he'd hung up the phone and buried his sister, buried her for a second time. He'd brought in a trusted crew to deal with the cleanup, but he'd insisted on taking care of Marie-Laure himself. He owed her that much. As he covered the grave with the last of the dirt, he felt almost nothing, not even sadness. It wasn't his sister he buried, but a stranger. His real sister had saved them all by being willing to die with her priest. Stabbing Marie-Laure instead of Søren had caused the chaos and confusion that had given him the two seconds he needed. If he ever doubted Nora's love for Søren before, he would never do it again.

With such thoughts in his head he fell asleep. When he woke, night still surrounded them but he sensed he and Nora were no longer alone.

Kingsley reached out and found the bed empty. He heard something and turned over. A few feet from the bed in Anya's large rocking chair sat Søren. In his arms he held Nora wrapped up in a blanket. She barely made a sound but from the shivering of her body, he could tell she sobbed against his chest. Of course she wept after all she'd been through. The breakdown had been inevitable.

He watched them together, watched Søren bending to kiss her forehead, to whisper in her ear, watched her wear herself out with crying until she finally fell asleep.

Sliding out of bed, Kingsley pulled on his pants and came over to them. Søren opened his eyes. Kingsley laid a hand gently on Nora's head.

"For a split second, I almost considered killing her," Kingsley confessed in French. "When I thought she might kill you to save herself."

"But then?"

"Then I remembered who she was. And I remembered who I was."

"I never forgot who you were," Søren said, slowly starting to rock again in the chair. Nora slept against his shoulder, her face tearstained but peaceful.

"I'm glad one of us didn't." He caressed Nora's hair before taking a step back. "I'll leave you alone with her."

Søren shook his head.

"Stay. Please."

Kingsley smiled at him through the dark.

"'Jacob have I loved,'" Kingsley said in English once more. "'Esau have I hated.' Romans 9:13. I paid attention in school sometimes."

"Not nearly enough attention."

"I was preoccupied."

"Obviously. You learned all the wrong verses. First Samuel 18:1. 'And it came to pass, when he had made an end of speaking unto Saul, that the soul of Jonathan was knit with the soul of David, and Jonathan loved him as his own soul.' First Samuel 20:16-17. 'So Jonathan made a covenant with the house of David, saying, "Let the Lord even require it at the hands of David's enemies." And Jonathan caused David to swear again, because he loved him: for he loved as he loved his own soul.' Second Samuel 1:26. 'I am distressed for thee, my brother Jonathan...thy love to me was wonderful, passing the love of women.'"

Kingsley stared at Søren and found he couldn't speak.

Søren smiled at his sudden muteness.

"Don't get into a scriptural pissing contest with a Jesuit priest, Kingsley," Søren chided. "You'll lose every time."

"I'm happy to lose this contest."

"Go back to bed," Søren said. "Obey me one more night."

Kingsley knelt down at Søren's feet and rested his hand on Nora's hip right under where she'd been kicked. They'd both been wounded for their sins, and both found their healing at his feet and in his arms.

"Every night."

# 45
# THE QUEEN

The next morning Nora woke up and knew she would be all right. It might take a while, might take a few more midnight crying jags in Søren's arms, but she'd get there. She'd get her spunk back, her spirit. Right now she just felt empty and tired and really fucking hungry.

She took a long shower and dressed in her own clothes that Grace had washed for her. Jeans, a white T-shirt and her boots. Finally she felt almost human again.

That human feeling momentarily faltered when she walked past Wesley's room. She wanted to talk to him again, make sure he was okay. When she reached his bedroom door, she heard the sound of lascivious laughter, a sigh of pleasure, followed by the unmistakable sound of a teenage girl having an orgasm. It hurt to hear but she made herself listen, anyway. She took it like penance. She'd hurt Wesley...worse, she'd harmed him. Now he found healing with someone else. Good for him. He deserved it.

She kissed her fingertips, and touched the door. She walked away and let Wes and Laila take their comfort in each other.

Grace had taken it upon herself to cook a big breakfast for them all. They assembled in the dining room, she and Søren, Kingsley and Grace. Nora studied Grace for any signs of awkwardness or regret about submitting to Søren last night. But instead Grace appeared radiant. She looked rested and happy and she and Søren acted like old friends and nothing more. She still couldn't believe Grace had gone through with it, but not many women after getting to know Søren could resist the temptation of a few hours alone with him, even if it meant submitting to pain. And although Grace had been doing Søren and Nora a favor by giving him an outlet for his sadism, Nora had made sure to get something out of the deal herself.

"You get my priest for a night, I get one more night with Zach," Nora had said last night.

And Grace, who never ceased to surprise her, had only laughed and said, "A night? For one night with your priest, you can have Zachary all week."

"Bring it," Nora said, and they'd sealed the deal with a fist bump.

They all gathered around the table for what promised to be a gluttonous full English breakfast. But the peace of the moment shattered when Søren posed a question that left them all quiet.

"Where's Laila?" he asked. No one answered.

Nora reached for the toast and Søren intercepted her hand. He took it, kissed it and looked at her with quiet determination.

"Eleanor, where is my niece?"

"Still in bed."

"Her flight leaves in a few hours. I'll go wake her up."

"No, I'll do it," Nora said, standing up.

"And where is Wesley?"

"Probably sleeping, too."

"Eleanor, answer me."

"I'm not one hundred percent certain I know where Laila and Wesley are."

It was true. After all, a point-one percent chance existed they might have been abducted by aliens in the past five minutes.

Søren rose out of his seat and headed to the entryway. Nora had to run to beat him.

"Don't." She braced herself in the doorway barring his exit.

"Eleanor, get out of my way."

"They're together right now—Laila and Wes. They spent the night together. They're still together. And if you don't want to traumatize your niece for the rest of her life, you'll leave them alone."

"Me, traumatize her? She spent the night with someone she barely knows who is in love with someone else."

"And she had a damn good time doing it from what I overheard."

"Eleanor…" Søren said in a tone so sharp she could have cut herself on it. "If you don't get out of my way right now—"

"You'll what? Beat me up? Or, as we call it, foreplay?"

"I'm not joking. Get out of my way this instant." He eyed her with barely restrained fury.

"No. You and I have put Wes through enough pain and drama to last a goddamn lifetime. If spending some private time with Laila makes him feel better, then fine. Laila got kidnapped and held at gunpoint. If she wants a few hours' distraction with a gorgeous, sweet kid like Wes, we're not going to stop them."

"You aren't. I am. So help me God, Eleanor, she is only eighteen—"

"So the fuck what? I was seventeen when you and I fooled

around the first time. Remember that night? You didn't seem to mind I was a seventeen-year-old virgin. And you also didn't mind you were a thirty-one-year-old Catholic priest. My priest. You remember that?"

"This is an entirely different situation." Søren took a menacing step forward but Nora stood her ground.

"Why? Because she's your niece? Fuck you, I'm somebody's daughter. I know Mom would love to come do what you want to do to Wesley right now."

"I'm not having this conversation with you."

Søren started to push past her and Nora put a hand out, grasping the door frame.

"You go another step past me and you will never see me again," she said, her voice low and menacing. "If you dare interfere with Wes's chance at happiness, even a few more minutes of it, I will run so fast and so far from you even God and all His angels won't be able to hunt me down. You and I have been playing this game by our rules for twenty fucking years and it is way too late for you to be pulling this vanilla bullshit on any of us right now. We know who you are. We know what you do. Every single one of us in this room has the bruises to prove it. So unless you want to lose me and lose me for good this time, you will sit your ass down and eat your goddamn breakfast and you will leave Wes and Laila alone. Otherwise, I will disappear from this life and the next life. I will make sure I die first and whether I'm in heaven or hell, I will bar the gates behind me so you can't even touch me in the afterlife. Say, 'Yes, Mistress,' if you understand."

"Eleanor…"

"Say it. Say it if you ever want to see me again." Nora felt like a corpse struck by lightning and jerking back to life. "I left you before. By God, I will do it again. This time I won't come back."

It was the only hand she had to play and she wasn't bluff-
ing. She stared at him. He stared at her. Wars had been started
with less fury than she felt at him right now. No way in
hell would she let him humiliate Laila and Wesley for doing
nothing wrong at all. Laila was eighteen, not even fifteen
like Michael was. Wes was twenty and a college student, not
thirty-three and a Catholic priest like Søren had been their
first time. They had nothing to apologize for, nothing to be
ashamed of. They'd committed no sins and she wasn't about
to let Søren punish them for one night of pleasure.

"I mean it," she said when she saw the war raging in Søren's
eyes. "You know I mean it."

For a few more terrible seconds Søren remained silent. She
knew her entire future hung in the balance even more now
than it had two days ago when she held her and Søren's lives
both in her hand. She could forgive Søren any hurt he'd ever
caused her in her entire life. But she would not, could not,
forgive him if he hurt Wesley. That she could not allow.

"Yes, Mistress," he finally said, and Nora nearly sagged
with relief. But she didn't relax, not yet.

"Good boy. Oh, one more thing."

"What?"

Nora slapped Søren so hard across the face that he gasped
from the pain of it. Søren looked at her in pure unadulter-
ated shock.

"I have wanted to do that for nineteen years, you preten-
tious, overbearing, self-important hypocrite. You made me
water a goddamn stick for six fucking months."

The last words she almost shouted as years of pent-up rage
rose up in her like an army with banners aloft ready to die
and ready to kill.

"Kingsley," she said, looking past Søren, "I'm leaving. If

he tries anything before Wes and Laila come up for air, shoot him."

She couldn't remember the last time Kingsley looked so delighted.

"With pleasure, *Maîtresse*."

Nora turned on her heel, leaving everyone—Søren, Kingsley, Grace, Wes, Laila and all the bad memories of the past few days—behind her.

"Nora, are you all right? Where are you going?" Grace called out after her.

"Thirty-six hours is about my upper limit for wallowing. I've got places to go, people to beat."

Nora slammed the front door behind her and the sound jarred her back to reality. She had no car, no keys, no money on her. Nothing. That's okay. Never stopped her before.

Wesley's Mustang was parked out front and Kingsley's Jag. She was rather fond of Wes and King today. Only one option remained.

Nora found the keys waiting in the ignition of Søren's motorcycle.

"Arrogant prick. Maybe you'll finally listen to me now. Told you to get a fucking disc lock for your bike." She started the priceless vintage Ducati and let her guts lead the way out of the driveway. Instead of heading home, her guts aimed her straight at Manhattan. Fine. So be it. New York, it is. Kingsley said Griffin was watching the Empire while they were gone. A little afternoon delight with Griffin and Michael would do her nicely today. And if not, surely Sheridan could be persuaded to come over and play awhile. She'd be elbow-deep in that little girl before dinner. And tonight, she was getting shit-faced. Now that was what the doctor ordered.

As the miles flew past her, the realization that she'd actually slapped Søren in the face started to sink in. Not only had she hit him, she'd hit him harder than he'd ever hit her. That slap was one for the record books. He'd be lucky to not have a black eye from that bitch of a slap she laid on him. On top of that, she'd done it in front of Kingsley and Grace. No doubt Søren would beat the holy living hell out of her for this. The various punishments and tortures he'd lay on her danced in front of her face. He'd probably have to invent some new form of sadism to punish her latest crimes. Or he'd choose the worst possible punishment for her of all—enforced and prolonged celibacy.

Whatever it was it would hurt. It would be brutal. It would be torture. It would be pure Søren at his most sadistic.

She couldn't wait.

# Part Seven

# CHECKMATE

# 46
# THE QUEEN

*December 21, eighteen months later*

Nora tied a red ribbon around the box and using scissors and tape fashioned an elaborate bow. Céleste showed much more interest in the boxes than the presents so Nora made sure to give Kingsley's daughter the best boxes in the world. Christmas was so much more fun this year now that she had children to buy presents for. Kingsley and Juliette's little girl had come screaming into the world only two months before Zach and Grace's son, Fionn. A boy and a girl. Perfect. She was already planning their first date.

"So I got my tickets to Paris. I leave the day after Christmas. You're not going to miss me too much, are you?"

Søren turned around on the piano bench to face her. He'd been playing Christmas music all morning while she decorated the tree and wrapped the gifts. Hard to believe it would be Søren's last Christmas at Sacred Heart.

"I'll try to survive your absence. No promises."

"Be strong. I'm only gone one week."

"Are you going to tell me why you're going back to France?"

Nora didn't answer at first. She hadn't told anyone about Marie-Laure's revelation that Kingsley had an illegitimate son living somewhere in the south of France. Marie-Laure might have been lying, playing with Nora's emotions. She didn't want to set Kingsley up for disappointment. Instead, she'd quietly hired a detective to find Nicolas. She'd seen a few pictures and he certainly looked like he could be Kingsley's son. But she wouldn't know for certain until she looked him in the eyes. Kingsley had taken to fatherhood better than anyone could have dreamed. Céleste had the most doting French papa in the world. Why not give the little girl the gift of a brother? Anyway, she had to try. From the moment she'd learned about Nicolas she felt possessive of him as if he were her own. The day after Christmas she'd meet Zach in Paris and together they'd hunt the kid down. Zach had lived in France a few years and knew the country much better than she did. Plus Grace had promised her a week with him. She planned to cash that chip in and find Kingsley's other progeny.

"I'm looking for something," she said to Søren, and left it at that.

"Something?"

"I'll tell you when I find it. If I find it."

"You're being mysterious."

"Entirely on purpose and mainly to annoy you."

"It's working."

"You know I'm a writer. I can't tell you everything in the beginning. Then there's no point to the story."

"But you will tell me?"

"Eventually, I promise. Soon as I get back."

"I'll hold you to that." Søren came over to the tree and

surveyed her work. "Very good work on the tree. I see you managed to avoid any inappropriate ornaments this year."

"I'm still putting the Christmas shark up on the tree when I find it. What is Christmas without the Christmas shark?"

"I can't even begin to answer a question of such theological import without at least a week of prayer and fasting first." He raised his hand to the little plastic hart that hung on a silver string from one of the higher branches. She'd given him the little hart years ago as a Christmas gift. Every year it had found its way onto his Christmas tree.

"Can you hand me that box over there? I have to wrap Fionn's last gift."

Søren handed her a small box and Nora shook her head.

"The other one please."

"No...I think that's the right box."

Nora looked up at him suspiciously. She put her scissors down and studied the small box wrapped in red paper.

"It's your birthday, not mine."

"Open the box, Eleanor."

"I'm supposed to give you presents."

"You've already given me your present. Now it's your turn."

"What is it?"

"I have no idea," Søren said. "I suppose you'll have to open it to find out."

Nora removed the red paper and found to her delight, and horror, a tiny black box on the inside.

"Oh, my Lord."

"Open it, Little One. Don't be scared."

She opened the box and found a silver necklace on a bed of velvet. On the chain hung two silver bands.

"Søren, not this again..." she warned.

"They're wedding bands."

"I know they are. We can't get married. We get married

and you get excommunicated. That's how it works. I've been excommunicated before. It's not fun."

"You are worth the risk."

Nora picked up the rings and noticed the engraving on the bands. One word on each ring. Her ring said *Forever*. It was the promise she'd made him that night so long ago when he'd pulled her ass out of the fire. She didn't even have to look to know his ring bore the promise he made her. *Everything*. The fire of her teenage infatuation with Søren had burned itself out years ago. In its flames a love made of iron had been forged. It could survive any blow, any trial. Even this trial.

"I made God a deal a long time ago," she said, meeting Søren's eyes. "If I didn't take you from the church He wouldn't take you from me. That's the one promise I've ever made I will die before I break."

"I'm not asking you to marry me. Not now. Not ever. I won't ask you to break your promise to God and I won't break mine, either. I'm only asking that you wear these. Consider them…very small collars." He smiled and she knew she couldn't say no.

"I'll wear them but you should know, it doesn't matter to me that we can't get married. I belong to you. I always will."

Søren clasped the necklace around her neck and the cool metal of the rings tickled the skin of her chest.

"Yes, you do." He leaned forward and kissed her. "Forever."

"Forever."

He pulled back and she exhaled heavily. Wedding bands. Ridiculous. But they were very pretty, she had to admit that. She supposed this meant they were engaged. Fine, let Søren think they were if that made him feel better. At least he'd tried to make an honorable woman out of her. No, they would never get married. Not now, not ever, and they both knew it. But the future did hold the prospect of more time together.

Six months ago Kingsley had announced that he was giving up his Empire, passing the keys of the kingdom to Griffin, and moving to New Orleans to start a new operation—smaller, more intimate. Less an Empire and more a private kingdom. New York had far too many enemies, far too many powerful people who he'd pissed off. He planned to start over in New Orleans, the perfect city for a man with a Haitian lover, and a quarter-French, half-Haitian daughter. Kingsley made his announcement and the next day Nora started house hunting. When Søren told her one month later that he'd accepted a full professorship at Loyola University in their Pastoral Studies department, she couldn't even feign surprise. Of course he had. And for his birthday today, she'd given him a box with a key in it—a key to a house in New Orleans' Garden District, a house hidden far from prying eyes, a house where he and she could be alone together, where he and Kingsley could be alone together.

He'd looked at the key and he'd looked at her. Nora had said, "You would have done the same thing for me." They said no more about it. They didn't have to. Things had changed between him and Kingsley since her week in Kentucky with Wesley. One night two weeks after her rescue she came to the rectory and found it empty. When Søren arrived home hours later and slipped into bed with her, she could taste Kingsley on his lips. She'd only laughed, called him a "big blond slut" and fallen asleep across his chest. They'd all looked death in the face thanks to Marie-Laure. When they looked away they saw one another, saw how all three of them belonged together, and they would never let anything or anyone divide them again. If Kingsley went to New Orleans, there would be no question. Søren would go, too. So would Nora.

She and Søren never spoke of his nights with Kingsley, as she never spoke of her phone calls with Wesley. After a few months, she could even ask Wes about his relationship with Laila without wanting to commit seppuku. Last year she'd cried alone at her kitchen table after Wesley told her Laila would be moving to Kentucky to go to school. Apparently there was some all-girls college not far from Wes's house that had an equine program. How convenient. But that was it, the last time she'd cried over him. Now she could think of him without pain, remember without hurting.

And life was starting to get really interesting.

Twenty years ago Søren had been sent to Sacred Heart in Wakefield, Connecticut, as a temporary fill-in for an ailing Father Greg. His "temp job," as she dubbed it, had turned into a calling that had taken him away from his Jesuit brethren. Now two decades later, he would rejoin them. A difficult transition, but still, it was life out of the small parish fishbowl, life outside the scrutiny.

"Eleanor?"

Nora realized she'd been doing nothing but staring at the rings on the silver chain for the past five minutes.

"I'm all right. I can wear these. But don't tell anyone we're engaged. Number one, we aren't. And number two, an engaged Dominatrix is a boner-killer, and I've got to be tough for the New Orleans scene. I'll be the new kid at school."

"I would never presume to tell anyone anything so horrifying and slanderous. And you'll have the entire town under your heel in a month."

"Good. I like the sound of that. Okay." She took a shallow breath to steady herself. "Now can I please have that box I asked for, sir?"

"I'll give it to you now. You'll earn it later."

Nora wrapped Fionn's last present, a Catholic Bible with his name engraved on it—*Fionn Aaron Easton*. She had already declared herself his godmother and hadn't taken any argument from Zach about it.

*Nora, you and I have slept together. I don't know how appropriate it would be for you to be my son's godmother.*

*When has the appropriateness of something ever been a deciding factor for me doing anything?*

*Well, I suppose I can't argue. Especially considering…*

*Considering what?* Nora had asked but Zach hadn't answered her.

Søren watched over Nora's shoulder as she wrote the name on the gift tag.

"Fionn," Søren said, narrowing his eyes at the name tag.

"What?"

"I've been meaning to ask you something. Do you know if Fionn is a family name?"

"No idea. Grace's mom's Irish. She said it was an old Irish name."

"It is. Fionn or Finn refers to the legendary Irish warrior, Fionn mac Cumhaill, or Finn McCool. It's very interesting."

"So why is that interesting?"

"Because Grace has red hair, and Zachary's hair is black."

"So?"

"Fionn means—" Søren paused and stared at the name tag again. His eyes seemed to lose focus a moment, as if he were remembering something.

"What?" she prompted.

Søren met Nora's eyes.

"The name 'Fionn' means blond."

Nora narrowed her eyes at Søren.

"Søren…that night you played with Grace, by any chance did you two—"

Before Nora could finish her question her phone started to emit the familiar strains of "Englishman in New York."

"Hold that thought. It's Zach. Booty call."

Nora brought the phone to her ear.

"Zach, I hope you finally have my synonym for *thrust,* noun form. Otherwise, I'm hanging up on you."

"Don't hang up. I'm not calling to talk to you."

"Are you calling to sing to me?"

"I need to talk to Søren, and I don't have his number."

"Why do you need Søren? Spiritual crisis?"

"Of a sort."

Zach sounded serious, uncharacteristically serious. Usually their phone calls were full of nothing but fighting and flirting.

"What's going on?" Nora asked. "You can tell me."

"I will. But I need to talk to Søren first."

"Is everything all right? You're kind of scaring me here."

Zach laughed on the other end, a warm, slightly sheepish laugh.

"It is all right, I promise. Just been putting off this conversation for a long time. Can I have Søren's number?"

"No. But you can have Søren. He's right here."

Nora handed Søren the phone. He gave her a look and she only shrugged.

"Zachary?" Søren paused and listened intently. After a few seconds his eyes widened hugely.

Nora's heart raced. Something was up. Something big. She prayed it was something good. He reached out and cupped her face with his slightly shaking hand.

Whatever it was she knew that it would change everything forever, although she couldn't say why.

"What is it?" she mouthed at him, needing to know the answer, unable to wait another moment.

Søren laughed.

* * * * *

If you've enjoyed this Mills & Boon® book.
We'd love to hear from you at
**millsandboon.co.uk**

*There are some books you never forget.*
*Some stories that can change your world.*
*This is one of them.*

Author Nora Sutherlin thought she knew everything
about being pushed to your limits. But in a world
where passion is pain, nothing is ever that simple.
Now Nora must face up to the choices she has
made...and to the man she left behind.

*A story about discovering who you really are...and
who you want to be;* The Siren *is a love story that
will leave you bruised, shaken and begging for more.*

**The Original Sinners**

The Siren • The Angel • The Prince • The Mistress

**www.millsandboon.co.uk**

0712/MB394

*She wanted him…*
*More deeply, more strongly than*
*she'd wanted anyone*

Nora Sutherlin is hiding. On paper, she's following her master's orders—and her flesh is willing.

But her mind is wandering to a man from her past, whose hold on her heart is less bruising, but whose absence is no less painful. Instead of letting him make love to her, she'd let him go.

*'Dazzling, devastating and sinfully erotic'*
—Miranda Baker

### The Original Sinners
The Siren • The Angel • The Prince • The Mistress

**www.millsandboon.co.uk**

1012/MB401

*Her only weakness, his deepest desire*

Two worlds of wealth and passion call to Nora Sutherlin
and, whichever one she chooses, it will be the
hardest decision she will ever have to make.

Wes Railey is the object of Nora's tamest yet most
maddening fantasies. He's young. He's wonderful.
He's also thoroughbred royalty and, reuniting with him
in Kentucky, she's in his world now. But Nora's dream
of fitting into Wesley's world is perpetually at odds
with the relentlessly seductive pull of Søren—her owner,
her lover, the forever she cannot have. At least,
not completely.

### The Original Sinners

**The Siren • The Angel • The Prince • The Mistress**

**www.millsandboon.co.uk**

# TAKE A STEP
## *DEEPER INTO THE SHADE*

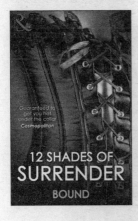
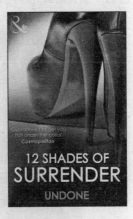

Inside each volume of *12 Shades of Surrender* you'll find six shocking and liberating romances, with similar themes to *50 Shades*.

*Short, sharp and totally unforgettable,* these scorching hot, powerful love stories will stay with you long after the final page is turned.

*Welcome to the darker side of romance.*

'Guaranteed to get you hot under the collar'
—*Cosmopolitan*

**www.millsandboon.co.uk**

0912/MB395

**THEY CALL ME 'WITCH'**

**THEY CALL ME 'HARLOT'**

**THEY KNOW NOTHING OF WHO I AM**

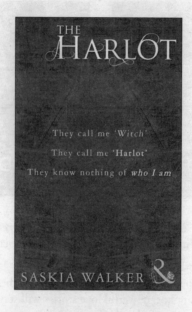

'One of the queens of erotic romance'
—*Romance Junkies*

'Lush and erotic'
—*Romanceaholic.com*

'Sizzling hot'
—*RT Magazine*

**www.millsandboon.co.uk**

0713/MB421